ANDREW O. LINDSAY

ILLUSTRIOUS EXILE

A NOVEL

PEEPAL TREE

First published in Great Britain in 2006
Peepal Tree Press Ltd
17 King's Avenue
Leeds LS6 1QS
UK

ISBN 1 84523 028 0

 Peepal Tree gratefully acknowledges Arts Council support

ILLUSTRIOUS EXILE

Dedicated with love to my children

Colin, Donna, Benjamin and Tristan

EDITOR'S NOTE

During the summer of 1997 I was in Guyana, engaged in research into the background of the British surveyor Charles Barrington Brown. My father-in-law, the late Denis Williams, was the founder and director of the Walter Roth Museum of Anthropology in Georgetown, and I was visiting him there when a wooden box was brought in by members of a team who had just returned from investigating a deserted Wai Wai village in the far south of the country. A brief report in the *Stabroek News* the following day commented:

> No human remains were found in the village, which consisted of seven thatched huts, a cooking area and a central *umana yana*.[1] A number of artefacts were found. These included beads, pottery, and a selection of arrows and fishing spears, tipped with bone. Of particular interest was a small mahogany chest, seemingly of European manufacture, which had been sealed with balata,[2] presumably to ward off the effects of damp. It was found in the roof space of the *umana yana*, which indicates that it was regarded as something of a tribal treasure.

Columbus sighted the Guianas in the fifteenth century, and there has been a long history of colonisation in this relatively small area on the Atlantic coast of South America, sandwiched by Brazil and Venezuela. French Guiana (*La Guyane Française*) remains a *département* of France to this day, while Dutch Guiana, now Surinam, became an independent Republic in 1975. Guyana, home of the once great sugar plantations of Demerara, Essequibo and Berbice, held the colonial status of British Guiana until 1966, becoming a republic in 1970. So although it was not unusual to find evidence of European presence in these parts, it was surprising to find it in a Wai Wai settlement, for even today this remote tribe has limited contact with the outside world.

The box was about sixteen inches by fourteen, and about a foot deep. The lid was slightly domed, and there was a brass carrying-handle on top. It was not possible to date it with any accuracy, but it was certainly not modern. It clearly contained something, because it was rather heavy for its size, though it made no sound when shaken.

Dr Williams and the team members decided to open it straight away. Inside were three volumes bound in leather, all the same size – eleven inches by nine – and about an inch in thickness. Together they formed a hand-written diary in English, and the use of the long 's' placed it at the end of the eighteenth century at the latest.

The title page of the first volume showed the diary to have been written by a Mr Robert Burns, who described himself as 'Erstwhile Poet, and Farmer at Mossgiel, Ayrshire'. The first entry was dated 1st July 1786. The fact that the diarist had been Scottish was not unusual, given the large number of Scots who emigrated to the Indies in the eighteenth century either in search of a fortune, or simply to escape the depressed economic conditions at home.

As a Scot with a literary background I was intrigued by the discovery of the journal and delighted when Dr Williams asked for my assistance in evaluating its content. There was, of course, no question of the volumes being removed from the country, and since my time in Guyana was limited to a few weeks each summer the diaries were photographed, enabling me to work in the UK.

The task of transcription and editing has occupied many years, and it is only since taking early retirement in 2002 that I have been able to devote myself to it full-time. It has been an interesting task, and my only regret is that Dr Williams passed away in 1998 and so did not live to see the completion of the venture for which he always expressed the greatest enthusiasm.

The three volumes that make up the journal, and the small chest in which they were contained, are on display in the National Museum of Guyana in Georgetown. The photographs used in preparing this edition have been sent to the Caribbean Research Library of the University of Guyana.

I have taken the liberty of making minor editorial alterations to the text. The author occasionally observes the practice of allocating capital letters to nouns, but this has not been shown. He frequently employs the ampersand (&), for which 'and' has been substituted throughout for the sake of consistency. The spelling of past participles has been modernised: for example 'spared' rather than 'spar'd'. Where words are indecipherable or doubtful, that fact is indicated by asterisks, together with a suggested reading. Deletions are indicated within square brackets. All words underlined in the original have been italicised.

Burns did not subdivide his text into paragraphs, possibly to conserve space. Where he is reproducing conversation, in particular, this can make the journal difficult to follow, and his text is therefore laid out according to current usage. He does not always employ inverted commas, which are provided. He frequently follows the common eighteenth-century convention of abbreviating proper names to a capital letter followed by a dash. This now appears unnecessarily mannered, and can sometimes give rise to confusion, so names are supplied in full except in a few cases where it was not possible to identify the person referred to. I have done the same where the author uses dashes to disguise profanity or indelicacy. His scorings-out have been restored in square brackets. Abbreviated forms such as 'sev^t' (servant) and the like have been filled out. There is an overall lack of consistency in the author's spelling. Forms such as 'chearful', 'oblidge' and 'chuse' are to be found together with their present spellings, and words such as 'honour' and 'favour' are frequently spelt with 'or'. He seems unable to decide on the spelling of 'receive' and 'believe'. The spelling has therefore been standardised in accordance with modern convention. These emendations to the text of the journal have been made for the convenience of the modern reader.

The poems within the text give every indication of being final copies, for Burns apparently discarded or destroyed his early drafts. He describes how he first sketched out his ideas 'on any old scrap of paper that comes my way' and he writes about how he 'cleared out a great bundle of my rough scribblings and jottings'. There is evidence that he occasionally reviewed his work retrospectively, for there are several alterations and corrections, which have been reproduced since they supply us with an insight into his process of poetic composition and revision.

For the simplicity's sake his continuous text has been divided into sections, each made up of a year's entries. Notes are a necessary evil, though every attempt has been made to keep them to a minimum. There is a glossary of words that might be unfamiliar, and a bibliography that will be helpful to any reader wishing to investigate this historical period in greater depth.

Burns mentions 'handwritten copies' of poems he had already written before the commencement of the journal, several of which he refers to in the course of the text. These had apparently been passed on to his brother Gilbert Burns 'for safe keeping' before the journey to Jamaica. Although they have never come to light, there is at least a chance that they may still exist in private hands, and there is scope here for further research and investigation.

Andrew O. Lindsay

Goed Intent   Cellardyke
West Bank Demerara   Fife
Guyana   Scotland

April, 2005

Journal

of my Sojourn
in the
West Indies

Comprising an Account of the Island
of Jamaica; its Inhabitants; the Workings
of its Plantations, and other Observations
Relating to Life in the Tropics

by

Robt Burns, Esq.

Erstwhile Poet, and Farmer at Mossgiel, Ayrshire

Commenced on the first day of
July 1786

Oh, fond attempt to give a deathless lot
To names ignoble, born to be forgot!

Wm Cowper

1786

Saturday, July 1st. Old Rome Ford, near Kilmarnock. Have today purchased this quarto volume and two more similar for the purpose of keeping this account of my existence, which is today most wretched. My Commonplace Book, in which I have not had the inclination to write since last October, and my handwritten copies of my poetic works, of which I had such exalted and alas! unfounded hopes, are now with my brother Gilbert for safe keeping. I see no reason for further encumbering myself with them, for in truth I am most heartily sick of the whole process of literary endeavour. I think Mr Cowper has hit the mark very truly, for if ever a man was 'born to be forgot' then I most assuredly am that most miserable of beings.[1]

Wilson, that scoundrel of a publisher in Kilmarnock, has dealt with me most shabbily. I know my poems were of merit – are of merit! – yet my fondest dream, which was to see them in print, has now been summarily dashed. A number of my patrons having withdrawn their support, he now declines to proceed with the venture, and 'begs' to inform me (I would make him beg most abjectly if I had him within reach of my foot!) that my poetry is 'lacking in the necessary refinements required by readers of good taste, and whose expectations are for the purest of sentiments, combined with felicity of expression'. Damn the man! It makes me sick to write down his words! My Cotter contains all the felicity of expression that even the most refined of Englishmen could ask for.[2]

Has the miserable blockhead even taken the trouble to read it? I had no mercenary motive; I did not submit my manuscript in any spirit of vanity; nor was I foolishly desirous of seeing my name in print and being called a clever fellow. Why should my address to the mouse be dismissed as uncouth while some simpering, insipid piece of drivelling shit is held up for universal admiration on account of its 'felicity' of expression? The answer is that the Scots tongue lacks the 'necessary refinements', or so the confounded oaf would have me believe. I do not believe it! I cannot believe it! And yet I must perforce accept it. Why should English be a superior mode of expression? What of divine Fergusson, most miserable of mortals, yet blessed with the richest gifts the generous Muse could bestow, had anyone possessed the sense to listen?[3] Why should Euterpe not breathe in the bardie's ear with the homely accents of the stubbled fields and the draughty barnyards as well as in the drawling accents of the idle fop? Why should the misty plains of far-off Arcady deserve more critical attention than the wind-blasted moors of Ayrshire? Worth is inherent: it cannot simply be conferred by a classical reference here, a nymph there, or an anglified dryad lurking in the undergrowth. I know it is possible to create beauty out of truth, however humble that truth may be. Truth *is* beautiful. Now I have had to advise those other good souls who would have subscribed to my productions that their confidence in me as a poet has been misplaced.

Ignominy is heaped on ignominy. Jean, whose condition can no longer be denied or concealed, has been back in Mauchline these six weeks, and her father has now taken out a warrant of arrest against me, demanding the sum of forty pounds as a settlement upon the unborn child, forcing me to sneak from hiding-place to hiding-place like the meanest and most despicable felon with the merciless legal pack at his heels.[4] I am here at the home of Mrs Allan, my mother's half-sister, but dare not remain much longer. Hamilton writes to tell me that Daddie Auld[5] and his pack of holy beagles are determined to have me attend church in order to undergo public humiliation and castigation in the cutty stool as a fornicator. It seems I shall be damned to eternal hell-fire if I deny his bidding. For my own part, I shall most assuredly be damned if I submit to anything of the kind while that old lecher Fisher looks on with his habitual mim-mou'd expression of sanctimonious virtue. Even if the miserable hypocrite had a spark of forgiveness in him, which I much misdoubt, he will never forgive me for my piece at his expense which earned him the justly-deserved epithet of Holy Willie, and 'set the whole warld in a roar o' laughin' at him'.[6] Hell hath no fury like an elder scorned.

I can no longer remain in Scotland. I already feel the bitter pangs of exile tear at my heart, and emigration to the West Indies is now not so much an option as a dire necessity. I had hoped to purchase my passage to Jamaica with the proceeds of my verses but now that hope has gone, and the sum of £9 is quite beyond my present means. I have written to Gilbert apprising him of my desperate situation, and begged him to take care of my little Bess.[7] He is my last hope now.

July 6th. Greenock. I have found refuge in the home of James Campbell, and his dear daughter Mary is to join us from Coilsfield on Friday. I have better news to write today. Gilbert has written to say that he has approached Hamilton, Aiken, McMath, and Richmond and that they have promised to forward me by carrier the sum necessary to [~~pay for~~] finance my journey.[8] All being well, the draught should be in my hands within the next few days. Earlier today I went to visit the master of the *Nancy* at the docks, Captain Smith, and he foresees no difficulty provided the requisite monies are forthcoming: indeed he expressed the most cordial hopes that I might resolve my present difficulties, and said he looked forward to making my better acquaintance during the voyage. He hopes to sail at the beginning of September, though the exact date is dependent on the delivery of certain items of cargo. He spoke with enthusiasm about Jamaica, on which subject he seemed very knowledgeable, and enquired kindly about my plans. I explained to him that I had obtained the post of book-keeper on a sugar plantation near Port Antonio. At this he raised his eyebrows and appeared mightily impressed, though I know that the promised salary of £30 a year is but a modest sum, and in truth I am filled with trepidation about my duties, which I fear will be little more than desk-drudgery.

He informed me that Port Antonio is a respectable village on the north-west of the island. The capital Kingston is a lively place, by his account, and is the main port of the island following the destruction of Port Royal in an earthquake. I enquired of him whether there was any risk of further destructive visitations of nature, at which he laughed very heartily and said that all this had been many years in the past and that I would have nothing more to contend with than the attentions of the Jamaican women, whose beauty he praised in the most extravagant terms. To this I made no reply, mindful of the tokens and vows I have exchanged with Mary, the most warm-hearted and charming young creature as ever blessed a man with generous love. I hope within the next few days to finalise our attachment in a manner fitting to one who leaves behind him his days of riotous folly, to face a future in which the star of sobriety and industry shall reign in the hitherto tumultuous firmament of his nature.

Monday, July 10th. Greenock. I am today the happiest of men: indeed I wonder what merits I possess to make me deservous of such perfect felicity! Mary – that dear, good woman! – has consented to become Mrs Burns, and to share whatever Fate has in store for us in the Indies. I have divulged to her all the secrets of my bosom, for I am determined that there should be no secrets between us, and she has forgiven me all of my excesses, and avowed that she will willingly have me as I am. I pray that I may be worthy of her, and the trust she has placed in me. We are lodged separately in the home of her father, and are determined to behave with the utmost propriety and decorum, despite the ardency of our reciprocal attachment. As befits a prospective son-in-law, I have spoken in private with Mr Campbell, who gave me a courteous enough audience, and asked for the hand of his daughter, and a father's blessing upon our union, and laid before him our plans for our life together in Port Antonio. He did not say much, but I formed the impression that he was not entirely displeased.

I then made a very frank confession of my faults, admitting that in the past I had been too readily led into dissipation and mischief, though in mitigation I offered the plea that it was the unsettled circumstances of my life which had tempted me to take refuge in the pursuit of a frenzied gaiety akin to the madness of an intoxicated criminal under the hands of the executioner. I told him of Bess, and how she would be cared for by Gilbert, at which he looked very gravely at me, saying that he hoped that I would do my duty, to which I asserted most sincerely that I would, and had indeed made certain material provisions in that respect. It was painful to tell him about Jean, and though I did not attempt to deny my paternity of the yet-unborn child I told him the truth, *viz.*, that her father had absolutely forbidden the match, and indeed had torn up the agreement which I had sought to make with his daughter in order to legitimise her position. I said that in these circumstances I had for some months been determined to regard this liaison as irrevocably terminated. I swore that I had no other attachments whatsoever, and that my intentions towards his daughter were entirely honourable, and that if he could bestow his blessing on our union, he would find me everything he could desire in a son-in-law.

I had to endure an uncomfortable homily that lasted for some time, but in the end he relented, and when Mary was given leave to join us, he bestowed the father's blessing that we had sought. We have exchanged written promises, and those, together with the Bibles we gave to each other that day in May, have united us as one.[9] Thank heaven for Aiken's endeavours on my behalf! for I would not be a bigamist for all the world. I know that marriage is appointed by God and I shall never quarrel with any of His institutions!

August 14th. Greenock. We have been very throng with preparations for the Indies, and fully resolved to take the opportunity of Captain Smith, but my plans have been deranged altogether. I went to see Dr Douglas yesterday, it being the Sabbath, and found him with a Mr and Mrs White, both Jamaicans. The *Nancy* sails to Savanna-la-Mar, which is on the south-west coast of Jamaica and some two hundred miles from Port Antonio, as I now discover. The journey to the plantation would cost my master Charles Douglas upwards of £50, almost two years' salary. The risks of undertaking such hard travelling in the hot sun are too much, especially if Mary is to share them with me, for there are great risks of being thrown into a pleuratic *(sic)*[10] fever that it would be foolhardy to ignore. Dr Douglas regrets that the passage is out of the question. However another vessel, the *Bell,* sails from Greenock bound for Kingston on the twentieth of September: Captain Cathcart is an intimate of Mr Gavin Hamilton's, and is as good a fellow as the heart could wish, and with him we are destined to go.

August 16th. Greenock. A letter today from that good soul Dr Douglas at Old Cumnock who confirms my appointment and salary. In a little over a month Mary and I shall be on our way. I must confess that I am filled with some trepidation at the prospect of a journey of such length, even if we are fortunate enough to have favourable winds: not so much on my own account, for the rigours of farming have rendered me largely impervious to physical privation, but for Mary, who is altogether of a more delicate constitution. She is nursing her brother Robert at present, who is ill with fever. I have given all of my affairs over into the hands of Gilbert, and so everything is in order and nothing remains but for us to gather our belongings and await the appointed day. As for other matters, I am now under little apprehension about Armour, for although his warrant is still in existence, Jean will not take any step against me without letting me know, as nothing but the most violent menaces could have forced her to sign the Petition. She is filled with the pangs of approaching travail, and I am most anxious for her situation. She would gladly now embrace the offer that she once rejected, but it shall never more be in her power. I have written to Richmond in Edinburgh and Muir to bid them farewell.

August 25th. Greenock. Since I penned the foregoing entry, I have had some leisure – a rare commodity! – to consider my own feelings as the day approaches when I shall step on board the *Bell,* and leave my native Scotia. Not least of these are my perceptions of how I stand in relation to that tremendous Being, the Author of existence. How shall I meet the reproaches of those who stand to me in the dear relationship of children, whom I am shortly to desert in the smiling innocence of helpless infancy? I have too frequently wandered from that order necessary for the perfection of His works, and yet He has never forsaken me! I have seen myself alone, unfit for the struggle of life, shrinking at every rising cloud in the atmosphere of fortune, adopting the pining, distrustful snarl of the misanthrope, and only in recent days have I understood that this world is indeed a busy scene, and Man a creature destined for a progressive struggle. I possess a warm heart, and inoffensive manners, and now at last I know that there is something to be done. Amidst the novelty of West Indian scenes, with Mary, I am determined to leave behind all these pangs of wretchedness and stabs of remorse which have settled themselves on my vitals like vultures, and let each day be a prayer of thanks to Almighty God, who has blessed me with immortality and lighted up Reason in my breast!

Monday, September 5th., Greenock. Gilbert writes to tell me that Jean has just brought me a fine boy and a girl at one throw! God bless the poor little dears! While I was quite resolved to tread the path of quiet and methodical routine, and reconciled to having two youthful dependents, I now find myself with three! Although I am not under the least obligation to her, I feel her situation most keenly, and console myself with the knowledge that Gilbert will do his utmost for her. I would have been driven to distraction by today's news but for the understanding and solicitude of my dear Mary, a sure antidote to the anguished conscience which would otherwise have made me unfit to read, write or think. I am thoroughly conscious of her deep attachment to me; in all housewife matters she is eminently mistress, and in short I can hardly fancy a more agreeable companion for my journey of life. I am all of a turmoil today, and given to weeping, though whether they be tears of joy or of sorrow I can hardly tell.

My brother-in-law Robert is somewhat improved, but the strain on my Mary has taken its toll, and she is greatly fatigued. Today when I saw the dark shadows under these wide blue eyes, I realised, for the first time, how great is the leap of faith which enables her to abandon her home and her family to travel with me to a life of which she knows nothing. I pray that I can be a worthy husband to this woman, for if ever an angel walked on earth, radiating noble qualities, it is she. The love I have for her is founded on the sacred principles of virtue and honour, and it is love like this alone that can render the married state happy. People may talk of flames and raptures as long as they please, but it has always been my opinion that the married life, properly speaking, can only be friendship in a more exalted degree.

September 10th. Ten days remaining. Have been to see the *Bell* – a fine, square-stemmed, full-built Carwell brigantine constructed here in Greenock only two years ago; twin-masted and (so her Master, Captain Cathcart, proudly informs me) measuring 173 tons.[11] Our accommodation is necessarily somewhat cramped, but it is clean and in good order. I am endeavouring to set my affairs to rights while Mary spends time with Robert, who is happily convalescent, but still appreciative of the devoted nursing which she provided, angel as she is! Have written to Richmond with news of Jean, and promised him a sonnet from the Indies.

September 13th. Tempus fugit, only a week remaining. I have procured all the clothes I shall require for Jamaica, and packed them in the trunk. Mary is doing likewise. By the time we have finished, I wager it will take three strong men to lift it!

September 18th . Since I last wrote I have made a final visit to Mossgiel and taken proper leave of my family. Mindful of Armour's determination to have me thrown in prison, I was very discreet about it. I would have liked to see Jean and the twins, but dared not risk it. In my absence Gilbert will have to assume the role of *pater-familias*, which will be a hard struggle for him, particularly now that he also has wee Bess to consider. William said that he had half a mind to come to Jamaica with me, but I have persuaded him to persevere with the saddle-making. He gives up too easily. My sisters have accepted my departure quite stoically, though little Isabella wept bitterly at my going. My mother was very practical and sensible – indeed, she made no more fuss than if I had been going to Kilmarnock. She made me promise to write as soon as I arrived, and counselled me to wear a hat in the sun. My brothers and sisters are all younger than I am, but our mother is fifty-four, and, as I do not know when I shall return from the Indies, there is a possibility that I might never see her again.

My little Bess is walking now, and it nearly broke my heart to see the joy in her eyes as she ran towards me when I arrived. She had been playing with her little dolls, an activity that keeps her amused for hours. She greeted me with an eager cry of Da-da, little knowing that I would soon be bidding her a long farewell. She is too young to understand what is happening. I shall write to her; and I have made it clear to Gilbert that he must tell her of me as she grows up. Who knows when we shall be reunited?

September 19th. No time to pen more than a line or two. Our trunk dispatched to the *Bell*, and all preparations concluded. Very tired. Our last night in Scotland – who knows what lies ahead? We have tried to conjecture what the journey will be like, but are unable to do so. Now that all our preparations are finally made, I feel a curious emptiness and aimlessness. I have been pacing about in an irritable and irresolute state of *ennui,* restlessly seeking something to occupy my attention, and finding nothing.

I was half-minded to write a poem, but my thoughts will not settle – they fly around in my head like autumn leaves in the breeze. Enough – I must be patient.

Wednesday, September 20th. I am writing this in our cabin on board the *Bell*. The die is cast; we are at sea! For so long I have been thinking of this voyage, and now that it is under way at last it is difficult to believe that it is really happening. At the moment of embarkation I was agonisingly aware that I was quitting my native soil: indeed, at the moment of setting foot on the gangway I suffered such a sharp pang from that knowledge that I thought I would weep. However, for Mary's sake I am endeavouring to speak positively about our journey. We sailed at about nine o'clock in the morning, and with favourable winds we soon left the Clyde and headed south. We were no great distance from land, and from the left-hand side of the ship (which I shall have to refer to as port in future!) the Ayrshire coast was clearly visible. When Captain Cathcart pointed out a distant cluster of buildings and steeples and told me it was Ayr, I found myself gazing at it with a terrible, empty sense of loss. Yonder were the scenes of all my youthful exploits; yonder was Jean with the two bairns; yonder was Bess; yonder was Mossgiel. How often had I looked out over this very stretch of sea, watching the sails of passing boats, and wondering whither they were bound! How many people, I wondered, secure on *terra firma*, were watching the *Bell* now? Did they realise that a poor wretch, formerly one of their number, was even now gazing shorewards with a heavy heart? Before long, the town was lost to view. There is such a fearful finality about this. I have written some verses that came into my mind more or less unbidden; I had vowed to myself never to touch poetry again, but it is difficult to lose the habit. Here it is, not more than an hour or two old –

Fareweel, fareweel

> Fareweel, fareweel, auld Mauchline toon:
> Fareweel ye banks of Ayr!
> Fareweel ye bonnie banks of Doon
> And the lass I'm leaving there!

> My ain dear Bess, ae fare-thee-weel
> For ever as we part:
> What earthly balm can ever heal
> A father's broken heart?

I've kenned fu' well mischanter fell
Thro' years wi' mis'ry fraught,
And now I brave the ocean's swell
To seek I know not what. [¹²]

Fu' mony a tear for mem'ries dear
Maun fa' tae blin' my ee,
As now I steer tae exile drear
Far ower the ragin' sea.

We passed by Ailsa Craig, which is exceeding massive at close quarters, providing a safe haunt for vast colonies of birds that make their nests on the cliff faces. It is a desolate place, and has about it the ghastly, eldritch eeriness of complete isolation. I had seen it a thousand times from land, and it was exceedingly novel to have a new perspective on it. What mysterious operations of nature placed it here, I cannot imagine. It is quite enough to make the hair bristle on one's neck to think of it!

It began to grow dark, and too cold to remain on deck. We repaired to our cabin, which has two bunks, a wash-stand, and room for little else save the great trunk, which contains our worldly goods, and occupies almost the entire floor space. A single port-hole gives us a view of the sea in the day-time, while two candles, in iron brackets, provide our light at night. I have pressed the top of the trunk into service as a writing-desk of sorts. It is all rather uncomfortable and cramped, and our only consolation is that it is temporary – in five or six weeks, all being well, we should be in Jamaica. This evening we partook of our first meal in the galley. The cook is called Kenneth McEwan: an oldish man with a permanent stoop which probably comes from spending so much of his life bending double in order to avoid dashing his brains out on the low ceilings and unexpected beams which have already dealt me one or two nasty bumps on the head. He served us up with a reasonably palatable platter of fish and boiled potatoes.

The motion of the ship is only very slight. Mary has already ensconced herself in her bunk, which she professes to be very comfortable. I am too weary to write more for today, and the poor light is paining my eyes.

September 21st. We awoke early after a very indifferent night. The movement of the ship caused me to start up several times, wondering where I was. There were all manner of sounds that rendered sleep impossible – the creaking of ropes; the flap of the sails; the clumping of the crew's boots as they moved around the deck above us, and the constant slapping and swishing of the sea against the side of the ship. I went up on deck, but there was no land visible, just the ocean, as far as the eye could see. Captain Cathcart was at the wheel, and bade me a civil good morning, and hoped that everything was to my satisfaction. He tells me that our course will take us south, between Ireland and England, as far as the English Channel, where we expect to meet a small convoy of vessels in whose company we shall proceed. This is to reduce the risk of attack by French ships, which has been known to happen more than once. We then make for the Azores, where, all being well, we shall pick up trade winds to speed us on our way westwards across the broad Atlantic – to Jamaica! – to our new lives!

In addition to Captain Cathcart, there is a First Mate, Mr Houston; and a Second Mate, Mr Galbraith, to whom we were introduced today. They are fine genial fellows. Our health is in the hands of a Dr Lockhart whom I have not yet had the pleasure of meeting, and I gather that he keeps pretty much to himself. There is only one other passenger, a tall, surly youth of about nineteen called Currie, who sedulously avoids everybody. The Captain tells me that he comes of a good family, but has brought some sort of disgrace upon himself, and so is being sent to Jamaica to mend his ways. The crew are six in number, I believe, but I do not know their names. While we are housed below deck in the centre and stern of the ship, they have their quarters at the front – or for'ard, as Mr Galbraith reminded me this morning. We can hear them moving about their duties, but as there is little to see on deck we remain below most of the time.

September 22nd. Another sleepless night. We have been bidden to dine with Captain Cathcart this evening. Mary is in something of a flutter of anticipation, though given the cramped nature of the dining accommodation, I hardly think it will be a very grand occasion. Yet I can see that one of the vicissitudes of the voyage will be the fearsome ogre Boredom, and so any diversion will be welcome. The Captain told me he had heard that I had something of a literary reputation, and hinted strongly that a poetical offering in the form of a toast would be welcome, and so, in some haste, I have done what I can.

September 23rd. At last, a good night's sleep – perhaps the inevitable consequence of the toasts yestreen! We were a party of six: our-selves; Captain Cathcart; Messrs Galbraith and Houston, and the hitherto invisible Dr Lockhart. He is a corpulent gentleman, with an extravagantly sanguine complexion. The mysterious Mr Currie had opted to dine alone in his cabin, which I felt was unduly churlish of him. McEwan excelled himself in the galley and served us quite a feast of boiled chicken and beef. These are the last of the fresh victuals brought on board, and from now on we will have to make do with the salted provisions laid aside for the journey. There is, however, no shortage of rum, brandy and whisky on board, and it circulated very freely after we had dined. The Captain said a few kind words about me, and paid some pretty compliments to Mary, which made her blush, and then I was invited to say my piece. I am happy to say that it was received with vociferous enthusiasm that was most gratifying to Mrs Burns and myself; the play on words in the final line – though hardly very original, to my mind – being much commented on for its cleverness. It went as follows –

A Toast to the Ship's Company

God bless the Captain of the *Bell*!
God bless her gallant crew!
In every skill they do excel
To bring us safely through!

To each and every one I call:
'Pray charge your glasses, fill them well!'
And now THE TOAST: Unite us all
In Friendship sound as any *Bell*!

I believe the Doctor had had considerable recourse to the whisky before sitting down to dine, for his speech rapidly became entirely incoherent. He also seemed inordinately keen to engage me in conversation, which was embarrassing, for the more his inebriation worsened, the more clearly did he believe himself to be making perfect sense. I must own that I could make nothing at all of what he said to me, and could only reply in a vague fashion, hoping that I was telling him what he wanted to hear. After about half-an-hour of mutual incomprehension he put his head on the table and, to my relief, fell fast asleep. I caught the Captain's eye, and he gave me an ironic look as if to say that this was nothing new. I fervently hope that neither of us falls ill during the passage.

I must confess to being rather unsteady on my feet when I finally arose from the table. Mary and the others very charitably opined that this was only due to the motion of the ship. At any rate I tumbled into my berth and enjoyed the soundest sleep I have had for weeks.

Alone on deck this morning, I saw the lad Currie standing with his hands on the rail, head bowed, the very picture of dejection and woe. I hate to see suffering in another, and went over with the best of intentions to introduce myself and wish him good morning. On discerning my approach, however, he moved off abruptly and walked to the other side of the ship, averting his face as he did so and putting up a hand as if to wipe away tears he did not wish another to see. I deemed it best to leave him alone for the moment, but I must ask the Captain more about him. Perhaps Mary will be able to engage with him and bring him out of his brown study. She has the sweetness of disposition that would melt the hardest of hearts.

September 24th. Sabbath Day. Some time within the next few hours we are expected to sight the other vessels which will cross the Atlantic with us, as we are presently not far from Land's End. Since there is nothing to be seen but endless sea on every side, I find it difficult to understand how it is possible to determine where we are. Mr Houston has shown me the workings of a sextant, a sort of telescope on a frame. The telescope is inclined to find the angle of the sun above the horizon, this angle being indicated by a lever on a curved scale. At night, the stars may be sighted in like manner. From a comparison of such observations with tables in an almanac, the navigator may thereby determine latitude, which is the distance north of the equator. There is more difficulty with longitude, which is the distance east or west of a given point. When Mr Houston was a young man he says he used to have to measure angles between the moon and certain nearby stars, and have recourse thereafter to the almanac, but now this is accomplished with the aid of a special clock called a chronometer, kept safely in the Captain's cabin. I found the explanation of its operation difficult to follow and am glad to leave this complicated business to those who know what they are about. Everything seemed clear as Mr Houston was expounding it to me, yet within ten minutes my poor brain was utterly confounded by the effort to recollect it.

This afternoon I had the chance of a few words with the Captain, and I took the opportunity to mention my encounter with Currie on deck earlier, and suggested that Mrs Burns might be able to break down the barriers that prevent him from being civil. When I said this, he looked very grave and declared that he did not think the idea a good one. I pressed him for a reason, which at first he would not vouchsafe me; but when I persisted, he explained that the young man had committed some heinous felony, and, his parents having some influence with the authorities, had been offered the stark alternative of either answering to the Law, or voluntarily accepting exile in Jamaica. Fear of imprisonment, or worse, had persuaded him to pursue the latter course. I enquired what his offence had been, but Cathcart declared firmly that this was a confidential matter which he was honour bound not to discuss with anyone. All he could say was that he would strongly advise against Mrs Burns having any contact with him, especially on her own. This has whetted my mental appetite and given rise to all manner of lurid suppositions, but I suppose I must follow the advice of the Captain.

Just before it grew dark this evening, another two ships came into sight, and are travelling on courses parallel with our own. We are headed for Finistère, which is the name of the most north-westerly part of France, and hoping that our numbers will safeguard us from any unwelcome molestation from French vessels.

September 25th. The sea was rough today, and it is proving difficult to write. I spoke to Mr Houston, who laughed and told me to wait until we reached the Bay of Biscay. I do not know what he meant by that, but I can imagine that it means worse to come. Mary has been feeling queasy, and remained in her berth today, declaring that she did not wish to eat. Mr McEwan brought some soup and bread to our cabin and explained that however ill one feels, it is always best to eat something. She obeyed his instructions, and declared herself a little better afterwards. I took a glass of rum this evening, which appears to have settled my stomach a little.

September 27th. We have rounded Finistère and have entered the Bay of Biscay. I could not write yesterday, for Mary was very sick. The motion of the boat grows steadily worse, and it is difficult to move about without falling over. The Captain has warned us against going on deck, for the planks are wet, and there is the possibility of falling overboard. It is difficult to write.

September 30th. If this continues we shall surely die! Oh Jesus.

Sunday, October 1st. Thank God, we are through the worst of it! I shall cast a tactful veil over the physical privations and unpleasant details of the hellish business. Instead, I have tried to write about it, not in any serious way, but rather as a flippant, silly means of putting the wretched experience behind us. This is my emetic offering, *spewed* forth, as it were, on the altar of the Muse! –

To the Sea-sickness

Pair mortal! Nature's less than kind,
When least tae suff'rin' he's inclined:
Tho' emerods plague his behind
    Wi' itchin' rare,
Just one can drive him oot his mind –
    The *mal-de-mer!*

Whiles wi' his cronies he converses,
Whiles sits he scribblin' at his verses,
Whiles, too, his sorrow he immerses
    In guid strong whisky:
He'll rue the day his ship traverses
    The Bay o' Biscay!

His cabin floor tilts up then doon;
His heid gaes birlin' roon and roon;
His groanin' belly's oot o' tune –
    Pale is his hue:
He kens the time is comin' soon
    That he maun spew!

He finds nae place tae lay his heid:
The nausea swalls wi' cursèd speed:
Pair sowl! He wishes he was deid:
    And safely beerit.
If Clootie's hell-fire were decreed,
    He wadna fear it!

He dabs his foreheid wi' a cloot;
And whimpers like an injured brute;
Heaves heart-felt groans, and rins aboot,
    Maist like tae greet:
And then the grue comes belchin' oot
    Tae file his feet!

Will respite come? Forget the notion
O' happy cure, or magic potion!
The hale damned warld is still in motion:
    The wild seas roar!
And, tossed upon that monstrous ocean,
    He spews once more!

O Thou! whose hand doth calm the sea,
I humbly pray on bended knee:
To Thy great pow'r and majesty
   I do defer:
Have mercy, Lord, and mak us free
   Frae *mal-de-mer!*

I crept out on deck this afternoon. No one else was there. Above me the sails were taut – crackling, snapping and creaking in the wind. All around was the cold, grey vastness of the ocean – it makes me feel small, insignificant and vulnerable. This boat, which seemed so large and fine in Greenock, seems tiny in the face of the prodigious hugeness of nature.

Mary is weak but appears otherwise none the worse. We have been to the galley and taken some food. Later we spoke at some length about how we feel about this journey, and what we have left behind us. For the first time we were completely frank with each other. Perhaps it has taken the storm to make us understand the reality of our situation. Mary is leaving behind two people she loves dearly: her father and her brother Robert. Dear soul, these are the only relatives she has in the world! For my part, I have my brother Gilbert to think of, but also Elizabeth Paton, and her daughter by these tempestuous loins – my tiny, darling Bess. There is Jean, and the two bairns. I am burdened with responsibility and guilt, and yet Mary enjoins me to think of the future. At this time we need each other more than ever.

Her view is that the past is the past, and that nothing can be gained from dwelling on it. Indeed, she has preached me quite a sermon on the need to look to the future. She declares that if I do not do so, then I shall become morose, which will make me a poor husband and companion. She is, of course, completely correct, and I have kissed her a thousand times and promised her that while my past can never be forgotten, I shall never permit it to dominate my thoughts. Although she is frail in body, she is a veritable Prometheus of mental fortitude.

October 2nd. Sighted land today on the port bow – see how I now use the seaman's language! – and am told it is Spain. Before long we shall head to the Azores. Captain Cathcart has pointed them out to me on his chart – a few small dots, which means little to me save for the realisation that there is but little in the way of dry land on this earth, amidst seemingly endless, desolate oceans.

Mary is reading *Pamela*, which keeps her entertained.[13] She tried to read some of it to me today, but the only pleasure I took from this came from the sweet sound of Mary's voice. The book I find execrable. The adventures of the witless woman are related in a series of long, rambling letters to her aged parents, which we are expected to believe she somehow finds time to write. Nothing of any consequence happens in the book, and to judge from the title, nothing will. She is the subject of the licentious attentions of a fushionless ninny called Mr B – quite why, I cannot imagine, unless he derives pleasure from observing the daft hizzie scribbling her tedious epistles. In my opinion, young Pamela would have been very much the better for a robust rogering twice a day with a good vigorous pintle rammed up to the hilt in her spleuchan. It would also make the book a deal more interesting. Mary was very shocked by these sentiments, which she finds excessively impolite, and mightily disrespectful to Mr Richardson. When I asked whether she would prefer to live a life of virginal virtue or connubial pleasure she protested with a blush that this was not the point. We argued for a while over this, and the upshot of it was that we betook ourselves to my berth where we surrendered ourselves to delicious amorous passions unknown to the tediously celibate *dramatis personae* of Mr Richardson's novel.

October 3rd. Still heading south. It is now noticeably warmer on deck, and as today was bright and sunny, we spent some time there. It is good to breathe the sea air, and we were more gay than we have been of late. Tomorrow we shall have been two weeks into our voyage, and we have gained what the Captain calls our 'sea-legs', so that we are unaffected by the movement of the ship.

At lunch-time Dr Lockhart honoured us with his presence: the first time we have seen him since the evening we dined together. He was not drunk, but neither was he sober, and he was perspiring very copiously. His conversation was limited to the alarming topic of scurvy, to which seafarers are especially liable. The symptoms are in the highest degree unpleasant: one bleeds under one's skin; one's joints ache intolerably; one's gums bleed and finally rot away until one's teeth fall out. He described all of this in exact and gruesome detail – he seemed unaware of the effect he was having on our appetites. Fortunately this ailment can readily be prevented by eating certain fruits, which is why we are served the juice of fresh limes with every meal. He told us that the late Captain Cook had made this discovery, which is why his crew had enjoyed good health during very long voyages. The good Doctor then launched into a tedious account of Cook's expeditions, growing quite sentimental and misty-eyed in the process. It took us a good hour to escape.

October 4th. Mary has been reading this journal and has made a suggestion concerning my style. Hitherto, recounting what has been said to me by others, I have been at pains to reproduce the gist of their words as accurately as I can. But Mary has asked me why I do not reproduce conversation *verbatim.* My first reaction was that I had only seen this done in the pages of fanciful novels, such as the wretched *Pamela*, where fictitious characters are made by the author to address each other, whereas my journal is entirely factual – a report of events as they happen. Mary contends that it makes no difference, and indeed claims that the accurate reproduction of discourse would increase the veracity of the account. I pointed out that I could not possibly remember accurately every word spoken to me, far less recollect conversations in their entirety several hours after they occurred. She argues that I would not have to do so, but merely set down those parts that I could recall.

I am intrigued. If I look at the few lines I have just written, my paraphrase of Mary's words – and my own – is entirely accurate. Yet these are not the words we actually used. If my memory serves me well she asked, 'Why don't you write down what people really say, Robert?' Then I said, 'You mean like characters in novels? But that's fiction, Mary. You canna write a journal that way. It's a description of real things.' Mary: 'What difference does that make? If you consider it, you'd be describing conversations more correctly if you wrote down what people really said – not what you decide they said.' I said (I think), 'How the devil could I remember every word ever spoken to me, lassie? It would tax my silly brain beyond endurance!' Then she laughed, and kissed me, and said (I remember this clearly enough), 'Dinna be daft, Rab, just the bits you remember!'

We have compared the two foregoing passages. I contend that the first is the more elegant of the two. She agrees that it may well be more refined, but that the second version is preferable because it gives a much clearer impression of our conversation. She likes the details about the kiss, and our little affectionate names for each other, which of course I did not mention in my 'elegant' version.

What a remarkable woman Mary is! I think that she is probably quite correct in what she says.

October 5th. Ten in the morning, and the Azores are in sight. I use the plural, but in fact only one island is visible, and that, I am told, is Saõ Miguel, the largest of the group.

There has been much activity on deck, for we are changing course and heading west and something to the north. We are also entering the realm of shockingly vast distances, for Jamaica is still some three-and-a-half thousand miles distant. The Captain says we have already covered some twelve hundred miles, which is hard to believe, although I am sure it is true enough. If the winds hold favourable, then we should make Jamaica in about thirty days.

October 6th. I rose early today, and lay silently for some time, thinking of the terrible finality of the decision we are making. Although I am entirely in accord with Mary's determination to look to the future rather than the past, I still bear a heavy heart. Mary was asleep, so I dressed quietly and went out on deck. There was nothing to be seen but the terrible loneliness of the ocean. Yet above the mast there was a gull, soaring effortlessly on the same breeze that filled our sails. Where had it come from? Something about the moment touched me deeply and I have spent today trying to force it into verse in the English mould, with the following result –

Lines composed at dawn upon seeing a solitary gull above the main-mast

Thro' taut-braced rig the salt wind sings:
The wind blows fair, the wind blows fair –
You soar above with outstretched wings:
Free as the air, free as the air.
Oblivious to my hopes, my fears,
My world of disappointed hopes and tears,
You follow [~~where~~] as the helmsman steers:
A spirit rare, a spirit rare.

Our [~~ship~~] barque heads far from Scotia's shore:
This star-girt dawn, this star-girt dawn –
My native land I'll see no more:
These days are gone, these days are gone.
And when I think on those I leave,
Full many a heart-felt sigh I heave:
Departed bliss I hourly grieve
To think upon, to think upon.

O! fellow-traveller o'er the mast,
And foaming swell, and foaming swell –
Thou hast no cause to rue the past:
I wish thee well, I wish thee well.
When storms and tempests do impend
To sheltered rest you'll safely wend:

But where my flight shall find its end
I cannot tell, I cannot tell.

Mary has read it. I have assured her that it is in no way indicative of gloom or pessimism, but simply the product of a transient state of mind. I have explained that sometimes, when things touch me, I have to write about them to purge them from my mind. She says the verses are very beautiful, and I hope that this may indeed be the case. Perhaps this is what I strove for as I wrestled with rhythms and rhymes, and trying to make something from an ephemeral experience. But I am spent and weary after writing out the final draft. Like a woman giving birth, I am heartily glad to have the whole business done with, the process of creation being a wearisome one. To make matters worse, it is not something that needs to be done at all.

Mary and I had a curious conversation this evening. She had been sitting with her book in her lap, but she suddenly put it away and turned to me.

'I have been thinking about Jamaica,' she said.

'What about it?' I replied.

'I have never seen a Negro.'

'Neither have I,' I said. 'What of it?'

'It will be strange, will it not?'

'I had not really considered the matter,' I said. 'I am sure that it is nothing to trouble yourself about.'

I have been too preoccupied with making good my escape from Scotland. Soon I shall be employed on a plantation, and yet have given far too little thought to my own likely feelings on the matter. I remember when I was a lad of fifteen or so, when I had just begun to commit the sin of rhyme, there was much talk about a Joseph Knight[14]. He was a Negro slave who had been brought to Scotland, and he took his master to court to obtain his freedom on the grounds that the state of slavery is not recognised in our Kingdom. I remember thinking that it was a brave thing to do. I know what the abolitionists are saying about the trade, and I feel an instinctive sympathy with their views, so why do I go to be a poor Negro-driver? I take refuge in the hope that the trade may soon cease, and that I shall not find the situation of the slaves to be as terrible as some would have us believe.

Sunday, October 15th. I have not written for a few days, as there has been an unpleasant incident with Currie. The day following my last entry, he decided to end his voluntary isolation, and appeared at table while Mary and I were finishing breakfast, taking a place opposite us.

He is not a prepossessing-looking lad. His hair is long and greasy, tied back with a grubby ribbon, and his face is thin and unhealthily pallid. His mouth was turned down in a sort of sneer, though whether this was his natural expression or not I could not say. He said nothing, but looked at us as if it was beneath his dignity to speak first.

'Good morning,' I said, civilly enough.

'Good?' he replied.

'I'm so glad that the sea is calm again,' Mary said with a smile. 'We were quite ill when the ship was crossing the Bay of Biscay. Wasn't it dreadful?'

'You were quite ill, were you?' he said derisively, in an exaggerated English accent. 'Well, well, you poor souls.'

I took immediate exception to his tone.

'I'll thank you to speak more politely to my wife,' I said.

'I'll speak the way I choose,' he retorted.

'Not to my wife.'

'What are you going to do about it?'

At this point I was on the verge of losing my temper, and in another few seconds I would have reached over the table and grabbed the impudent young cub by the throat, but Mary put her hand on my arm and suggested we leave the room.

'That's right, take him away,' said Currie as we departed. I fancied I saw a triumphant look on the cub's face, and was on the point of breaking free and kicking him around the cabin two or three times.

'Let him be,' said Mary quietly, sensing my fury. When we reached our cabin I told Mary that if the young fool behaved this way again he would have cause to regret it.

'Let's just keep out of his way,' Mary said. 'He's obviously very angry, and has forgotten his manners.' My opinion was that he would find his manners being mended very sharply if he ever crossed me again. Mary – ever patient and charitable – took the view that the boy was evidently upset at being sent away all alone, and having to begin a new life in a strange country, and was attempting to conceal his feelings behind a veneer of aggression.

As usual, I am sure she is right. However I do not find it in my nature to walk away from any insult, particularly an insult to my wife. She has made me promise to avoid him.

We did not see him for the remainder of that day, but the next day he was on deck when we went up to take some air. Obedient to my promise, I steered Mary to the other side of the boat, but when he saw us he came over and, leaning on the rail, began eying Mary with open licentiousness. I felt my blood begin to boil.

'Let's go below, Robert,' she said.

'Robert!' snorted the lad in a disdainful echo.

It was quite obvious that Currie had taken a dislike to me on sight, for I have given him no cause whatsoever for offence. Mary and I agreed that I should speak to the Captain about it before things went any further, and I was able to do so that evening.

I explained that I found the boy's attitude inexplicable, and that although I could handle his rudeness to me, I would not be able to account for my actions if this discourtesy extended to my wife. Cathcart agreed that it would be best for us to keep away from him as much as possible, but acknowledged that if he deliberately chose to provoke a disagreement then something would have to be done.

'I can't permit fighting on my ship, Mr Burns,' he said. 'I can fully appreciate your situation, but I represent the law on this vessel, and I cannot condone violence. But now that you have made me aware of the situation I shall be alert, never fear. However, I would counsel you never to leave your wife alone.'

'Do you think he is a danger to her?' I asked.

'He may be. Be careful.'

Three or four days passed without incident. The damnable thing about being at sea, even in a well-equipped and thoroughly modern craft like the *Bell*, is the impossibility of ever escaping from one's fellow-voyagers. Even in our cabin, only the thinnest of partitions separates us from the one adjacent, which is Galbraith's, and it is possible to hear the sound of every movement he makes when he is at home. Outwith the cabin, be one above or below deck, one is forever encountering others. For the first few days after leaving Greenock, we were constantly saying 'Good day' or 'Excuse me' or 'No, please do go first', but by this time we had adopted the shipboard practice of largely ignoring others. So we still saw Currie; but although he did not speak directly to us again, he has acquired a disconcerting habit of staring at Mary from a distance, which irritated me greatly, though I tried not to show it.

Yesterday things came to a crisis. Currie came on deck at about ten in the morning, much the worse for drink. We tried to ignore him, but he began speaking to himself in a way which was clearly designed to be overheard. His words were slurred, but those we heard were directed at Mary and were lewd in the extreme. I do not propose to sully the pages of this journal by setting them down here. We went below immediately, and I bade Mary remain in our cabin with the door locked while I went to find Cathcart and apprise him of the situation.

He was in his cabin. He readily agreed that Currie had gone too far, and proposed that he and a couple of members of the crew should lock him safely away until he sobered up, at which time he would be properly cautioned about his conduct. However he was nowhere to be found on deck. We went below and sought him in his cabin, but he was not there either. It was purely fortuitous that I decided to go to my own cabin, to tell Mary what had been decided upon.

To my horror, Currie was there. He had forced Mary into a corner, and with one hand was holding a knife to her throat, while with the other he was fumbling in her clothing, plainly intent on violating her honour. I was so appalled that in that instant I was unable to move, until Currie turned with a snarl and lunged towards me. I stepped back as he swung the knife at me. It was my good fortune that he was drunk, for the blade missed, and stuck in the frame of the doorway. I seized him as he made to pull it free, and the crewmen, who are great strapping lads, also took hold of him, and together we bore him to the ground.

Once he was safely secured, I rushed to comfort Mary, who was sobbing pitifully. She was unable to speak at first, but after a few minutes, brave girl, she began to compose herself, and was able to give her account of what had transpired. A few moments after I had left to talk to the Captain, she had heard a knock at the door. Thinking that I had returned, she had unlocked it. Currie had pushed his way in, held the knife under her chin and threatened to cut her throat if she cried out.

I was all for hurling the villain overboard there and then, but the Captain had him placed in irons and secured in the hold, where he is to remain until we reach Jamaica, when he can be handed over to the authorities.

'Did he imagine that he could get away with it?' I asked.

'It was the drink, I expect,' said the Captain.

'But there is nowhere to run on board ship!'

'Quite so. He must have lost his reason altogether. Not for the first time, I fear, which is the reason for his banishment.'

I was annoyed to hear this, for had we known that we were sharing the *Bell* with a dangerous lunatic then we might have been able to take better precautions. However, Mary has not been injured, which is the main thing. Lockhart opined very weightily that she was shocked (which I thought was obvious) and prescribed brandy (which did not surprise me greatly, as he has more than a passing acquaintance with its sedative effects). Mary and I have talked through the incident over and over, and anger has now given way to relief.

October 17th. Today we were very surprised to awaken and discover that the ship is passing through great floating mats and rafts of seaweed. At first I thought that we must be close to land, but Mr Houston says that this is a frequently observed phenomenon in these parts. Although the weed is not sufficiently thick to impede our progress, there are reputed to be huge floating islands in which hulks have become hopelessly entangled, and that these derelict ships may still be sighted, their sails rotted, and the bleached bones of their crew lying on deck. I do not know whether this is true or not, but we have spent much of the day scanning the horizon in search of marooned galleons. Needless to say we did not see any.

October 18th. The seaweed has gone. There was a very balmy feel to the breeze this morning, and it seemed to me that the sea is more blue than it was before. Overhead was a massive sky, stretching to limitless horizons in every direction.

I have spent some time today trying to speculate what our life on the plantation will be like. I imagine it will be much like any other farm, except that the crop will be sugar cane, and the workers will be Negroes, who are best adapted to the climate. I look forward to seeing the fields of banana and ananas, which must be a wonderful sight in the tropical sun. As for my duties as book-keeper, I assume that I shall be helping Mr Douglas by keeping his accounts in order, and arranging for the plantation produce to be sold. I do not envisage these duties as being particularly onerous – certainly nothing like the miserable, backbreaking travail I was compelled to endure at Mossgiel! I am not indolent by nature, but the prospect of a little lethargy has undoubted appeal. Until I set foot on the *Bell*, I do not think I had passed a single day without feeling compelled to accomplish something, and the enforced idleness of these past few weeks has been curious, but not unpleasant. I may even return to poetical composition in these new climes if I can find a dusky Muse to guide my pen.

We have just been out on deck. A moonless night – such darkness! We walked to the bow, hearing the creaking of ropes, and the rush and hiss of water as the prow cut through the ocean. Extending to every horizon, the wide expanse of heaven was lit with countless points of light! To look upwards gave us such a giddying prospect of vastness that we had to hold on to the ship's rail for support.

October 19th. Last night Mary told me that she believes herself to be with child. This is the most wonderful news, and I am not ashamed to admit that I wept for joy when I heard it. When I told the Captain that I was to be a father he clapped me on the shoulder and said that

I was a lucky fellow. He hastened to bring out a bottle of usquebaugh and we had several brimming bumpers to celebrate the occasion. We may have over-indulged somewhat, for I have a headache today, but that does not in any way detract from the joy I feel. I am full of plans, though Mary, ever practical, tells me that we shall have to wait and see what our circumstances in Jamaica will be. Our coming child represents a final break with the past, a tangible token of the new life we have determined upon.

Friday, October 20th. We have been exactly a month at sea, and we may reach port within the week. The Captain has said that we should see land within a matter of hours, and we have been eagerly scanning the horizon today. After so many days at sea, it seems hard to believe that there is any land at all upon the surface of the earth! Mr Galbraith came and stood with us for a while, and made a show of sniffing the air.

'Aye,' he said sagely. 'We'll sight Hispaniola in the morning. I can smell it in the air.'

'Smell?' we asked.

'Aye. A seasoned sailor can smell land. Take my word for it.'

We were not sure whether to take him seriously or not. I sniffed at the air myself, but it seemed no different.

October 21st. We are in the Indies at last, for to port we can just make out a distant mountain ridge, very hazy, which we are told is indeed the island of Hispaniola. How strange to think that Christopher Columbus must have enjoyed the same vista on his voyage of discovery! The island is Spanish, though the western part – Saint-Domingue – is French, and yields huge quantities of sugar from its plantations.[15] Our course lies along the northern coast, thence through the Windward Passage, which is the strait separating two of the greatest islands in the Caribbean Sea, Hispaniola and Cuba.[16]

October 22nd. I have spent today in composing a poem for Mary. Recent events have shaken her considerably. This will be the first poem I have written for her alone. I am now more than ever determined to think no more on what might have been, and to concentrate instead on the future that we shall share together, united in the tender bonds of mutual devotion.

My Ain Dear Wife

Were all the wealth of Croesus mine,
And finest silks, and rarest wine:
Had I domains in foreign land,

With rod and sceptre to command –
I'd trade it all to pass my life
With thee alane, my ain dear wife.

But if the Fates decreed it so,
Barefoot and penniless I'd go
To labour long at toils obscure,
And vilest hardship to endure –
And yet I should embrace such strife
If thou wert there, my ain dear wife.

I gave her the final copy and she was very moved by it. I have told
her that although I have done my best to express my emotions, mere
words cannot convey a fraction of what I truly feel. The knowledge
of her new condition is the perfect expression of our felicity, and I
am surely the most blessed of men.

October 23rd. Little to do today. I have been reading through this
journal with Mary, who says that in years to come it will serve to
remind us of times past, or auld lang syne, as that exceedingly
expressive Scotch phrase has it.

We have been on deck, looking at the distant land. It is very
mysterious and beautiful: much more mountainous than I would
have believed, with soaring peaks crowned with great white clouds.
The sea is very blue, the breeze is warm; it is altogether an idyllic
picture. I am not quite sure what I expected the Indies to look like
– I think I fancied the islands to be small and flat – but the grandeur
before us exceeds all expectations. Mr Galbraith was on deck, and he
tells us that Jamaica is much the same, though on a smaller scale.

October 24th. Very heavy rain today, which has kept us confined
below decks. The winds are very strong and so our progress is rapid.
Cathcart says we have passed through the Windward Passage. I am
impatient today, and for the first time on the journey I have felt,
quite literally, cabined. Mary is still engrossed in her Richardson.

October 25th. Preparations are being made for landfall. I have been
wondering how Currie is faring in the hold. Mary believes that his
behaviour was attributable to the drink, and is of the opinion that he
will be thoroughly contrite by this time. Her composure and
magnanimity astonish me! She has suggested that I should try to talk
to him. Now that I feel more calm, I may well do so. I am sure that
ten days spent in sober and solitary contemplation will have had a
salutary effect on his manners.

October 26th. We should be in Jamaica tomorrow, if the winds continue. Today I asked the Captain's permission to speak to Currie, for I am anxious to know why he behaved as he did. Cathcart agreed, on the condition that he be present. Accordingly we went down into the hold where the young man is confined, and found him a very sorry spectacle indeed, with heavy manacles on his wrists and ankles. When he saw me approach he cowered back, expecting to be struck.

'What dae ye want?' he said, attempting bravado, but with a tremor in his voice.

'I'm not going to harm you,' I said. 'I just need to know why you behaved as you did.'

He muttered something about having had too much to drink, and not remembering anything about it.

'But you took a dislike to me right from the outset,' I insisted. 'What the devil did I ever do to you to justify your antagonism?'

'You didna have to dae onythin',' he grumbled sullenly. 'There was I, bein' sent awa on ma ain. A disgrace tae ma family, as they keep tellin' me. An' there was you, wi' the bonnie wee wife and never a care in the world. Why should you get tae tickle her tirlie-whirlie while I lay in ma chaumer on ma lane playin' wi' ma pego? I just took a scunner, that's a'. I canna mind daein' whit I did tae yer wife. God man, I was bitch-fou. The drink does that tae me.' He looked up at the Captain. 'Whit'll happen tae me?'

'That will depend on Mr Burns,' said Cathcart. 'I shall have to hand you over to the powers-that-be in Kingston. I have heard that conditions in Jamaican jails are grim. But if Mr Burns saw fit, he might be able to arrange for charges to be dropped.'

'You'd surely no' see me in the jail?' said Currie, looking at me in supplication. All I could see was the vivid mental image of this disgusting creature holding a knife to the throat of my wife, and advancing towards me with murder in his eyes. He had shown no remorse – offered no apology – and I found his language repugnant.

'Would I no'?' I replied coldly. 'I'd see you in hell if I could.'

'Ye miserable, grace-prood bastard,' he screamed. 'I dinna want the jail! It's no fair!'

'Aye, you'll get your fairin', ma buckie,' I said with some relish. Then I went out, with Cathcart following, ignoring the oaths and imprecations hurled at our backs.

'Do you think I was unfair?' I said, when the hatch had been secured.

'Not a bit of it,' he said. 'He's a complete scoundrel. I'll put in a full report, of course, but he'll probably get off pretty lightly. Your wife was not physically injured, after all, and he'll probably claim that his head was turned by an attractive woman, and that he behaved as he did through a combination of youthful exuberance and strong drink. The courts in Jamaica tend to act with considerable leniency where the accused is a white man. He'll obviously stay mum about the reasons for his being sent abroad.'

'So he'll walk free?'

'Probably.'

'Then I shall go back down into the hold and throttle him.'

'You can't do that. If this had been a military ship I could have had him flogged, which is no less than he deserves, but I do not have that authority.'

I feel very angry at the turn of events. Is there no justice for those who have been wronged? Why do the wicked thrive?

As I have been writing this account of the day's events, Mary has been busying herself with packing our belongings into the trunk. We seem to have been an age on board ship, and although we are relieved that the voyage is nearing its end, we are almost sorry to be leaving our cosy little cabin, which had become quite a home to us.

Friday, October 27th. In Jamaica at last![17] When I went on deck this morning, land was in sight, and the crew were bustling around in preparation for docking. There appear to be great hills in the interior of the island, but, as the upper slopes were shrouded in dense white clouds, I could not guess at their height. As we drew closer to land, we could see little villages along the coast. We dropped anchor outside Kingston harbour, awaiting the arrival of the pilot who is to steer the *Bell* to her berth. We soon found ourselves surrounded by a host of small boats, expertly and energetically paddled by small, black-eyed children, almost naked, some with black skin, others with brown. They shouted to attract our attention, offering us coconuts, bananas and other fruit unfamiliar to me.

By and by the pilot arrived. He was an energetic, cheerful man with weathered skin and pale blue eyes. He appeared to know Captain Cathcart pretty well, for he greeted him familiarly. The anchor was pulled on board again, and the *Bell* moved forward slowly with only a little sail. As we entered the mouth of the harbour, we could see Port Royal to our right, but we would have been unable to dock there because all of the buildings were shattered and roofless, and the few that remained standing were leaning at all angles. The quay was littered with debris, and the harbour itself was filled with ships that had sunk. We have learned since that a hurricane struck here last week. I had not believed that wind could inflict so much damage.

The pilot steered us very slowly into Kingston harbour, through a forest of swaying masts. It began to rain, and by the time our moorings were secured, it had intensified into the heaviest downpour I have ever experienced. The port itself, so far as I could see through the vertical sheets of rain, consists of an untidy conglomeration of wooden wharves or jetties, with a collection of dilapidated buildings fronting the quayside, all made of wood, and painted a variety of garish colours. There are huge palm trees a short way off, and the rain made a great hissing sound in their drooping leaves.

After a short time the deluge ceased, and the sun came out, so that within a few moments everything was steaming. The effect of the heat was to summon up all manner of unfamiliar and unwelcome odours, each vying for supremacy in my quailing nostrils. There was, of course, the reek of tar and fish, which I dare say is to be found in any port, but augmenting this were effluvia of an unfamiliar and altogether noxious kind, probably arising from the rotting fruit I could see floating in the harbour. To add to our misery, the sun encouraged flies, which fortunately do not sting, but which settle on one's face in an abhorrently persistent way. Everywhere around us was a terrific bustle and din. The wharfs were full of commotion and activity: the rattling of carts; cracking of whips and the yelling of drivers. Mary tried to wear a brave face, but I was fearful for her, particularly in her present condition. We are in a permanent sweat. Captain Cathcart had word that a carriage would be here tomorrow to convey us to Port Antonio, and so we were to remain on board in the meantime. I must confess I was not sorry to hear it, for it will take us some time to become accustomed to this climate.

Currie is no longer on the *Bell*. The Captain gave him into the hands of the constabulary, together with a full written account of the incident that led to his arrest. I asked if we would called to give evidence at his trial, but it seems that this will not be necessary.

A customs official came aboard; the hatches were opened, and we encountered our first Negroes. They came on to the ship at about two in the afternoon – a team of about a dozen powerfully-built fellows who busied themselves silently and methodically with emptying the hold. We were on the deck, and at no great distance, but they ignored us completely. Their skins are exceedingly black, yet the palms of their hands are pink. Their hair, which is jet-black and very curly, lies close to their scalps, and is wiry-looking. We particularly noted their lips, which are very full; and their noses, which are more flat and wide than the European variety. We would have observed them further, but it seemed ill bred to stare.

It is now dark, and we are preparing for our last night on the *Bell*. The harbour noises have given way to the sound of raucous singing from the various rum shops on the front. It is very hot in the cabin, but we had to close the porthole after an enormous moth entered and fluttered round our candles. It is hard to believe that we are actually here, despite the evidence of our eyes and ears and noses.

October 28th., Port Antonio, New Cumnock Estate. We have finally arrived at the plantation after a perfect nightmare of a journey. Early this morning we said our farewells to Cathcart, Galbraith and Houston. The good Doctor, unsurprisingly, was still abed. The *soi-disant* carriage turned out to be a massive four-wheeled cart drawn by two horses. We were obliged to sit on some sacking in the back, with our trunk. Our coachman, if I may dignify him with so grand a title, was a taciturn Negro who spoke less than a dozen words to us during the entire journey. To be charitable, I allow that he had scant leisure to indulge in polite conversation, for the track – I cannot call it a road – was the most execrable imaginable. After only a few miles we were quite black and blue from the jolting and lurching of the wagon. Mary was visibly upset and distressed. We had no protection from the elements, and had to shield ourselves from the sun with handkerchiefs. At around noon, it rained with a vengeance, so that we were soaked through.

The journey seemed interminable, taking us up by zigzags into what our driver told us were the Blue Mountains, over a high plateau, and then down again. By the time we reached the estate, it was dark, and Mary was almost insensible with fatigue and misery. I pray that the experience has not put our unborn child at risk. For myself I am completely exhausted. I have a host of impressions and details to be set down, but they will have to wait until I recover.

I am writing this at a plain wooden table in what I assume to be our quarters. Having settled Mary, I really am too fatigued to describe it any further. Our driver told us that we would find Mr Douglas at the 'Great House' in the morning, and then rumbled away in his wretched cart. All I want to do is sleep.

October 30th. We have been to the Great House to meet Mr Douglas, a tall, spare man of about fifty. He has a mass of white hair, and huge shaggy eyebrows which, taken together with an aquiline nose, give one the impression of one of the fiercer Old Testament prophets.

He expressed his regrets at the rigorous nature of our journey, explaining that his carriage, which would have been more comfortable, was quite unsuited to the mountain road. He is a person of few words, and he looks as though he finds it painful to smile, which gives him a severe air of stern authority. His wife, on the other hand, is all geniality and generosity; she made a great fuss of Mary, and insisted that she should feel free to call round at any time. They were gaily talking about the correct clothes for the climate while Mr Douglas and I made a tour of the plantation.

I did not quite know what to expect, but this is perfectly extraordinary. The Great House would bear comparison with the grandest residence in Scotland, and is surrounded by lush, verdant gardens. Close by is a veritable township. There is the mill itself – a most imposing stone building – and next to it the boiling house, the curing houses and the still house, which are scarcely less impressive. This is surrounded by neat and well-tended streets where there are lodgings for the overseers, a smithy, and several carpenters' shops and cooperages. Beyond these are stables and farm buildings, and a whole town of Negro houses. There are two hundred and seventy slaves on the plantation, which extends to over nine hundred acres. A third of this is standing timber, and a further third is given over to the cultivation of yams, corn, bananas and plantains to sustain this metropolis, which is a bustling market town in its own right. Indeed I believe that even Ayr on a market day could not match this place for commotion and industry. It really is most remarkable, made all the more so by the heat, and the smells – most of which I do not recognise – and the sound of voices shouting in dialects unknown to me.

The remainder of the land is given over to the production of cane, which yields, I am told, around 200 hogsheads of sugar per annum, and 130 puncheons of rum.[18] When Dr Douglas first mentioned the word 'plantation', I had fond notions of a few fields of sugar-cane and had not envisioned anything on so vast and organised a scale. It will take some time to find my way around.

Mr Douglas says that I may have a week's furlough before taking up my duties. I am relieved, for both Mary and I are still feeling the effects of the journey. Last night, on going to bed, we were convinced that the room was in motion. When I stand still for any length of time I am quite certain that the ground is moving beneath my feet, so that I find myself swaying to keep my balance, no doubt giving a passable impression of a hopeless inebriate. Mr Douglas tells me that this is very common, and that it may take some time before one's sense of balance acknowledges that the sea journey is over.

We are housed very comfortably in a wooden cottage not far from the Great House: the other overseers and book-keepers also live in this part of the plantation. We have three rooms: two are bedrooms; the other a spacious chamber which serves as both kitchen and a living room. It opens on to a balcony at the front. It is well furnished with windows, which are necessary to admit any breeze, for it is very hot. These are not glazed, but furnished with shutters hinged at the top, and held open with poles. It is strange not to have a fire-place, but since there is no winter here, it would be quite superfluous. There is a garden at the rear, but it is very much overgrown, having been neglected for several months.

The mosquitoes are infuriating. It is quite impossible to keep them out, and they are present in such large numbers that I am bitten constantly. For some reason, they leave Mary alone, and while I am glad for her, I wish I could discover her secret. At night we have a net which hangs over the bed, but however assiduously I arrange it to exclude these insects, there is always one of the brutes which manages to get in, and the first I know of it is the whining sound it makes as it flies past my ear. By the time I have risen and lit a candle, it has vanished into some obscure corner of the bed, and the act of rising and opening up the net only allows others to enter, and so the wretched performance goes on until one is quite worn out by it. I have only spent two nights here, and each morning I have discovered a fresh crop of lumps that itch maddeningly, though scratching only makes them worse. I was bitten badly on the first night when I neglected to lower the net. Fortunately the bites themselves are harmless.[19]

We have a servant! I have always regarded a servant as something of a luxury only to be enjoyed by the well-to-do, as has Mary, and so this is an unfamiliar experience for both of us. The first we knew of it was when there was a knock at the door yesterday. When I opened it there was a young Negro lassie there, with a basket of provisions, who asked me if I was 'Massa Burns'. She marched in, seized a broom and began to sweep the place out. That done, she unpacked her basket and began to prepare a meal. Her name is Adah, and her conversation is limited to two words: 'yessuh' and 'nosuh'. She comes and goes as she pleases, and is content to ignore us while she does her chores. Yesterday we had chicken, cooked rather dry, and coated with some piquant herbs or spices which were quite new to me, served up with a sort of thin, flat bread. Today we had a fish stew with rice. Mr Douglas had a couple of hammocks brought over with his compliments, and I have rigged them up on the balcony.[20] Already Scotland seems exceedingly distant. I try to imagine what

kind of life Mary and I would have had together had we remained
there. We should eventually have achieved a tolerably comfortable
domesticity, I dare say. Yet as I sit at this table, hearing the crickets
outside; watching my precious Mary sleeping in her hammock;
seeing the fronds of the banana-tree waving in the warm breeze – the
bananas point upwards, by the way – I had always assumed they
hung down! – and see through the open doorway the bed where we
sleep as a respectable married couple – all of this seems like a dream.
Everything is so different from the familiar mundanities of Ayrshire.
I confess that it frightens me somewhat, for I know so little of the
quotidian realities of life here. It makes me uneasy to be reliant on
others in everyday matters.

Now that she is largely recovered from the journey, my Mary
bravely pronounces herself perfectly content, although I am sure
that she must have qualms. She has never spoken about her brother
Robert or her father, and this silence is a mark of her strength just
as surely as my diffidence in broaching the subject is indicative of my
weakness. Yet as I look over and see her slender form in the
hammock, I feel very responsible for her, more so than I have felt in
respect of any other person in my life. And soon we shall have a little
one to bring up – Mary believes that we should prepare ourselves for
the birth next March. Here we are, cotters in the Indies! May we also
'Be blest with health, and peace and sweet content'![21]

November 2nd. We have had the opportunity to see something of Port
Antonio, which is only a short distance from the plantation. The
town itself is of no great size – what there is seems dusty and noisy,
and extends along the shores of two bays, called West Harbour and
East Harbour, separated by a narrow peninsula with an island at its
end. The water is wonderfully clear and blue, and it is a joy to see the
little boats plying to and fro. What is most delightful is the lushness
and profusion of the vegetation. The hillside behind the town is
completely shrouded in green; everywhere there are giant palms
with long fronds, and brilliantly coloured flowers the likes of which
I have never seen before and whose names I do not yet know.
Everywhere we go we are treated with the greatest possible deference.

I have made a start in clearing our own garden, for the mosquitoes
hide among the weeds, and I would like to grow some vegetables, as
I did at Mossgiel. The best tool for this purpose is a long, broad-
bladed knife called a matchet, the same implement as is used in the
cutting of the sugar-cane. However it is difficult to work for long in
the heat, and the task is taking longer than I anticipated.

We have a neighbour, a Mr Garvie, who came by this afternoon. He is responsible for Mr Douglas's business interests in Kingston, and undertakes the purchase of slaves from Messrs Coppels, the leading traders on the islands. I would place him at about sixty years of age. The skin of his face is very lined, wrinkled and leathery-looking, doubtless the result of years spent in the tropics. Like Mr Douglas he does not smile much, and his manner is very formal. He expressed the greatest possible surprise that I was working in my garden.

'Why on earth are you giving yourself the trouble?' he said.

'Because it is all overgrown, and I want to plant some vegetables.'

'I don't mean that,' he said. 'I mean, why are you doing it yourself? There are nearly three hundred slaves here.'

I said that it had not occurred to me to instruct a slave to clear the garden, and that I assumed that their duties with the sugar cane occupied them fully. I also said that as a newcomer I was not sure whether I had the authority to give orders in such a way.

'Authority?' he said. 'Good gracious, man! You cannot be seen doing such work! You simply find an able-bodied neger[21] and tell him what you want done. Do you want me to organise one for you?'

I thanked him, but said that I would rather do the work myself. He looked at me very strangely, and went away shortly after. I know that slaves work on the plantation, but it seems wrong to ask one to carry out a task I can do perfectly well on my own. I had not realised just how much power I had simply by being white. There is something rather uncomfortable and unsettling in the realisation.

November 6th. Monday, and my first day at work. I had supposed that as a book-keeper I would be employed in a stifling office with nothing but dusty ledgers for company, but nothing could be further from the case. I am to supervise the work of the mill, together with another exile from Caledonia, John Armstrong, a cheerful Borderer who has been here for ten years. The only book-keeping to be done is a tally of the quantity of the juice extracted from the cane. It is a very interesting process, I am told, though I have yet to see it in operation. The mill only operates when the cane is being cut, and it is not being harvested at the moment, which is something of a disappointment. Armstrong tells me that when the mill is idle, we are expected to assist the overseers in their general supervision of the orderly workings of the plantation. This is not particularly difficult, since there is a clearly established routine. He says that the slaves work quite cheerfully and diligently while they are being observed, though their efforts tend to diminish when the overseers are not present. Between harvests, their main duty is to keep the growing cane free of weeds, which grow very prolifically in this climate, and this is a task in which their women and children are expected to take part. The production of food for the plantation provides a constant occupation for large numbers, as does the tending of livestock, for there are over a hundred cows here, and about seventy mules that are used for transport.

Today for the first time I was able to see the slaves at work. They seemed to be very happily engaged in their activities, and gave a respectful salutation to us as we passed. They were attired in plain cotton shirts and short trousers. But for their black skins, they might have been farm labourers anywhere.

'Mr Douglas is a good master,' said Armstrong, when I remarked on this. 'His slaves are well treated and they know it. It's in their own interests to get on with the job, because they know they'll be properly fed and comfortably housed if they do. There are always a few difficult cases – idlers, malcontents and malingerers – but not many. Mr Garvie makes his purchases with great care.'

There was something about the word 'purchases' that I found distasteful. I am not a fool, and was aware that slaves had to be bought, but it was not something I had really thought about. What touched me on the raw was the *casual* way in which Armstrong spoke – as if a slave was a simple commodity like a pound of nails or a length of timber. The Knight case came to my mind again, and I found myself wondering how anyone could possibly *own* another person.

'What price must one pay for a slave?' I asked.

'I believe their current value is forty pounds or thereby. When you consider how many we have here, that represents a huge investment, and that is why it makes good sense to look after them. A great deal of money is spent on maintaining their health – there is even a hospital for them.'

'And is this general practice?' I asked.

'Unfortunately not,' he replied with a grimace. 'There are plantations where conditions are very bad – usually the ones run by attorneys.'

He explained that he knew many plantation owners who disliked the climate, and preferred to remain in Scotland where they could enjoy their huge fortunes without having any direct contact with the reality on which their wealth was based. Apparently such proprietors appoint an attorney to run the plantation, and such posts are eagerly sought-after. They provide an excellent income and the more disagreeable duties can be delegated to the overseers. I learned that since the attorney has no personal interest in the estate, he can treat the slaves in any way he pleases, and brutality is commonplace. Of course, such an attorney would ensure that in addition to his salary, he pocketed a sizeable additional income by understating the production of the plantation, and selling sugar and rum for himself.

'Our plantation is not run that way,' said Armstrong. 'Mr Douglas is always on hand, and he has the best interests of the slaves at heart. They know that. Goodness, man, they are far better off here.'

He went on to explain how Joseph, our head cooper, had learned his trade here on the estate, and now travelled around other plantations, offering advice and helping to train other slaves who showed aptitude. He was allowed to charge for these services, and keep a proportion of his earnings after a percentage has been paid to Mr Douglas. Sooner or later, said Armstrong, he would purchase his own liberty, and set up in business on his own.

'This is a very civilised plantation,' he insisted, 'and Mr Douglas is rightly proud of it.'

He has given me even more to think about. Adah had prepared a meal for us, and I could not help but contrast my situation now with those cold November nights at Mossgiel, when I would stagger back home, numb with cold and nearly dead with fatigue. Truly a remarkable change in my fortunes!

November 13th. Monday again: a week has gone by almost without my knowing it. I can now find my way around the plantation, and the slaves recognise me.

To my astonishment – many things have surprised me of late! – I have discovered that the operation of the estate is much more complicated than I had supposed. Answerable to the overseers there is a contingent of the most dependable and trustworthy slaves, who actually undertake most of the work of supervision as well as the allocation of duties. In return they are granted special privileges. Only the head driver is permitted to wield the lash, and I am mightily relieved to learn that such punitive measures are almost unheard of on this plantation. I know that I could never strike a fellow-mortal with a whip to compel him to do my bidding – the very thought sickens me.

The slave village is marvellous to see. It is quite extensive, and very neatly laid out. The Negro women are very house-proud, and each home is neatly painted or whitewashed, and the little yard swept. Their clothes are simple, but very clean. I have not had the opportunity to view the interiors of the houses.

Until I came here I had assumed that all Negroes were the same, but I am told that this is not the case. There are Ibos, who are said to be very gentle by nature, and who make good domestic servants, although they are unsuited temperamentally to field work. The menfolk are very idle, and expect their women to wait on them constantly. There are Mandingoes, who have straight hair, and straight noses, and who are reputedly descended from the Moorish people. Many of them can read the Koran, which is their Bible, and they view Friday as a holy day. They are quick to pick up skills such as carpentry and leather-working – Joseph, our head cooper is one. Most of the field labourers are Coromantees. The French and Spanish will not employ them, because they have been associated with past rebellions, but ours are very well behaved.

Mr Douglas allows his slaves to have their Sundays at leisure, which gives them time to see to their crops. They may disport themselves as they wish, though the playing of musical instruments and dancing are forbidden, save on special occasions, for it makes them too excitable. I was surprised by this, but Armstrong says that dancing has invariably preceded rebellions on other estates, of which there have been several over the years, and that Mr Douglas is quite adamant on the point.

Mary goes almost daily to see Mrs Douglas. None of the other overseers is married, and she is the only other white woman on the plantation. I am glad she has company, for I had been afraid that she would be bored when I was not at home. Although she tries to keep out of the sun in the middle of the day, her skin has darkened. She is apologetic about it, but I have told her that I do not hold with the opinion that a chalky complexion is a sign of breeding.

'No doubt Pamela was as white as milk,' I said, teasing her. 'After all, she was so busy with her letter-writing that she never had time to go out of doors.'

I wonder if Negroes burn in the sun, or whether the darkness of their skin protects them? I must ask Armstrong about this.

It has come as a surprise to me to discover that such a large proportion of my colleagues on the plantation are also from Scotland, but I am told that this is not unusual, and that there are great numbers here, and indeed everywhere else in the Indies. Many have come to these parts out of economic necessity because Auld Scotia offers but a poor living, as I well know.

Jamaica is beautiful, but one can still see the effects of the hurricanes that wrought terrible devastation in 1780 and again the following year. I believe that upward of twelve thousand slaves perished of famine during these awful times, and in the lean years that followed, and the island is only now recovering. That is why such a considerable proportion of this plantation is given over to 'pens' that help to sustain everyone who lives here – slaves and masters alike.

November 21st. This week I am supervising in the cane fields. In addition to weeding, a section is been replanted with small cuttings called ratoons. It takes them less than a year to attain a height of fifteen feet or so, when they are ready to be harvested. The slave women make a hole in the ground with a dibble, and drop the shoots in. Children fetch water, which is poured into the holes, and the cutting firmed in place with the sole of the foot. It is important that the cane is evenly spaced and planted in straight lines – a long piece of twine is used for the purpose.

The planting party is under the supervision of an elderly slave called Gregory. He is a gentle soul, with white hair, and only two teeth left in his head. He tells me that he was born here on the estate, before Mr Douglas's time. I said that I expected he had seen many changes. He said that he had – I cannot set down his words, as Mary would wish, for to be candid I did not understand all that he said, and do not know how to spell the parts that I was able to make out – the slaves speak a kind of English, but with an accent to which I have not yet become accustomed. He could recollect being whipped when he was a young man, for stealing vegetables. The old master had once ordered a man's foot to be cut off for running away, summoning a doctor to carry out the operation. But these were in the old days, and Gregory was of the view that Douglas was a good master, a view he repeated rather more often than was necessary.

He spoke about something called 'merunes' which had been the cause of a lot of trouble. When I went to the Great House this evening to fetch Mary home, I had the opportunity of a few words with Mr Douglas, and mentioned this to him.

'He means Maroons,' he said, 'but it has nothing to do with their colour – it's a Spanish term, I think.[23] When the Spanish left Jamaica, they let their slaves free, and they established settlements in the hills. They would attack plantations, and there was eventually a full-scale war with them. It was impossible to defeat them, and in the end a treaty was agreed. It's held so far. But that's why it is so important to run contented estates – if there is a hint of rebellion, we'll have the Maroons down upon us in an instant. They're a formidable lot. One of their leaders was a woman by the name of Champong Nanny – the Jamaican equivalent of Joan of Arc. Next time you see Gregory, ask him to tell you the story about her fighting methods, particularly when returning musket fire.' I said that sounded very intriguing, but he would not be drawn further.

Mary has been in excellent health and spirits this week. She has penned letters to her father and her brother; and I have done my filial duty and written to my aged mother, assuring her that my hat never leaves my head from morn to night. Mr Garvie took the mail to Kingston on his last visit, and made the necessary arrangements for us. We both feel much better for having done this, though it may be February before the letters arrive.

I have been asking Armstrong what is to be done about mosquitoes. I had hoped that he would be able to suggest some infallible remedy, but his only advice is to wear a sock over one's head with small eyeholes cut in it. As far as burning in the sun is concerned, he says that it also affects Negroes, though not to the same extent. Obviously the effects are not so noticeable, but he has seen black skin peeling just as white skin will do.

I have cleared the yard, and am now wondering what I can procure to plant in it. Adah is amused by my horticultural efforts. She treats Mary with great deference, but scolds me as if I were a naughty child. When I come in from the yard, she looks pointedly as my boots, and goes for the broom, saying 'Yuh makin' de house dutty again, Massa Burns?' I think it amuses her to have her little womanly authority over the 'Massa'. Mary and I have concluded that we do not know what we would do without her. I asked her how she came by the name of Adah, and she explained that this was the name given to her by Mr Douglas, and that her real name is (I think, having asked her to repeat it several times!) Mawunyaga Adumensa, though she only uses this when she is among her own people.

Since our arrival I have not been able to contemplate composing poetry. I do not find it easy to write descriptively, attempting to paint wild or exotic scenes in fine words. It is mostly the small incident that touches me. Moreover, I find I do not have the time. Perhaps I should have worked more assiduously at versifying while I was on the *Bell*. The plain fact is that I cannot write to order, though once an idea seizes hold of me, I am fit for little else until I have it on paper.

November 23rd. The planting is finished, and I have been supervising the still, where the estate produces its rum. The process involves the fermentation of molasses, which is the residue from the sugar-making. There are three large vats for the purpose where the dark, sticky molasses are combined with dunder – the dregs from the cane juice, which ferments naturally. Water is added, and the action of the dunder coverts the sugar to alcohol, much as yeast will act in bread. The smell is absolutely appalling. An instrument called a hydrometer is lowered into the malodorous mixture to determine when the fermentation is complete. The mixture is not drinkable at this stage, and pipes convey it down to the distillation vessels that resemble oversized copper kettles. Fires keep the mixture on the boil – these are fuelled by stuff called bagasse, which is the name given to the sugar cane that has been crushed, and allowed to dry. The alcohol finally emerges in a slow trickle from a coiled tube, immersed in water, in which it has condensed. This finished rum is directed into puncheons, which are propped in place with the bunghole uppermost.

It takes two or three days to fill a puncheon, but it would take an eternity without constant vigilance to ensure that the workers do not appropriate it for their own use. The slaves are very fond of rum, but Mr Douglas is concerned about the possible consequences of drunkenness, and insists on an overseer being present in the still-house at all times. Such are the privations of being in such a place that we are only there for two days at a time.

It is impossible to remain there for more than ten minutes and remain sober. There are only a few small windows, and these are securely barred. The doors must be kept closed and locked at all times. The heat of the fires under the still, and the sharp fumes of the rum combine to make you light-headed almost immediately. After an hour, a terrible headache develops, and by the time another overseer comes along, you are staggering about.

Charles, the slave in charge, seems quite unaffected by it all. He is a Foolah, and a Muslim, and so does not drink alcohol, though he must absorb vast quantities of it through the pores of his gleaming black skin. He is a massive man, which perhaps protects him from the pervasive vapours. For his work, he requires at least three assistants, and unsurprisingly there is no shortage of volunteers for the job; they work for but three hours at a time, and often have to be carried out insensible. From my own observation, it is very clear that they do everything they can to appear unconcerned about the proximity of the rum, yet as soon as one's back is turned they have found some pretext to approach the channel which feeds the puncheon, and to scoop some quantity of the liquor surreptitiously into their mouths, believing themselves to be unobserved. And indeed they might well succeed in this, but for the fact that they quickly fall over and have to be carried away, quite drunk.

Any desire one might otherwise feel for the demon alcohol disappears completely when one is required to maintain oneself in such close proximity to the revolting substance. These last few days I have been arriving home of an evening very much the worse for wear. Adah finds this in the highest degree entertaining, and greets me with a cry of 'Oh ho Mistah Burns, yuh bin drinkin' rum all day?' I really do not share her amusement, nor does Mrs Burns, who has to forego my company and put me to bed.

Monday, November 27th. Thank God I have returned to duties in the fields and the open air. I had a confounded aching in my wretched skull that lasted the best part of two days, and I can form a pretty near guess as to the cause of it, but now my head is clear again. I own that even the thought of rum makes me quite ill.

When with Mr Douglas the other night, I had the opportunity of examining briefly an essay on slavery that has recently been published. I think the author's name was Clark.[24] Mr Douglas expressed the greatest possible displeasure with it. I asked him in what way he found it offensive, and he jabbed at the word 'human' that formed part of the title.

'That is what is the matter with it,' he snorted. 'How can anyone be so deluded as to imagine that the savage is 'human' in the same way as you or I are human? I grant you that he has two legs, two arms and a head, but so has an ape. Is it any wonder that the savage and the ape come from the same continent? Is it not obvious that they are closely allied? I grant you that when they have been taught to speak, and given clothes to wear, and shown how to perform useful tasks they may acquire some of the trappings of humanity, but God has ordained them for our use and no amount of sentimental philosophy will change that fact!'

He thumped the pamphlet on the table repeatedly as he spoke – I had never seen him lose his composure before. I asked if I could borrow the tract in order to form my own opinion of it, but he made some remark about filling my head with foolish and dangerous notions, and so I forebore to press him. I said I was surprised to hear him speak so disparagingly of the Negroes, for he had always given me the impression that he treated his slaves pretty decently.

'Of course I treat them decently,' he snapped. 'It is in my interests to do so. If they rebelled, or grew sick, or ran away, then where would I be? Where would *you* be, Mr Burns, eh? There's not a slave in Jamaica better treated than my boys. But you have to remember what they are. Don't start to attribute them with fine feelings and noble sentiments, because you can take it from me that they do not possess any. Do you know how many slaves there are in Jamaica? A quarter of a million, Mr Burns! That means eight blacks to every white man. Can you even begin to imagine the scenes of chaos if they were all suddenly set free? What would happen to the plantations? What would happen to England if there were suddenly no more sugar to be had out of the Indies? And what would the slaves do? Where would they live? How would they support themselves? Before this blockheaded buffoon began scribbling his ridiculous, pious meanderings he should have considered the realities of the case. I'll wager he has never set foot on a plantation.'

There was much more of the same. I left for home feeling somewhat uneasy. It is certainly true that the slaves here are well treated, and in return they appear cheerful and diligent about their duties. I have no doubt that their situation here is much better than their savage state in Africa. However, something within me reacts with distaste to the notion that they are not human. When Adah teases me about my dirty feet, and makes to beat me with the broom, she is behaving in the same way as any high-spirited servant lassie. She may be a slave, but she exhibits all of the qualities of *homo sapiens*; and if she is indeed human, which I believe to be true, then how can she be ordained by God for my use, as Mr Douglas avers to be the case?

December 5th. Mary continues in good health. She tells me I have gained weight – if so it is thanks to Adah's cooking. I have been trying to make something of the yard this week but am much vexed by my failure to grow anything but copious quantities of rank and odiferous weeds. Adah finds this hugely diverting, and laughingly offers to cook them for me. For someone who is not officially to be regarded hereabouts as human, she nonetheless displays an engaging sense of humour. Her devotion to Mary is immensely reassuring to me.

Very throng this week with the weeding. It is very hot, and sometimes I almost – I say almost! – long for a guid dreich day, and a fine penetrating drizzle, driven by a nipping wind. It will be winter in Ayrshire; the ground will be hard with frost; and Gilbert will be ending his work for the day, all muffled and begloved, with his breath hanging about him, white and vaporous. Yet here am I, sweating in a light cotton shirt. In Mossgiel, there will be the bleating of sheep, and perhaps the bleak cawing of crows in the branches of trees, bare of leaves now, black and bleak with rime, while here, the twilight outside is filled with the tropical chorus of frogs and crickets in the verdant foliage. Were it not for the damnable mosquitoes, I would believe myself in paradise.

December 12th. I have grown pretty well used to the climate – I still
feel the heat, of course, but I have learned to take life at quite a
different pace. I recollect well the first few days I spent here,
wondering at the way in which everyone strolled slowly around, as
if they had not a care in the world, even when they were engaged on
the most pressing business. I have a staunch ally in Adah, who
admonishes Mary severely if she so much as lifts a finger. She lies
down to rest each afternoon for two or three hours, in order to avoid
fatiguing herself, and until the nine-month race is run I have insisted
that she refrain from any activity which will tax her. What it is to be
a husband, and to have a wife so gratefully and fully devoted to me!

What can I say of the conjugal state? Well, I divide the scale of
good-wifeship into ten parts – good nature, four; good sense, two;
wit, two; personal charms – by which I mean a sweet face, eloquent
eyes, fine limbs and a graceful carriage – all these – two. As for
fortune, connections, noble birth – I would not give a whit for any
of them. My Mary must be the paradigm against which all other
wives should be judged, for I cannot conceive of any other man
enjoying the perfect companionship and happiness which she brings
to me. We may never accumulate much by way of worldly riches or
gear, yet I hope that our child may inherit the rich legacy of her
mother's goodness of character.

December 19th. We have been invited to the Great House on Christ-
mas Day, to partake of a formal supper with Mr and Mrs Douglas.
I gather that this is something of a ritual invitation, extended to all
overseers and book-keepers when they reach the end of each year on
the plantation. Mary is all of a flutter – Adah and she have spent
hours fussing over every garment in her wardrobe, and are still
nowhere near a decision as to what she will wear on the night!

I asked Gregory today about Champong Nanny – the matter had
escaped me until now – and he was at first very gratified to hear that
I had acquired the rudiments of Jamaican history. I said that I had
heard that she had employed some unusual methods of combat, and
desired him to let me know what they were.

'She brave fighter,' said Gregory.

'Is that all?' I said. 'I thought that she used special tactics when
fired upon.'

Gregory's eyes opened wide in surprise, and then he burst out in
mighty guffaws, slapping his thighs in merriment, bent double with
hilarity.

'What on earth is the matter?' I asked.

'Oh Massa Burns!' he wheezed. 'Don' ax me tuh tell yuh!'

'Why on earth not?' I said in vexation. He would say nothing, but burst out into laughter again. For all my efforts, I could get nothing out of him. Every time he started to speak, he would collapse in paroxysms of mirth. It is all very frustrating, and I shall have to ask someone else.

Monday, December 25th. Christmas Day, and supper at the Great House. We dressed our best for the occasion, and I believe we made a very handsome couple. We sat at a very fine table of dark, polished wood, set with delicate white chinaware and silver cutlery. Two Ibo boys were in attendance, dressed in the most impeccable livery – deferential and efficient. We dined on beef, perfectly served up with a tasty gravy and potatoes. There was wine, and much rarefied conversation. I was asked about my poetic endeavours, which appear to have been the subject of correspondence between my employer and Dr Douglas in Cumnock. I freely owned that I had once been pretty sure that my poems would have met with some applause, but was now content that the roar of the Atlantic would drown the clamour of censure; and that all of my pretensions were now behind me; and that any future visitation of the Muse would be a purely accidental encounter. I said that I knew that Fancy and Whim might make me zigzag in my future path of life, but my intention was to proceed with the most determinate integrity and honour. It was a pompous little speech, no doubt, but I have an instinctive dislike of being sounded out, particularly where poetry is concerned. It is too damned personal to discuss with anyone else.

There was more wine, more brandy, and more convivial chatter. The evening finally ended with Mr Douglas reading from his great Bible, in tones that reminded me of the patriarch Cotter. As his text he had selected the Gospel according to the first chapter of St John, *videlicet –*

He was in the world, and the world was made by Him, and the world knew him not. He came unto His own and His own received Him not.

These divine words are supremely moving, but, blasphemous though it may seem, I cannot help but apply them to my own situation. I did not seek or claim to create anything distinctive in Scotch poesy, but I put forward my best endeavours and was spurned. I wonder how many other obscure individuals such as myself give of their utmost, only to experience rejection?

By the time we left, I was feeling morose, but Mary chided me gently, and persuaded me that it was only the brandy, and reminded me of how much she loved the poems I had written for her. She is right – the only way to go is forward!

December 31st. This is the last day of the month; and of the year, and tomorrow's rising sun shall usher in the dawn of the year of our Lord 1787. I am writing this brief entry before the festivities begin, feeling it safer to do so while sober. Armstrong has come around with a bottle of whisky, determined to celebrate Hogmanay in true Scotch fashion, although it is the Sabbath Day. I fear that Mr Douglas would disapprove mightily, and I think that we shall end up notoriously bitchified ere the year is out!

1787

January 1st. Awoke late this morning with a pounding head, for which I only have myself to blame, and have determined never again to succumb to the seductress Drink.

January 4th. A letter today from Gavin Hamilton. My family is all in good health, and Gilbert is having more success with the farm, which pleases me greatly. He was always one to persevere, and in every sober qualification he has ever been my superior. Jean is well, and the twins, whom she has named Jean and Robert, are thriving. My little Bess is well, but Gilbert says that she enquires after me a great deal, and on being told that I am in the Indies, asks that she may be soon taken there to see me: poor child! she can have no inkling of how far away her father is! I must write to her. There is not much else in the letter: he writes that if I were to return I would find little altered. How strange to peruse his epistle, penned in a wintry Mauchline. I feel an oddness, as if it has come from another world altogether. Mary has read it and says that she hopes it will not make me melancholy. In honesty it does not do so, but rather engenders a gentle wistfulness of the soul.

January 10th. Praise be to a benevolent Deity for the simple pleasures of domestic routine! There are men, I know, who despise the conjugal situation, speaking of marriage as if it were some ghastly ordeal, and of their wives as if they were veritable Maenads. Does not 'conjugal' derive from *jugum*, a yoke? I have heard them bewail the need to do an honest day's work, or turn their hands to even the most elementary of household chores. I well remember occasions in Poosie Nansie's with the tippenny flowing copiously when anyone would have thought that the daughters of Eve had been ordained for the sole purpose of rendering life intolerable for men. I blush to own that I expressed myself as being in agreement with those silly senti-ments. Ah, the foolishness of youth! At the end of this month I shall attain my twenty-eighth year, and with the *gravitas* of middle age, a proper appreciation of those blessings which adorn it, *videlicet*, a charming and devoted wife; a profession that sustains me without undue effort; a pretty home; a cheerful and tireless domestic; robust health, and shortly a little one to adore. Who could ask for more?

January 17th. Mary is looking radiant, and says that being with child suits her. She thinks that the confinement will take place towards the beginning of March. Adah fusses over her constantly. Today I came home from the plantation to be met on the threshold with a wagging finger and a vehemently whispered admonition: 'Missiz Burns sleepin', so yuh betta mek no noise less yuh wants *trubble!*' Sometimes I wonder who is the servant in the house! She was born here in Jamaica, and seems perfectly content with her situation. The fact that she is owned by Mr Douglas, who could sell her if he wished, does not appear to concern her in the slightest. In consideration of her feelings, Mary and I have avoided using the word 'slave' in her presence, but she herself has no such compunction. The other day I spilled some broth on the table, and was about to mop it up when Adah snatched the cloth from me.

'Hey, Massa, no reason fuh yuh tuh clean when yuh've a slave in de house,' she said, quite without irony, and in the most matter-of-fact way.

'I don't think of you as a slave, Adah,' I said.

'No?' she replied, with a smile. 'But dat's what I is, all de same.'

'Well, maybe. But I mislike the word as it applies to you. We're very fond of you, Mrs Burns and I.'

'Dat don' change nuttin'. We all slaves, Massa Burns! I works fuh *you* – *you* works fuh Massa Douglas – an' Massa Douglas works fuh de sugar traders. No diff'rence. We all gat jobs tuh do.'

She went on to explain that she had lived all of her nineteen years on the plantation. Her parents worked here, as well as her two brothers, one of whom was apprenticed to the blacksmith, and so could look forward to a prosperous future. What, I wondered, was her ambition in life?

'Mebbe fin' me a white man and have fair chil'n,' she said impishly.

'Why on earth would you want to do that?'

'T'ink 'bout it,' she said, with a laugh, as she walked off. I did not quite know what to make of her remark at first, but I *have* thought about it and have concluded that there is logic in what she says. I know that children of black women and white men are spared from slavery, and as free coloureds they enjoy many privileges. I suppose that after two or three generations of this it may be difficult to detect the presence of a Negro ancestor. It saddens me, however, to think of any ambition based on a desire to resemble in ever-greater degrees one's oppressors. Adah possesses not a single drop of white blood, yet for all that she is, I realise, remarkably fine looking – though in outward regard quite different to a white woman. She has, in short, a beauty which is peculiarly her own, and it is a matter of regret that she should feel obliged to deny this to future generations in order to gain full social acceptance for them.

Oh, the disgrace of having black skin! Oh, the dread connotations thereof – blackheartedness; the black arts; blackmail; the Black Death! What a blackguard must every Negro be, by virtue of his ebony hue, fit only to have his unworthy name written in a Black Book by the sooty Prince of Darkness himself!

January 25th. Yesterday I had some trouble with Aquinas, a young slave who has newly joined the great gang.[1] He refused to work, saying that he was sick, though to my mind there was nothing wrong with him. Gregory prodded him with his stick, but the lad only made the most desultory attempts, and as soon as he was left on his own sat idly on the ground, with the sulkiest expression imaginable. Gregory was determined to have the young scoundrel given a good flogging, but I dislike violence, and decided on another approach.

'So you are sick, eh?' I said.

'Yessuh.'

'Dear me,' I exclaimed, with solicitude. 'I am very sorry to hear it. We cannot have you out working in the sun if you are unwell, can we?' He looked at me oddly. 'No,' I went on. 'We shall have to look after you. Come with me, Aquinas.'

I took him to the hospital, and made him sit in the porch while I had a word with the person in charge, a peevish fellow called Simpson who styles himself a doctor, though I have my misgivings. I explained that there was nothing wrong with the boy except an acute dose of sloth, and that I had a shrewd suspicion that at the end of the day he would miraculously recover, and desire to be off.

'A malingerer, eh?' said Simpson. 'What are you bringing him here for?' I explained my strategy, and then brought the patient in.

'This is Aquinas,' I said to Simpson. 'He's complaining of feeling sick. I think you'd better take a look at him.'

'Very well,' said Simpson, and made him sit on a bed. He prodded him all over, looked down his throat, into his ears, shaking his head and tut-tutting all the while.

'Aye, it's a very bad case,' he said at last.

'What is it, doctor?'

'In my professional opinion it's a severe case of *lethargitis*, made worse by excessive indolence of the *gluteus maximus*.'

'Oh, surely not?'

'I'm afraid so.' Throughout all of this, Aquinas was looking at us with increasing agitation.

'I really is sick?'

'Oh yes, you need bed rest and regular doses of cinchona. With luck you'll recover.'

I left as Aquinas was being put to bed. That evening I returned to check on his progress, to find that immediately after the first dose of cinchona he had declared himself suddenly and completely cured. However, as I had agreed with Simpson, he was being kept in bed and made to continue with the treatment. In the morning I looked in on the way to work. 'How are you feeling today?'

'I's better, Massa Burns!' he exclaimed. 'I's truly better. I don' need no more'f dat stuff.'

'But are you well enough to work?'

'Yes! Oh yes!' he begged. 'I's well enough. Lemme go tuh work!'

'What do you think, doctor?' I asked.

'Well, I don't know,' he said. 'It's a strange illness. Sometimes the patient feels better, but then they get sick again.'

'Don' say dat, man,' Aquinas implored. 'Yuh *knows* I is better.'

'Do I?' I said. I wouldn't want you out in the fields and falling ill again.'

Eventually we relented. Of course, he knew perfectly well that we had seen through his strategem and turned the tables with our own.

It is my birthday today – twenty-eight years. Adah was very merry about it and said that I would soon require a walking stick. She had prepared a veritable feast, with a spicy stew of chicken, which she knows I adore. 'Massa need plenty nourishin' food now he a' ole man,' she said with a sniff as she served it up. I know she was speaking in jest, but in all seriousness I actually feel younger. Before we came here, my joints were prone to rheumatics in the cold weather, but now I no longer feel these debilitating cramps and twinges, and my hair and my nails seem to grow more luxuriantly than before.

I went down to watch the great gang in the cane field. The rate at which they work is truly prodigious. One team cuts down the cane while another stands by ready to gather up the felled stalks and strip off the leaves. When this has been done, the next team gathers the stalks into bundles, and loads them on to the cart. By the time it is full, another is waiting to take its place, and so the whole procedure is continuous. Nothing can be allowed to pause for a moment – if any group should cease work, then everyone else is quickly affected. The plantation is like a complex machine with many moving parts, each one depending on scores of others. The men perspire copiously, and their hands are sticky with the cane juice. I have tried to cut cane myself, and after a few minutes I was too exhausted to continue – it never fails to amaze me how these fellows manage to labour for hours on end.

February 10th. As the date for Mary's confinement approaches, Mr Douglas has referred us to a Dr Morton who has a practice in Port Antonio. We paid him a visit today and were favourably impressed. He examined Mary and declared her to be in excellent health. The baby is kicking lustily and in his opinion the birth is due in about a month's time, at the beginning of March. He has promised to attend to the delivery in person, and we feel that we are in good hands. Mary was very pleased with the excursion, for she has not recently had the opportunity to venture further than the Great House and its immediate environs. It was November when she last visited the town, and she only saw a little part of it then, so we instructed our driver to take us on a more minute tour of inspection. There were some very picturesque streets, with prettily painted wooden houses; with the sea a perfect blue and the backdrop of the wooded hills made a delightful setting. Presently the driver took a wrong turning, and so we were obliged to pass through a very squalid area. The smell was insupportable, made worse by the intense heat; great swarms of flies buzzed around us, settling on any exposed part of our bodies they could find. Our progress was hampered by little Negro children who hastened towards us, and tried to thrust themselves close, stretching their hands out in supplication. Our driver had to threaten them with his whip, but there were many of them, and for a moment it looked alarming until he was able to increase speed and leave them behind.

February 14th. The feast of St Valentine – I seem to recollect that the unfortunate man was clubbed to death for some reason, so why he became the patron saint of sweethearts I do not know. I spent a few minutes in composing some lines for the occasion, which I copied and set down where Mary would find them. I do not regard them as anything more than passable, but Mary was very pleased with them.

For Mary

'Midst Mother Nature's fairest flowers
The sweetest bloom of all thou art:
Grant me a place, ye Heavenly Powers,
Forever in my Mary's heart!

February 20th. A little concerned about Mary, who has a headache – to be fair, she complains but little, and makes light of it, saying that it is only a chill. She appears a little flushed, however. Adah has made her drink a toddy that she concocts with molasses, and hot rum, into which she squeezes the juice of two or three lemons. Our child kicks most powerfully now. Mary teases me by saying that it must assuredly be a boy, with muscular ploughman's legs inherited from his father. I have been most amused by young Aquinas lately, who now does the work of two men, and redoubles even those noble efforts whenever he sees me.

'How are you today, Aquinas?' I'll ask.

'Very well, Massa. Oh yes. Dat medicine, he mek de sickness go.' He knows very well my subterfuge, but he bears no grudge, and in fact it has become something of a joke between us.

February 21st. No improvement in Mary's chill – if anything it is worse. She has pains in her limbs and her back. Her face is flushed and her tongue is very dry, so that she has to have water constantly by her. Adah is extremely solicitous, and has been bathing her forehead. This afternoon she began to suffer bouts of shivering. She continues to claim that it is just a trifling indisposition, but I confess it worries me, particularly in her condition. I went to see Mr Douglas, and the upshot is that we have had Mary moved into the Great House where there are better facilities. Adah has insisted on going with her. At first Mr Douglas was reluctant to permit it, saying that Mary would have plenty of servants to take care of her, but Adah was adamant on the point so in the end he had no option but to relent. Had I not been so concerned about my wife, I would have found it a diverting spectacle to witness the owner of the estate being browbeaten by one of his own slave girls. In any event I am relieved that Adah is with her. Simpson has attended in his professional capacity, but had nothing very helpful to say save that she should be kept as cool as possible. Dr Morton has been sent for, and has promised to be here tomorrow morning. I am sure that it is nothing serious, but it is important to take all precautions. I have been sitting in her room writing this. The headache is very bad, her face is red and she is extremely restless. Tonight I noticed a slight rash on her arms, which is probably just the fever. Adah is constantly by her side with a damp cloth to keep her cool.

February 22nd. There was no improvement this morning. Dr Morton came at about ten, and examined her with great thoroughness. I had hoped for some reassurance, but instead his sombre diagnosis appalled me so much that the strength went from my legs and I had to sit down. Overnight Mary has developed spots on her limbs and body and some of these are bleeding slightly. All of these symptoms taken together point indisputably to hospital fever. [2] In the normal course of events, her youth and strength would probably enable her to pull through. However the imminence of the birth is a drain on her energy, and the situation must be regarded as grave. He says that there must be someone with her at all times, and that she must be made to drink as much water as possible to replace that lost through perspiration. Duty calls him back to Port Antonio this afternoon, but he promises to return tomorrow and remain with her until, as he puts it, 'matters are resolved'. I do not know what to think. I am quite numb with it. I cannot even begin to contemplate the prospect of [losing] No, I cannot even write the word – to do so is to admit a possibility too dreadful to imagine.

February 23rd. This morning Mary has an apathetic look, and appears not to know me. The doctor is here, and his presence is reassuring, but in reality he can do little. He says that there is naught to do but to sponge her down with antiseptic lotion, and to ensure that she has plenty of fluid, duties that Adah carries out most assiduously. That lass has not slept since Mary was brought here. Morton has ordered the windows opened to admit fresh air during the day. He opines that a little rum mixed with water may be of some benefit as a stimulant. Meanwhile my poor wife inhabits her own hell of shivering, muttering delirium, and I curse my inability to be of assistance. She is very great with child, and Morton declares the birth to be imminent.

February 24th. Matters go from worse to worse. My darling has lapsed into unconsciousness, and I can do nothing but sit by her bed, weeping, and calling down God's wrath upon this damned country, the heat, the wretched mosquitoes. Why did I ever think to bring her with me to this awful place? Why could I not be the one to be suffering so? What harm has she done to anyone to deserve this?

February 25th. At about noon today Mary gave a cry of 'Robert!' and tried to sit up in the bed. She had been sleeping, albeit restlessly, and we were quite startled by this sudden change. She has been delirious and confused, but now she looked at me with perfect recognition. Morton, who had been dozing in a chair by the window, came across at once. 'Oh Robert, it's the bairn!' she said, and then fell back with a gasp of pain. To my horror I could see a bright patch of blood on the cotton sheet that covered the lower part of her body, spreading even as I watched. Dr Morton ordered me from the room. Am sitting with Adah and Mrs Douglas, and writing this account, for there is nothing else I can [*entry incomplete*].

February 28th. The last link with my native land has been severed; my last hope has gone; the very reason for my life has been taken from me. The dear wife who would have grown old by my side, and the son who would have grown up to be a man – a pride and comfort to me in my old age – are now confined together in the earth. I have just returned from the hellish duty of supervising the obsequies for my dear dear Mary, and a stillborn son no less precious to me. There, I have written it down. Everybody that I love, in 'one fell swoop' – two innocents cut down by the remorseless and unfeeling tyrant *Death*. How could God have looked down and not intervened? How can I believe in a God who can allow such a thing to befall? Of all nonsense, religious nonsense is the most nonsensical. The Reverend Pomposity who officiated (I forget his name already) informed me that 'God works in mysterious ways', but had I not been so abject with misery I would have been inclined to express doubts as to whether He works at all. I find nothing mysterious in what has transpired. What a transient business is life! What is there here for me now?

March 4th. Rum is a grand thing for dulling the senses! Oblivion! Nepenthe! When I am quite sober, I endeavour to understand what has happened, but am swamped by misery and anger. Then I turn to the nipperkin, and it brings a most welcome fuddling of the sense, though when the fumes of intoxication clear away I'm left once again contemplating my situation with a terrible clarity, and with an aching heart, so that I reach for the jar again. Adah, bless her, is as distraught as I. Yet she will not let me alone, damn her! (What a fool I am, to have blessed her and consigned her to perdition within two sentences!) But she insists on making me eat when I have not the stomach for it, and she chides me constantly about the rum until I grow irritable with her. Why am I writing this? What a slave-driver is Habit! I only need to turn back a few leaves to see the felicity I once enjoyed, and to touch the very pages that Mary touched as she [*remainder of sentence deleted and heavily scored through*]. I suppose that I am writing it for myself now.

March 5th. Last evening, grew excessively morose, and must have consumed rum very immoderately, for I have no recollection whatsoever of retiring for the night. As I awoke today and opened my eyes I was vaguely aware of Adah rising from my bed, and leaving the room. I rose hastily and questioned her about what had transpired the night before. She told me (I cannot set down her exact words, for this has shamed me deeply) that I had fallen asleep on the floor, and had been very sick, and that she had been obliged to clean me up, undress me, and drag me bodily to bed. She had remained with me because she feared that I might be sick again. I said that I hoped no impropriety had occurred, and she retorted with some asperity that she was sorry to think that I could entertain the thought that she would have permitted any familiarity in the bed of her late mistress.

Mary is everywhere in the house. At any moment I expect to see her walk through the door; and the echo of her voice is forever in my ears. Her little belongings are scattered where she last left them, which I find pitiful in the extreme. I am sitting now with her hairbrush, which retains the revered smell of her soft, fair locks. Dear Christ, how can I live like this? How can I exist?

12th March. To work today, for the first time [~~since~~]. Others uncomfortable around me and for my part I was glad of it, for I have no inclination to expose my feelings to anyone. Everything around me seems remote and unreal; when people speak, their voices seem distant, nothing to do with me. Slaves treated me with solemnity and unusual respect. I am living inside myself. Home again, and glad of the rum-jug. [~~I should~~ *entry abandoned*.]

March 17th. I am still seething with anger which only the exercise of supreme self-control was I able to prevent from violent expression. I entered the boiler house on an errand, and I overheard Jock Gilmour talking to Armstrong. Unobserved, I was about to announce my presence when I realised that they were talking about me and, foolishly, paused to hear what they were saying. Armstrong, good man that he is, was expressing the opinion that I had been very melancholy of late, to which Gilmour gave a kind of snort of derision.

'He'll be getting plenty o' braw houghmagandie wi' his neger bitch,' he said with a coarse laugh. I felt the blood rush to my face, but after a moment I turned and walked out. So that is what Gilmour thinks. As if any woman could be anything but the glimmer of a farthing taper beside the cloudless glory of my Mary in Heaven! Does he really believe that I could besmirch her memory so? How little he knows of me, or of plain decency! I shall be even with him for this, and if he ever dares to say such a thing to my face then I shall not be accountable for my actions.

March 24th. Saw Garvie earlier, and am assured by him that this is indeed the date. He looked at me very oddly. Not sure about the last few days. Not been at work this past week. Too much rum, to be honest. Have just awakened, fully clad, in bed, but sun is going down. I cannot remember. Must have slept all day – nay, been insensible. Adah not here, but she clearly has been. The place is tidy and clean. I have a fearful awareness of being unable to go on. The cup that cheers, then. Who cares?

March 28th. Adah comes and goes, grumbling a great deal. Since that embarrassing occasion a few weeks ago she has said little to me, and does not banter with me as before. It occurs to me that she misses Mary almost as much as I do. She has tidied her things neatly away – I know, for I watched her do it – and she wept piteously as she did so, until I felt the tears start in my own eyes, and had to flee the house. At times I think that both of us are keeping the house unchanged and in a state of readiness to welcome Mary through the door to a joyous homecoming after a long absence. Alas! it is only pretence, but it brings comfort of a sort.

April 3rd. Mr Douglas has been to see me, and I fear I did not make a good impression. I have not shaved for several days, nor have I changed my clothes during that time. He came at about eleven in the morning, and already I had made considerable inroads into the rum.

'When are you thinking of putting in a day's work for me, Mr Burns?' he said, wrinkling his nose in distaste. I wanted to placate him, and make some reference to my general sense of wretchedness, but I slurred and stumbled over my words and felt damnably frustrated and angry with myself.

'You know we are all very sorry about what happened,' he went on in a less stern tone. 'But now it is time for you to take control of yourself. That your loss was terrible is undeniable, but you must not let it be the ruin of you, man.' I managed to nod in agreement, and to look shame-faced. 'There are too many memories here,' he said, looking around. 'I can find you another place quite easily.'

I am to move tomorrow. He says I can take with me any personal keepsakes I wish, and Mrs Douglas will arrange for the disposal of Mary's wardrobe. He says that this is for the best, and I am sure in my mind he is right. However in my heart it feels as if I am abandoning Mary, and to dispose of her clothes seems sacrilege.

April 4th. Here I am, ensconced in new quarters. They are much the same size as the previous, and it did not take long for Mr Douglas's boys to transfer my humble effects. Mr Douglas has made it clear that I may have two or three days to settle in, but that from the start of next week he expects me at work as usual. I have my table, where I am writing this. Two o'clock, by the sun. I rigged up a hammock earlier. Time to toast my new bachelor accommodation – adequate, but cheerless, as befits one in my solitary and spouseless station. I have written to Gilbert with my news.

April 5th. I have had quite a day of it with Adah. Apparently she had been sent packing by Mrs Douglas after Mr Douglas had set in motion the process of my removal. I had, frankly, been too full of rum to appreciate what was happening, and last night – well, the less said the better. This morning I dragged myself from bed and searched around for something to eat, but it was a vain quest – nothing. In my bleary state came the realisation that for all these weeks there had always been food – either served to me by Adah or left on the table for me to have cold. I had relied upon her totally for these most elementary needs, and now she was gone. This drove me into a veritable brown study, and I was wondering what on earth I should do when I became aware of raised voices outside. I discovered Adah, with a great basket on her arm, marching purposefully towards my balcony, pursued by two of Mr Douglas's boys.

'Lemme be,' she was yelling over her shoulder at the boys. One of them – Luke, I believe he is called; a tall fellow with a limp – stopped when he saw me, but continued to shout out.

'Massa Douglas goin' be powerful cross when he hear yuh come here. Yuh goin' git a terrible whippin', Miz Adah.'

'Go tell de Massa dat I don' care 'bout no whippin',' riposted Adah as she reached the balcony and began to climb the stairs. 'Massa Burns, he need me. Massa Douglas easy find 'nother girl fuh de kitchen. Go tell'm.'

With this she marched through the door, and somehow it seemed that she had taken charge – I cannot explain it – as if there was now order where there had been chaos. 'Well, Adah,' I began, realising that anything I said would sound ridiculous, 'it really is very kind of you to come here . . .' I stopped when I saw the expression on her face. She put the basket down on the floor and came to stand in front of me, arms akimbo.

'Who gwine look afta' yuh, now Missiz Burns ain't here no mo'?' She was weeping, I could see, though I could not tell if they were tears of sorrow, anger or frustration. For the first time in the six months I have known her I looked properly into her eyes – they were of a very dark brown, almost black, and the whites were exceedingly clear. Her lip trembled. It was full, and the colour of a ripe plum. I had never been as close to her before.

'Who gwine look afta' yuh, Massa?' she repeated.

'You've always been very good,' I said.

'I don' mean dat. I don' mean cookin' and keepin' de place nice. I mean who's gwine look afta' yuh? When Missiz Burns was alive, God bless 'er, yuh'd not be standin' here lak dis, wid de rum on yuh breath and yuh clothes stinkin'. Lemme tell yuh sump'n', Massa. De white man come, de white man drink de rum, he git sick, he git dead. Yuh wanna git dead, Massa Burns?'

'I can look after myself,' I said, feebly.

'No, Massa. Yuh cyan't. Yuh gonna die fuh sho'. Who's gwine look afta' yuh?'

I had nothing to say to this, for she was absolutely right, and I knew it. The next thing I knew was that she was clinging to me, weeping very piteously and begging me not to send her away, but to permit her to remain to take care of me. Her entreaties were so touching that I agreed at once, and went directly to the Great House to confirm the arrangement with Mr Douglas. I had not anticipated any problems, but I found him surprisingly reluctant on the matter.

'Oh very well, if you must,' he said, with what I felt was very bad grace. 'Mind you, most of my other book-keepers seem to manage on their own. Adah's a strong girl, and to be frank, I could put her to better use in the fields. Still, you've had a bad time of it, and I expect you've grown accustomed to having your domestic needs attended to.'

'She has been very good,' I said.

'Oh yes, I dare say. She is clearly devoted to you. I am sure that she will cater for your every . . . ah . . . need.'

'What d'you mean by that, Mr Douglas?' I asked, irked by what he implied.

'Nothing. But you're a white man without ties, and she's a healthy young creature with all the carnal appetites of a black woman.'

'I don't think of Adah in that way,' I said with some heat.

'Well, that may be. Very commendable, to be sure. But in what . . . er . . . *way* does she think of you?'

'I am sure she does not entertain any of the thoughts you attribute to her. She merely wishes to be of service to me.'

'Hmmm. I am older than you are, and I have considerably more experience in these matters. Young Adah has ambitions, and mark my words, you are a means to an end.'

'I think that you'll find yourself to be mistaken,' I said stiffly. 'Our relationship is entirely proper. I merely wish to retain her as a servant; and for her part, I believe that looking after my household is all the reward the lassie desires.'

'Oh very well,' he said. 'Have it your own way. Your colleagues will draw their own conclusions, of course, but that is their privilege.

When a white man takes a black woman into his house, there is generally only one reason for it.'

I went away feeling angry. I remembered what Gilmour said, and how much it had upset me; also in my mind, to be honest, was what Adah said about wanting 'light chil'n'. God knows that [when Mary)] I never thought of Adah in any prurient way. I do not consider myself a prude, and God alone kens about me and the lasses, but – Adah?

April 7th. That damnable girl is determined to keep the rum from me. She has hidden the household supply, and refuses to divulge its whereabouts. I made something of a fuss about it, and she said that if I wanted rum then I only had to ask and she would bring me some. I commanded her to do so at once, and she duly complied, fetching me a tiny measure in the most minuscule glass imaginable. I downed it in an instant, and bade her bring more, to which the hussy replied that she would do so after carrying out the duty she was engaged in. I told her that it was devilish inconvenient, at which she sniffed disdainfully and walked away. I called after her, asking her who was master in the house. She had the gall to say that if I had my way, the rum-jar would be master. Impudent bitch.

April 10th. Back at work, and not a particularly auspicious start. In fact I am minded to seek out Mr Douglas with a view to negotiating a passage back home. I am sick of this place. This morning I met up with Jock Gilmour; I had not forgotten his remarks. Admittedly he was unaware of the fact that I had overheard him, and was much more polite and circumspect when we met face-to-face today.

'Good to see you back, Mr Burns,' he said, rather too jovially. 'We were all sorry to hear about . . . you know.'

'That's all right,' I said. 'I'd really rather not speak of it, if you don't mind.'

'Oh no, no to be sure,' he said, smirking. 'Still, you're well enough set up, so I hear.'

'What d'you mean?' I shot back. The smirk disappeared, and was replaced by a look of wide-eyed innocence, which I found equally irritating, because it was transparently insincere.

'Nothing at all, Mr Burns!' he exclaimed. 'Nothing at all! All I meant was that you've got someone to look after you – Adah, I mean – and . . . well, that's good. To have your meals cooked and your clothes washed. We're not all so lucky! No indeed! But no one begrudges you that for a second. We are all pleased that you are being cared for, after the terrible things you have been through.'

He walked away, and joined another group of men some distance away, and after a few moments I heard a coarse laugh go up. I knew fine the reason for it, but there was no point in making a scene. Later on I was passing the mill, and I thought I heard a call of 'Hey Burns! How's Adah?' but when I turned, of course no one was looking my way. I find it maddening to be goaded thus. On many plantations it is commonplace for the overseers to do with the slave women as they wish, though Mr Douglas strongly discourages it here, unless the woman is agreeable to the arrangement. I have heard of a plantation near Savanna-la-Mar where the late owner, a Mr Thistlewood, had sexual congress with almost every slave woman on his property, notwithstanding suffering very badly from syphilis. It was his habit, when receiving callers, to offer them a slave woman for their carnal gratification with as little thought as another might offer coffee, or a seat by the fireside. It is even rumoured that Thistlewood kept a diary of his disgusting dalliances, though I dare say accounts of the man are much exaggerated.[3] I suppose simple souls like Gilmour imagine that I am no better than Thistlewood.

April 12th. It would be less than honest of me if I claimed that I have never thought of what it would be like to bed Adah. I was not destined to be celibate, and the promptings of the flesh have been growing more insistent of late. There is no denying that she is an attractive creature. Her skin is very dark, and of an extremely fine texture. As for her height, she is of middling stature, very slender about the waist, with shapely hips and firm, high breasts. Her hair is black and exceedingly fine, and standing out like a halo around her head. Her eyes are large, and of a very dark shade of brown. That she is desirable is, to my mind, beyond doubt; but the attraction that she exercises is radically different from anything of my previous experience: that is to say, fair-skinned Ayrshire lasses. I have heard it said that union with a black woman is perverse and unnatural, since they are not like us, and since Nature clearly intended that black and white, which were created separately, should remain separate. Such is the theory, though I have observed nothing of it in practice, and am inclined to dismiss it as nonsense. If one were to pursue the argument to its logical conclusion, one would have to espouse the ludicrous notion that red-haired men should marry red-headed women only, and that laddies from Mauchline must needs limit their amorous horizons to no further than Tarbolton. But I am not inclined to view Adah as inherently inferior. This, I realise, is what separates me from the likes of Gilmour – who is a hypocrite because he despises black women whilst at the same time not hesitating to use them for his lewd pleasures, and mistakenly assumes that I am the same. Whatever my thoughts on the matter, nothing is likely to come of it. I have taken such a high moral stance over the propriety of my domestic arrangements that I should look exceedingly foolish if I were to succumb to temptation now!

April 15th. Tomorrow I am to accompany Mr Garvie to Kingston. Mr Douglas says that I should gain experience in the business of slave purchase, and must go to the auction of the cargo lately landed. We are to purchase young females, for there are fewer children being born, and with slaves now costing almost fifty pounds *per capita*, it clearly makes sense to produce our own. So says Mr Garvie, ever an enthusiastic apologist for the economic case. What he says makes sense, I suppose, although I find it offensive to think of slaves being bred like so many cattle. Part of the problem lies in the fact that the womenfolk choose to suckle their children for as much as three years, which, during this time, renders them infertile. The death rate among children is very high, though this has improved of late thanks to inoculation against the smallpox and cleaner living conditions, on this plantation at least. When I told Adah that I would be away on business for a few days, it was clear that she had already heard about my errand, and my fears about offending her sensibilities proved groundless.

'Ev'body knows 'bout de auction.' she said. 'De men, dey axin' Massa Garvie tuh bring back wives. Massa Garvie, he choose good. When dey come, dey 'fraid, but we takes care of'm, and dey soon 'appy 'nough.'

I would have thought that you'd have found a husband by this time,' I said.

She snorted. 'I don' want no 'usband.'

'Don't you get lonely?' She looked at me oddly and shook her head. It appears that if she had been a field slave, then she would probably have settled down with a man by this time, out of simple necessity, but those who work with the 'Massas' are viewed as superior in status, and can afford to pick and choose. I had never thought of it before, but I do provide her with a roof over her head, and she eats the same food as I do, although she declines to sit at table with me. I am well aware of how arduous the field work can be and so there is no doubt that her position is a privileged one.

April 21st. We have returned with six female slaves. I did not enjoy my experiences in Kingston, and I am anxious to set the details down before making a determined effort to forget what I have seen.

The journey was long and unpleasant. Kingston itself was hot, crowded and dirty, with much jostling and bustle in the streets. When we arrived at the dock, we found that the ship with its human cargo was moored offshore, and little wonder, because the stench emanating from it was insupportable, even at a considerable distance. I really find it impossible to express just how horrible and ghastly it was to stand on the quay-side and look out at that huge, grim vessel, all sails furled, with hundreds of black figures seated on deck. All of the hatchways had been opened, and gangs were at work below deck, scrubbing and scouring with boiling vinegar, the pungent smell of which, mingled with the stink of urine and excrement, was enough to turn the strongest stomach. What it must have been like on board the vessel itself I cannot begin to imagine.

Before they are brought ashore the slaves are fed; they are washed and oiled, and their heads are shaved. Many of them are sick from the journey, and indeed up to a third usually die within a month or two of arriving in Jamaica. Mr Garvie tells me that the captains are often quite unscrupulous, and will resort to all manner of chicanery in order to represent even the most wretched specimen as being in robust health. The most common ailment on board slave ships is the bloody flux that is generally fatal, the sufferer's bowels voiding constantly, causing a debility from which recovery is unlikely. Ship's surgeons are often commanded to stop up the anuses of such afflicted souls with wadding in order to conceal the symptoms, and it is essential to check every slave in this respect before making a purchase. We watched as the slaves were brought ashore by boat, and led, naked and chained, to the auction yard. Such pitiable expressions! What must they have been thinking? First of all the appalling privations of the journey, and now the fearful ignominy of being herded like cattle in front of their prospective purchasers. I am told that by way of cruel jest some slaves are told that they will be eaten by the white men, and to judge by their terrified expressions they believe it. One thing is certain – they know that their miseries are far from over, and although they cannot guess what lies ahead of them, they clearly understand that it will be terrible.

We saw a few young girls that Mr Garvie considered might be suitable. They were around thirteen or fourteen years of age, by my reckoning – old enough to work in the fields, and of a suitable build for child-bearing. Mr Garvie was hopeful of a bargain, because there is less demand for girls, who must be regarded more as an investment that delivers its yield in the longer term.

The auction was an experience I never wish to undergo again. One by one the wretches were stood on a little raised platform, to be prodded and scrutinised by the plantation agents and owners. Some of the males attempted to put up some kind of resistance, but were quickly cowed with the whip. It is shocking to see the women submit to the awful humiliation of having their private parts minutely examined and probed. Most pitiful of all is the consternation of the children, wrenched bodily from their parents, wailing and screaming; and the anguish of these parents as their little ones are dragged away, never to be seen again.

The male slaves were auctioned first. Purchasers are very particular about the stature and complexion of their slaves, and the highest prices were fetched by those of the blackest sort with curly hair, and of a middling stature. We saw some with a more yellow skin and straight hair, but Mr Garvie says that they are more likely to be troublesome and adapt less easily to the rigours of life in the fields.

When it came to the turn of the women to be auctioned, the young strapping ones with full breasts quickly sold for a good price. Garvie got his bargain: we were able to obtain three girls at thirty-five pounds each and a further two for thirty apiece. We bought one more: a very young one, perhaps ten years old, and blind in one eye, which deformity enabled Mr Garvie to hold out for the very low price of ten pounds. He told me that she was otherwise a sturdy enough specimen, and that her affliction, though unfortunate, was unimportant. Once we had settled the account, we supervised their removal to the wagon, amidst such a screaming and screeching that we were near deafened by it. Mr Garvie got a kick in the shins from the biggest of the girls, and the one-eyed minx clawed at my cheek as I hoisted her up, so that I almost dropped her. Once they were shackled in place, they became a little more subdued. I tried to remonstrate with them, and explain that we meant them no harm, but they naturally did not understand a word of English, and to judge from their shocked expressions I might as well have been telling them that they were destined for the cooking pot.

I fetched some food and gave it to them, and they consumed it hungrily. As they were eating I again spoke softly to them, and they looked up at me – this is a moment which will haunt me for the rest of my life; I mean the memory of these tearful young eyes, in which there resided such an agonising infinity of pain, fear and incomprehension. It cut me to the heart; I felt profoundly ashamed. Murder is sinful, but what we were doing was worse. It was taking life – not granting the peace of death, but forcing the captive to endure a personal hell. Henceforth these innocents would live, but only on our terms. How can this be anything other than sinful? The journey back was a nightmare. It rained; our pathetic human cargo wailed and sobbed, and my mind was filled with memories of the last time I travelled this way, with Mary by my side.

When we reached the plantation Mr Garvie went to the Great House to confer with Mr Douglas. I unshackled the girls, and gave them over into the keeping of a group of women from the slave village, who greeted them with huge kindness and affection, and bore them off with maternal solicitude. I came back home here in an extremely sombre frame of mind. Adah was very animated, and pleased to see me; she began to question me about my journey, but I told her that I did not feel much like discussing it at present, and she has left me alone to write this. Never before in my life have I witnessed so much MISERY as in these last few days, and what makes it much worse to bear is the realisation that I have actively assisted in the process of imposing it. I have not been honest with myself. I am ashamed now that I paid so little heed to what Wilberforce and the rest were saying before I booked my passage. So many excuses! I had never seen a Negro – slavery was something that happened in distant lands – others were better qualified than I to pronounce on the matter – I was too busy pursuing my own affairs to give the issue serious consideration – there was no one with whom I could discuss it – I even thought it an English problem, and hence for them to solve! My hot-headed eagerness to leave Scotland overwhelmed completely whatever scruples I possessed. Even more reprehensibly, I consoled myself with the foolish notion that there might be some way of reconciling slavery with my principles. To be sure, most of the slaves on the estate appear content, but like a fool I have allowed myself to ignore the fact that they *do not belong here*. God forgive me.

April 22nd. I have managed to procure some rum today (which was not difficult) and I have sternly ordered Adah to leave it alone. I just need to blot out these past few days. It is raining, and I was thoroughly soaked at work; now all I can hear is a cacophony of dripping, splashing and trickling – everything is sodden, water-logged and depressing. I am finding it hard to live with myself. It had been my intention to sit this evening and attempt to gather my thoughts, but I only become more confused. That confounded slave auction! Those poor, wretched girls! I know it is wrong, but here I am, entirely dependent on the iniquitous system that requires such dreadful things to happen. I have been thinking about returning to Scotland. Gilbert could do with my help, and there is my little Bess, who will very soon be three years old. There is Miss Armour, and my little Robert and Jean. I thought I had a future here, but that hope has been dashed. I must have a word with Mr Douglas about it. God, I wish the rain would stop!

May 1st. I saw Mr Douglas, who gave me a very cold reception. When I told him that I was considering returning home, he raised his eyebrows, sniffed, and asked me what had prompted my decision, and I explained that I had found the slave auction repugnant, and the whole business of purchasing the girls very upsetting.

'You are too sentimental, Mr Burns,' he said. 'I told you before that it is wrong to think of them as if they were our equals.'

'They're different,' I replied, 'I won't deny that. Their skin, their hair, the shapes of their noses – all unlike ours. But inwardly . . .'

'Please, please,' he remonstrated. 'This is foolishness. You've no doubt been reading Monsieur Rousseau and he's filled your head with these fanciful notions.[4] It simply is not sensible to imagine that these savages were living in some kind of Garden of Eden before they were brought here. Ask anyone who's been to Africa! How do the slaves reach the coast in order that they may be shipped here? They are brought by their own kind, Mr Burns! Savages! They are enslaved by their own people, who deal with them mercilessly. Cruel though it may seem to you, these girls you brought here will find their circumstances vastly improved on this plantation. They are fed, they are clad, they receive the attention of a physician if they require it. In return they give their labour. What's wrong with that? We all have to work.'

'But, Mr Douglas,' I replied, 'what if the situation were reversed? How would you feel if you were plucked from your home, packed into the hold of a ship and . . .'

'But that can never be!' he shouted. 'Do you not perceive the hand of God in this matter? We were ordained the masters of the earth, and all that is upon it. We have conquered the oceans. Look at our great buildings! Consider our advances in science! Think of Shakespeare, think of Milton! Is there any way in which the primitive savage, in his native state, could even begin to aspire to such heights? The girls you brought here will, in time, learn to be civilised, as you and I are. Now, I grant you that the transition to a new way of life may be distressing. But in the end, they will be grateful for it.'

'I wish I could believe you,' I said.

'Why don't you ask Adah?' he replied. 'Faced with the choice of remaining where she is or returning to Africa, what would she do?'

'But she was born in Jamaica,' I said.

'What difference does it make? If the uncivilised state is as congenial as you seem to imagine, and if life here is as intolerable as you claim, surely she would wish to return? She has grown up appreciating the advantages of our way of life.'

'At least she does not work in the fields.'

'Oh, Mr Burns,' he said, with a laugh. 'What is wrong with working in the fields? Have you not spent wearisome hours following the plough? Were you not in bondage to Mr Hamilton, who charged you ninety pounds a year for the privilege of wresting a living from the wet clay?'

'I was not a slave.'

'No? I'm sure there were many occasions when you wished the burden of the farm didn't lie on your shoulders alone, that someone else would see that your needs were taken care of, come what may.'

'But I was free to leave that way of life,' I said. 'The same cannot be said of your slaves.'

'We're all slaves, in some respect,' he said. 'You probably consider me very fortunate. But I have concerns that you cannot imagine. I am at the beck and call of my bankers, who own me more completely than I own these girls. Everything is precarious in the extreme. A poor harvest – a rebellion – a sudden fall in sugar prices – any of these things could ruin me overnight. And then where would I be? What benevolent master would care for me? What would become of the people on the plantation? What would become of *you*, eh?'

There's no arguing with Mr Douglas. He's been very good to me, and he's clearly sincere in his beliefs. He steers well clear of the multifarious abuses that bedevil this island. But, as ever, I left his presence feeling that I had not properly stated my case. As for my return to Scotland, that seems unlikely for the moment. Mr Douglas is right – we are all slaves. I recollect Adah saying much the same.

May 3rd. Visitors at the Great House today – the Honourable Someone-or-other, a lanky, chinless idiot with the voice of a donkey. To think there was a time when I found it impossible to believe that anyone possessed of a title could also be a complete ninny! The Honourable Nonentity was accompanied by his wife (whose name escapes me) – a great, bloated, disgusting, perspiring creature – and their daughter, a rather fetching lass of about nineteen called Miss Josephine, who affected an air of complete *ennui* throughout the duration of the visit. Mr Garvie and I were invited to meet them. We were served tea in the garden, and I was able to persuade the daughter to walk with me under the trees. It is a long time since I have had the opportunity to speak with a pretty white girl, but it was an excessively disappointing conversation.

'What brings you to Jamaica, Ma'am?' I asked.

'Oh, Papa has business here,' she said, with a roll of the eyes, and a silly grimace.

'And how do you find the island?'

'Tedious in the extreme. The climate is insupportable.'

'I see. Have you found anything to your liking here?'

'Very little. I dislike the blacks. They stare, and one constantly has the feeling that one is being mocked behind one's back.'

'Does one, indeed?' I replied.

'Yes. And the flies are disagreeable.'

'Indeed. And when will one be returning to England?'

'Next week. Papa has already booked our passage.'

'I trust one has a pleasant journey.'

'Thank you.'

I walked her back to the tea-table, where her obese mother was fanning herself, displaying huge sweaty patches under her oxters, and complaining about something or other to Mrs Douglas, who was politely pretending to take an interest. The Honourable Shit-for-brains was holding forth, but I could decipher little of it, and, to judge from their expressions, Mr Douglas and Mr Garvie were faring no better. Miss Josephine sat down with a sulky expression and ignored us all. After about half an hour of this I'd had enough. My Lady's grumbles – about the climate, the food, the people, the travelling, the insects, and the servants – were growing too tedious to bear; while Milord's incomprehensible neighing and braying was giving me a headache. As for little Miss Sulk, moping and scowling, the less said the better.

When I arrived home, Adah was sweeping the floor with set features and unnecessary energy, clearly in an ill temper.

'Whatever is the matter?' I asked.

'Nuttin',' she replied curtly. 'Jes' let me be so's I c'n do de sweepin'.'

I sat down to work with some papers, and she continued her rather ostentatious housework, picking things up, dusting them, and slamming them down again so that the whole house rattled. I tried to ignore it, but eventually it became too much.

'Do you think you could make a little less noise, Adah?' I said, in exasperation.

'Got to mek de house nice, case de *white girl* come callin',' she said, with heavy emphasis.

'What white girl?' I asked in bewilderment.

'Yuh spend de aft'noon wid she. I see'd yuh on de lawn of de Great House, when I's fetchin' de vegetables. 'Spec' yuh enjoys bein' wid a white woman 'gain. 'Spec' yuh likes she pretty white dress and she pretty yellow hair. If she come callin' . . .'

I laughed out loud. 'Adah,' I said, 'no white girl is going to come calling. That young lady you saw me with was a guest of Mr Douglas, and she'll be leaving for Kingston tomorrow. And let me tell you something, I found her company dreary and tiresome beyond endurance. I am very happy that I shall never see her again.'

'She pretty, though,' said Adah, with a little pout.

'Not as pretty as you,' I replied.

Her eyes grew wide. 'Yuh t'ink I's pretty, Massa Burns?'

'Of course you are,' I said lightly.

She has been in an excellent frame of mind ever since. I suppose it was natural that she should imagine that I would be attracted to the one white woman of marriageable age who has visited the plantation in all the time I have been here. It had not occurred to me that she might be jealous.

May 5th. Morning in the fields with the second gang. On the way home I passed by the slave village to enquire after the girls we brought here from Kingston a couple of weeks ago. I was able to see two of them, who had been adopted by Martha. She is an elderly woman, no longer capable of hard field work, but very useful nonetheless, for she tends to young women in their confinements, and is also much respected for her knowledge of African medicine which has saved several patients who have been declared hopeless cases by Simpson. [I wish I had thought to]. They looked clean and presentable, with cotton dresses. At first, they were a little alarmed to see me, and ran to hide behind Martha's skirts until she coaxed them out. As African names are deemed unsuitable, they have been named Tabitha and Theresa. I must seek out the others.

This evening I have been engaged in some morose poetical scribblings, but the Muse has deserted me; the lines are awkward; the rhymes seem forced and trite, and I have lost patience with it. Since the events of February I have been trying to collect my thoughts together, but they are still too confused to be set down in these pages. It is much easier to seek solace in drink, though this only postpones the day on which I must face up to facts.

May 12th. Confined to bed with a confounded chill that has me all of a shiver. Cannot write much.

May 22nd. My little Bess is two years old today, no doubt toddling happily around Mossgiel, wondering where her father is. Here I am, *sans* wife, *sans* child, *sans* everything. I wonder what I did to deserve this. I know that I have been less than perfect, and I wonder which of my demerits lead to my present situation. Over the past few weeks I have been reconsidering my relationship with the Almighty, and have come to the sorrowful conclusion that RELIGION is nothing more than a cruel delusion. What rational mind can believe in a Deity who allows the wicked to prosper, but visits his rage on my innocent Mary, and my helpless son? What kind of God finds it necessary to include mosquitoes, yaws, marsh fever, bloody flux and syphilis in his creation? When I look back through these pages I see how assiduously I have refrained from writing out in full any word that might have given offence to the Almighty – why? What good has my deference done to me? As for the idea of life after death, that is surely the most foolish fiction of all, appealing only to credulous and simple minds. If there had been a form of existence beyond the grave then most assuredly my darling Mary would have found some way to reassure me that we should be reunited. Instead I am faced with the shocking intransigence of death. Granted there is an end to pain, care, woes and wants – but that is the only blessing, and we have no need of a God to take credit for it, since it is no more and no less than what happens to a piece of broken machinery. If my pocket-watch were sentient, would it be gullible enough to believe that on the day its mainspring broke it would be elevated to some watchmaker's emporium in the clouds, to be lovingly restored, to keep perfect time for evermore? Does a lamb, being led to the slaughter, entertain for one moment the belief that after the agony of the knife comes a blissful eternity of gamboling in lush green fields, watched over by an indulgent shepherd? Why, then, are we so naïve and fond as to believe in a fantastical heaven? I think, therefore I am, said Descartes – very wisely – and it follows as surely as death follows life that *non cogito, ergo non sum*. When our brains have ceased to operate, then we are no more. Ashes to ashes, dust to dust – but let no one pretend there is anything more to it than that. We are all playthings in a vast, chaotic and brutal game of chance where there are no rules. All the nostril-sniffing sanctity in the world cannot alter that fact. That is all life is. There is nothing mysterious or divine about it. We are like children staring at the clouds, pretending to discern faces and shapes where none exist – worse than that: claiming that failure to observe a pattern is a signal proof of how skilfully it has been concealed. If I say to Adah that there is an invisible person in the room with us, then she will look around and tell me that she sees no one. If I then say to her that this proves the existence of that invisible person, by virtue of the fact that invisible persons cannot be seen, then she will no doubt tell me that I am a fool, and quite correctly so. When I ask for proof of God's existence in the midst of terrible personal privations, I am told that it is precisely because of his mysterious incomprehensibility that I should believe in Him. There is no God, and anyone who thinks otherwise is guilty of the most foolish self-deception.

I'm glad to have set this down at last. I shall have no further truck with this grand fallacy, which talks so pompously of things which matter nought except to pious rogues like Fisher, reverend grannies or daft auld wives. I have to accept that Mary is dead and gone. I do not now believe that she has ascended to heaven, or that we shall be reunited when it is my turn to die. We made the most of life together, and now it is all over: any consolation must come from my memories, rather than any senseless notions about an after-life. Although it may seem contradictory, I am glad that her remains lie where they do, in a secluded graveyard, well tended and shaded by trees. Leaving aside the supernatural fiddlesticks, there is a fine solemn dignity about the place. The Muse has been prompting me, and I am at work on some sketches that may come to something.

June 5th. I have been in a self-pitying state, my foolish mind so hebetated by rum that my witless pericranium is fit for nothing. Most assuredly it is not what my Mary would have wanted; indeed, I can all too easily imagine how she would have chided me if she had seen me during these last weeks and months. It is time for me to be a man again, albeit a man burdened with the deepest care, and a stranger forever to the careless bliss I once knew. I have long been impressed with the poetry of Mr Gray, particularly his exquisite Elegy, which pours its moving flow warm on the heart, and today I have completed my own verses on that most sombre of preoccupations. The act of bringing them forth has been of some help to me, I think.

In Memoriam

I

The leaden clouds hang brooding, dark and low
Above the grassy grove in which I tread;
No thought within my heart but black with woe;
No living soul but I, amongst the dead.

II

Each sculpted stone, each melancholy cross
Tells of a life imbued with vital breath,
And stands, mute testament to grief and loss,
As transient life gives way to endless death.

III

Here lies a mother, once with family blest,
Who knew the joys of parenthood's sweet trust:
Her infant son now shares th'eternal rest,
And both alike repose in mingled dust.

IV

If earthly sins of mine deserve such pain
The fullest expiation would I give:
But, wan and hopeless, I entreat in vain,
Condemned to walk alone, to mourn, to live.

V

This sacred earth was hallowed to the Lord;
And all who were His servants loyal:
Now twice-fold blessèd is this precious sward,
By virtue of thy presence 'neath its soil.

VI

Shall future generations bow the head
O'er this, the holy earth in which you lie?
And shall they weep, in presence of the dead,
Reflecting that they too are doomed to die?

VII

The day gives way to night, and restless woe:
Alas the day we reached Jamaica's shore!
Tomorrow dawns another day for me, but O!
For thee, my love, that sun shall rise no more!

VIII

Farewell, thou steadfast lodestone of my life!
Farewell to thee, who heart was fully mine!
Farewell my fond, my own, my cherished wife!
Farewell from one whose very soul was thine!

June 6th. Today I saw at first hand a case of yaws, quite the most
dreadful affliction imaginable. I had slipped in some mud, and in

striving to retain my balance wrenched my knee very painfully. Feeling sorry for myself I hobbled to the hospital to see if Simpson could give me some liniment. He was occupied in dabbing at the wounds of a male slave of about thirty. The miserable wretch was covered with suppurating, ulcerated sores that stank most abominably. His flesh in places had been eaten away so that the very bones were exposed, and he was screaming in pain as the festering lesions were scraped clear of dead, pus-ridden matter. There is nothing to be done for this condition. Plentiful rest and a good diet can bring about a degree of healing, but once the disease has gained a hold the victim is never free of it again.

I quite forgot my own suffering, and limped back home, absurdly grateful for my own inconsequential infirmity. As the evening wore on, my knee began to pain me more, and I grew irritable because of it, grumbling at Adah a good deal, though it is not her fault. She has brought me some hot rum – O! unexpected generosity of spirit! (in both senses of the word, for she certainly served a brimming measure!) – and insists that when I retire she will give the offending knee a *proper doin'*, whatever that may be.

June 7th. I must injure my knee more often, for Adah's *proper doin'* has not only effected a cure, but was, I must confess, a most delightful experience. When I had donned my nightshirt – more for the sake of modesty than necessity, for I normally sleep scuddy-naked – she made me lie down, and sat on the edge of the bed with her back to me. She then applied palm oil to the offending part, before using light pressure with her thumbs to rub away at the sore place. At first it was mightily ticklish, and I could barely keep still. Then she began to work away on the muscles above the knee, and it was the most soothing of sensations; indeed so pleasurable that, as the stiffness left my knee, it began to threaten an appearance elsewhere. Finally she took hold of my foot, and began to knead the sole and the bases of the toes. I could never have envisioned anything so relaxing, and I have only a vague recollection of Adah saying 'Jes' relax, Massa Burns' before awakening this morning, much refreshed, and with hardly any pain at all. The girl is a wonder, and it has crossed my mind more than once that if she can bring such delicious pleasure by ministering to the extremities, what heights of delirium might be achievable if she applied her skills in more sensitive regions, so to speak.

'Where did you learn to do that?' I asked.

'It ain't nuttin' much,' she said, shrugging. 'Lotsa slaves gits sore, and most women knows 'bout de healin' touch.'

'Well, it was extremely effective,' I said, feeling it better not to disclose the other thoughts I had been entertaining. 'Thank you very much.' She shrugged again, giving the impression that it was hardly worth mentioning, but I find it difficult to credit that she is so innocent as to be unaware of the effect of her 'healing touch'. During the day she has contrived to catch my eye on a number of occasions, and I could swear that there is a glint of mischief there. I am sure that I shall not give that salacious Gilmour and his odious ilk anything to snigger at. [All the same, if I could only persuade her to].

13th June. Rain, rain, rain. There is no doubt that Jamaica can be a pleasant enough place when the weather is clement, but at times like this it fully earns its title of the piss-pot of the universe. The rain is PISSING down – there is no other word for it. There – I have written the word! There is too much prudery in the world, and no all-seeing God to be offended.

June 17th. Have re-read the previous entry, in which I detect the influence of a tipsy Muse. I would never knowingly cause offence to others, but I see no need for genteel circumlocution. I never show this diary to anyone, now that Mary is gone. Adah cannot read. Really there is no need for a diary at all, but sheer force of habit compels me to set my thoughts down, as an aid to reflection. I dare say that when I return to Scotland, it will serve to refresh my memory when I tell my little Bess of her father's adventures!

There is much grumbling talk among the slaves today. There is trouble of some kind on the Harmony estate – I could not discover what it was, for they leave off talking about it when they see an overseer. Some of them have relatives on that estate.

June 18th. I passed by the infirmary today to enquire after the poor individual with the yaws; to my surprise he has been discharged, and is being attended to in the slave village. Simpson says that native cures can be more effective than anything he has to offer, and seemed quite put out by having to admit to what he evidently regarded as his own failure.

'What sort of cures?' I asked him.

'Oh, how would I know?' he growled. 'They get all sorts of leaves and pieces of bark, and boil it together. There really is no reason why it should have the slightest medicinal effect, and yet it does seem to have some healing influence. God knows why.'

'Should you not try to obtain some of their ingredients for yourself, and investigate their effects?' I suggested. 'Who knows, you might discover some new remedies.'

'What?' he exclaimed. 'Are you suggesting that I have might have
something to learn from ignorant black savages?'

'Well, no,' I said, unwilling to offend him on such a delicate
matter as his professional competence. 'But if they do manage to
effect a cure, then it might be interesting to investigate how it's
achieved. There may be plants unfamiliar to us which have curative
powers we know nothing of.'

'Damned superstition, more likely. They even eat dirt, some of
them.' He did not seem inclined to pursue the conversation further.

This afternoon I met up with a party of children and old women
on their way home from a day's weeding. Among them I recognised
the one-eyed girl I helped to purchase in Kingston. She looked very
smart in a little cotton dress and a bright kerchief binding up her hair.
Martha, who was with them, introduced her as Athena. I patted her
head, and told her she was a good girl – she understood nothing of
what I said, of course, but gave me a cheerful grin anyway. As I walked
off I reflected on how curious it was that this African child would grow
up named after the Greek goddess of wisdom. It is as if my Bess were
to be seized and carried off bodily to Africa, there to be named after
some female divinity in a pagan pantheon unheard of in Scotland.

June 20th. There is still more muttering about a bad situation which
is developing at Harmony, and apparently growing worse. I know
that the *régime* there is far less liberal than our own, but the fear of
rebellion haunts even the most generous and enlightened planter. I
have not had the opportunity of enquiring of Mr Douglas what the
matter is, and none of the other overseers has heard anything. Today
Adah came to the house with Theresa and Tabitha, who entered
with extreme diffidence, and stood in a corner staring shyly when
they saw me.

'I see you've met the newcomers,' I said.

'Oh yes, Massa Burns. Dey's me sisters.'

'Don't be silly,' I said. 'They can't be your sisters: they've only
been in Jamaica for a few weeks.'

'I knows dat,' she said. 'But dey's still me sisters.'

'I see. What you mean is that you've adopted them as if they were
your sisters. You don't have the same parents – you're just looking
after them.'

'No, but dey's still proper sisters.' This developed into a long
discussion about family and kinship that fairly baffled me. I had
always understood words like 'brother', 'sister', 'aunt' and 'uncle' to
have perfectly clear meanings, but among the slave people they are

used in a much looser sense. Adah's real father is, I gather, alive and
well; yet she claims to have at least two others who fully qualify for
the title. She also sees nothing in strange in the fact that some of the
plantation women have several 'husbands' – though they do not
solemnise such unions with any ceremony. I know that Mr Douglas
views this as evidence of shameless and indecent behaviour, and I'm
well aware that Gilmour and his lubricious sort argue that if these
women are so free with their favours then there's no harm in their
having their way with them. Certainly if anyone is seeking a proper
family among the slave ranks – I mean a husband and a wife, and little
bairns 'who round the ingle form a circle wide' – then they will surely
be disappointed. Is it for us to censure them? When they arrive here
they have no family, and no blood-ties. Is it so very surprising that they
form new ones, simply to support each other? Theresa and Tabitha
could not wish for a more conscientious guardian than Adah. Were
she their real sister, they could hardly fare better.

June 27th. The plantation has been in a state of alarm for the past few
days, for there has an attempted rebellion on the Harmony planta-
tion – an ironic appellation! – not twenty miles away. This is what
all of the murmuring among the slaves has been about. The estate is
run by an agent, a Mr Solway, whose name, like that of Thistlewood
at Savanna-la-Mar, is a byword for cruelty and ill treatment. For this
reason he has had problems with runaways hoping to reach the hills.
Lately he imported a dozen dogs from Cuba, massive beasts by all
accounts, trained to pursue fugitives and rip them to shreds. Their
very presence on the plantation struck terror into the hearts of slaves
but, far from rendering them more amenable, incited them to
insurrection. Two or three days ago the Great House was attacked
in the night and set ablaze. Solway managed to make good his escape
and summon the militia, who arrested a dozen ringleaders. Two
were shot dead on the spot for attempting resistance, and the others
will surely be hanged.

   Joseph, one of our ablest coopers, has been to see Mr Douglas,
begging his intercession with Mr Solway in the matter. It seems that
his brother is one of these arrested. Joseph claims that he was
nothing more than an innocent bystander, but being a Coromantee
was immediately locked up under suspicion of trouble-making.
Quite a crowd gathered outside the Great House while Joseph was
inside, and for the first time since my arrival here I sensed danger in
the air. None of the slaves would meet my eye, and many of them
were talking animatedly in their own languages. However every-

thing was resolved when Joseph reappeared, announcing that Mr Douglas had promised to intervene and would, if the authorities permitted it, purchase Joseph's brother and bring him here. The general mood of the slaves improved immediately, and I think that Mr Douglas has made a very wise decision.

July 8th. The name of Champong Nanny was raised again in conversation within my hearing, and at last I have discovered why she is such a memorable heroine. I had asked Gregory on several occasions, but he simply refused to tell me, dissolving into fits of embarrassed laughter every time I broached the topic. Up until now I had failed to understand his reticence, but today all is clear. Outside the mill house, a group of boys were chattering idly away as they worked, and I overheard the name 'Nanny', followed by loud guffaws. Anxious to lay this silly mystery to rest, I went across and said:

'This Champong Nanny of yours certainly was a great fighter, wasn't she?'

'Oh yes, Massa,' they replied earnestly in unison.

'And when she was attacked by musket-fire, she certainly knew how to fight back?' This was as far as I had ever got with Gregory.

'Yessuh.'

'So how did she do it?'

'Yuh don' know 'bout it, Massa?'

'No. I'm waiting for you to tell me.' They looked at each other, grinning, and clearly uncertain as to how to proceed.

'Come along,' I said sternly.

'Well, Massa,' said the biggest lad, 'when de English shoots at Nanny wid de muskets, she turn roun', an' she bend over, and she catch de bullets in she ARSE, and then she FART so 'ARD dat de bullets shoots back an' KILLS de backras ... Oh, beg pardon, Massa,' he concluded, suddenly horrified. 'I didn' mean nuttin', Massa. I didn' mean to say dat bad word.'

The other boys clapped their hands over their mouths, caught between appalled shock, and doing their utmost not to laugh aloud at the discomfiture of their fellow.

'That's all right,' I said. 'Thank you for telling me the story.'

As I went off, I could sense their consternation – not over the indelicacy of the anecdote, but for the use of the word 'backra' which, as they well know, gives me perfect justification for ordering a severe flogging.[5] Of course I shall do no such thing.

As for Champong Nanny – well, now I know why she is a legend in Jamaica. I am not sure that I would wish to put her methods to the test; indeed, I suspect that the lady in question belongs more to the realms of mythology than fact. That is of little consequence: I have rarely met with anything in history which interests my feelings equally with the story of Bannockburn – a gallant nation devoting themselves to the rescue of their bleeding country. Why should people not believe in their heroes and heroines, and enjoy a modicum of licence in elaborating the legends surrounding them? I'm sure that there were many Scotch kilts raised to display derisive buttocks to the English foe. Why should Nanny be any different? And if she contrived to return fire, so much the better for her!

July 16th. Joseph's brother Jacob has been brought here by the militia, after Mr Douglas interceded at the very highest level. All the overseers were called together to receive him, and Joseph was also summoned to attend. Mr Douglas spoke very sternly to them both, and said that he expected exemplary behaviour, to which they very readily agreed. Of course they could hardly have done otherwise. Jacob is a fine looking man, though the livid marks on his body show that he has been severely dealt with whilst in captivity. He holds himself well, and has a direct gaze characteristic of a man who takes pride in himself. I daresay Mr Solway found it insolent – it could readily be construed so by one who insists on fawning servility.

Adah cut her hand today, and I bound it up for her. It is not serious, and will heal in a day or two. However while tending to her I recollected the poignant words of Shylock to the effect: 'If you cut us, do we not bleed?' Her hands are very small, and the palms pink, soft and delicate. I felt a sudden wave of protective emotion towards her, and I believe she must have sensed it because she returned me a look of tender affection for a brief moment before withdrawing her hand, and resuming her usual flippant manner. I am growing very fond of her, and I am certain that the warmth of feeling is reciprocated. My thoughts are all of a turmoil. If she were a white servant girl then I am sure that I would have pressed my advantage long ere this. Yet about Adah there is what I can only describe as a *distinctiveness* – not merely in terms of her black skin, but in the curious social arrangement in which we are both trapped – I could demand her compliance, but to do so would be to do her disrespect – the fact that I have the right to take her is sufficient reason for not doing so. She is far too remarkable to be used as a means of sordid gratification.

July 17th. The Reverend Pomposity has been to visit. His real name is Caldwell, I believe. He is an unhealthy-looking man in his late forties, with gingery hair and a pleuk-covered face. He goes everywhere in the black garb of the minister, and never relinquishes his periwig, even in the heat of the day, so in consequence he perspires constantly and stinks of sweat. I had not seen him since these dreadful days in February, and little good was he then as far as the dispensation of comfort was concerned. He did not appear altogether overjoyed to see me, and I jalouse that Mr Douglas had persuaded him to call. After accepting a chair with some reluctance, and casting a fastidious glance around the room, he enquired how I was coping with my loss. What adequate answer is there to such a fatuous question? I was certainly not able to supply one.

'God works in mysterious ways,' he observed. This irritated me, just as it had done at the time of the funeral.

'I wonder that anyone can believe He works at all,' I said. He looked startled at this.

'I trust you are not having doubts, Mr Burns?'

'Doubts?' I said, with a bitter laugh. 'What kind of God took my Mary from me? What kind of God found it necessary to create disease if He loves us so much?'

'It is not our place to question the divine will, or to fathom God's inscrutable purposes,' he said, growing flushed now.

'How convenient,' I said, pleased to see that I had riled him. 'We simply must accept His benevolence in providing us with yaws and mosquitoes, must we? I tell you this, Caldwell, I would rather believe in no God at all than believe in a God filled with hatred and spite; a God who punishes the innocent and rewards the guilty. No, Mr Caldwell, I cannot and will not believe in such a God.'

For a moment he was speechless. 'Suffering is sent to try us,' he spluttered. 'We grow purer for having passed through the furnace of tribulation.'

'Is that why He gave you pleuks all over your face?' I said. It was unkind, but I was unable to prevent myself.

'There is no need to be offensive,' he said. 'It is just a burden I have to bear.'

He looked very sad when he said that, and I very nearly felt a mild pang of compassion for him. 'I'm sorry, Mr Caldwell,' I said in a calmer tone. 'I cannot share your certainty in religion.'

He asked if that was why I had not been attending divine service, and I was about to reply when Adah passed through the room. I noted that the reverend Ninny cast her a glance in which opprobrium and lubricity were present in equal measure, though he attempted to conceal the latter. It was the kind of look I have frequently observed on the face of that miserable hypocrite Fisher, as he ushered the young women of the parish into the kirk of a Sunday morning – all his seeming solicitude concealing the corruption within.

'Who is that, Mr Burns?'

'That is Adah, my housekeeper.'

'I see,' he said, in a tone I did not much care for.

'What do you see?' I asked.

He had the grace to look abashed. 'Nothing. I intended no disrespect.'

'I hope not, Mr Caldwell.' I stood up, and he flinched as if he feared I was about to strike him. 'If you will excuse me, I have pressing business to attend to.' He scurried away like a frightened animal, and I do not expect he will come calling again.

July 20th. We are doing pretty well for provisions here although the word from Kingston is that there are shortages in many places, the reason being that since their conflict with Britain, the former American colonies have not been inclined to trade with Jamaica. In consequence, there is a dearth of grain, and there still remains the legacy of the hurricanes of seven years ago. C[larke?][6] has taken the matter in hand, and we have heard that the appropriately named HMAV *Bounty* has been dispatched to the South Seas to fetch breadfruit plants that should flourish in our fertile soil. In the meantime we have to make do with salt fish and boiled plantain, a dish that sustaineth the body but wearieth the palate.

August 3rd. I fear I have offended Mr Garvie, who is a devout man, and who was lecturing me today about predestination, a topic on which I invariably stumble. He was talking about the omniscience of God when I interrupted him.

'Tell me, Mr Garvie,' I said, when I finally had the opportunity. 'Is it your belief that God is all-knowing?'

'Yes,' he said.

'And mankind is His creation?'

'Of course we are.'

'Very well,' I said. 'Since God is all-knowing, then He knows the outcome of all things, for everything that happens to us is a part of His great purpose.'

'That is correct.'

'I see. So when I believe I am making a choice, then God knows already what that choice will be?'

'Yes,' he said.

'Tell me,' I said, 'am I correct in believing that Adam was created by God?'

'Of course,' he said, testily. 'You have read the book of Genesis, I hope?'

'Certainly,' I said. 'I just wanted to be sure. Now, God told Adam not to eat from the Tree of Knowledge. Why did He do that?'

'Because He wanted Man to remain innocent. Had Adam not eaten of the fruit, then he and all of his descendants would have inhabited Eden for ever.'

'So you and I would have inherited an earthly paradise.'

'Indeed we would.'

'Tell me, Mr Garvie, would it not have been simpler to place Adam in a paradise where there was no temptation to sin?'

'Ah!' he said, wagging his finger. 'That's the whole point! Adam was given a clear instruction by God. He knew what would happen if he disobeyed that instruction. But the temptress Eve seduced him, and he yielded to her will, rather than the will of his Maker.'

'From what you have told me, Mr Garvie,' I said, 'one thing seems clear. An omniscient God knows the outcome of all things. This means that God created Adam, knowing full well that he would disobey. In other words, Adam's choice was not a free choice at all, he was merely doing what had already been preordained.' Mr Garvie began to protest, but I had the bit between my teeth now.

'So,' I went on, 'God had already seen into the far future with His divine gift of omniscience. Adam was merely a pretext for God's real plan, which was to create a world of danger, disease and death, populated by miserable sinners who could be made to suffer agony in this world, before being mercilessly punished in the next.'

'That is a gross travesty of the truth!' he spluttered.

'It seems to me,' I said, 'that God had the choice of creating a world of joy or a world of misery, and He chose the latter. I cannot say I am impressed.'

'Who are you to challenge the Scriptures? Who are you to deny God?' I felt that I had perhaps gone too far. The man was purple in the face. Why is it that the pious can never discuss their religion calmly? They invariably become angry and defensive, and begin to shout about blasphemy.

'This is blasphemy, Burns,' he said, sure enough.

'I only intended to clarify some contradictions,' I said. 'If there is no free will, then Adam's choice was already made when God created him. So we should blame God, not Adam.'

'You dare to blame the Almighty?' he shouted. 'I'm glad Mr Douglas hasn't heard your sacrilegious nonsense. You should get on your knees and beg forgiveness!'

'What would be the point? Either I'm doomed to perdition or I'm not, and praying will make no difference if God has already made up His divine mind regarding my fate in this world and the next.'

He walked away, very surly, and I heard his door slam behind him as he went into his house.

August 19th. The Sabbath, a day of brilliant sunshine. I went fishing with Armstrong. We found a fellow in Port Antonio who was happy to take us out in his boat in return for some trifling sum, so we instructed him to take us to the middle of East Harbour. It is the most beautiful bay, almost entirely landlocked, and from our vantage point on its still waters we could look shorewards, and admire the lushness of the gentle slopes on which our plantation stands.

The water was about fifty feet deep and astonishingly clear – we could see the bottom quite clearly – indeed it almost made one's head spin to look down into it, as if we were somehow suspended at a great height instead of floating on water. Our captain gave us a couple of lines that we dangled overboard, and between us we managed to pull half a dozen small fish on board. There is something very peaceful about being on water, and we soon tired of fishing, sitting instead in a silent reverie, enjoying the gentle motion of the boat. I was reminded of these weeks on the *Bell*, and how I often used to lie on the berth with Mary, sleepily aware of the sounds of the ship, and its slow rocking movement. For a time I felt quite the miserable widower, but when I opened my eyes and looked again at the beauty of the scene, my *ennui* soon took flight. I remember looking at the scales of our little fish, and how they glistened and sparkled in the sun, and thinking how beautiful they were.

On my return, Adah expressed her delight with my piscatorial prowess, and has served up as a delicious meal. These days of leisure are good for me: I need to devote more time to simple relaxation and solitude. The quotidian routine allows no time for contemplation.

August 24th. Gregory was complaining of pains in his chest today, so I sent him home. I have noticed that on a few occasions lately he has been very tired-looking.

'Don't come back to work until you feel better,' I said.

'Yuh nuh gwine send me tuh Simpson fuh de cinchona?' he asked, with a feeble smile.

'I'll send you to Champong Nanny if you're not careful,' I said. 'If you see her bending over, then you'd better run.'

'Yuh knows 'bout Nanny? Oh Lord!' He gave a wheezing laugh that degenerated into a cough.

'Off you go,' I insisted, and obediently he tottered away on his stiff old legs.

August 26th. We have had to dispense with the services of our head sugar boiler, Ezekiel, who was drunk today, and not fit for his duties. The contents of the grand copper had begun to ferment by the time we realised anything was amiss. Our head driver would have flogged him, but Mr Douglas intervened and instructed that the miscreant be made to work with the weeding gang, which comprises only women and little children, and this will be a greater humiliation than the lash. He will be permitted to return to his normal duties when he has demonstrated that he can remain sober.

August 28th. We have all been very saddened by the death of Gregory, who passed away in the middle of yesterday afternoon. His end was very peaceful – according to Martha, who was tending him, he simply fell asleep and never awakened. Her diagnosis was that he was 'jes' plain wore out'. To think that it is less than a week since we shared our last little joke together! It is hard to believe that he is gone, but I am glad that I was able to show him an act of kindness at the end. Mr Douglas provided a handsome coffin, and has cancelled all work today and tomorrow, generous gestures that have much impressed the slaves. Martha was insistent that I should attend the funeral and I understand this to be an unusual honour.

I have just returned from that solemn occasion. The body was borne to the grave in a great procession, everyone decked out in their best finery; clapping their hands; dancing, and singing and wailing in the most doleful tones. The number of mourners must have been upward of two hundred, and their chanted dirge was in the highest degree affecting. I have heard a good deal of dour Presbyterian voices raised in pious expressions of grief, and, for all that, sounding very much like the grudging execution of an unpleasant duty, but this afternoon the lamentation came from the heart – it soared – it froze the marrow to hear it. I did not understand any of the words, but that did not make the slightest difference. I have long cherished a belief that melody *per se* not only enhances language – as witness our incomparable Scots airs – but actually transcends it, reaching into the very soul. So I was very moved as he was laid to rest with the greatest dignity imaginable, whereupon rum and tobacco and food were placed with him in the grave to sustain him on his final journey.

The Africans believe that a dead man's soul rejoins those of his ancestors, and that he returns to his native land, free at last from the chains of bondage. As a doctrine goes, it is to my mind as good as any other. With the burial over, more food and rum were produced, and the celebrations commenced. These are expected to continue well into the night, but I felt it tactful to withdraw at an early stage, having paid my respects with due deference.

September 3rd. I have been considering the funeral, about which some of the overseers – particularly Gilmour – have been very disparaging, calling it heathen superstition, pagan nonsense and the like. That it was a pagan ceremony is true, but what of that? The evident sincerity of their belief elevates their philosophy to a level far above that displayed by the sanctimonious cleric, mumbling platitudes to the gullible. I have whiled away a few minutes with my goose-feather in the composition of a few lines on the subject –

Epitaph for Gregory

Here lies a man who knew no prayerful fraud;
Whose priestless pilgrimage has duly passed:
And if, indeed, there be a loving God,
Release his unchain'd soul to wander free at last.

Of course Gregory has no headstone, such a luxury being unknown to the slaves, but I shall give a fair copy to Martha and read it to her.

September 13th. The mood of the slaves is improved, for the Harmony malefactors have been spared the gallows. It all worked out rather amusingly, and justice has been served in a manner worthy of the divine Nemesis herself. Mr Solway, in his flight from the plantation, had made no provision for the feeding of his pack of hellhounds, and none of his servants dared go near them. As a consequence, the creatures were ravenous and unapproachable by the time he returned. Notwithstanding, he rashly entered the enclosure where they were penned up, carrying a bucket of raw meat, whereupon the brutes flew at him in a fury. It was only by good fortune that he was able to effect an escape, but even so the word is that he was severely bitten. The authorities, far from taking pity on his plight, have instead formed the opinion that the animals are far too dangerous to be kept on the plantation, and that their presence there was provocative. They have decreed that although the damage to the Great House cannot be condoned, his actions had done much to incite the slaves to an act of destruction. It is likely that they will be treated quite leniently. It is good to see that there is some justice.

I have had to endure a lecture from Mr Douglas on the subject of the little poem I wrote for Gregory. Somehow he has heard about it, and it has displeased him greatly. He took the greatest possible exception to the phrase 'prayerful fraud' – being himself a very devout person he was shocked at what he viewed as atheist sentiments.

'You're a Christian, aren't you?' he said, with asperity. 'So what is this "fraud" you speak of?'

'If you or I were compelled to worship some pagan idol, then that would be a fraud. Gregory had his own beliefs, and it would be wrong to condemn him for that. For him, our God must seem irrelevant.'

'This is coming dangerously close to blasphemy, Burns,' he said, colouring in anger. 'The world was created by God. The Bible tells us that quite clearly. You know as well as I do what the Good Book has to say about false gods. "Thou shalt have no other gods before me", isn't that what the commandment says? Eh?'

'Yes, but Gregory didn't know anything about that,' I said. 'How can you blame him for believing in something else?'

'We're all children of God,' he said, in the kind of voice that I am sure that some of the Old Testament prophets must have used in making their pronouncements.

'If Gregory had been baptised, and lived a good Christian life, would he have gone to Heaven?'

'Certainly.'

'So there will be Negroes in Heaven?'

'"In my Father's house are many mansions". The Good Lord will provide for all true believers. Each will be rewarded.'

'Do you believe that the distinction between master and slave will disappear in the next world?' I asked.

'No one can define Heaven in earthly terms,' he replied. 'We will all be equal before the Lord.'

'Why are we not equal before the Lord here on earth?'

'Because the Lord has ordained it thus! I find your wilful obtuseness on the point most exasperating, Burns.'

'But does the Lord not also tell us to love others as we love ourselves? How can this be reconciled with enslaving them?'

'Anyone would think that you were becoming an abolitionist, man! I treat everyone with the respect and decency appropriate to his situation. Have you ever known me to treat one of my slaves with unkindness?'

'No, of course not.'

'Then you ought to know better than to provoke me in this way.'

'I do not seek to provoke you, Mr Douglas,' I said. 'But it seems to me unsatisfactory to claim that the situation of being a slave is somehow an accident of birth. Surely it is a situation which you impose willy-nilly.'

'I did not impose it,' he replied with some heat. 'I simply take things as I find them, and try to deal honourably with everyone according to his station. What is so wrong with that? What would you have me do? Set the slaves loose, and leave them to fend for themselves in the forest, or in the gutters of Port Antonio? Leave the cane to harvest itself?'

'No, but . . .'

'Then kindly think before you speak in future. And I must ask you to stop putting ideas into the slaves' heads.'

He stalked off before I could reply.

September 20th. A new fellow started here today, by the name of James McLehose, formerly of Edinburgh. He made a good impression upon me: a tall, good-looking fellow though inclined a little to fat under the chin; blue eyes which met mine steadily, and a firm handshake. He had been in the legal profession, but not found it conducive to his taste, and had come to the Indies to make his fortune. For a time he had been in Kingston, and is now to take up the post of overseer in the distillery. Fatigued by the journey, he has been given leave by Mr Douglas to rest for a few days, and to settle himself in. He sought me out at supper, desirous of conversation with a fellow countryman. This began in a civil enough fashion, which became ever more convivial as the rum-jug passed between us, until at last we were singing songs together and pledging everlasting friendship, forever united by the bond afforded by John Barleycorn – or John Sugar-cane, I ought rather to say. This morning I feel decidedly the worse for my carouse, but what else can I do? The warmth of the rum in my belly may be short lived, but it is an opiate to the memory while it lasts.

September 24th. Most evenings spent with McLehose these past few weeks. He is an uncommonly entertaining fellow, and has me in fits of helpless laughter with his mimicry of the fine primsie gentry in Edinburgh. He asked me if I had ever been married, and I said that I had, albeit briefly, tasted the pleasures of the state of matrimony, and related the melancholy story of Mary's death, at which he seemed most affected, saying it was a damned shame. I enquired about his own marital state, but he seemed rather evasive on the subject, and I jalouse that there are matters there which he does not care to speak about. I know that Adah does not approve of McLehose, though she shows him perfect courtesy when he is in the house. It manifests itself in small ways, and without knowing her as I do, no one could possibly be unaware that anything was the matter. Mostly I notice a tension in the jaw muscles; she also employs an irritating sniff when she is in his presence. She counters any suggestion of disrespect by the assumption of an excessively deferential politeness when she addresses him.

September 28th. McLehose made an appearance at dinner in the Great House yesterday evening with a mulatta, which caused something of a [stir] *frisson* in the assembled company. Nothing was said, in so many words, but I rapidly sensed that Mr Douglas regarded the introduction of the lady into our society as a breach of etiquette. However she spoke and conducted herself with perfect correctness and indeed refinement. Her name is Ann Chalon Rivvere, and she is certainly a rare beauty, with long black hair, a rather haughty expression, and a most captivating smile. I gather she is a free coloured, and was (ostensibly at least) a housekeeper for Mr MacGregor, the agent on the Fraser estate, until he died from fever last October. I would guess her age to be about eight-and-twenty years. McLehose is clearly greatly enamoured of her, as was evident throughout the evening, for he had eyes for no one else. For my part, I own I found the situation rather amusing, but Mr Douglas clearly did not, and withdrew shortly after dinner, bidding us rather a curt goodnight, and vouchsafing Miss Rivvere little more than a stiff and unsmiling bow. McLehose seemed perfectly oblivious to the embarrassment he was causing.

At about nine, I went back to my quarters. I was on the point of preparing for bed when there was a knock at my door, and McLehose let himself in.

'What do you think of her, Burns?' he demanded, helping himself from my store of rum, and sprawling in my best chair with the air of one well contented with life.

'Miss Rivvere? She is certainly a bonny woman.'

'I'm glad you think so,' he said, grinning. 'She really is quite out of the ordinary, you know. The way she speaks, for instance. One would never believe she was Jamaican. And she is perfectly fluent in French.' He went on to recount her multifarious talents and accomplishments in exhaustive detail, always with one eye on me, as if he was awaiting approval or endorsement on my part.

'I'm glad you're happy with her,' I said, when at last I had the opportunity. 'A man needs a good woman, and it does no harm, provided he has no other attachments.'

At this he flushed slightly, and his geniality left him. 'What do you mean by that?'

'Nothing,' I replied, somewhat taken aback. 'It's none of my business what you do. You are free to do as you wish. I hope you'll be very happy with her.'

He stood up and paced across the room a few times, obviously ill at ease. 'Yes, I am,' he said, but somewhat defensively, in my opinion. There was a moment of awkward silence, and it occurred to me that he was very drunk, but like the habitual drunkard, succeeding in concealing the fact with a skill born of long practice. Suddenly he guffawed aloud, and pointed over at Adah.

'That's a fine specimen you have there,' he remarked, quite unconcerned that she could hear him. 'I wonder you haven't thought to get between her legs. Or maybe you have. It's no business of mine of course, but if I were in your shoes . . .' He grinned and made a suggestive gesture, all the while leering at me in a disgusting manner.

'I do not think it is appropriate to discuss such matters in the presence of the lady concerned,' I said. 'After all, I wouldn't hold such a conversation in the presence of Miss Rivvere.'

'Oh come on, Burns,' he declared. 'A lady? Whatever are you thinking of? Ann is a free woman, but this Adah person is just your . . . oh, really . . . you do not seriously suppose that she is of the same standing?' He began to laugh quite heartily.

'I believe that all women deserve respect, whatever their standing,' I said, rather coldly. 'Now if you will excuse me, I must retire for the night.'

He rose, a little unsteadily. 'I didn't mean to upset you,' he said.

'That's all right. I'm very tired, that's all.'

He went out, staggering a little, and I was glad to see him go. As I closed the door I could see Adah standing very still at the table in the little kitchen, with her back to me, and her head bowed. I went over to her at once and saw that she was weeping.

'So I's yuh *specimen*,' she said. 'What's a *specimen*, Massa Burns?'

'Don't trouble yourself,' I said. 'He had no right to speak that way.'

'Dat's where yuh wrong, Massa Burns. All de white men, dey all git de right tuh speak dat way.'

'They may have the right, but not in my house. Another thing – just because they *have* the right, it doesn't follow that they *are* right.'

'Is I a lady?'

'You are a woman, just like the Rivvere *specimen*,' I replied. To my relief she gave a little smile at this.

'An' all women deserves respec'?'

'Yes, they do.'

She remained motionless for a moment, then said: 'Yuh good man, Massa Burns. I likes yuh style.' Suddenly she turned, put her arms around my neck and planted a clumsy kiss on my startled lips, before running off into her own room.

During the course of writing this evening, I have more than once arisen and gone to her door, standing there irresolute. I do not think that she would deny me. Perhaps even now, in the darkness, she is awaiting me. But I, who have always sought intimacy at the earliest encounter – and never known rejection! – now find myself unaccountably diffident. Whereas, for many, blackness invites a contemptuous sensual licence, with Adah it has engendered in me an unaccustomed deference; for despite her servile status and her imperfect English, she is an exceptional woman. More than anyone else, she demonstrated true devotion to me and to Mary from the moment of our arrival, and since Mary's death she has been a perfect model of solicitude. It would, I believe, be utterly contemptible of me to return this devotion by going to her bed, and extorting the West Indian equivalent of *droit de seigneur*. I want her; she very probably wants me; everyone assumes that we [fʊ] regularly frolic together in bed; and yet here I sit, knowing that she is in an adjacent room, but determined to sleep alone, in perfect propriety. That I admire and esteem her is true, and if these are crimes then I am the most offending thing alive.

October 1st. An amusing incident today. Toby and I were standing waiting for some timber to be brought to repair the roof of one of the storage sheds. Toby's friend Martin was to fetch it with a horse and cart, and indeed we could see him in the distance, making very poor progress, for he seemed to be experiencing the greatest difficulty in keeping his horse on the road. After ten minutes, during which time he had not progressed as many yards, I let out a sigh of vexation.

'What on earth is the matter with Martin?' I said.

'He's a lazy 'arse,' said Toby. I was quite taken aback by this, for I have never known him to say a bad word about anyone, far less to employ indelicate language.

'That's rather a disrespectful thing to say about Martin,' I said.

'I don' mean no disrespec' fuh Martin,' he said.

'Well, calling him a lazy arse isn't particularly respectful, is it?'

He looked at me in puzzlement. 'I didn' call'm dat. Martin nuh lazy. It's his 'arse dat's lazy.'

'But that's very much the same thing, isn't it?'

'Nosuh. I mean de 'arse dat pull de cart. It's a lazy 'arse.'

'Oh, you mean horse?' I said, with belated comprehension.

'Yessuh. Like I say, Massa Burns, a lazy 'arse. Wha'd'yuh t'ink I say?'

'I thought you said, "he's a lazy arse".'

'Not he *is* a lazy 'arse. He *'as* a lazy 'arse. An 'arse 'as four legs, Massa Burns. Martin git two legs.' He suddenly grinned. 'Oh Massa Burns, yuh t'ink I call Martin an *arse*? Oh nossuh! I nuh use bad words. Nuh me, suh!'

I thought I had pretty well mastered the Jamaican version of English, but there are still pitfalls aplenty!

October 3rd. We have had word that the Americans have set up a Constitutional Convention in Philadelphia. This new nation, by nature of its very vastness, presents to my mind almost insurmountable difficulties of governance. Each individual state, which may be larger than Scotland, naturally wishes to preserve its own distinctive identity. Imagine these formidable conflicts of allegiance multiplied over the face of a whole continent! It is a brave venture indeed.

October 14th. Sabbath. Adah has gone to spend the day with her family, and I took the opportunity to take a solitary walk, following some of the leafy pathways that wind around the plantation. Sometimes I meet with others as I wander pensively, and they wonder why I am short with them when they try to fall in beside me with their foolish, inconsequential bletheration. I care not if they consider me reclusive and odd. Today was good because I met no one; I was *alone,* to relish the smell of the air; the vastness of the clouds; the perfection of flowers, and the songs of birds! Now that I have returned, I feel that my mind has cleared, and I have resolved a few matters.

Item. I am growing very fond of Adah, and although I have never tried for familiarity I have often dreamed wistfully about it. I am prevented by my pride – having assured everyone of the pristine propriety of our domestic arrangements – and also by her inscrutability. I have seen one or two of the plantation girls who disport themselves in a very lewd manner, but Adah has dignity and strength, and has been an excellent housekeeper – to spoil this with clumsy, hot-blooded advances would be quite wrong. Our relationship proceeds with complete decorum, and I shall keep my amorous inclinations to myself.

Item. McLehose is an entertaining fellow, but I am not sure that I should spend so much time with him. There is coarseness beneath his urbanity and for all his bluff heartiness and seeming openness I feel he is hiding some secret. What is more, I was offended by his rudeness to Adah. I shall not eschew his company altogether, but I mean to avoid indulging in these interminable post-prandial carousals that leave me with the devil of a headache the next day.

Item. I must write home more often; I am daily determined to do so, yet I cannot summon the resolve to lift the quill. I believe I'm prevented by the knowledge that nothing I have to impart from Jamaica would made sense to Gilbert, and so, when I do write, I restrict myself to simple facts, and formal expressions of affection. What interest would he have in a description of the workings of the mill-house; an essay on the sounds the crickets make at night, or a treatise on sugar cane? Yet these are the very matters that occupy me constantly! When he writes, it is somewhat the same – I have a dwindling sense of Mossgiel, or of Bess, or of the Ayrshire woods and riverbanks where I used to wander! Nevertheless, I have determined to make a greater effort to be an assiduous correspondent.

Item. The question of slavery – would that I had an answer! Before I left Scotland I really did not know what to believe. On my arrival here, I had hardly arrived at an opinion before another one developed, and I found myself caught up like a scholar who studies for a lifetime only to realise how little he knows. The more I see and hear of slavery, the more confusing it becomes. I understand what Wilberforce is saying, and every fibre of my being cries out in revolt at the notion that one man should stand in dominion over another on the grounds of privilege, rank, and – yes! – colour! Yet here I am, part of the whole trade. And here are slaves who run their own affairs; transact business; are cared for in their old age, and possess, even bequeath, property. This hardly corresponds with the abolitionists' picture of vile oppression and servile chains. I have been here for barely a year, and I think I have much to learn – I have scarcely set foot beyond the plantation all this time, and I have yet to see how slaves are treated elsewhere. I have heard stories, but one cannot always believe what one hears.

October 29th. The weather has been very stormy lately, with much rain, but providentially little damage. This is the season of the year when hurricanes strike, and although we have been spared here, word has reached us of disaster at Montego Bay two days ago, where whole plantations have been levelled and very many persons killed.

Mr Douglas says that we no longer have anything to fear for the moment, as the storm, though exceedingly violent, is relatively small in area, and if it has struck the east of the island then it will continue directly on its way, leaving us alone. This is welcome news, but what of the next hurricane? The damnable thing is that there is nothing anyone can do by way of self-preservation.

October 31st. The storm has almost gone; there is just the occasional gust of wind to remind us of it. As tonight is Hallowe'en, I have been telling Adah about some of our quaint Scottish superstitions, many of which were related to me by my mother and Betty Davidson, who was related to us in some obscure way and occasionally came to visit us. What a treasury of tales they had! How many times did we sit by the ingle, shivering in delighted terror at these daft tales!

'We git ghosts in Jamaica,' said Adah. 'We git duppies!'

'Duppies?' I said. 'What are they?'

'Dey's *bad*,' she said. 'Afta people die, dey comes back.'

'All ghosts come back,' I said.

'Yuh nuh un'erstan',' she said. 'Dey *really* comes back. Dey comes out dey graves, and dey walks!'

'That's impossible.'

She shook her head vigorously. 'Plenty people seen'm. Duppies cyan't say nuttin' an' dey cyan't eat nuttin'. Dey kin turn deyselves inta an'mals. Dey kin go t'roo walls. If a duppy speak tuh yuh, then yuh's dead fo' sho'!' She shivered, and I could see that she believed in her duppies. Outside there was a sudden, violent flurry of wind, and she gave a little squeal.

'It's just the wind, Adah.' I said. 'Now, come and sit here by me and I shall tell you a ghost story.' She came to me eagerly, and I told her a long, rambling tale about a miserly old lady whose most precious possession was a gold locket. Her daughter coveted it, and hoped that one day it would be hers. Eventually the old lady died.

'Did she git de locket?' asked Adah.

'No, she did not.'

'Why?'

'Because,' I said, 'the old lady left a will, and in the will it said that she had to be buried wearing the locket. So of course that is what happened.'

'So dat's de end'f de story?'

'Not quite,' I said. 'The daughter was determined to have the locket. So on the night after the funeral, she took a spade, and she went to the grave-yard . . .'

'. . . tuh dig up de grave!' said Adah, with wide eyes.

'Yes. So she dug down and opened the grave, and sure enough, there was the locket on the dead woman's breast. So she pulled it off; put it in her pocket, and then filled the grave in again.'

'She gwine be sarry she done dat. Dat's a bad, bad t'ing.'

'On the way home,' I said, 'she was walking slowly because it was a very dark night – like tonight – and a very windy night – like tonight. And as she walked she thought she heard something behind her.' Adah's eyes grew even wider.

'Wha' she hear?'

'It sounded like footsteps.'

'Oh Lordy.'

'So she began to walk more quickly. When she got home, she opened the door, looked behind her, and standing there *was her mother!*'

'She come fuh de locket!' she said with a gasp.

'So she ran to her room, but there was nowhere to hide. Then she heard the footsteps of her mother *coming . . . up . . . the . . . stairs!*'

Adah said nothing, but here eyes did not leave mine. I could swear that I heard her heart beating.

'So she climbed into her bed and pulled the covers over her head. As she lay there, she could hear the footsteps of her mother *coming . . . across . . . the . . . room!*'

Adah moved even closer to me, breathing rapidly with excitement.

'So as the poor girl lay there, she realised that her mother was leaning down to *whisper . . . in . . . her . . . ear,*' I said, leaning down and placing my lips very close to her ear, reducing my voice to the merest fraction of a hushed *pianissimo*. '*And . . . the mother . . . said . . . GIVE ME MY LOCKET!*' I suddenly yelled, *fortissimo*, grabbing her by the shoulders. She shrieked aloud, jumped on to my lap and clasped me tightly. When she had recovered herself, she scolded me a little for frightening her so much, but within a few minutes she was laughing, and asking to be taught the story.

It is late now, and I must finish. How soft and warm she is! Did I contrive the story to make her leap into my lap, or did she use the story as a pretext? Something is changing between us.

November 15th. There is nothing so tiresome as a drunk man pretending to be sober, as evidenced by McLehose this evening. He came round unannounced with a bottle of Antigua, trying rather too hard to pronounce his words correctly. Adah was in the process of rubbing palm oil on my feet, so I was not overly pleased with the intrusion.

'I thought we might have a glass or two of this,' he said, waving the bottle at me, and making himself at home. Adah gave him one of her looks as she left the room. He poured out two enormous measures, and swallowed his with a few gulps.

'Ah,' he said, licking his lips, 'there's nothing like it! I've been waiting all day for that.'

It was perfectly clear that he had been drinking all evening. He launched into a voustie lecture about his favourite subject – himself. He had been a great lawyer in Glasgow; he kenned Lord So-and-so and Lady Such-and-such; he had defended all of the most difficult cases – oh, he was the brightest star in the legal firmament. He poured himself another large measure with a shaking hand.

'And the women, Robert,' he said. 'They simply wouldna leave me alone! The letters I have had! The invitations! I think it's the wig and gown. I used to cultivate a stern, haughty expression in court – women admire that, you know. I could have taken my pick!'

'So what brought you to Port Antonio to be an overseer?' I asked. He looked at me rather blearily and remained silent for a while.

'Edinburgh!' he said at last. He speech was very slurred by this time. 'Have you ever been to Edinburgh, Robert?'

'No.'

'A wise decision on your part.'

'It wasn't a decision,' I said. 'I never had the opportunity. But what does Edinburgh have to do with your decision to leave Scotland?'

'Things happened,' he said morosely.

'What things?'

'Oh,' he said, 'you get involved with . . . this and that. Glasgow is governed by commerce; Edinburgh is governed by gentility. If the high and mighty turn against you, then there are few options left.'

I would like to have discovered more from him, but there was a knock at the door, and when I opened it there was Miss Rivvere.

'Ah, Ann!' said McLehose, trying to stand, but stumbling rather badly and having to hold on to the wall. 'Wah-jan-ish?'

'Time to come home, James,' she said in a voice that had an edge of steel to it. 'You will excuse us, Robert.'

'I wish you both good night,' I said, and she led him off into the darkness.

Adah resumed her ministrations with the palm oil, which was very relaxing, and now I am completing this journal for today. I wonder what drove McLehose from Edinburgh?

November 20th. When Adah came this morning I was surprised to see that she had applied some kind of white powder to her face. When I asked her the reason for it, she replied that she had wanted to make herself look lighter. Frankly it made her look rather ridiculous, and I told her to wash it off.

'But I wan' be pretty lak Missiz Burns,' she protested.

'Don't be silly, Adah, I said. 'You're much prettier without it.'

'I wan' be lak a white lady.'

'You can't change the colour of the skin you are born with,' I said. 'You can't change your height, or the colour of your eyes, can you?'

'No, but I wan' look mo' light.'

'Look Adah,' I said. ' If I painted my face black, would that turn me into a black person?'

'Well, no.'

'You see? I've got straight hair, and my mouth and nose are the wrong shape.'

'But yuh gat real dark eyes, jes' lak mine,' she said.

'That's true. But we shouldn't try to change the way we look.'

'Yuh t'ink a black specimen lak me cyan be pretty lak a white lady?'

'Of course you can,' I said. 'You *are* very pretty.'

We had quite a discussion about it. I cannot understand why she should want to paint her face. But for some Jamaicans a great ambition is to pass for white. Black skin may admittedly be the outward badge of slavery, but it is the slave trade that has made it so. This desire to resemble the Missiz and the Massa annoys me a little. What have we done to deserve emulation?

December 2nd. Woman is the blood-royal of life; let there be no degrees of precedency between them, whether rank or colour, it makes no difference. Let them all be sacred! I am writing this all back-to-front, *alors, commencez au commencement!* It all began this morning when Adah was kneeling to scrub the floor. She was wearing a loose chemise and by accident or design it had fallen open, revealing her breasts, which were small, but exquisitely shaped and well proportioned, with dark nipples. I confess that I could not take my eyes from them, so that when she looked up and found me staring, I was covered in blushing confusion, and hastily made to apologise.

'That's all right,' she said, quite unconcerned, and making no attempt to cover herself up. 'Yuh looks all yuh want.'

She gave me an arch glance which was very eloquent, and returned to her floor-cleaning, swaying her whole body to and fro in a suggestively rhythmical manner. I had to go out at that point, but spent a substantial proportion of the day in an enjoyable reverie. On my return at the hour of six or thereby, she had discarded her outer dress altogether, and her modesty was preserved only by the longitude of her chemise, which was sorely scanty.

'Me dress git dutty,' she said. 'Anyway, I's too hot.'

I could think of nothing to say. In the course of serving up my meal – a process which involved leaning over the table a great deal more than was her wont, as well as bending to pick up things which had unaccountably fallen to the floor – it became obvious to me that she was perfectly naked beneath that thin cotton garment. As I was finishing my food she came and sat opposite me – something which she had never done before – and began to eat a banana, looking coyly at me all the while.

'Are you all right, Adah?' I asked.

'Oh yes, Massa Burns. 'Cept me leg git terrible cramp. D'yuh t'ink yuh c'd give it a *doin'* fuh me? Sorry tuh ax yuh, but it's hurtin' real bad.'

'Well, I expect I could try,' I said, seeing where this was leading. I suppose that had been inevitable, the only question being when, and on whose initiation! She kept up the pretence of the cramp very well at first, lying back on my bed with the martyred air of one in the throes of the most excessive discomfort; she directed the application of the palm-oil to a point just above her right knee, groaning in a most affecting way, and, during my ministrations, wriggled around in a way which exposed her most intimate charms. Then she announced that the cramp had shifted to her other leg, at a spot much higher up, and directed my hand to it. Within a short time it was impossible for either of us to masquerade any longer, all play-acting was rapidly abandoned, and very soon the Temple of Venus had yielded – not at all unwillingly! – to the strong and resolute on-slaught of the battering-ram, whose robust and stalwart action led to a rapid triumph! – the joyous culmination of the campaign! – a sudden outpouring of rapture! – a massive ejaculation of ecstasy! Jean was always obliging and tender in love-making, but rather passive. Mary (rest her soul!) was affectionate and very willing, but although she professed to like it very much, I am quite sure that I enjoyed the act more than she did. Without disrespect to either of these fine women, I must say that Adah's ardour is of quite a different order. She is a strong, supple lass, and she cooperated with such violent enthusiasm that Corporal Pintle, having 'discharged' his duty most effectively, is quite bruised from his early evening skirmish! When I had recovered, I discovered that Adah was already up and about, properly dressed once more, and seeing to her duties as if nothing had happened between us. I felt awkward about this.

'How's the cramp now, Adah?' I asked her. Her face broke into a radiant smile, and I realised that she was feeling as diffident as I.

'Oh Massa Burns!' she exclaimed, 'dat's de best doin' I ever had!'

I asked her if she would share my bed from now on, and she has willingly agreed. Now that the domestic *status quo* has been changed, we shall have to decide how we present ourselves to the world – but enough of that for tonight. As I write up this account of the day, I can hear her singing cheerfully to herself in the bedroom, awaiting me; and despite his heroic exertions, Corporal Pintle is eagerly standing to attention!

December 16th. My travails in the fields by day are as nothing compared with the joyous exertions of the nights: *hic labor est!* On my homecoming she serves me up our meal, which we can scarce eat for eyeing each other in the most licentious way imaginable; and hardly have we eaten the last mouthful than we betake ourselves to bed, where I am positively overwhelmed by such a variety of lascivious caresses that my head is swimming with it, and as for the Rod of Aaron – the Staff of Life! – such constant rogering would wear it away to a shadow, were it not for its mysterious powers of regeneration, which astound me. I had always thought myself quite the virile fellow, but my stamina is being sorely tested! I have attempted, with some difficulty, to persuade Adah not to call me 'Massa Burns'.

'I a'ways calls yuh dat,' she argued. 'Anyway, yuh is me massa. I's jest yuh specimen,' she added with a cheeky grin. This has become a term of endearment, and I truly believe that she has no idea what the word signifies, despite my attempts to elucidate her.

'Don't be silly,' I said, 'and anyway I'd rather you didn't.'

'Well, what yuh want I call yuh?' she asked.

'Just use my name.'

'Call yuh "Robert" like Missiz Burns? Oh my!' She clapped her hands over her mouth and shook her head.

'Well, Rab then. Some of my friends used to call me that.'

'Rab,' she said, tentatively. 'Rab. I'll try dat.'

Since this conversation, she has done her best, but still falls back on 'Massa' occasionally, to which I respond by calling her 'Miz Specimen' while tickling her, causing shrieks of laughter and giggling. In the company of others – notably McLehose, who is liable to drop in of an evening without notice – she reverts to being formal and deferential, although behind his back she has the saucy habit of making droll faces and suggestive gestures which are in the highest degree distracting. More than once I have had to feign a fit of coughing in order to prevent myself from laughing out loud. He knows about Adah and me, of course, and is not in the slightest judgemental about our liaison, taking the view that it was bound to happen eventually.

December 25th. Christmas Day, and no work on the plantation. It is late: I have been to the Great House for dinner, but am feeling morose because I remember the last occasion I attended with Mary. It seems impossible that it was a year ago! We were so happy then, and with so much to look forward to! This is not to denigrate in the slightest what Adah has done for me of late, and I know that this appears ungracious to her – it is not intended to be.

I attended dinner on my own, mindful of Mr Douglas's reaction to Miss Rivvere a couple of months ago. If he was offended by the presence of a free coloured, possessed of every social accomplishment, then I fear he would suffer an apoplexy if he were expected to entertain one of his own slaves at table! Adah, bless her, has not mastered what might be termed the niceties of social decorum – nor does she perceive any need to do so. Within the confines of our own house, I am of the same opinion. I am not ashamed in the slightest by the vernacular nature of her speech, or by the fact that she prefers to eat with her fingers. I am actually rather proud of the way she stands up for herself. However I am mightily vexed by my inability to acknowledge her openly and freely, as McLehose does with Rivvere. No one would blame me for taking my casual pleasure with her – it is the fact that we care about each other which would cause mortal affront to Douglas, and ribald amusement to the likes of Gilmour. Our situation, which harms no one, and should therefore upset no one, might also create difficulties between Adah and her own people, particularly the young menfolk, who are naturally liable to feel resentful when a white man lures away a prospective mate! Of course, if I could procure her manumission, then matters would be different. I have not mentioned this to Adah, for I would first have to discuss it with Mr Douglas, and I do not judge the time to be propitious.

December 31st. I heard the other day that there is great excitement in Berlin, where a certain Herr Achard claims to have discovered a most excellent and infallible method of producing sugar, not from cane, but from beets! We have had many a laugh over the foolishness of the notion!

1788

January 6th. The Sabbath day. Leisure to sit down and write at last. I have a very pleasant spot here at my window where I have placed a small, plain table. On it is this journal, an inkwell, my quill, a sheet of blotting paper and *c'est tout!* I require nothing else, and indeed I am seldom happier than when I am simply sitting here daydreaming. Adah has finished her little chores, and is asleep in a hammock. Everything is very quiet apart from the incessant chirr-chirr-chirr of the crickets. One could be in paradise.

I think that my life has entered at last into a period of stability, routine and contentment. In a few weeks I shall attain my twenty-ninth year. I have mastered the workings of the sugar mill, the boiling house and the distillery. I have made my mark with the slaves; the other overseers treat me with respect, though I know that they gossip about me when my back is turned. Mr Douglas is a good man to work for. The conditions on this plantation are humane and well ordered. Adah keeps our modest home neat and clean, and grows vegetables in a little pen close by. We live together in perfect happiness, keeping ourselves to ourselves as much as possible. I have managed to save upwards of thirty pounds of my salary during the time I have been in Jamaica, for there is little on which to expend it, and my needs are modest.

The beginning of the year is a good time for contemplation. Now that I am settled here, I need to start thinking of the longer term. In another three years I ought to have amassed a hundred pounds or so. This would enable me, on returning to Scotland, to throw in my lot with Gilbert at Mossgiel and help his situation, which I fear is precarious. I would also be able to resume my acquaintance with the Muse Calliope and her sisters, and perhaps try again with my poems. I have not felt the urge to write much since coming here, nor is it easy to gain access to books, although Mr Douglas has a few in his library, which he is good enough to allow me to borrow.

The matter of the slave trade is giving rise to much debate at home. Mr Wilberforce is to place legislation before parliament and it can only be a matter of time before this becomes law. The outcry of the anti-abolitionists is unsurprising as they contemplate the loss of a lucrative industry. For them, the ghastly death-toll of fifteen thousand miserable souls a year is less important than their own vast profits, fine town houses and verdant country estates. However there is a distinction to be drawn between the abolition of the *trade* and the removal of the institution of *slavery* itself. Even when the ships stop bringing slaves over the Atlantic, the plantations will still be here – and emancipation will be a long time coming, I fear.

But life is very pleasant for the moment. I can do no more than follow the wise precept of Horace: *carpe diem, quam minimum credula postero!*[1]

January 18th. I have always considered Mr Douglas to be a fair man, but flinty-bosomed by nature; puritanical rather than tolerant, and totally indifferent to the promptings of sentiment. But there is another side to him, I think. One of the slave women has suffered the loss of an infant only a month or two old – a distressing circumstance which, unsurprisingly, I am unable to contemplate without becoming tearful. I would have thought that Mr Douglas would have regarded this as a trivial matter, but instead he has been to the slave village early today and spent some time with the woman, commiserating with her for upwards of half an hour. The other slaves were mightily impressed by this, for a social call by 'Massa Douglas' is unheard of, and for him to come on such an errand of mercy is in the highest degree unusual. He has always been held in high regard by his workers, but his standing has risen still further today.

I spoke to him this afternoon, and remarked that it had been a very decent gesture on his part.

'Aye, so you think I've gone soft, Mr Burns?' he said in his usual gruff manner, as if any show of emotion was something of which to be ashamed. 'Well, it's nothing of the kind. The child would have grown up as a valuable worker, and I don't want the mother pining away, for she'll be of little use to me if she does. I was just checking on my assets.'

'I believe you went to render the woman some comfort,' I said.

'Believe what you like. I've got a plantation to run, that's all.'

He did not wish to pursue the matter. But is there is a human side to the man after all; perhaps even a conscience?

February 12th. Adah is indisposed – the monthly affliction of womankind. She assures me that it is not painful, yet she appears very sad and tearful about it. When I asked her what the matter was she appeared evasive.

'Nuttin's de matter,' she said. 'Me jest a little sad, dat's all.'

'Sad about what, Adah? You must tell me.'

'Nuttin'.'

'It must be something.'

'Nuttin'. Well, nuttin' much.'

'What, then?'

'Cyan't say. Yuh mebbe git vex.'

'Don't be silly.'

She stared down at the floor. 'When de bleedin' come,' she said at last, 'it mean no pickney dis time.' She looked up at me with big eyes. 'Me wants yuh pickney, an' dat's why me's sad. Miss Rivvere's gwine 'ave a pickney. Me wants tuh be a bellywoman lak she.'

I held her and reassured her. To be honest it had not crossed my mind that Adah might be concerned about having a child, though I remember Mr Douglas saying something about her having ambitions and using me as a means to an end.

I mentioned this to McLehose and asked him what the status of any future child of our union would be. I was assuming, *tout naïf,* that if there were a child then it would be free, but I was in for a shock.

'Free?' he said. 'Not at all. Adah has not been manumitted, and she remains Mr Douglas's property. This is also true of her issue. Your child would belong to Mr Douglas.'

'That's ridiculous!' I said.

'Not really. As you well know, it is far better to breed your own slaves than to rely on the trade.'

'Let us suppose that Adah and I have a son,' I said. 'Does that mean that when he's old enough he'll be put to work in the cane?'

'That's up to Mr Douglas, of course, but I don't think it's very likely. He wouldn't be given manual work.'

'I'm damned if any child of mine is going to be a servant or slave to anyone!' I said. In truth I felt a huge sense of indignation.

'As I said, it's up to Mr Douglas. He seems content to let Adah remain in your house. Most probably he'd make no demands on the child. He's a decent sort.'

So any child of mine – a son or daughter of Robert Burns, a free man! – shall be a slave, though spared field labour and given *lighter* duties – thanks to *lighter* skin! Today I believe I have understood for the first time what it truly means to be 'born into slavery'! I mean what I said to McLehose – I am damned if any child of mine is going to be a slave to anyone! I shall have to procure manumission for Adah in the event of her ever being with child.

February 14th. A letter from Gilbert today. The farm is proving difficult; the weather has been frosty; last year the spring came very late, and the crops were very unprofitable. Although he does not say as much, I believe that my suspicions about the farm are correct, and it strengthens my resolve to return to Mossgiel when I have suffi-cient funds to do so. It is strange to hold his letter in my hand, and think of him writing it, so far away. Poor Gilbert, he is quite exhausted by the farm; he would be happier at almost anything else. Bess will soon be four years old; apparently she prattles incessantly, and he assures me that he speaks to her about me, and tells her that I shall return home when I am able. The twins, Robert and Jean, are thriving. I shall write to him today, with my news. I have to tell him about Adah – perhaps I shall also amuse him with an account of the legend of Champong Nanny!

I often think of the cottage in Alloway where I was born, and compare its thick-walled solidity with the humble little house where I am sitting. But as Ramsay says, it is a 'cosy but and a canty ben,' and as *I* always say – 'Better a wee bush than nae bield'!

February 24th. Hurry, indolence and fifty other things conspire to keep me from my journal. In truth, nothing of any note is happening to me, and rather than fill these pages with reams of inconsequential nonsense I shall, I think, visit them again when the Muse prompts me, or when I have something of moment to record.

March 17th. Charles Edward Stuart is no more; I hear today that he died in Rome on the last day of January. I am no Jacobite, though I seethe with rage each time I think of the cursed commissioners who sold our nation away for their own vile gain. But tonight, in a mood of mawkishness (doubtless aided by the rum) it seems to me that something intangible yet precious has slipped away, never to return. Did I cling to the last vestige of a forlorn hope that Scotland might one day return to being the nation it was? I have penned some tipsy sentiments on the subject, which would no doubt earn me opprobrium or worse in certain quarters, but since my bibulous scribblings are never likely to see the light of day, I felt no constraint in giving vent to my feelings on paper. As I began to compose the lines, I had in my mind a picture of the exiled Prince languishing in some mean Italian lodging, and thought to write some fine English verse, but the Muse took me in another direction.

Whaur's Auld Scotia noo?

We're ruled by haughty England's law
Our passions tae subdue, man:
Charlie's awa; we're losers a' –
So whaur's Auld Scotia noo, man?

A nation sold for English gold
By sic a dastard crew, man!

What price the pride o' days of old?
And whaur's Auld Scotia noo, man?

Oh Wallace, hero of renown –
How sairly wad ye rue, man,
Tae see our crown in London Town –
For whaur's Auld Scotia noo, man?

Gie fools their gowd, and silks, and wine:
Sic trash we maun eschew, man!
But as for what is yours, and mine –
Oh, whaur's Auld Scotia noo, man?

March 30th. I have often wondered how Adah manages to keep her teeth so white. I occasionally use my finger to rub my own with alum if I can get it, and I even employ a piece of sharpened wood to dislodge pieces of food. Yet my gums pain me, and I have had toothache recently, while Adah's teeth appear to be in every respect perfect. Today I came across her while she was about her ablutions and found her poking into her mouth with a twig. When I asked her what she was doing, she showed me how she chewed the end of the twig until it was soft, and used this to rub her teeth and her gums. I asked her if any twig would do, and she told me that there is a particular one that grows wild – when chewed it releases a substance that helps to prevent the teeth from discolouring. I have asked her to fetch a few for me.

Adah's skin is always soft, whereas my own is dry from constant exposure to the sun. Ever solicitous, she has made me some balm from coconuts. She did this by grating coconut into water and allowing it to stand for a few days, by which time a layer of oil had formed on the surface. It is very soothing when rubbed into the skin, and exudes a rich scent reminiscent of the yellow gorse blossom on a summer's day.

April 12th. Mr Douglas has insisted that I borrow the 'Olney Hymns', no doubt for my moral edification. Although the volume purports to be the work of John Newton,[2] I discover that some of the hymns are by William Cowper, whose work I have always admired, and so I have been reading through them with some pleasure. Hymn 3 is particularly fine. There is a noble, spare simplicity in his description of the 'peaceful hours' which, having departed, leave 'an aching void the world can never fill', though I am less impressed by the metaphor of the 'feeble worm' in No. 22. Mr Newton's work is variable in quality; his hymns are really sermons in miniature, doubtless written for particular occasions, and on occasion somewhat trite. On the other hand, he has moments that are inspiring – anyone who has suffered privations in this world must surely recognise the 'dangers, toils and snares' through which we have passed, and long for an 'amazing grace' to lead one 'safely home'.

April 13th. The Sabbath. I am still reading Newton. The analysis of poetry is always a stimulus to the mind, and between the covers of this volume I can discern true sublimity as well as the fustian commonplace. Mr Newton seems at his best when he is simple and philosophical, but his verses on Esau,[3] to take but one example, seem ordinary and rather unworthy of the rest – the 'morsel of meat' is a phrase I do not altogether like. His treatment of the Biblical story of the widow is poor; the second verse in particular seems very dull and pedestrian.[4] But his hymn on Grace is magnificent in the simplicity of its vocabulary and the effortless ease with which the sentiments are expressed.[5] I have turned to it again and again. There is a deftness about the interplay between the wretchedness of being 'lost' or 'blind' and the joy of being 'found', or regaining sight – and all in six-and-twenty words! I wonder to what air the hymn is sung?

My pleasure in the verses does not make me religious, but they move me very much – the expression of simple faith always excites my envious admiration, and the words of the Bible can move me to tears by their beauty. But my faith has gone.

May 6th. Today I returned the hymnal to Mr Douglas. He asked me if I approved of the work, and I said that some of the verses had affected me very deeply.

'So what do you think of Newton, then?' he asked.

'He appears to be a very pious and thoughtful man,' I said.

'Aye. He's a man of the church now: a curate.'

'Now?' I said. 'What was his profession before he became a curate?'

'What do you think?' Mr Douglas had that mischievous look in his eye, and the suspicion of a smile on his normally stern face.

'I really could not say. A schoolmaster perhaps?'

'No, no, he was not a schoolmaster.'

'A doctor then?'

'No, Robert.'

'I cannot guess.'

'He was captain of a slave ship.'

'Surely not?' I said.

'Aye. By all accounts he treated his cargo with the utmost

decency, and was very much respected. It goes to show that a man can be a Christian as well as a slave owner. Anyway, I am glad you enjoyed it.'

Having made his point, he went off humming to himself, leaving me very pensive. I do not understand how Christianity and slavery can *ever* be reconciled – how can a man fetter poor Negro wretches in the cruel holds of his ship, and then produce such exalted verses about Freedom and Grace? The words could almost supply an anthem for the Negro people, yet they emanated from the pen of a slave trader!

I shall have to do something about the pain in my tooth. I believe they look whiter since Adah introduced me to the miraculous twig, but the sore tooth is black, and the gum around it greatly inflamed.

May 15th. Miss Rivvere fast approaches the time when she must be delivered, and McLehose is full of excitement. He was here yesterday evening, and we made the most of a bottle of very fine Antigua, which was greatly superior to the rum we produce on the plantation.

'I'll sleep well tonight,' he said, as we poured out the last measures.

'You'll no' get much sleep when the bairn comes,' I said. 'Sometimes they yell all night.'

'Oh, I ken,' he said. 'I mean, that's what I've heard,' he added, and I thought he flushed a little, though I expect it was the rum. 'I heard a funny story the other day. I must tell it to you.'

He began to chuckle to himself. 'Yes, it was a conversation overheard between a mulatto and a poor white. Each thought himself superior to the other – the white man because of the colour of his skin, even though he hadn't a farthing to call his own, and the mulatto because he was free and had become successful in business. D'you follow so far?'

'I think so.'

'Right. Well then. One said to the other . . .'

'Which one?'

'Oh sorry, the white man. He said to the mulatto – did I mention that they were in a rum shop, by the way?'

'No.'

'Oh, sorry. I'll start again. The mulatto and the white man were sitting in a rum shop.'

'And you overheard their conversation,' I said.

'Yes.'

'When was this?'

He snorted. ' I didn't *really* overhear it. It's only a story.'

'Go on,' I said.

'Right. The white man felt he was superior to the mulatto, so he said, "Boy, go fetch me a rum!" The mulatto went to get it, and while he was away, the white man took the mulatto's hat and spat in it.'

'Is that the story?' I asked, seeing that he had begun to laugh quite heartily.

'No, no, there's more. The mulatto could see what had happened, but said nothing. When the white man had finished, he shouted out again, "Boy, go and fetch me another rum!" And guess what happened?'

'He spat in the hat again?'

'Yes! God, you're sharp, Robert.'

'How much longer does this go on for?' I asked.

'Wait, wait. When the mulatto comes back, he sees what's happened, but he says nothing. When the white man finishes, he sends the mulatto to get another rum, and spits in his hat again. The mulatto comes back, hands over the rum and sees again what's happened.'

'And he says nothing.'

'No, no, that's the whole point. This time he does say something.'

'What does he say? "Stop spitting in my hat"?'

'No. Just listen, Robert. This is the best bit. He said to the white man, "I wonder when it will all finish?" And the white man said, "What do you mean, finish?" And the mulatto looked very sad, and said, "All this rudeness. All this sending people to fetch things. All this spitting in people's hats. All this pissing in people's rum."'

He was barely able to deliver the last sentence for giggling, and as soon as he had done so, he collapsed in laughter, with tears streaming from his eyes, slapping at his thighs. I thought it was a very amusing story, but I was determined to have some fun of my own.

'Who pissed in the rum?' I asked, feigning incomprehension.

'Why, the mulatto of course.'

'And the white man didn't notice? I think I'd notice if somebody pissed in my rum.'

'Yes, but that's not the point,' he said testily. 'The point is that the white man believed he had the mulatto's willing compliance, whereas from the very outset the mulatto had been showing his disrespect by . . .'

'Yes, I understand that part,' I said. 'And the point of the story is the unexpected revelation that the mulatto is not referring merely to things that the white man has done to him, but is revealing his own iniquitous action that had hitherto been undisclosed.'

'Damn it man. You spoil the story by dissecting it like that.'

I laughed, and patted his shoulder affectionately. 'Och, I was only teasing you. It's a very good story and I'm sure I shall tell it often.'

'Is that the end of the rum?' he said, looking at the bottle. 'It seems to have gone down very quickly.'

'That's the end of the Antigua,' I said, standing up. 'I'll fetch some of ours. Oh and by the way, McLehose . . .' I wagged an admonitory finger at him. 'Don't you dare spit in my hat while I'm gone!'

'And don't you dare mistake the rum jug for the chamber pot!'

So the evening was very convivial although I paid the price for it this morning with a wretched headache. The tooth is giving me a lot of pain. I must attend to it.

May 22nd. The tooth has gone! I could stand the pain no longer – I was pacing the room, demented! – so off to Simpson I went. He looked at it, and told me to sit down and drink some rum before the operation. This I did, and when I began to feel the pain abate somewhat, he took a forceps from his pocket; told me to open my mouth; seized the tooth, and with one deft twist removed it. It was over very quickly, though he told me that the tooth was so rotten that it would soon have fallen out of its own accord. He advised me that it was important to avoid infection of the bleeding gap in the gum, and said to rinse it well with rum – I did so, and I swear it was more painful than the toothache had been. I am to rinse with salt water every few hours until it heals. What a relief to be rid of it!

Bess will be three years old today. Of my three living children, she is the only one I have ever seen. I should have liked to see the twins before I left Scotland, but Armour would have had me before the magistrates. I often wonder what Bess will look like as she grows.

Charles, the Foolah, died suddenly yesterday, and his place in the boiling house has been taken by Ezekiel, one of the assistants in the distillery. He is an able man, but we shall have to keep a close eye on him, because he has proven himself too partial to rum in the past, and the post of head boiler requires above all a clear head, there being no part of the process of sugar-making that is more important.

June 12th. McLehose's woman, Miss Rivvere, has been delivered of a little girl called Ann Lavinia. The man is in great spirits, and can talk of little else. I called on them to offer my congratulations and to admire the newcomer, who is bonny enough, with dark eyes and a lusty bellow. Miss Rivvere is delighted that the infant has the naturally pale complexion of the father. They have asked me to be the lassie's godfather, which is a great honour, and I assured them I would fulfil my duties to the letter. While I rejoiced for them in their hour of happiness, I confess I also felt something of a pang in my heart, imagining my own situation had my Mary not succumbed to illness as she did. But there is nothing to be gained from dwelling on the past, or on (dolorous phrase!) *what might have been*. I have no complaints. My little household is harmonious and pleasant and my every need is catered for. We arise just before dawn; Adah prepares breakfast, and when the plantation bell is rung at six I am ready to commence work. When I return home, my evening meal is ready. Our evenings are mostly spent in conversation, though occasionally I borrow a volume from Mr Douglas's library and immerse myself in it. When there is a holiday we work in the yard or make little repairs and improvements to the house. We keep to ourselves and are well content to have it so. If Adah were to have a child, then my happiness would be complete.

June 30th. So there is to be an Estates-General in France. Louis has spent all of his money in support of the American war – the *people's* money, rather, for the fine Lords and Ladies can contribute nothing whatever, as they must have their fripperies; mansions; servants; fine clothes; powdered wigs and gilded carriages. Meanwhile the country is bankrupt, and the privilege of paying taxes is, as ever, magnanimously conferred upon the poor, who cannot afford to eat. We have our Negro slaves; France has *les pauvres*. Generations of inhumanity, cruelty, exploitation and rapacity have brought us to this, and I am fearful of where it may end. To my mind it invites catastrophe when power and wealth are filched by the Few, while the Many are treated with contempt. It is almost thirty years since the Tacky rebellion here, but no white man can afford to forget the terrible lesson of history – how simple it was for Tacky and his followers to seize the Frontier and Trinity plantations, killing every white man they found there, and how rapidly the rebellion spread across the island. What took place here could so easily happen in France. Even here the Maroons could easily rise again.

We usually hear news in a garbled form at third and fourth hand from those who have lately arrived in Jamaica – sometimes we procure a copy of the *Royal Gazette* but it is generally several weeks old, and its reporting of events in Europe is very limited.

July 2nd. I am to go to Savanna-la-Mar for a few weeks to assist on the plantation of Mr McPherson, an acquaintance of Mr Douglas. Two of his overseers having lately died, he finds himself in need of assistance until others can be recruited and trained. I understand that my duties will be in the boiling house, where the hands are incapable of working without supervision. I shall continue to draw my salary here, and in addition Mr McPherson has promised to pay me four Jamaica pounds for my services.

It is an exciting prospect, but the single drawback is that Mr Douglas flatly refuses to let Adah come with me. This has upset the domestic harmony of our little household, and despite her copious tears and heartfelt supplications, I have had to tell her that I cannot persuade my employer to change his mind.

'She'll be better off here,' he said, when I remonstrated with him. 'She can move back in with you on your return, and in the meantime she can work here in the house for me. I will not put her in the fields.'

I have collected what I shall require and am to leave on Saturday.

July 5th. Early morning. I leave at nine o'clock. Adah is utterly miserable, but I can do nothing about it except to put on a brave face and assure her, with a cheerfulness I am far from feeling, that I shall return as soon as possible. Now that the hour of departure is imminent, I realise how much I shall miss her.

'Yuh gwine fin' anudder specimen I 'spec', she said sadly.

'Don't be silly, Adah,' I said. 'I don't want to be with anyone else.'

'Yuh promise?'

'Of course I promise,' I said, but she did not seem convinced, poor lassie.

July 10th. Savanna-la-Mar. I have many impressions to write down. After a tearful parting from a wailing Adah, I climbed into the carriage that Mr McPherson had sent for me. I had not realised how lengthy a journey it would be. Port Antonio lies in the north-east, and Savanna-la-Mar is situated in the south-west, so they are divided by very nearly the full length of the island, which is, I believe, about one hundred and fifty miles.

Our drive took us through Kingston, and onwards down the south coast. Surely Jamaica must be the loveliest island in the world! With nothing to do except gaze at the scenes that surrounded me, I had the leisure to enjoy the journey, and I could scarcely believe that such perfection existed. We passed through groves of palm trees; neatly tilled pens; vast plantations, and little clusters of houses by the road – above us always the radiant sky with small clouds that mimicked the cotton in the fields; the warm tropical sea glistening and sparkling on our left; blue horizons in the distance and the mountainous wooded spine of the island rising on our right. It was an idyllic picture – to do full justice to it in words would challenge the abilities of far more talented writers than I.

The only blemish lay, not in Nature itself, but in what Man has imposed upon it – I mean the sight of hundreds of Negroes and their womenfolk toiling in the fields; carrying water; loading carts; driving cattle; weeding – *in fine*, engaged in every sort of menial pursuit imaginable, to the accompaniment of the shouts of their masters, and the cracking of their whips. On my own plantation the Negroes are, for the most part, compliant and respectful, but from what I now saw it was clear that my limited experience does not reflect the general state of affairs on the island.

At nights we had to lodge at plantations along the way, where my driver was evidently known.

Mr Douglas had warned me that McPherson's plantation was run on less benevolent principles than his own, but this did nothing to prepare me for what I found when we arrived at the gates. As we turned from the road and headed down a track towards the main buildings, I saw a gibbet from which was hanging the remains of a slave, greatly decomposed and surrounded by a great swarm of flies. The stench was intolerable. The driver said nothing, but continued to a large wooden house where I alighted and went to the door to announce my arrival. A man came out and introduced himself without any cordiality as MacPherson. He was an odd looking person – a little older than myself; squat; corpulent and red-faced; with a large nose; a pendulous lower lip; a prominent Adam's apple, and no chin worth speaking of.

'So you are Mr Burns,' he said. 'What do you know about sugar boiling?'

I gave him an account of the skills I had acquired, and he nodded in satisfaction. 'I'll give you the rest of the day to settle in,' he said. 'Tomorrow you can make a start. The negers are useless on their own. A whole batch was ruined yesterday. They allowed the juice to stand for too long and it wouldn't set. I gave them a damned good flogging, but it made no difference.'

'I could not help noticing that a slave has been hanged,' I said.

'You were meant to notice,' he said, with a chuckle. 'The negers certainly do. There's nothing like a hanging to keep them in order.'

'What was his offence?' I asked.

'He ran away,' said MacPherson. 'He'd done it twice before. This time I made an example of him.' He spoke of it in a matter-of-fact way, as if the taking of a man's life was a commonplace incident.

'That was rather an extreme measure, surely?' I said.

'You can think what you like,' he said, 'but I'll thank you to keep your opinions to yourself. I sent for someone to supervise the boiling house – if I'd wanted sermons I'd have sent for a priest.' He turned and left me.

I settled into my accommodation, which is spartan but adequate for the short time I shall be here.

When I inspected the plantation later, my misgivings increased. The slaves were very ill clad and poorly nourished; most of them bore the traces of the lash, and several among them wore iron fetters on their ankles. They looked sullenly at the ground as I passed. The estate buildings were not in good condition; there was little evidence of weeding having taken place, and near the kitchens a great heap of discarded food gave off a disgusting smell.

I met the other overseers in the early evening; meals are taken communally. There are a dozen or so fellows – I cannot remember their names, and I was not very taken with any of them. They made little attempt to welcome me or include me in their conversation, which was vulgar in the extreme, mostly to do with the carnal pleasures they enjoyed with the slave women. I made my excuses as quickly as I could.

July 11th. It has been a long hard day, but at least the sugar boiling is under way. I found the boiling house in a state of disarray – there was no fuel for the fires, which had been allowed to go out; the coppers were dirty, and the five Negroes who were waiting for me were clearly convinced that they were going to be flogged again. It is my rule to speak to them firmly, but with courtesy, and of course I do not care to carry a whip. This approach succeeded, as I had hoped it would, and within an hour or two we had restored order. I allocated two men to the task of fetching bagasse and stoking the fires, two more to stirring and skimming, and the other to testing the sugar to determine when it would set when removed from the heat. I quickly realised that there were two reasons for past failures. One, they did not realise that the cane juice must not be allowed to stand or it will begin to ferment, and will never set. Two, their evident surprise at the fierceness of the fires confirmed my suspicion that they had not been properly instructed in the importance of temperature in the process.

By the afternoon we had our first batch of sugar, and the molasses had been gathered up and taken to the distillery. The men have been accustomed to working for twelve hours at a stretch, but as soon as I was sure that they had mastered the process I sent them away, and commandeered another five in order to teach them the process, reminding the first gang to return at six o'clock on the morrow. In this way there will always be hands in the boiling house who are reasonably fresh, and understand what has to be done.

I remained until late, and propose to go in early tomorrow. I made a brief report to my employer. How I wish that Adah were here, with her cheerful laugh and her bustling ways.

July 12th. The Sabbath. Work as usual. There have been no disasters overnight, and everything is proceeding smoothly. The hot juice is slow to set, however, and I have consulted with Sam, the head driver, about the manure used on the canes, and the nature of the soil. As I had thought, the soil is acid, and today I added a small quantity of lime, which has solved the problem. The workers were very surprised when they saw me doing this, and I took some time to explain that they had to taste the juice before it was set to boil, and according to the sharpness of the taste, to add the lime accordingly. I have made one man alone responsible for this, and stressed to him the importance of his job. The first time he tried on his own he added too much, so the juice was spoiled and had to be thrown away. He cowered when I ordered this to be done, thinking that he would be beaten, but I explained it again, and before the day was out he was working confidently. The others are becoming adept at their various tasks, and there is a fine heap of bagasse drying outside, so we never lack for fuel.

Before I leave, I shall write some notes for MacPherson, detailing everything that is necessary for the running of the operation. I smile to think that I was once a ploughman, trying to wrest a precarious living from the soil, and here I am now, a master of some consequence on a plantation.

July 16th. A new overseer has appeared. He is a young lad from Bristol, and only just arrived on the island. His name is Edward Harvey, and when I met him today he seemed quite overwhelmed by everything, particularly the hanged man at the gate. I am to instruct him in the sugar boiling, and when he has mastered it I can return to Port Antonio. I shall not be sorry to do so.

Since I arrived, I have kept very much to myself. With my two little teams – ten men in all – I have no problems. They have lost their initial manner of hostility, and we engage with each other civilly enough. I am pleased about that, for they work harder and have even begun to show an interest in what is going on, and can be left unsupervised in the knowledge that they will not neglect their duties. In the fields it is different. The lash is used as a matter of routine. Yesterday one of them, whose only crime was to steal some food from the kitchen, was given 150 lashes by MacPherson in person, with the assistance of his son, a lad of about seventeen. There are slaves on this plantation who have had hands cut off, and one who had his foot amputated for running away. These brutal mutilations are attended by a physician specially hired for the occasion to ensure that the patient does not bleed to death. Word has it that young MacPherson takes particular delight in inflicting pain – he has been known to bind a slave to a tree, lash him mercilessly until his back is a mass of bloody welts and gashes, and then to rub salt, pepper and lime juice into the wounds, enjoying the screams of the hapless victim.

No one appears to find such behaviour out of the ordinary, and it pains me that I am obliged to keep silent about it. Nothing like this could ever happen on the Douglas estate. What infuriates me is the knowledge that such viciousness has exactly the opposite effect from that which is intended. It does not make the slaves work harder; it does not diminish their desire to escape – all it can ever secure is an increasingly reluctant cooperation.

MacPherson has an English wife who never leaves the house. I have only seen her briefly at a window, a pale slattern with sallow skin and limp hair, grown old before her time. Her toad of a husband sleeps with his Negress housekeeper and anyone else who takes his fancy, and the son's accounts of his fornication with the young girls in the slave village are the subject of ribald comment among the other overseers, who appear to find it very entertaining. I remember that Thomas Thistlewood had a plantation hereabouts, and it would appear that his despicable habits have been widely emulated. Almost too horrible to mention is what he termed Derby's dose, whereby one slave was compelled to void his bowels into the open mouth of another, whose jaws were then wired shut. I would like to believe that there is nothing intrinsically so vile in human nature – yet I fear that the likes of MacPherson and his pup may not be so uncommon in Jamaica. If the slaves should ever rise up on this plantation, the two of them will be torn to pieces, and frankly I would not be sorry.

July 20th. Sabbath. Edward is an attentive pupil and he has learned everything I taught him. He is obviously not sure how to behave towards the Negroes, and appears intimidated by them. For the moment there are no problems, but once I am gone I have no doubt that the others will instruct him in their ways. In short, he shall become a brute.

In another week or so I am confident that the boiling house will be in safe hands. In the meantime I am writing notes to leave with my employer. I cannot say how much I am looking forward to returning to my own plantation, and to Adah. Although I have missed her, I can now understand Mr Douglas's wisdom in refusing her leave to come here.

July 27th. Sabbath. My notes are finished, and I am very proud of them. Together they form a comprehensive guide to everything that goes on in the boiling house, and I believe that they will prove of value, not only to MacPherson, but also to anyone desirous of learning about the process.

I went up to what passes here for the Great House – a sprawling wooden edifice, its boards unpainted and bleached almost white by the sun. I knocked, and the housekeeper answered.

'Yuh wants de Massa?' she said. She showed me into an dirty room in which papers and documents were scattered untidily on every available surface, including the floor.

'Oh it's you, Burns,' he said, in his ill-humoured way. 'What do you want?'

'I've come to give you this,' I said, handing over my little treatise. He looked at the first page or two without any great interest, and laid it down on a chair.

'So you have whipped them into shape?' he said.

'I didn't find it necessary to use a whip,' I said. 'The main thing is that between them, the two gangs can keep the boiling going constantly while the cane is being crushed. If you look at what I have written you'll see that . . .'

'Yes, yes, I'm sure. And the new man?'

'Young Harvey is doing well. In each of the two gangs the duties have to be divided, and it is advisable to have one man in charge so that when the overseer is absent . . .'

'In charge? A neger in *charge* of my sugar? I think not.'

I could see where this was leading, and decided not to press the point any further. To be honest I had no wish to debate anything with the man – all I wanted was my money, and a seat in the carriage to take me back to Port Antonio.

'My work is done. I believe I have four pounds owing to me.'

'Four pounds?' he said. 'That was the sum agreed for a month. You have only been here a little over two weeks. No, no – two pounds is all I can offer.'

I explained that I had laboured extremely hard and so had accomplished a month's work in half that time, and in addition had produced a written account of the process, which was more than I had been contracted to do. He hummed and he hawed, but I stood my ground, and eventually we settled for three pounds, which he gave me.

I am to remain here tomorrow and the next day, for the driver is needed on other business, and on Wednesday I am to be conveyed back to Port Antonio and Adah.

August 3rd. Back in Port Antonio! A week has passed since I wrote, so I must begin today by giving an account of my last two days in Savanna-la-Mar, and the rather violent conclusion to my visit.

I knew that young MacPherson was in the habit of going down to the slave village in search of young slave girls, ordering them back to his house and bedding them. On the afternoon before I was due to leave I was in the boiling house with Edward when I heard shouting in the distance. Two of the overseers came past at a run, and my immediate reaction was that insurrection had broken out. We headed towards the source of the sound, and when we arrived, we could see young MacPherson in a clearing with a young slave woman. He had flung a rope over the branch of a tree and bound her hands with one end, then hauling on the other so that she was pulled nearly off the ground and suspended by her wrists.

'So you think you can refuse me, do you, you black bitch?' he was yelling. 'Not good enough for you? My God, I'll make you sorry for it!' Mouthing threats and imprecations he advanced on her, tore down her shift and began to lash at her with his whip.

I had been labouring with suppressed anger for many days, and this was too much. I know I can be impetuous, and I acknowledge that on occasions I have done and said things that should not have been done or said, but I make no excuses at all for what I did next.

Taking a rawhide whip from the man next to me – he barely noticed; his attention was elsewhere – I went forward, and with all the strength I could muster I swung the heavy leather thong so that it wrapped around young MacPherson's body with what was, to my ears, the most wondrously satisfying crack. He cried out, but did not know who had struck him until he turned and saw me.

'If you are such a brave young master that you can flog a helpless woman, then maybe you can flog me,' I said, and hit him again. He released his grip on the rope, and the woman covered her modesty before running off. He came flying at me, but I easily side-stepped him and caught him fair and square across the back of his shoulders, splitting the thin cloth of his smock and drawing blood. He yelled in pain.

'Aye, now you know how it feels,' I said, advancing on him.

'You cannot do that,' he said, his voice wavering.

By way of reply I lashed at him again. He began to blubber and run around the clearing, and I followed him, striking at him again and again. All of this time the overseers had been gaping in astonishment, but now, realising that their own positions would be in jeopardy if they stood by and did nothing, they advanced upon me in a body. There was nothing I could do – I was knocked to the ground and kicked all over. When they had rendered me pretty well *hors de combat*, they went off in a body, presumably to make their report to MacPherson. I was eventually able to stand, and I hobbled slowly back to my quarters in anticipation of a visit from MacPherson *père*, which indeed was not long in coming. A furious battering at my door signalled his arrival, with his whimpering son at his side and a crowd of truculent overseers behind him.

'What the hell do you mean by taking a whip to my boy?' he shouted, his face red and his eyes almost starting from their sockets. 'My God, I'm going to have *you* flogged for this!'

'I don't think so,' I said. 'He had it coming to him. The lassie had done nothing wrong, and your boy's behaviour was inexcusable.'

'He can do as he likes! This is my plantation! My God, you are going to regret this!'

'You shall regret it even more if I report your behaviour to the authorities in Kingston. I'm thinking about that man you hanged. Under the terms of the new law passed last month, you could find yourself in prison for that.'

'Law? What law?' he said. 'Never heard of it.'

Neither had I, but he had begun to look anxious.

'You are a long way from Kingston,' I said. 'News travels slowly. But that will be no defence when you find yourself in court faced with the confiscation of your property. There will be a thorough investigation, and it will involve not just you, but anyone else who may have had a hand in it.' I looked at the overseers as I said that, and they also began to look uncomfortable.

'Confiscation? Confiscation? What do you mean?' He looked worried now.

'If you or any your men lay a finger on me, you will find out, I promise you,' I said. 'You've got your boiling house working; you've got my notes for your future use, and your son has had a thrashing that he well deserved. I've done you a favour.'

'Have him flogged,' snivelled the pup, but his father ignored him.

'I want you off this plantation now,' said MacPherson. 'You can find your own way back, but I'm damned if it'll be in my carriage. Take your things and go.'

Thus it was that I found myself walking into Savanna-la-Mar, where I was able to procure a carriage to take me to Kingston. There I rested up for a day before finding transport back to Port Antonio.

On my arrival, I reported to Douglas, who looked at my battered and dishevelled appearance with great concern.

'What on earth happened to you, Burns?' he said. 'Have you been trying to add prize fighting to your list of accomplishments?'

I told him what had taken place, and he listened intently.

'So you thrashed MacPherson's boy?' he said.

'Yes. And I'm not sorry.'

I do not know how I had expected him to respond to this – most probably with disapproval at the very least, or with another of his moral lectures, but to my amazement he flung back his head and guffawed. I had never seen him laugh before, and I was taken aback.

'Oh Robert,' he said, wiping the tears from his eyes, 'always the man of principle! Well there's no harm done. You did a good job for MacPherson, and I dare say his lad deserved it. If what you say is true, then the boy behaved disgracefully: if I had been his father I'd have flogged him myself. I'm just sorry you had to suffer for it. Well, Adah is here. When she has finished what she is about I shall tell her you have returned. She's been mightily morose, and I dare say she'll be pleased to have you back.'

It was with a sense of huge relief that I pushed open my door, and saw once again these familiar surroundings that I have come to call home. I had barely begun to unpack my things when Adah burst through the door, shrieking with delight, and flung herself into my arms, which was damnably painful, though I did not mind it. When she saw my bruises she was appalled, and bade me tell her the whole story, which I did.

'Dat boy deserve he whippin' fo' sho',' she said. 'Yuh done good. Lemme tell yuh sump'n,' she went on, looking at me very earnestly. '*Yuh is my man.*'

The words seemed to float silently in the air between us for a long time. It was, I realise, a declaration of love and commitment that had not come easily to her. After the sorrows and vicissitudes of my life, she is a treasure beyond compare; an angel come to fill my life with light – more than I deserve.

She brought me the rum jug, and began to rub my aching shoulders gently, promising to give me *a proper doin'* when I am done. Happy my lot – to be a willing votary of both Bacchus and Venus!

August 20th. I have not written these past few weeks, as I have been kept busy about the place, and, since life has resumed its normal routine, there is little to report. My injuries have healed completely and I am none the worse for the Savanna-la-Mar episode. Indeed it was good for me, for it has given me cause to reflect on the nature of persons such as MacPherson, Thistlewood and their ilk.

Whence this hatred of black people? Have the Negroes enslaved us, carried us from our native shores to work under the hot sun? Have the Negroes persecuted us, or committed offences against us? Have they violated our womenfolk? They have done none of these, and yet the detestation of Negroes is everywhere plain to see. 'If you prick us, do we not bleed?' said Shylock, and why may a Negro not say the same? Indeed, he must feel inclined to declare, 'If you wrong us, shall we not revenge?' Is it fear of revenge that makes us cruel?

White men know nothing of Negroes, whether it be their languages; their customs; their religious observations; their mode of dress; their music; their loves or their loyalties, and it is this ignorance that forms the pernicious root of the hatred. Ignorance, as Mr Pope might have said, brings with it the bliss of not having to face distasteful facts, and God forbid that any white man should have his bliss shattered by having to learn a rude lesson!

Together with this hatred, must be considered the question of power. If I hate my neighbour in Mauchline, I cannot pick up a cudgel and beat his brains out with it, for the law exists to protect the innocent, to punish the guilty, and to show no partiality. But imagine if the law were taken away? Would I beat the wretch? Worse, would I enjoy it? I am in a weak position morally, for I beat that lad of MacPherson's, and I confess that I gained a measure of satisfaction from doing so. However it is not the same, for I was acting in the absence of law, and seeking to do what every instinct tells me was *right*, so I assumed the mantle of law and imposed a sanction in accordance with the common understanding of what we call *justice*. But when justice is found wanting, and nothing remains but the sanction – what then? For the answer to that question, look at Thistlewood and his kind. They are brutes because there is nothing to prevent them from being brutes. Mr Douglas has the power and the right to flog and hang his slaves, but he chooses not to do so, for he possesses a moral code that prevents him, just as it would prevent me. He pretends that his devotion to the wellbeing of his slaves is a matter of simple economy, since it means that he does not need to purchase replacements, but I know there is more to it than that, even if he will not admit to it.

I have always considered that the best dominies are those who need little resort to the tawse; the worst are those who cannot parse a sentence without beating half-a-dozen children while they are about it. Wherever we see brutality we see a weakness concealed; wherever we see a tyrant, we see a man who is afraid.

September 1st. I must have been blessed, all unknowing, with the gift of prophecy when I threatened MacPherson with talk of a new law, for a new code *has* been passed. I am reading of it in the *Royal Gazette*. Under the provisions of the code, any slave accused of a capital offence must now stand trial in a slave court, in the presence of a jury. At first sight this seems excellent progress, but on further perusal I am not convinced that it brings with it any advantages. The existence of a separate court merely serves to emphasise the *differences* between the Negroes and the white persons of the island – if we are to have the rule of law, then surely it must apply to all? These slave courts are empowered to mete out death and disfigurement of the most horrible kind. I read too that the slaves' right of assembly has been curtailed and that any slave practising obeah, or claiming to have magic powers, may find himself under sentence of death or transportation. So a measure presented as being in the best interests of the Negroes only imposes still more opportunity for oppression, and a sanction for still more cruelty.

What kind of reasoning is it that declares that a slave who has run away must be *ipso facto* guilty of rebellion? Why is it a capital offence to attack a white man, whereas attacking another Negro is punishable, at most, with a few lashes? I read with incredulity that the judges are empowered to order that ears be cut off, may at their solemn discretion determine whether it be the right or the left ear; the upper or lower part of it; how close to the head it may be severed, and exactly where it may be nailed, be it to the gallows or a cottonwood tree. Noses may be slit open; feet may be removed; brands may be applied. To be sure a white man may stand indicted before the assizes and be sentenced to hang, but I have never heard of a white felon being condemned to bodily mutilation as part of the sentence!

Calaloo again this evening. Adah does her best, but I tire of the same old fare day by day. Recently I have found myself longing for a *haggis*, that epitome of fine Scots *cuisine*. Oh, to smell the fragrant steam as it boils; to see it on the platter, awaiting the sharp knife; and oh, the joy as the warm richness spills out! It is a dish that deserves a grace all to itself! My mouth is watering as I write. Although I have never cooked it myself I have watched while my mother did so, and

I am sure that I could manage tolerably well if I had the ingredients, though I do not know whether they may be obtained on the island. I asked Adah if she had heard of haggis, but she had not.

September 3rd. There are few sheep on the island, except in St Elizabeth parish, so obtaining the stomach of one would appear to be next to impossible. But there are goats everywhere in the greatest of profusion, not much different in size or in feeding habits, and one of these must furnish my requirements. I asked James about the constituents of haggis, much to his amusement.

'You surely aren't proposing to cook *haggis?*' he said. 'In *Jamaica?*'

'I don't see why not. All I need to know is what goes into it.'

'Well, you'll need suet.'

'What is suet exactly?'

'I'm not sure. But you need it, I'm sure.'

'All right,' I said. 'I'll find out. You need oatmeal, I think.'

'Yes. Liver, too.'

'Aye. I remember my mother used to boil it up and let it dry so that it could be grated. There were onions forbye.'

'And scraps of meat chopped up. You boil it first, and keep the juice to mix up the rest with. You'll let me try this haggis of yours when it's ready?'

'Of course. What else?'

'I can't think of anything. I never did any cooking when... I mean, men don't cook, do they?' He flushed a little, as if he had let something slip.

Mrs Douglas was able to tell me that suet was just another name for the hard fat surrounding the internal organs of sheep and cattle, and I now think I have the recipe for a fine haggis. All I have to do is to assemble the ingredients – first and foremost the goat's stomach.

September 6th. Wet and stormy today, with very strong winds. The end of the hurricane season is in sight, but we cannot take anything for granted yet. Field work finished early; the sky is leaden, but I am home at last.

I have been gathering together all that is necessary for my haggis, including a large pot to boil it in. The oatmeal was easy to obtain and we have plenty of pepper and salt. I had more difficulty in obtaining the necessary parts of a goat. There is a fellow on one of the pens who keeps goats and does butchery, and I went to him earlier today. His shop, if you can call it that, was just a couple of rough planks set up underneath a leaky palm thatch. Various animal parts were laid out, and other pieces had been hung up under the thatch, or lay scattered about on the ground. I was glad of the rain, for it kept away most of the flies that had been attracted by the smell. He gave me some liver, assuring me that it was fresh, and certainly it was still bloody enough. On the matter of suet I had more difficulty making myself understood. He had clearly never heard the word, so I pointed to an open carcase and indicated the fat adhering to the inside.

'Yuh wants dat?' he said, amazed. 'Yuh cyan't eat dat!'

'That's what we call suet,' I said, patiently. 'Please cut me some.'

He did so, looking at me very strangely as he laid it in front of me. 'Yuh want anyt'in' else?'

'Yes. Give me a goat's stomach, please.' He looked at me.

'A stummick? Yuh wants belly meat?'

'No, I want the stomach itself – the tripes, the thairm, or whatever you call it.'

'De guts?'

'Yes.'

He rolled his eyes, picked up a knife and rummaged around inside a goat that had already been partially dismembered, returning with some dripping loops of gut. 'Yuh want me clean it?'

'Please.'

Holding one end of the guts fast with one hand, and pulling with the other, he firmly squeezed the loops, which discharged their malodorous contents with a splatter on to the ground. He then returned and laid them on the counter. I indicated that I required nothing else, and he wrapped the motley selection of offal in a piece of dirty cloth and watched as I picked it up, with an expression on his face that made clear what he thought of the dietary predilections of white men.

On my return, I laid the items out on to a table, much to the amusement of Adah.

'Why d'yuh bring all dis dutty meat?' she exclaimed, holding her nose.

'It's not dirty,' I told her, though I had to admit that it looked something less than appetising. I set her to chopping up the suet into fine pieces while I hacked at the liver, pulling out the threads and veins before setting it on a fire to boil. This left the stomach to be dealt with. I discarded the parts I did not require and scraped it until it was clean, washing it thoroughly with salt and water.

'We gwine eat dat t'ing?' said Adah with some trepidation.

'We don't eat that part,' I said. 'We stuff everything else inside and boil it.'

'I sho' am glad tuh hear dat!'

We have just completed our tasks, and set everything aside. Everyone thinks me mad, but we shall see. Tomorrow is the Sabbath, when I shall have leisure to prepare my haggis! I have invited McLehose and Ann to come in the evening and partake of our feast.

September 7th. This afternoon Adah and I prepared the haggis. The liver being cooked and cooled, we shredded it finely, then added the chopped suet and onion, a portion of oatmeal and a goodly quantity of ground pepper, mingling this together to a paste with a little of the water in which the liver had been boiled. With a piece of twine I securely tied off one end of the stomach, which I stuffed firmly with the mixture. We then set a large pot of water to boil over the fire, and put the haggis in.

'How long we cook dat t'ing?' asked Adah.

'I don't know. Two hours at least, I should think.'

Adah boiled up some plantain and yam to accompany the dish, then came back to examine the progress of the main course.

'What if de string come off?' she said.

'Then we shall have haggis soup,' I said.

Fortunately the string did not come off, and the haggis was simmering very nicely by the time McLehose and Miss Rivvere arrived, with little Ann Lavinia. The women made a great fuss over the little girl, talking to her, stroking her black curly hair and playing with her fingers and toes; McLehose and I took a glass of rum together, and we were a very cheerful party by the time supper was ready.

Bowls were laid out, and with great ceremony Adah brought the haggis to the table where I stood waiting with my knife. It looked very plump and fine, giving off a grand steam, and McLehose clapped his hands with delight when he saw it.

'Man, you've outdone yourself!' he exclaimed. Miss Rivvere was not so sure, and I could see her exchanging quizzical glances with Adah.

'Is this the haggis James has been telling me about?' she said. 'It looks very peculiar.'

'You'll like it fine, Ann,' said McLehose. 'In Scotland this is a rare treat for us – I never thought I'd see one here. Go on, Robert, cut it up!'

I delivered myself of a few *extempore* lines in praise of Scotia's nourishing national dish, comparing it most favourably with some of the foreign trash so esteemed by the high and mighty, who grow feeble and sickly in consequence, then I plunged my knife into it, sending its contents gushing on to the platter. Adah served the yam and plantain, and then a portion of haggis to each person.

I took my first mouthful, but alas! it bore no resemblance to the haggis of my memories. To be sure, it looked very much the part, and in texture it was pretty well the same, but the proportions of the mixture were wrong – there was too much suet and pepper in it, and the only word I can use to describe the taste is *goaty*. McLehose tried very bravely to praise it.

'It is quite good, really,' he said, wiping his forehead. 'After all, it is the first time you have tried to make it.' Adah sampled a little, and hurriedly followed it with a huge mouthful of plantain to conceal the taste. As for Miss Rivvere, observing our reactions, she tasted a tiny piece and then pushed the rest to the side of her bowl. There was an embarrassed silence as everyone wondered what to say, so I decided that the only thing to do was to pre-empt the general opinion.

'It's hellish, isn't it?' I said.

'I can't eat it, I'm afraid,' said Miss Rivvere. 'I'm sorry.'

'Him try real hard fuh mek it nice,' said Adah sympathetically.

'Don't be too hard on yourself,' said McLehose. 'It's not that bad. It can't be easy to get the correct ingredients here.'

'At least you did try,' said Miss Rivvere.

'I'll wager it's the first time anyone has tried to make a haggis in Jamaica,' said McLehose. 'You'll go down in history, Robert!'

Everyone began to laugh; we passed the rum jug around, and Adah fetched some salt fish, which together with the yam and plantain and some bammy furnished us an excellent supper. The offending haggis was put outside, where one of the plantation dogs soon ran off with it. We ended the evening very merry, and no harm was done, but in future I shall leave the cooking to Adah.

October 3rd. It is now eight years to the day since the terrible hurricane destroyed Savanna-la-Mar, and many of the plantation's workers have keen memories of it. But the skies are clear today, and we are spared the fell visitations of nature.

Gilmour, in his usual coarse way, was making rude remarks about the Negroes' inability to read or write, calling them ignorant. He himself cannot read without following the words with his finger and sounding out the letters to himself, and when it comes to writing in the plantation logs, his best efforts amount to little more than an illegible scrawl. Yet this fine man of letters condemns the Negroes for their stupidity! Can he not see how ridiculous it is to expect such skills from people who have not been taught? I dare say that if Solomon himself were to be plucked bodily out of Egypt and thrust into the cane fields with a matchet, we should reckon him to be foolish and possessed of very little ability. How many Solomons have we shipped here to the Indies to toil in our fields?

October 17th. I have been in Kingston for the last two days to arrange for the delivery of provisions to the plantation, and what a fortunate encounter I had! I was in a stationers on Wednesday, procuring some paper and ink, when I was aware of another man, about ten years older than myself, engaged in similar business. As he paid for his purchases, it was clear from his speech that he was a fellow Scotsman, so I greeted him in a friendly fashion, and we struck up a conversation. We soon discovered that we had much in common, and so we spent the remainder of the afternoon very happily in a rum shop.

He told me his name was Hector – a fine Trojan appellation! – and he shares my passion for poesy. Unlike myself, he has the leisure to pursue it, for he recently received a legacy, and so is under no obligation to work. He was greatly interested in hearing my opinions of slavery, for he was once employed as an overseer like myself, and has written a small treatise on the subject. His views were rather similar to those of Mr Douglas, though he expressed them with less dogmatism. He also showed me some of the poetry he is writing, and I found him a man after my own heart – his verses were beautifully crafted and extremely simple in expression, unlike some of the dreary, Latinate nonsense that seeks to impress though long words, unnecessary classical allusions, and convoluted, protracted clauses that mean little. We might have spoken for many hours, but I had business to attend to, and so I had to bid him a very reluctant farewell.

He will be returning to Edinburgh soon, and when my time comes to return to Scotia's shores I must seek him out.[6]

November 1st. Confined to bed the last few days with a rheumatic fever. My limbs ache, and I am only now beginning to crawl about. Today I ventured out of doors for the first time, but I remain very weak. Adah has been attending me most devotedly. She has been treating me with a concoction that she makes from the leaves of a chilli plant. Although applied cold, the effect is very warming, causing the skin to flush as if sunburned. I have been so poorly that I was scarce able to hold my pen.

November 10th. I have returned to work. The pain in my joints still afflicts me a little, but this has been improving daily, and although I feel very tired, I can no longer bear the tedium of enforced leisure! Rather to my chagrin, I find that the plantation has run perfectly smoothly without me.

November 14th. Problems on the plantation with a slave called Punch. He refuses to work, claiming that he is the victim of a duppy sent by Hercules, who is in the same gang. The two men have been at loggerheads over a woman called Minerva, and in my opinion all Punch's talk is just a pretext to make trouble for Hercules. He says that the duppy comes in the night and throws stones at him – he has several bruises that he is eager to show us, but I am convinced he has inflicted them upon himself. George and I saw Punch together and warned him about malingering, but he was very adamant and animated, declaring that the injuries were caused by the duppy, and that Hercules had sent it.

We spoke to Hercules, who denies all knowledge of the matter, as well he might, since the practice of obeah attracts the severest penalties. For all his protestations, there was something about his demeanour that made me suspect he knew more than he was prepared to admit, but the idea of a spirit throwing stones is so ludicrous I cannot believe it. Mr Douglas has been told about it, and he has ordered that Punch should be kept in the hospital overnight.

Adah has been teasing be about the haggis, and I am sure I shall never live it down. Every time she brings me a meal she apologises for not serving it boiled in a 'stummick'. She has been extremely affectionate since my return from the MacPherson plantation.

I told Adah about the behaviour of Punch, expecting her to share my amusement but she was very serious about it. I told her it was foolish to believe that a spirit could throw stones, but she did not agree.

'Ev'body knows duppies kin t'row t'ings,' she said.

'Well I don't believe it,' I said. 'I never heard of such an idea.'

'Yuh's in Jamaica.'

She looked frightened and unsettled. I know that she knows of many strange and dark customs that I cannot even guess at, and I respect her ancestral beliefs and the ancient Jamaican lore she grew up with. All the same, I do not believe that there is any supernatural basis to the Punch matter. Tomorrow, I dare say, the whole business will be settled.

November 15th. This affair with Punch is decidedly odd. When I went to the hospital, he was sitting in bed with a bandage on his head. Once we had moved out of Punch's hearing I asked Simpson how the patient was faring. He thought that either Punch was very resourceful or there was something strange going on. He had been sleeping in his room when he had heard a sharp sound, followed by a shout from Punch. He had found Punch bleeding from a wound on his head. He showed me a jagged stone about the size of an egg. 'The window was closed,' he said, anticipating my question, 'and I am sure that Punch did not bring it in with him.'

'He must have done,' I said. 'What does he say?'

'He says a duppy threw it. Anyway the wound is real enough.'

'I expect he struck himself on the head, shouted out, and then threw the stone against the wall,' I said.

'I expect so,' said Simpson. 'I'll keep a closer eye on him.'

'Search him to make sure he does not have any more stones,' I said.

'I've done that already.'

I told Adah about all of this, and she is more convinced than ever about the duppy. She says that it has been set to work by some ill-intentioned person. I asked her if she really believed that Hercules was responsible, but she seemed unwilling to talk about it. She said that someone would have to 'pull the shadow' – whatever that means – and that only an obeah man could do such a thing. The practice of obeah being punishable by death, she was rather evasive in response to my questions, but I sensed from what she was saying that obeah men are still to be found. George, who has been told everything, says that the duppy can be exorcised, or, if it can be prevented from returning to its grave at daybreak, it will be rendered harmless.

November 16th. I was not able to go to the hospital this morning, so the events of last night were reported to me by George. Apparently Punch has taken another attack, and the floor of the hospital was littered with stones. I went round this evening before returning home, to find Simpson quite bemused by the whole thing. He showed me a pile of a dozen or so stones that he had picked up from the floor.

'I don't know what to think,' he said, lifting a stone. 'I can't account for it at all. I intend to talk to Mr Douglas about it.'

Talk of the duppy is now rampant on the plantation. There are rumours that Hercules has been seen throwing coins on to a grave, and pouring rum, but nobody has any evidence of this, and he continues to protest his innocence.

November 17th. A further attack last night. Simpson has quite lost his nerve, and refuses to have Punch in the hospital any longer. George is taking him to see an obeah man – at least I assume that is what he intends to do, though everything said on the subject is expressed by means of elaborate circumlocution. Mr Douglas knows about it, and indeed I think he may have suggested this course of action, but he cannot be seen to be any part of it.

When I saw Simpson he was at a complete loss, poor fellow. He is a man of science, believing that every effect must have a cause, yet he cannot account for the stones.

McLehose and Ann came by this evening with their daughter, who is now five months old. She is a beautiful child, and they can talk of nothing else but her little accomplishments. Adah fears herself to be infertile, which I find difficult to believe, given that she is in every respect an extremely healthy young woman. I know nothing of medicine, and I cannot talk to Simpson on such a delicate matter, so I do not know how this will be resolved.

November 18th. George and Punch returned to the plantation this afternoon. They were both very reticent about where they had been and what had transpired, but Punch looked much happier than of late, and George has assured me that the matter has been dealt with. We must wait and see what tonight brings.

My own view is that Punch has been playing a trick at our expense to escape work, and win over Minerva, who now lives with him. It is significant that he was only injured by the stones when there was no other person present. I tend to believe that he had some accomplice throw stones through a gap in the roof in order to scare Simpson, and lend credence to his claim.

November 19th. Punch had a peaceful night, and is quite his old self. This is exactly what I thought would happen. He has Minerva and so there is no more need for drama and pretence.

My joints have now ceased to pain me, thanks to Adah's liniment. When I think of how many of my countrymen are afflicted with the rheumatics, I am sure that her recipe would prove very popular if made available in Scotland!

December 5th. Hercules died suddenly last night. He did not appear when the plantation bell rang, and when someone went to fetch him, he was found dead in his bed. Simpson had a look at him and said that he could see no reason for it: in every respect the man appeared to have been in good health. Inevitably there is open talk of witchcraft, and the suggestion that Punch may have cast some spell of his own as revenge for the duppy. Mr Douglas has been to see George and made it very clear that such talk is to stop.

Adah is convinced that the death is the result of obeah, and I cannot persuade her that it might have a simpler explanation, such as heart failure, which can bring about death without any external signs to see. She responds by saying that she is disappointed that I do not give more credence to what she tells me.

Am I wrong to dismiss obeah out of hand? Do I indeed display the arrogance that I condemn in others? Although reason tells me that Hercules would have died whether or not this duppy business had happened, there is now a small part of me that suspects that the whispers on the plantation may be correct, and that there are forces at work here that are beyond my comprehension.

December 20th. To Port Antonio with Mr Garvie to fetch a few bushels of nails, for the recent weather has damaged a number of roofs that must now be repaired. We had a pleasant drive there – the harbour always presents a delightful prospect when the weather is clear, and I never tire of the blueness of the sea, having been used to the grey-green waters that wash the Ayrshire coast. Mr Garvie was about some business or other in a notary's office, and I was standing outside, watching the comings and goings, when I felt a hand clapping on my shoulder. I turned round to find myself face to face with a fellow I had never seen before.

'It's Harrison, isn't it?' he said, with the greatest show of friend-liness.

'No,' I said, 'I think you must be mistaken.' I could see now that he was ill kempt and swaying slightly on his feet. He frowned in puzzlement.

'I was sure you were Harrison,' he said.

'My name is Burns,' I said.

'Pleased to meet you, Mr Burns,' he said, seizing my hand and shaking it a little too vigorously. 'My name's Peacock, by the way.' The only other person I have ever met with that name was a scoundrel of the first water that I knew in Irvine and, related to that particular rascal or not, I did not wish to become acquainted with this individual. However I did not wish to appear rude, and besides I had to wait for Mr Garvie. 'It's always good to see another white face,' he went on. 'You get tired of all these neger faces, don't you? What brings you to Port Antonio, Mr Burns?'

'I work here.'

'Do you indeed?' he said. 'That's good, that's very good. In fact I'm available for work myself.' I could smell the rum on his breath now. His speech was slightly slurred, and he appeared to be having some trouble remaining upright. 'Perhaps you could put in a word for me, eh?'

'I am not in a position to advise my employer,' I said.

'No, no, of course not,' he said. 'The fact is, you yourself may be able to help me out with a little problem I have encountered. You see, I appear to be experiencing a temporary shortage of funds at the moment. I shall have money tomorrow, but in the meantime, necessity compels me to ask whether you . . .'

Just then Mr Garvie came out of the office and saw me with Peacock, who advanced towards him with an outstretched hand. 'Peacock's the name,' he said, 'I was just talking to my friend Mr Burns here.'

Mr Garvie ignored him and indicated to me that we should return to the carriage, which we did with the importunate Peacock yapping at our heels.

'That's what Jamaicans call a 'walkin' backra',' said Mr Garvie, when we had finally left him behind, waving his fists impotently at us. 'Too lazy to work, and no money to get back to England. They turn to petty thieving, and keeping all sorts of unsavoury company. Jamaica could do without their sort.'

'It makes you feel ashamed to be white,' I said.

'Exactly. It gives the worst possible example to the Negroes, who imagine that this is how white people behave. We try to keep them away from the plantation because they are fit for nothing and they just stir up trouble. I'd have them all sentenced to transportation if I had my way, and given a good flogging into the bargain.'

I told Adah about the 'backra', and she said that her people called them 'red-leg trash' and regarded them with amused contempt. They come here, she said, with the promise of a good position, but being disposed to idleness, fall into dissolute ways, and generally end up begging or doing menial work.

December 25th. Christmas Day, and very hot in the sun. This is Thursday, and we are at leisure until Monday. I gave Adah a gift of a little chatelaine that I purchased in Port Antonio last Saturday, and she presented me with a broad hat that she had woven herself and which, she says, will protect me better from the sun when I am in the fields. She is fearful that I may suffer a *coup de soleil,* which affliction has been the undoing of many an otherwise sturdy soul. Well I remember my mother giving me the same advice before I left for the Indies! When I look at myself in the glass, I now see a darkened forehead and cheeks; I have grown a beard and I am sure that if Gilbert were to see me now he would hardly recognise his own brother, while Bess would flee from such a strange-looking man!

1789

January 25th. The Sabbath, and my thirtieth birthday. I must have a bent to idleness, for I have not taken up my pen these three weeks or more. Life proceeds very smoothly at present. Day flows into day, week into week – when I see my inkwell, I am filled with good intentions, but the warm incubus of Sloth smothers my resolve!

What a strange dream I have had! The weather has been unsettled and although there was no rain in the night there was a strong wind blowing, and the sound of it kept me awake. When I finally did sleep, I dreamt that I was in Scotland, standing near the old castle at Glengarnock, perched on its lofty outcrop, looming over the Garnock Water below. There can be few sights in nature so interesting and so melancholy as a castle fallen into disrepair, and few in Ayrshire so imposing as Glengarnock.[1] I visited it during the Irvine years, and it made so great an impression on me that last night I saw it plain in every detail – that massive tower, the remains of its vaulted roof! – gaunt, isolated and remote, its stones telling most eloquently of times long gone, a reminder of the impermanence of man and his works.

Then, as happens in dreams, I found myself in another place. I felt instinctively that I was in Ayrshire, but I did not recognise the spot. I was standing on the margin of a moderately sized loch where the cold wind hissed in banks of waving reeds and ruffled the waters, grey beneath a winter sky. At the other end of the loch, a mile or so distant, there lay thick woodland, and a small island not far from shore, on which stood a ruined keep. I made my way down the side of the loch, and entered the woods, following an overgrown track that took me at last to the edge of the water, with a clear view to the island; then I found myself standing on the island itself, surveying the ruined structure that occupied it more or less entirely.

There was no sign of human habitation anywhere for miles around, and in my mind I *knew* with certainty that no one had stood on this spot for a very long time, and that indeed I was the first to tread here since the building had been abandoned. It was a square peel-tower of no great size, surrounded by great banks of nettles and the indistinct, grassy contours of a long-abandoned courtyard and outbuildings. Inside lay a jumble of mossy stones and rotted timber where the ceilings and floors had collapsed. Looking up at where the roof had once been I could see the clouds driving across the sky. A spiral stair in a roundel led up to a doorway in the wall above, opening on to the empty air where the upper floor had once been.

Weeds sprouted in profusion from every crevice in the crow-stepped gables, and the wind moaned sadly through the window openings. With the irrational logic of dreams, I *knew* that I had lived here many years before, and was now returning like a ghost to haunt a once-familiar scene.

I awoke to the noisy reality of a Jamaican dawn, and the hissing of the wind in the palm trees. I felt low in spirits, for no reason that I am able to explain. For weeks at a time I scarcely think of Scotland, but perhaps there is a secret longing for home that comes unbidden to my mind when I dream, like a fish rising unexpectedly to the surface from the depths of some unfathomable pool. I know that no such place exists; I know that none of my poor ancestors lived in a castle, yet I find it difficult to forget my vision. Everyone knows that dreams are caused by some disorder of the nervous system, or proceed from some outward cause – in my case the sounds of the weather – yet those of Joseph were prophetic, so perhaps mine also has some profounder meaning – does the castle represent Auld Scotia, that venerable country of my birth, to which I belong in a way that I can never belong here? Does it reflect a sombre pensiveness in my nature, or an unconscious awareness of my own mortality?

January 30th. For as long as I have known her, Adah has kept me very amused with little stories about a spider called Anancy, of which she appears to have an endless store.[2] She rattles them out at a very rapid pace, with all manner of animated gestures, so that it is more in the nature of a performance than a recitation, and today I made her repeat one of her favourites several times at a slower rate so that I could transcribe it.

'Anancy tek de job to sweep de 'ouse,' she began. 'After he sweep de 'ouse an' git de pay, he buy a pig. When he gwine 'ome he needs tuh cross de stream but he cyan't git de pig across. He cyan't carry it heself and he nuh want pay anyone fuh help'm. So he see a dog comin' by. He say, "Br'er dog, bite dis pig, mek dis pig jump over de river, mek Anancy git 'ome." But de dog say no, cyan't do dat.

Nex' he see a stick comin' by, so he say, "Br'er Stick, lash dis dog, mek dis dog bite dis pig, mek dis pig jump over dis river, mek Anancy git 'ome." But de stick say no, cyan't do dat.

Nex' he see fire, an' he say, "Hey Br'er Fire, burn dis stick, make dis stick lash dis dog, mek dis dog bite dis pig, mek dis pig jump over de river, mek Anancy git 'ome." An' what d'yuh t'ink de Fire said?'

'I expect the Fire said no,' I said. 'So what happened next?'

'After de Fire say no, he see Water comin' down de road. "Good

Massa Water," he say, "I begs yuh out dis fire, mek dis fire burn dis stick, mek dis stick give dis dog a good lickin', mek dis dog bite dis pig, mek dis pig jump over de river, mek Anancy git 'ome.'"

'But the Water said no,' I added, and she grinned.

'Den he see a cow comin' down de road. So he say, "Br'er Cow, Br'er Cow, drink dis water, mek dis water out dis fire, mek dis fire burn dis stick, mek dis stick lick dis dog, mek dis dog bite dis pig, mek dis pig jump over de river, mek Anancy git 'ome.'"

'And the cow said no.'

'Yeah. So he see a butcha comin' along wid a big knife, an' he say to the butcha, "Hey Massa, tek yuh big knife an' kill dis cow, mek dis cow drink dis water, mek dis water out dis fire, mek dis fire burn dis stick, mek dis stick lick dis dog, mek dis dog bite dis pig, mek dis pig jump over dis river, mek Anancy git 'ome." But de butcha say no, cyan't do dat.

Nex' he see Rope comin' along, so he say, "Oh Massa Rope, please 'ang dis butcha, mek dis butcha kill dis cow, mek dis cow drink dis water, mek dis water out dis fire, mek dis fire burn dis stick, mek dis stick lick dis dog, mek dis dog bite dis pig, mek dis pig jump over dis river, mek Anancy git 'ome." But de rope say no.

So nex' he see Grease comin' down, an' he say, "Grease, I wanna ax yuh sump'n. Grease dis rope fuh me, mek dis rope 'ang dis butcha, mek dis butcha kill dis cow, mek dis cow drink dis water, mek dis water out dis fire, mek dis fire burn dis stick, mek dis stick lick dis dog, mek dis dog bite dis pig, mek dis pig jump over dis river, mek Anancy git 'ome." But ol' Massa Grease say no. So along come Mista Rat, and Anancy say, Hey Mista Rat, gnaw dis grease, mek dis grease grease dis rope, mek dis rope 'ang dis butcha, mek dis butcha kill dis cow, mek dis cow drink dis water, mek dis water out dis fire, mek dis fire burn dis stick, mek dis stick lick dis dog, mek dis dog bite dis pig, mek dis pig jump over dis river, mek Anancy git 'ome." But ol' Mista Rat say no. So den who d'yuh t'ink he see comin' by?'

I knew the answer, of course, but went along with the game.

'I don't know,' I said. 'Give me a clue.'

'Sump'n dat cyan chase rat.'

'A cow?'

She shrieked with laughter. 'Cow cyan't kill rat! An' we git de cow a'ready!'

'Oh. A dog?'

'No, he see *Puss* comin' down de road. So he say, "Sista Puss, kill dis rat, mek dis rat gnaw dis grease, mek dis grease grease dis rope, mek dis rope 'ang dis butcha, mek dis butcha kill dis cow, mek dis cow drink dis water, mek dis water out dis fire, mek dis fire burn dis stick, mek dis stick lick dis dog, mek dis dog bite dis pig, mek dis pig jump over dis river, mek Anancy git 'ome." So what d'yuh t'ink Puss say?'

'Tell me,' I said, knowing she could hardly contain herself. She took a deep breath and said then she was off.

'Puss say, *"Yes, I will kill de rat!"* An' de rat say, "Befo' yuh kill me, I will gnaw dis grease." An' de grease say, "Befo' yuh gnaw me I will grease dis rope." An' de rope say, "Befo' yuh grease me, I will 'ang dis butcha." So de butcha say, "Befo' yuh 'ang me I will kill dis cow." An' de cow say, "Befo' yuh kill me, I will drink dis water." An' de water say, "Befo' yuh drink me, I will out dis fire." An' de fire say, "Befo' yuh out me, I will burn dis stick." An' de stick say, "Befo' yuh burn me I will lick this dog." An' de dog say, "Befo' yuh lick me, I will bite dis pig." So de pig is list'nin' tuh what dey is sayin' and de pig say, 'Befo' yuh bite me, I will jump over dis river!" So de pig jump over de river, an' Anancy git 'ome, *an' it cost nuttin'!'*

She had made herself breathless and excited by this. I asked where she had learned it and she told me that she could not remember. I have a faint recollection of hearing or reading some nonsense about a house that Jack built, with rats eating malt, and 'maidens all forlorn', but alas! I cannot remember enough of it to give a rendition to match Adah's *tour de force!* [3] Now that I have written it down I must commit it to memory – it may improve my Creole speech, which I can only manage very indifferently, although I understand it well enough.

February 6th. Terrible weather today, with very strong winds, and everyone very fearful that there may be worse to come. Mr Douglas tells me that in the hurricane of 1780, tens of thousands of slaves starved to death because their provision grounds were all washed away. The sea swept inland for upwards of a mile, and large boats were carried by the waves for great distances, some coming to rest in treetops. As the water retreated it took everything with it – entire plantations together with all their cane fields; trees; houses; animals; overseers and slaves alike – all swept to their destruction in the deluge – drowned or smashed to pieces. This was in the west of the island, a fact that brings little comfort on days like this.

Today began bright and clear, but at around noon the sky became heavily overcast, and the wind rose to the point where all field work had to be abandoned. I can feel our house shuddering, and the gusts are making such a din that I can hardly hear Adah when she speaks. She is as fearful of the tempest as I am, but she attributes it entirely to the spirit of a dead obeah man called Plato.

'He a runaway like Tacky,' she explained. 'He like rum, so dey leave rum where he fin' it, and when he git drunk dey ketch'm.'

'When did this happen?'

'Befo' de storm. End'f seventy-nine. I was jest a pickney.'

'What happened to him?' I asked.

'Dey burn'm,' she said, with wide eyes. 'But befo' he die he cuss de island. He say dat befo' de end'f de year a big storm gwine come an' mek de island flat. Everybody t'ink he just a crazy man talkin', but sho' t'ing, it come true. An' de distric' where he git killed – *dat's de place de storm flatten most!*'

I can do nothing to shake Adah's conviction that this storm has a supernatural origin, indeed, as darkness starts to fall and the winds show no sign of abating, I could almost share her belief that there is a demonic force at work. It is the accounts of the great waves that make me most apprehensive. In the darkness, with our little lamps flickering, we are utterly helpless, and the first we would know would be when the waters crashed through our walls. However the plantation is at a reasonable elevation above the sea, and at least two miles from it, so I think we will be reasonably safe.

We have a little barbecue[4] outside, on which Adah sets our fish to dry, but the winds have carried it away. The shutters rattle, and I know that sleep will be impossible. *[End of volume one.]*[5]

February 7th. Confined to the house. It would be dangerous to venture outside, in this wind, which carries all sorts of debris along with it. A roof must have blown off, for we saw a great shower of shingles hurtling through the air like autumn leaves before thudding and clattering on to the walls of our house and the path outside. I am convinced that we are in the grip of a full hurricane, and Adah is certain that we shall be blown to pieces at any moment. Even though it is day, the sky is filled with low, black clouds that swirl and roil like baleful smoke as they speed over us. With our shutters fastened, I have had to light a lamp in order to write. The sound is the most fearful imaginable – like some monstrous beast battering and roaring in fury. The feeling of helplessness is the worst. We have nowhere to go, and can do nothing but cower here. I am packing this journal away now, for if we lose the roof, as seems likely, I do not want it all to be lost.

February 10th. Mirabile dictu! – the storm has passed, and our roof remained intact, Now we have a difficult time ahead of us, for the whole plantation is littered with palm leaves, fallen branches, broken planks and shingles that will have to be gathered up and burned;

also about a quarter of our cane now lies flat, limp and useless on the ground. Lush foliage has been driven by the wind into great heaps that steam in the sun. There is already a smell of decay everywhere. In the slave village there has been a great deal of damage. There is nothing for it – we must all join forces and try to rectify the situation.

I saw Mr Garvie, whose house is adjacent to mine, and asked him how he had weathered the hurricane.

'No harm done,' he said. 'And that was a storm, not a hurricane.'

'You mean it can be worse than that?'

'Worse?' he said. 'That was just a puff of wind, man! I was in Kingston after the eighty-four hurricane – that's before your time. You wouldn't have believed what the place looked like. Hardly anything left standing. The harbour was the worst part.' He shook his head. 'I'm a fairly hard-bitten chap, Mr Burns, and I have seen some unpleasant sights in my time, but that scene in the harbour will remain with me until my dying day. It was full of bodies, hundreds and hundreds of them. Not complete bodies either. It seemed as if half the population of Kingston had been dismembered by some fiendish butcher, and the pieces just dumped into the water. The sight was dreadful enough, but the stink . . . ugh, it's still in my nostrils. We had to organise teams to go out in little boats, and bring everything ashore. I can see them yet, with cloths tied round their mouths and noses, pulling arms and legs out of the filthy water and bringing them to the quayside. There was no question of proper burial either – we just loaded everything into carts and buried it in a field behind the city. You can see the place yet, if you care to look for it. I believe Savanna-la-Mar was hit even harder. So don't talk to me about hurricanes. I hope you never have to experience one.'

I am sure he spoke the truth, and I share his sentiments!

February 20th. It is as if the storm has never been; repairs have been carried out and the debris cleared away. Now we have sunny skies, and little wind. Life proceeds with very little incident.

March 15th. The Sabbath. The reason that I do not make more entries in this journal, perhaps, is that what was formerly strange and unfamiliar has now become normal and unremarkable. I suppose that every person coming here, be he a white man or a Negro, has to become 'seasoned'.

At leisure today, content with my lot, being of sound health, with few worries to concern me. Life with Adah is ideal. At times she chatters incessantly about all the doings on the plantation, at other times she is content to sit silently near me while I read.

I look back to those bleak days when I would go to bed alone and all a-shivering, despite the thickest flannel nightgown I could find, with the cold wind whistling down the chimney and the frost nipping my nose. Tonight I shall luxuriate in the warmth of a tropical night, listening to the chirping and chittering of the nocturnal lullaby, with the dark body of Adah beside me. What a marvel she is! Her hands in particular fascinate me: small and entirely black; the nails very pink, and the palms much lighter, criss-crossed with fine dark lines. She gives me so much pleasure that I almost wonder if she has cast some sort of obeah spell over me! To be sure, she lacks elegant manners and intellectual refinement, but in every other particular she is everything to me that a wife could be.

March 18th. One of Adah's many 'sisters' has given birth to twin boys, which is a matter for great rejoicing. As the father of twins I share her pleasure in this happy event, though sadly I have yet to see my own little ones, who will be three years of age now. Mr Douglas is pleased, for they represent a valuable plantation asset, and although I am instinctively repelled by the idea of birth into servitude, at least they will grow up in a secure environment, and will never experience the horrors of being forcibly transported from their native land.

I had believed that in Scotland the laws and regulations pertaining to slavery in Jamaica did not apply, and any slave setting foot on Scottish soil became a free man, and thereby entitled to the full protection of the law. Mr Garvie tells me that I am mistaken, and that the law decrees merely that while no slave may be compelled to return to the Indies, he must remain with his master nevertheless, as Joseph Knight was compelled to do. I am confused by the whole wretched business. I passionately believe that slavery is contrary to all moral principles, but what would happen if all slaves were emancipated tomorrow? Could they not indeed be given their liberty, but at the same time indentured to their former masters? The shame of it is that I can see no way forward that does not invite turmoil and discord.

It is, however, agreeable to note the large number slaves on this estate who, though turned seventy or more, are still healthy – evidence of the treatment they have received.

April 14th. Ezekiel, the head boiler, was drunk again today, and more cane juice has been spoiled as a consequence. He is full of excuses, claiming that the bagasse is damp; that the fires are poorly tended, and that the other workers are not stirring the coppers properly, but he is plainly negligent. Mr Douglas was very wrath, and took the unusual step of ordering George to administer a sound flogging. He has now been made to work with the weeding gang once again, and sternly warned that his next transgression will have even more serious consequences. He is disgruntled and is going about his weeding duties with exceedingly bad grace, muttering under his breath and, of course, blaming everyone but himself. The pity of it is that he is an excellent worker when he is sober; however I feel it would be best for one of the others to be trained to replace him.

April 18th. A sad event today. A child of two years was in the care of his mother, who was weeding, but, being unobserved for a few moments, fell into a drainage ditch and was drowned. The poor woman was inconsolable, and the sight of her clutching the tiny body, wailing piteously, was profoundly affecting. Adah has been weeping all day, for although she hardly knew the child there is such a sense of community among the plantation people that the death of one is an event that touches them all. Such an accident is uncommon on the plantation, though newly born children sometimes succumb to the locked jaw, which is invariably fatal.[6]

April 19th. The Sabbath. I attended the burial of the child who drowned yesterday: a scene of terrible grief and lamentation. That such ceremonies are necessary I do not deny, but I feel exhausted by the turbulence of my emotions. Any death is to be regretted, but the death of a child is surely the most terrible thing of all, for one can think of little but the waste of a life that has hardly begun.

Foolish people claim that Negroes cannot possess emotions as we do, but such a notion is entirely false. If anything, their suffering and misery is all the more intense, since they have little else in this world but each other. I was reminded of the grief I shared when Gregory died – today I was awed and humbled by everything. Their sorrow was expressed in song, the agony of loss expressed in surging, anguished harmonies that touched me to the heart. Such strains must be of the greatest antiquity; passed from mother to daughter through the generations, and are probably the same as would have been heard in distant Africa before this iniquitous trade was instituted. I understood nothing of what was going on, and indeed I almost felt myself transported to Africa, but I was deeply affected by it.

I remain even more convinced that life is merely the operation of chance. Why would any God permit the birth of an innocent child, knowing that its life would end so terribly?

At times such as these I feel very conscious of my own mortality.

Who knows what lies ahead? I cannot tell, which is a blessing – how could we bear to live at all if every day we were conscious of our relentless progress towards some hideous fate that we were powerless to avert?

May 9th. For the past few days we have had problems in the boiling house. No matter how much we boil the sugar, it will not set properly. The only possible explanation is that some foreign substance is being introduced into the coppers. My suspicions lie with Ezekiel, who has been in the highest degree surly and insolent since his flogging, though he has managed to keep away from the rum. I know that he would not be so foolish as to attempt any mischief if he believed himself to be observed, but I have no doubt that he would cause trouble if he could. This evening I intend to be on hand when the great copper is filled: I shall send him away on some trivial errand, and conceal myself in order to determine if he is indeed responsible for the problems. There is a storage space in the rafters of the boiling house, and from there I will have a clear view of the area below. I have asked Gilmour to join me.

May 10th. Ezekiel is in irons, and is to be taken to Kingston tomorrow to be charged with maliciously spoiling the sugar. We caught him *in flagrante delicto,* and an example has to be made of him. As the great copper was filling this morning, I went in with Gilmour, found a pretext to dismiss the workers, and sent Ezekiel off to fetch some water so that we were left alone. When he had gone, we secreted ourselves in the upper part of the building and waited. After about five minutes he returned with the water. Believing himself to be alone, he sat for a few moments, watching the juice run into the copper, then busied himself with stoking the fires. For a time his actions appeared entirely innocent. Then he went to the door, peered out to satisfy himself that no one was coming, and returned to the copper. Reaching behind it he pulled out a bag, and extracted a dozen or so lemons from it. There was nothing untoward about this, for the tart juice of the fruit is cooling and refreshing in the heat. I saw him take out a little knife, and proceed to cut all the lemons open. Having done so he squeezed the juice into the copper, returning the crushed skins to the bag. It was at once clear why the sugar would not set – any sourness prevents it from doing so.

   Gilmour and I shouted out, and climbed down to confront him. For a few moments he blustered, protesting his innocence, but when it was clear that we had seen the whole thing, and that this foolish denial of his guilt was to no avail, he fell silent, and his face assumed an expression of sullen resignation. The evidence of the lemons was damning.

We summoned George, who placed shackles on him, and we reported the matter to Mr Douglas, who listened to what we had to say with a very grim face.

'Well, he's had two warnings,' he said. 'I can't afford any more lost production. This was a deliberate criminal act, and I shall have to make sure he is dealt with.'

'What are you going to do?' asked Gilmour. 'You could hang him for this!'

Mr Douglas glowered at him. 'That's not my way, man, and you know it. I shall hand him over to the slave court. They will deal with him. You two will have to appear as witnesses, of course.'

"And what happens to Ezekiel meantime?'

'He goes to Port Antonio tomorrow and I'll enter the charges. If they have room in the jail, he'll be kept there. If not, we'll have to bring him back here and lock him up until the date of the trial is arranged.'

'It would be quicker to hang him yourself,' muttered Gilmour.

'Don't tell me my business!' snapped Mr Douglas. 'There will be no hangings on this plantation. I am not a judge, and I do not expect any man on this plantation to become an executioner. If a crime has been committed then the law will deal with it in the proper fashion.'

May 22nd. I have been a little morose this evening, thinking of Bess who is four today. Adah asked me what was ailing me, and I have told her all about my daughter, and the twins I have never seen. As ever, her pleasure in hearing what I have to tell her is diminished by the fact that she so badly wants a child of her own. She has been making herself sick recently by drinking some astringent medicine that she made by boiling leaves, and I have told her to desist from this, as she may do herself harm. I must speak to Simpson about it.

It has been impossible not to think of Ezekiel, languishing in jail at this very moment. It is likely that he will remain there for a month or two before the trial. I am not sure that I share Mr Douglas's confidence that the trial will be a fair one, and I am not sure what penalty will be imposed for the offence, but at least there will be a jury.

Despite the heat, I have felt all of a shiver since this afternoon and my head aches.

June 10th. I have been thoroughly debilitated with that wretched fever again, and have only now summoned up the strength to write. Adah has been giving me something bitter to drink and it has helped me to sleep soundly. For her sake, I am making light of this indisposition, but in reality it worries me a good deal, for it is worse than any chill and I fear that it may be a more serious illness of a recurrent nature. Simpson is not helpful, only saying that I should drink camomile tea if I can obtain it. I have found an infusion of ginger root to be effective, as it seems to restore my vigour somewhat.

June 23rd. There are rumours that Maroons have attacked a plantation in St Andrew's parish. If this proves to be true then it means serious trouble for us, for I doubt we could defend ourselves against attack. Mr Douglas is of the opinion that there might be another war, in which case our situation would be a very dangerous one, for the Blue Mountains overlook this plantation. They are formidable fighters, and so skilled in concealing themselves that I have heard it said that they can stand in undergrowth and remain unobserved by someone passing only feet from them. They attack silently by night, carrying off women for procreation together with any guns and powder that they can find. It is said that they are skilled practitioners of obeah, and can make themselves invisible, and that they will take their own lives rather than suffer themselves to be taken prisoner and enslaved. Mr Douglas is waiting to hear more, and if there is indeed an uprising afoot them we shall have to be issued with muskets.

June 30th. The Maroon story proved to be unfounded. What happened was that two runaway slaves entered the plantation by night, with the utmost stealth, and carried away a considerable amount of provisions and rum. When the theft was discovered, a party set out in search of the thieves who were found not a mile away, fast asleep having partaken of too much rum. We are relieved, but the threat from the Maroons is one that we can never allow ourselves to forget for a moment.

July 4th. A copy of the *Morning Star* has made its way here, dated 13th May, reporting at length on a very impassioned speech to parliament made by Mr Wilberforce the day previous, in which he argues most eloquently against the slave trade. He does not seek to point the finger of blame at the merchants who make their fortunes from it, but rather to engage in cool deliberation on a mighty subject. He has made much of the wretched conditions endured by slaves, and the lies told by those who extenuate their crimes by claiming that in the ships they are treated with all manner of luxurious indulgence. That they are guilty is not in question, but we are all guilty, and we ought to plead guilty, and not seek to exculpate ourselves by throwing the blame on others.

To understand the real horror of the slave trade, it is sufficient to catch the smell of a slave ship. If my well-intentioned but ignorant countrymen could experience this powerful, olfactory proof in their delicate nostrils, then the trade would be abolished tomorrow.

July 15th. I hear that a statue is to be erected in Kingston, depicting our most exalted Lieutenant-Governor, who is to leave his post in a few months. During six years of office he appears to me to have done very little except make himself rich beyond the wildest dreams of avarice. I know of no benefits the island or its people have gained in return; as for the Negro folk, he has done nothing for them at all. Despite his assurances, we have seen no sign of the *Bounty* with the promised breadfruit. I have pondered the matter, with this result –

On the statue of A[lured] C[larke]

Come, future generations, and admire the bust
Of one who ground the hapless Negro in the dust;
And view, with proper awe, that stern, commanding eye
Which watched with unconcern his faithful servants die.
That haughty brow, instinct with every Christian grace,
Tells of his zeal in treading down a captive race:
Each feature eloquent of one who served his Lord
By wresting riches from the Negroes he abhorred.

August 2nd. Circumstanced as I am here, I know that I could never have hoped to find a companion who could have entered into my studies and relished philosophy and literature with me. I esteem Adah very highly: she is a much-loved fellow-creature whose happiness or misery is entirely in my hands – who could trifle with such trust? She has a good nature; a sweet disposition, and a warm heart whose constant impulse is to please me, all set off to advantage by an alluring figure. It is churlish of me to set this down, and I am ashamed of myself to write it, but – I feel regret that there should be so many subjects we cannot discuss. She takes no interest in learning – a dozen times I have offered to teach her to read and to write, but she shows no inclination. If she has a fault, it is that she can never truly be a soul mate as Mary was. Yet in every other way she is everything I could possibly want or need.

August 25th. The trial of Ezekiel takes place in Port Antonio tomorrow, Wednesday, and Gilmour and I have to attend with Mr Douglas. McLehose is to accompany us, as he is a lawyer by profession. The charge is a serious one – deliberate damage of this kind carries with it the severest penalties, and I have the greatest reservations about the slave courts, especially under the recent code. Even if Ezekiel were entirely innocent I should be fearful of the outcome. As it is, the verdict is a foregone conclusion. I do not deny that the wretch should be punished, but I would not see him tortured and degraded.

August 26th. To Port Antonio this morning. The slave court is housed in a large wooden building in the main street, with the jail adjacent to it. There was a great, noisy crowd outside, consisting, I suppose, of the friends and relatives of those about to stand trial. Members of the militia, in their neat red uniforms, were on duty to keep order, and to deny entrance to all but those who had business inside. As witnesses, we were at once escorted through the throng, and admitted to the rear of the courtroom – as white men, we would have been allowed to enter anyway.

There was a trial in progress as we entered. The courtroom was square in shape, and we sat at the back, where there were five or six rows of uncomfortable benches, nearly all occupied. The windows were high up on the walls, stoutly barred, with their shutters only open a little way, so that the heat was stifling.

Facing us was a bench on a raised platform, behind which sat three magistrates, all white men, all wearing black robes and wigs. The magistrate seated in the middle was a florid man who wheezed as he spoke, and was obviously acting as chairman. The one on his right was a fat fellow who looked half asleep in the heat. The other had the look of a ferret, with a sharp nose and a gingery complexion. His lips were a thin, bloodless line, and he looked as if he never smiled. I remember a few church elders with very much the same facial expression, as if the Almighty had set out with the intention of fashioning a rat, but had changed His mind at the last moment.

Fixed to the wall at one side of the room was a kind of cage for the accused, the entrance to which, I assume, led to the adjacent jail, the whole thing designed in this way in order to frustrate any attempt at escape into the body of the court. There was a chair inside on which a young Negro was sitting. On the other side of the court was a stand for witnesses.

As we sat down a case was reaching its conclusion. The accused, a young Negro named Jeremiah, sat impassively in the cage. He had struck his master in the face a year ago, for which he had been severely whipped, and now he had apparently repeated the offence, breaking the nose of the said master.

The wheezing magistrate conferred briefly with his colleagues before asking Jeremiah to stand.

'The court finds you guilty of striking your master to his severe injury,' he said. 'We have to take account of the fact that this is your second offence, and accordingly the sentence of this court is that you should have your nose slit, your face branded on the left side, and your left ear cut off. The sentence is to be carried out immediately. Take him away.'

Jeremiah was led out, shouting his protests. Another prisoner appeared in the cage. The clerk consulted his papers and introduced him to the court as Gordon, from the Willoughby Plantation. The charge was that he had murdered William Branker, an overseer on the plantation, by repeatedly striking him with a matchet. The magistrate called for witnesses, and two overseers came forward to describe the attack in detail. When they had given their testimony, Gordon was given a chance to speak in his own defence. He launched into his version of events, rapidly becoming hysterical, and banging his manacled hands on the bars of the cage. He spoke so quickly that it was difficult for me to follow, and I shall not attempt to reproduce it *verbatim,* but the gist of the matter was that Branker had come to his house and demanded that he hand over his wife. When he refused, Branker had beaten him senseless, dragged the woman away in order to use her for his lustful gratification. In the morning she had returned, bleeding and bruised, and in a fury he had taken up the matchet and gone in search of the man who had treated her so cruelly, and brought shame on them both. When he had finished, the magistrate looked at his colleagues. The thin one indicated that he wished to ask a question.

'Tell me, Gordon, when you took up the matchet, did you intend to harm Mr Branker?'

'Yessuh.'

'And are you sorry that he is dead, and that you killed him?'

Gordon stared back defiantly. 'Nosuh. He done a bad t'ing. If I done dat t'ing to a white woman I'd be a dead man. I cyan't say I sorry I kill'm.'

The magistrates looked at each other and nodded.

'Stand up, Gordon,' said the chairman. The man did so. He must have guessed what the verdict would be, for the expression on his face was ghastly.

'This court finds you guilty,' said the magistrate. A moan ran through the court. Someone at the door must have run to impart the verdict to those waiting outside, because we heard shouts and wails.

'This was a terrible crime,' he went on. 'You forgot that both you and the woman you live with are the property of the estate, and it is for the estate, through its overseers, to determine what happens to you. Mr Branker was within his rights to act as he did. If you felt so strongly about the matter, then your correct course should have been to go to Mr Willoughby and explain your feelings to him. Instead you took the law into your own hands, and murdered an overseer in cold blood. What is more, you have told this court that you feel no remorse or contrition for the terrible felony you have committed. The sentence of this court is that you be taken from here to a lawful place of execution and given one hundred lashes, following which your right hand shall be burned in a fire, and then you shall be hanged by the neck until you are dead. Take him away.'

Two men came through the door to support Gordon, whose legs had given way beneath him. They dragged him out and the door closed.

We were all shocked by the severity of the sentence. Hanging would have been bad enough, but the lashing and burning beforehand was a wholly gratuitous cruelty.

'Is there not supposed to be a jury? Douglas asked McLehose.

'There should be, according to the code. The man was entitled to proper representation and to have witnesses called in his defence.'

Mr Douglas looked very grim. 'What can Ezekiel expect?'

'I'd have thought transportation at the most,' said McLehose. 'But this court seems to dispense justice as it pleases.'

'Justice?' grunted Douglas. 'It seems a strange kind of justice. I don't hold with all this slitting, branding and burning. It's a disgrace.'

'The code allows it,' said McLehose.

'The code stipulates a jury. This is all very unsatisfactory.'

'I agree,' said McLehose. 'But there's not much we can do about it.'

The next case was called.

This time it was Ezekiel who appeared in the cage. He had lost weight since I saw him last, and looked very listless as he sat on the stool.

'Well?' said the magistrate.

'Ezekiel, from the Douglas estate,' said the clerk.

'Read the charge to the accused.'

'The charge is that on the tenth day of May in the year of our Lord seventeen hundred and eighty-nine, you, a slave known as Ezekiel, the property of Mr Douglas, did maliciously introduce a harmful substance, namely lemon juice, into a boiling copper with the intention of spoiling the sugar therein.'

'How do you plead?' asked the magistrate. Ezekiel made no reply, but shook his head wearily. 'We'll take that as not guilty, then. Are there any witnesses?'

I arose and went to the witness stand. I could see the thin magistrate looking me up and down, and I realised that he enjoyed his position and the power that it gave him. The chief magistrate looked even more florid close at hand: a rivulet of sweat was running down his forehead from beneath his wig.

'What is your name?' he wheezed.

'Robert Burns.'

'And your occupation?'

'I am an overseer for Mr Douglas, the owner of the plantation.'

'Very well. Did you see the accused place the lemon juice in the copper?'

'Yes.'

'Did any one else see?'

'Yes. My colleague, Mr Gilmour.'

'I see.'

'According to the charge,' said the thin magistrate, 'the accused put a harmful substance into the sugar. But lemon juice is hardly harmful, is it?'

'Not normally,' I said. 'However, the sour taste of a lemon is attributable to the fact that it contains what we term an acid. If it is added to cane juice which is then boiled, it alters its chemical composition so that the juice will not set and form crystals as it cools.'

'So all the cane juice is wasted?'

'Yes.'

'Thank you.'

'Tell me,' said the chief magistrate, 'on how many occasions was the sugar spoiled in this way?'

'Three or four times.'

'And what pecuniary loss to the plantation was suffered as a consequence?'

'Twenty-five or thirty pounds. We also lost molasses for the distillery, so it affected our rum production.'

'I see. What did Ezekiel say when you and Mr Gilmour confronted him?'

I looked at Ezekiel who was hanging his head and avoiding looking at me. 'He tried to deny it at first,' I said. 'But I think he realised that it was pointless.'

'I see. You may stand down.'

I sat down, and they called Gilmour who gave pretty much the same account as I had done.

'Ezekiel,' said the magistrate, 'do you want to say anything before the court passes sentence?'

Ezekiel looked up briefly and shook his head.

'Let me remind you of the severity of the charge,' said the magistrate. 'Malicious damage to the fabric or the property of the plantation is an exceptionally serious matter. You have received all of the benefits the plantation has to offer, and in return you have had recourse to wicked, clandestine actions with the express purpose of harming your master. It is akin to treason. I would remind you that this is a capital charge, and the evidence against you is irrefutable. Unless you can give an explanation of your actions, then I shall have no alternative but to hand down the severest sentence it is within my power to pass.'

Ezekiel looked at him, and for a moment it seemed as if he was about to speak, but he shook his head again, with a look of infinite resignation. He was finished, and he knew it. I felt sorry for him – it is terrible to see such a look of utter hopelessness on a man's face.

'This court is adjourned for five minutes,' said the magistrate. 'If you have anything to say to us by way of mitigation we shall hear it from you when we return.' He stood and went out with his colleagues. Ezekiel buried his head in his hands.

'They mean to hang him for sure,' said Douglas, 'and Heaven knows what else besides. I'm not having this.' He got up, marched to the front of the court, and went through the door where the magistrates had gone. This caused some commotion in the court.

'Surely he can't think he can influence the verdict?' said McLehose.

We listened to the buzz of speculation around us. The minutes passed and it was fully half an hour before Douglas reappeared. We would have questioned him, but the three magistrates had followed him and the florid one was already rapping for silence with his gavel.

'Have you anything to say to us, Ezekiel?'

'Nosuh.'

'The court finds you guilty. We have considered the matter carefully, and the sentence of the court is that you be taken from here to Kingston, and from thence transported to Barbados on the first available ship.' It was a fair verdict and a popular one in the court. The thin magistrate glared venomously at Mr Douglas, who stared back impassively. Ezekiel was taken away and we left the court.

'What did you say to them, Mr Douglas?' I asked as soon as we were outside. He looked at me with a faintly amused expression.

'What makes you think I said anything to them?'

'You must have done,' said McLehose.

'Oh, I made a few wee observations. I commented on the lack of jury and defence counsel. I told them I did not believe it was a capital charge. I mentioned that I would be happy to have the case referred to the Supreme Court in Kingston, where the conduct of today's hearing could be reviewed. I may have said one or two other things – I can't remember. Anyway, justice has been done.' He would answer no more questions, and so we returned to the plantation.

Such was my experience of the slave court. Had Mr Douglas not been there, then Ezekiel would certainly have been mutilated and hanged. What hope is there for justice for the Negro people when the courts that are supposed to protect their rights are employed only to mete out degradation and humiliation – in other words, a very different justice from that to which a white man is entitled? Surely the very word 'justice' loses its meaning unless it applies equally to all!

My estimation for Mr Douglas has risen greatly today.

September 2nd. Such news in the *Gazette* today! The Bastille has been stormed and its prisoners released! That most potent symbol of arrogant despotism has been broken down and its stones, I hope, employed for nobler purposes like houses for the poor or hospitals for the sick. Cursed be the wretch who could plot the destruction of honest, innocent men who never offended him, and consign them to beggary and ruin! And blessed be the spirit of the PEOPLE and the sacred principle of LIBERTY! I hope that I would not offend Billy P[itt?][7] with such sentiments, but I am sure there will be glum faces in certain lofty and exalted quarters today, and *pourquoi pas?* Dare I allow myself to hope that humankind stands on the threshold of a better age, where man shall speak unto man as a brother, not as an enemy, and where compassion and benevolence shall replace self-interest and suspicion? Like Herr Handel, I shall sing a most exultant, heartfelt *Hallelujah!* should it indeed prove to be so.

September 9th. This morning one of the sugar boilers – a young lad called Scipio – somehow got his hand into the boiling sugar and the sound of his screaming was audible to the furthest ends of the plantation. When I came on the scene he was outside the boiling house and running about, in the most dreadful agony, clutching at his hand, to which the scalding liquid had adhered like glue. It took four of us to carry him to the hospital, where Simpson took one look and shook his head.

'We'll have to take the hand off,' he said. 'That damned sugar has burned through to the bone. What's your name, laddie?'

'He name Scipio,' said George, the head driver.

'Very well, Scipio,' said Simpson to the poor wretch. 'That's a nasty burn you've got there. If we don't do something about it now, it will mortify and you'll die for sure.'

We tried to reassure the lad while Simpson fetched his instruments. I felt queasy, but there was no way I could absent myself.

'De doctor say he tek de hand off!' he wailed, his jaw quivering in terror. 'Please, Massa Burns, tell'm he cyan't do dat!'

'The doctor will make you better,' I said. George gave me a sceptical glance, but said nothing. Scipio started to weep as Simpson came back, carrying a wooden box and a lamp.

'Lift him on to the table,' he said. 'You two – hold the burned arm still. George – hold his feet. Burns, hold his other arm.'

We lifted him up and, despite his wails and entreaties, held him down as Simpson had instructed. I was glad I was on Scipio's other side, for it meant that I could look away.

'Keep him absolutely still,' said Simpson, fixing a tourniquet in place. We bore down on him, so that he could do nothing but whip his head from side to side. His eyes were staring in terror.

'Now, Scipio,' said Simpson, in a gentler tone. 'You must be a brave boy. Hold still. I will be as quick as possible. Are you all ready?'

We said that we were. Simpson took a curved knife and with a circular movement drew the blade around the forearm, cutting through the flesh down to the bone all the way around. As blood began to gush from the wound, he took a smaller knife, held its blade in the flame of the lamp, and then applied it to the wound. There was a hiss and a reek of burning that turned my stomach. He repeated the process several times, sealing the blood vessels.

'Steady now,' he said, and took a small saw from the box. Scipio caught sight of it and fainted, which was a mercy. I looked away, but I could not close my ears to the sound the saw made as it rasped through bone. There was a thud as the severed hand fell to the floor. The whole operation had taken only a minute or so.

'All done,' said Simpson, and he began to apply a dressing to the stump. Weak at the knees, I stumbled outside and was sick. When I recovered my composure sufficiently to return, Scipio was lying down moaning, and Simpson was instructing a boy to sluice down the table and the floor to clear away the blood.

'Will he survive?' I asked.

Simpson shrugged. 'He's young. If the wound doesn't become infected he'll pull through.'

'I had not realised that it could be done so quickly,' I said. 'You did a good job.'

'We'll see,' he said. 'Leave him here for a day or two.'

I felt unable to return to work, and returned home to recount the story to Adah. She offered me food, which I had to decline. My thoughts are with Scipio, who began his day little suspecting that it would end so terribly for him. As I noted a few months ago, what a mercy it is that we cannot know what lies in store for us!

September 10th. Scipio is weak and in a lot of pain, but still alive. He is understandably upset and tearful but Simpson is confident that he will recover. The horror of the amputation is still with me – I do not know how anyone could endure such a thing and live.

September 27th. Scipio is recovered sufficiently to leave the hospital, and Simpson tells me the stump is healing without any sign of mortification. However he will clearly be unable to resume his duties in the boiling house, and Mr Douglas has arranged for him to train as a watchman, which requires honesty and vigilance, but does not involve any manual duties.

October 17th. I have spent the last few days at the McKenzie plantation at Hope Bay in the company of Mr Douglas for the purpose of advising the new agent there on matters concerning the running of the mill, which has newly been installed. I did not take this journal with me, and now that I am returned I am attempting to write today's entry in spite of the strident strains of Adah, who insists that she does not wish me ever to leave her again, and that even though it was only for a few days she missed me and wept constantly. Between her tears and caresses she rendered the process of chronicling quite impossible. Bless her heart – her devotion touches me, and I am humbled to realise how deeply she cares for me.

Regarding my visit, the agent, Mr Millar, is a pleasant man of about forty, and has come but recently to these climes, so has much to learn. The plantation is smaller than ours, but agreeably situated. The Great House, although on a less imposing scale than our own, is of new construction and well appointed. Our days were concerned with practical matters, and in conversation about the island; the intricacies of the sugar trade; problems with the cultivation of provisions; the procurement of slaves; the vagaries of the climate, and the thousand-and-one other little details that old hands such as ourselves take very much for granted.

It might have been a most enjoyable visit but for the presence of a house-guest, a Lady F[–], whose husband is visiting the island in some capacity or other at the invitation of the Governor. Our evenings were rendered perfectly intolerable by this creature. I would guess her to be some fifty years of age, a huge, shapeless, sumphish ruin of what might have been, many years ago, a ordinary-looking woman at best. The entire substance of her conversation was one continuous girn. Oh, the airs and graces she gave herself! In her powdered wig and padded bodice, she felt 'too hot', so an army of servants had to be constantly on hand to fan her; the mosquitoes bothered her and had to be 'dealt with'; a footman who (very understandably in my view) made so bold as to stare at this embodiment of petted, pampered, pompous fatuousness had to be 'punished with the utmost severity'. What amazed me was how her absurd whims and ridiculous opinions were received with a degree of obsequious, toadying deference that would have been laughable had it not been so damnably irksome. How I detest the arrogant, conceited dignity such individuals display when they are obliged to cope with reality. How I loathe the contumelious sneer of those whom accident has made our 'superiors'!

Your time has come and gone, Madame! *Ça ira, ça ira!* How I would love to see you tumble headlong into some foetid ditch; how I would roar with merriment to hear your shrieks, and your vain entreaties for assistance! What satisfaction and happiness it would give me to observe your futile flounderings in the mud to which you and your worthless kind are happy to consign Negroes in the pursuance of their duties!

I fear I am becoming quite the revolutionary! The latest from France is that the fine noblemen and the devout clergy feel disinclined to obey the orders of the Estates-General regarding taxation, and that in consequence the poor have risen up to declare themselves firstly the Third Estate and now the National Assembly. The Bastille is no more; powdered princelings and mitred hypocrites precipitately flee their fine *châteaux* and opulent palaces in terror, and *pourquoi pas?* Away with the parasites! *À la lanterne*, say I!

November 27th. The Sabbath. Adah is unhappy because she is still not with child. The McLehose infant is perfectly delightful, and we see her frequently, but each visit serves to make Adah even more dissatisfied with her position. On a matter so delicate I feel diffident about seeking medical advice, but I have contrived an innocent pretext, and procured from Simpson a copy of Dr B[uchan]'s excellent treatise, which deals most comprehensively and expertly with all the ills known to afflict mankind.[8] I was struck by his chapter on intemperance, wherein he rails against the Scots for their gross immoderation, which he describes as a relic of barbarity too often mistaken for hospitality. 'In Scotland', he writes, 'no man is supposed to entertain his guests well, who does not make them drunk' – too true an observation, I fear. On barrenness he states that its cause may be an irregularity or obstruction of the menstrual flux, though this hardly applies to Adah. Nor is she guilty of high living or want of exercise, both of which have an adverse effect on fecundity. He recommends a milk and vegetable diet; cold baths; exercise, and dragon's blood, whatever that may be. I would have thought such an item might belong more in a witch's cauldron than in a modern inventory of simples and medical preparations.[9] There are many interesting creatures in Jamaica, but I have never yet heard tell of dragons. The good doctor is also of the opinion that the male should also partake of the same regimen as the want of children is oftener the fault of the male than of the female, so I shall take his advice despite the fact that my loins have proved fruitful enough in the past. As for cold bathing, he recommends quick immersion. Cold bathing has a constant tendency to propel the blood and other humours towards the head, so it ought to be a rule always to wet that part first. By due attention to this circumstance, there is reason to believe that complaints that frequently proceed from cold bathing might be prevented.

November 30th. Adah and I have been practising cold bathing, and I am only now recovering from the first session. I ordered an old barrel from the distillery to be sawn in half, which provided a pair of capacious bathtubs. The yard at the rear of our house is not overlooked, so we have set our tub next to the wall of our house, and made a screen with canvas so that we can have privacy during our medicinal ablutions. The water was fetched from the pump in two buckets. I decided to bathe first, and, mindful of the advice of the good doctor, I lectured Adah very earnestly on the need to attend to the head first of all. I knelt in the tub with the expectation of being anointed gently, but Adah, who has refused to take the matter seriously, tipped the bucket over my head and ran away screaming with laughter. Forgetful of the fact that I was completely naked, I leapt from the tub to pursue her around the corner of the house, threatening to skelp her doup for her, only to realise that I had entered into full view of Mr Garvie, whose face bore a look of horror and amazement.

'What on earth are you doing, man?' he said, as I covered my private parts and began to back away.

'Nothing,' I said. 'Adah was giving me a bath, and . . .'

'A *bath?*' he exclaimed. 'Have you taken leave of your senses? What in Heaven's name do you want a *bath* for? And why is Adah running around like a mad woman? What in the world is happening?'

I was quite unable to proffer any explanation that would have made sense to him. When I was sure he had gone, I went in search of Adah, who was attempting unsuccessfully to conceal herself beneath the bed, and marched her out to the tub where, after a noisy struggle, we finally succeeded in carrying out the doctor's precepts. I do not yet know whether the treatment will prove efficacious, but if, as Buchan says, the cure lies in discovering a means of amusing and entertaining the fancy, then that object was most certainly achieved, for I have rarely experienced such a rumbustious rodgering as we two enjoyed that night.

December 1st. Little to report. I dreamt again last night of the castle. Once again I was standing inside, looking up through the broken roof at clouds moving across the sky. Again, the prevailing mood was one of loneliness and isolation. It was the plaintive sound of the wind that seemed to remain in my ears when I awoke – a fretful moaning, rising and falling like an endless cry of sorrow or grief – a threnody of remoteness and desolation. I normally sleep very soundly, and I do not know why my slumber should have been disturbed in this way. Perhaps it is the effect of the cold water yesterday, which may have driven malign vapours into my cerebellum, or else it signifies a rooted inclination to melancholy in my nature – I cannot tell.

December 3rd. I have read that there is a book newly published by a man called Equiano, which I am most anxious to obtain. Mr Equiano is a Negro, and he writes of his experiences both in captivity and subsequent to his manumission. This news fills me with a hopeful excitement, for I know of no Negro able to read or write, and from this it must surely follow that the stories of their lives could never be known from anything but their spoken narratives of what they have had to endure. But now such a narrative appears in print, and by all accounts very well written! It is surely to men such as this that Mr Wilberforce and his supporters must now turn as being the most authoritative and persuasive of witnesses. Who can tell more eloquently of the iniquity of the trade than those who have had to endure it? I have sent to Kingston for a copy.

President Washington now stands proudly at the helm of the world's newest nation, and not only has he pledged to pursue the course of virtue and the common good, but in publicly renouncing all pecuniary gain from his high office he demonstrates a level of integrity that should be demanded of all leaders of men. The Bastille has fallen, and a new Gaul arises, phoenix-like, from the smouldering ashes of the old. We are witness to the triumph of liberty and honesty over privilege, tyranny and oppression!

December 14th. Adah and I are persevering with the cold baths. Although they have yet to produce the effect for which they were instituted, I feel that they are beneficial for my general health, for the aches and pains that have plagued me in the past seem to have disappeared. Mr Garvie remains deeply suspicious about bathing, and has warned me that water will damage the pores of the skin. However I believe that Dr Buchan is nearer the mark.

December 25th. Friday, and no work on the plantation for three days. The overseers were bidden to the Great House at noon today where we partook of some very fine boiled meats, and heard Mr Douglas reading from the scriptures. He spoke with great fervour, and as I listened to his words I was reminded of the days, not so long ago, when I too had religion strongly impressed on my mind. I felicitate him, good man that he is, for having a solid foundation for his mental enjoyment, and I envy him his anchor of hope when he looks beyond the grave. I would dearly love to believe that Jesus Christ, whose natal day we celebrate, is no imposter, but when I consider the impositions that have been palmed off on a credulous mankind my doubts return. To be sure, I can *hope*; but I cannot *believe*.

1790

January 12th. With Mr Douglas today when he let slip a piece of unwelcome news.

'I've got a new man starting work next week,' he said. 'He's been in some sort of trouble, I gather, and he's been looking for employment.'

'What sort of trouble?' I asked.

'Oh, some sort of bother over a woman. I don't know the details.'

At this I felt a sort of premonition.

'What's his name?'

'Currie. My agent in Kingston has spoken to him, and he appears a decent enough sort.'

'If he's the same Currie that I know, then he's very far from being a decent sort,' I said, and related to him the incident that had taken place on board the *Bell*. Douglas listened sympathetically enough, I thought, but when I desired him to change his mind on the matter of hiring him he shook his head.

'It's a big plantation,' he said, 'and you'll probably not have much contact with him. Anyway, it's all in the past now, and I need him.'

I continued to make entreaties, but he was quite adamant. I cannot conceive of any human being I would rather have avoided, but I am powerless to change things. As I write, I have a strong, instinctive feeling that there is trouble in store for me. At any rate Mary is spared the realisation that her assailant is to be a neighbour.

January 15th. I have obtained a copy of Equiano's book, which is causing something of a stir on the island.[1] Wonderful. I read it with the greatest interest, amazement and joy that at last a Negro has written a full account of his vicissitudes. He does so without the slightest degree of self-pity, nor does he condemn all white people, but indeed praises those who have dealt with him fairly and honourably. His account of his suffering is timely, and must surely help to hasten the demise of the trade. His most telling argument is that the trade does not make any kind of financial sense, and that far greater fortunes are to be made by entering into commerce with the African continent. A country almost twice as large as Europe offers possibilities in commercial intercourse that could prove an inexhaustible source of wealth for our own manufacturing interests. Moreover, Africa abounds in all manner of useful treasures, so that industry, mining, farming and enterprise will have the fullest scope. In a word,

Africa presents an endless, unexplored field of *commerce,* and since
the manufacturing interest and the general interest are synony-
mous, as Equiano says, then the abolition of slavery would be a
universal good, as far greater fortunes could be made, to the benefit
of the African and the English people alike. With slavery cast aside
and the Negro people working *with us* instead of *for us,* how much we
could gain from each other!

January 24th. My natal day tomorrow, but much to do on the planta-
tion then, so as this is the Sabbath I am taking an opportunity to write,
though there is but little of interest to report, I fear. Adah is sad because
there is still 'no pickney', although we have followed Dr Buchan's
advice to the letter, and have come almost to enjoy our 'cold' baths,
though in these tropical climes, the water in which we bathe would be
considered warm enough for any aristocrat in the cooler lands with
which the good doctor was familiar.

In St Ann's parish, we hear that the still and the mill house have
been destroyed in a great conflagration, together with a cane piece of
five acres, the cause being a spark from a stoke-hole being blown on
to the roof of the mill, which was thatched. This is always a danger
when there are winds of any strength, and we shall increase our own
vigilance in future.

I have met with Currie for the first time since his arrival here –
his *intrusion,* rather – and it was much as I had feared. He means to
make trouble, I am sure. He was with McLehose and the others this
morning, doing his best to ingratiate himself with them, and when
I joined them he clearly recognised me at once, but made a great
show of ignoring me. I made a point of speaking to him on his own
when I judged the moment to be right. My intention had been to
seek some way in which we could agree to behave civilly towards
each other, but he clearly had other ideas.

'Aye, it's been a while since I saw you,' he said, ignoring my
proffered hand. 'I was locked up in the jail thanks to you.'

'I know that we have had our differences,' I said. 'Surely it is time
to put these behind us.'

'Behind us?' he said. 'Damn it man, ye hae a nerve tae speak o'
putting things ahent us. Hae ye ony idea o' whit the inside o' a
Jamaican prison is like?'

'I know you bear a grudge towards me,' I said. 'I think we should
just agree to keep away from each other. I promise I will not give you
any occasion for offence.'

'Ye're a fine one tae be talkin' aboot offence. I forgot masel' for

a few minutes, and I endit up gettin' locked in a stinking cell wi'
a dozen filthy negers. Ye'll never ken whit I had tae thole!'

'Aye, you forgot yourself all right,' I said. I could feel the rage
boiling and seething within me, but I knew that there was nothing
to be gained from showing it. 'Anyway, we're here now, so we may
as well make the best of it.'

'Ye've made the best o' it,' he said with a sneer. 'I hear that yer wife
died. Ye didna waste much time in takin' up with a wee neger hizzie.
Whit's she like, Robert? I'll wager she walks bow-leggit wi' a' the
rodgerin' she gets!'

I turned and walked off, leaving him mouthing obscenities at my
back. What have I done to deserve such treatment? I am the one with
a grievance, and I have to put up with this!

February 3rd. I spoke to McLehose today about Currie, and asked
him what he thought of the boy.

'Oh he's all right. He's a bit of a braggart. He doesn't like you
much, for some reason.'

I explained about the incident on the *Bell*, and he nodded.

'It was the drink, I expect,' he said with a dismissive wave of the
hand. 'Anyway, there was no lasting harm done in the end, and he's
paid the price for it. Just let him be.'

'I'm happy to do so,' I said, 'if he's prepared to do the same. But
every time I see him he provokes me.'

'He's only a laddie,' said McLehose. 'He'll settle down, just you
mark my words.'

He had come over to return the Equiano book I lent him, and I
asked him what he had made of it.

'Aye, it was interesting,' he said. 'It's bound to help the abolition-
ist cause. I doubt if Mr Douglas would think much of it.'

'I thought about asking him if he wished to borrow it,' I said, 'but
thought better of it.'

'You'd have had a six-mile sermon in return, most likely,' he said,
laughing. 'But, you have to admit, if emancipation came tomorrow,
then compare the Negroes from our plantation with some of the
poor souls we've seen elsewhere. Ours have skills; they practise
trades; they understand sugar production and distilling. When they
walk out of the plantation gate they will be able to put all of this to
immediate use, and to prosper in life. *And* they are not likely to come
back and burn the Great House down, because they will realise that
Douglas has worked very hard to put them in such a favourable
position. Mr Douglas has nothing to fear from the abolition of the

slave trade itself, because he seldom needs to buy slaves. He has nothing to fear from emancipation because his slaves regard him with respect and affection. But there are many in Jamaica who will be trembling in their shoes, I can tell you.'

I could see the merit in this argument. If all plantations were run on Douglas's lines, then Jamaica would be a safer place. I asked him about the mutual benefits of trading with Africa instead of seizing its people and carrying them off into servitude.

'I don't think Mr Equiano's ideas will come to anything,' he said.

'Why not? There are huge benefits for everyone – be they British or African.'

'I don't deny that Africa is a rich continent,' he said. 'There are probably resources there that we do not even know about.'

'And commerce is in the interests of all, is it not?'

'Britain has centuries of experience in manufacturing, trading and commerce, but Africa has none.'

'Then they will acquire the experience, surely?'

'From whom? Mark my words, we will teach them to accept cheap goods at high prices, and give them a pittance for what they have to offer us in exchange. It will be trade of a kind, but for Britain's profit alone. You must realise, Robert, that no one who has been a master will relinquish his power willingly, and no one who has become rich will stand idly by while others prosper.'

I told him that his view of humanity was somewhat jaded, and that I believed that Equiano's book proved that men of all races could and should work together to improve their common lot.

'What common lot?' he said. 'Look at the colossal fortunes made from sugar! You're a part of this commerce – how has your lot been improved? Do you think Douglas is a rich man? Do you want to know whose lot has been improved by commerce in sugar? Let me tell you.' He leaned forward and stared at me very earnestly. 'Next time you are in Scotland, look at some of the fine country houses our esteemed Mr Adam and his brothers are busy designing and building.² Trespass if you dare on the new landscape gardens. Admire the ranks of servants in livery, bowing their heads to the nonentity to whom all of this belongs. Then ask yourself – how much did all of this cost, and from whence did the money come? You know the answer, but I shall tell you anyway – it came from the commerce in sugar, for which you and I are paid a trifling sum, and the slaves are paid nothing at all. Do you think that such a human parasite, sitting in his grand estate, cares one whit about the common lot? Do you imagine that he wishes to improve the lot of Negroes in Africa?'

I had never seen McLehose so agitated. I have considered what he said and there is some truth in it. If you consider the matter, the only people I know whose lives have materially improved are the slaves on this plantation for whom Mr Douglas cares so diligently. There is a devil of a paradox in this.

March 1st. I have been very busy, and have not had the opportunity to write these last few weeks. Mr Douglas has purchased four more slaves, who were brought here today. There is a great excitement on such occasions, and the villagers vie with each other for permission to adopt a newcomer and take him into their homes.

I watched as they arrived and stepped down from the wagon, looking about them in bewilderment. I know in my heart that slavery is wrong, and it offended my soul to see these men stand there, confused and frightened, not knowing what was to happen to them. I know that Mr Douglas will care for them, and ensure that they are treated with every consideration for the remainder of their lives, but that knowledge is not sufficient to counter the deep sense of pity that I felt today. I have been so accustomed to the slaves here – and to Adah, of course – that I had almost allowed myself to forget that the presence of each and every one of them here in Jamaica derives from a scene of degradation such as this.

I was pleased to see the warmth of the reception they received from those who clustered around them, patting them on the shoulder and treating them with every kindness; indeed, I had a lump in my throat as I saw their anxious expressions give way to shy smiles. At times like this I despise myself for the position I hold here, and for remaining in Jamaica so long.

March 16th. For several weeks some of us have had misgivings about Absalom, the muleteer. He is a man of some substance, as he possesses three carts, and employs workers to deploy them about the plantation. When cane is being cut they are kept fully occupied in hauling it to the mill, but at other times they are free to hire themselves out in the surrounding district, and they make a good living from this.

Once a week Mr Douglas sends them to Port Antonio to fetch in the plantation provisions. Recently we have had the suspicion that their loads are too small, and that they are purloining the goods for their own use, but when questioned they were quite adamant that that they had fetched everything they had been contracted to collect.

Yesterday we set a trap by placing lookouts along the way, and sure enough, at a spot just outside the plantation the carts halted and quantities of vegetables and salt fish were thrown into the bushes, presumably to be collected later. This is a serious matter, and it was reported at once to Mr Douglas who called all the overseers together, and summoned Absalom and his men to appear before us. They looked mightily nervous when they arrived, and shuffled uneasily, staring at the ground.

'Your load was short again,' said Mr Douglas.

'Nossuh,' said Absalom. 'Dat's what dey give us.'

'You are not telling the truth, Absalom,' said Mr Douglas. 'It will go badly for you if you continue to deny it. Now where are the missing goods?'

'Dere's nuttin' missin',' insisted Absalom, shaking his head.

'Very well. Come with us,' said Mr Douglas, and together we walked to the place where the carts had been seen to pause. Absalom and his men began to look more and more dejected as we neared the spot, and when Mr Douglas silently indicated the food in the bushes they hung their heads and said nothing.

'What is that, pray?' said Mr Douglas. 'How did it get there?'

'Nuttin' tuh do wid us,' said Absalom.

'Don't be foolish, man!' shouted Mr Douglas. 'Tell me the truth!'

'Mebbe it fall from de cart,' mumbled Absalom.

'Nonsense. You put it there. Didn't you?'

'Yessuh.'

'Right. Now how many times have you done this? Tell me the truth, mind.'

Absalom began to cry. 'Two, mebbe t'ree time,' he stammered. 'I's sorry, massa.'

'So you should be. I pay good money to make sure that everyone on this plantation is properly fed, and because of your greed, your own people are getting less to eat. It is disgraceful.'

Absalom said nothing. He knew the offence was a serious one, and on most plantations he would have been assured of a thorough flogging at the very least.

'Very well, Absalom,' said Mr Douglas. 'This is what is going to happen. You will take a cart back to Port Antonio and load it with salt fish. You will pay for it with your own money. When you return, you will go to the slave village and make sure that every family receives a share. Otherwise I shall confiscate your carts, set you to work in the great gang, and order a good whipping into the bargain. Do you understand?'

'Yessuh,' muttered Absalom.

'Is that fair?' said Douglas.

'Yessuh,' he said abjectly.

'Very well. Get moving and see that it is done today, or you can expect a visit from George.'

'Yessuh.'

So the matter is solved without recourse to the lash, which satisfies me greatly. The punishment is a fair and just one, because the victims of the crime – the plantation people – are properly compensated for their loss, and the sting of Absalom's humiliation will be sharper than any whip.

April 5th. Monday. These past few days we have had some trouble with a group of lads of about seventeen years of age – they have lately started in the second gang, and are finding the work harder than they expected. They have been turning up at the hospital – or the 'hothouse', as they call it – claiming to be unwell, and wasting Simpson's time. All the same, Simpson is obliged to treat their concerns seriously, for the death of a single slave through disease is a serious loss to the plantation. By today there were no less than ten patients, lying very comfortably in bed, and Simpson was in despair.

'I can find nothing wrong with any of them,' he said. 'They look perfectly healthy to me.' I reminded him how effective the cinchona treatment had proved for a case of malingering.

'I'd thought about it,' he said. 'Mr Douglas has another idea, and he'll be here soon.'

I had to leave at that point, and so I was not present when Mr Douglas arrived. When I returned later, the hospital was empty, and Simpson was smiling broadly.

'How did you manage it?' I asked.

He laughed. 'It was Mr Douglas. They weren't expecting him, and I think they were a bit frightened. But he enquired after their health very pleasantly, and hoped that they would soon feel better, and then said that it was a great shame that they would be missing the dancing he had arranged at the Great House this evening. Well, hardly had he left when they all jumped out of bed, saying that the rest had done them good, and off they went to work!'

'Is there really to be dancing at the Great House?'

'Well, yes, but it will take place on the lawn in front of the House, with Mr Douglas present. There will be no rum, for one thing, and if it becomes too rowdy then it can be stopped. The dancing is only for the second gang, and they are all youngsters. They will have a good time.'

In that he was certainly correct, for as I write it is about seven in the evening, and I have been round to watch the festivities. I have returned home, but even from here I can hear such a beating of drums and a blowing of conch shells!

Adah's head was nodding in time to the music as she sat in her accustomed place by me, and I could see her shoulders and hands making little involuntary movements. I pointed this out, and she smiled.

'I likes tuh dance.' she said.

'Well, go ahead,' I said.

'Yuh don' mind?'

'Certainly not.'

So, to the sound of the distant drums, she danced, and it was the most graceful and natural thing that I ever saw. Her body became sinuous, moving in ways I could never have imagined, her eyes gazing beyond mine all the while. I wonder if Herod was bewitched by Salome in the same way? In dance she becomes entirely herself – I was utterly captivated, and I know that I shall never forget this evening.

April 19th. I have spent two days with the plantation children, examining them for chigoes on their feet.[3] If these are not picked out they can quickly cause an infection that makes walking impossible, and can cause permanent damage. Some of the mothers do not understand that these injuries are entirely preventable, and must be shown how to check their children's feet, particularly after they have been walking in grass.

On some plantations, mothers suckle their children for as much as three years, hoping thereby to avoid field labour, but Mr Douglas insists that the little ones be weaned at twelve months and placed under the care of a matron. In this way the mother can be assured that her child is being well looked after, and so return with confidence to work, although some do take their children with them.

The children are never idle, and it is good to see them with their little baskets, put to task around the plantation, keeping it tidy, chattering and laughing as they go.

May 1st. We have a new Lieutenant-Governor in the august person of Thomas Howard, Earl of Effingham. The sum of £4000 is to be spent on a week of celebrations, comprising three days of riotous feasting in Spanish Town, and a further two days of foolish dissipation in Kingston. I cannot conceive of anything more profligate and pointless! The sum of money is disgraceful – it represents as much as this plantation will make in a year, or a salary like mine accumulated for an entire century![4] And what will he do for us, I wonder?

He will sit in his official residence, collecting a huge salary, and doing very little but disporting himself in a pompous manner.

May 22nd. This is one date in the calendar that is forever precious – five years ago my little Bess came into this world, and today in particular I sit here and wonder about her. Would I even recognise her if I saw her? Would she know me if we were to meet again?

June 6th. We now know why the *Bounty* never arrived with our cargo of breadfruit. There was a mutiny on board, and Captain Bligh was set adrift in a small boat and arrived back in Britain only after terrible privations and a journey of many months. The *Gazette* records that he was tried in March for cruelty, but completely exonerated. I do not know when we shall ever have our breadfruit. The pens hereabouts are very productive, and even in the last year or two I have been aware that supplies are easier to find.

June 12th. Currie is obnoxious, and I am finding it difficult to control my mounting anger. He finds a ready audience in Gilmour and his ilk for all sorts of scurrilous stories about me, such as the suggestion that it was my liaison with Adah that precipitated the death of Mary. His treatment of the slaves is not good, and more than once Mr Douglas has had to caution him about his over-zealous use of the lash. Some of the girls in the weeding gang follow him around and he treats them with a lecherous familiarity that causes resentment in all quarters. For some reason he and McLehose seem to get on well together, but then McLehose likes to impress, and Currie is eminently impressionable.

July 3rd. I have finally decided to return to Scotland, though I have told no one as yet except Adah. Mr Douglas was very cool about it the last time I raised the issue, but I have been careful with my salary, and believe that I shall have sufficient for the passages and other expenses. I say 'passages' because Adah is very determined to accompany me, and 'other expenses' because I shall be obliged to purchase her manumission before she will be permitted to leave the plantation. The latter subject will have to be broached with Mr Douglas at some point.

I am weary of life here. It is not that cruelty is prevalent, as elsewhere on the island, or that my duties are over-arduous, or that the climate is impossible to bear. The truth is I feel a repugnance about the exploitation of Negroes that I can no longer live with. No claim to generosity of spirit can alter the fact that I am to some degree an efficient agent in this terrible business. When I hear of the atrocities committed not a dozen miles from here my blood boils. There is nothing I can do about it – I am part of it! – I cannot challenge it or confront it without destroying myself – and although there are those who would censure me for running away, I think that I will be of more use back home, where I will be able to add an authoritative voice to the increasingly clamorous chorus raised against the trade. How many of those decent principled souls have seen it at first hand, as I have?

When I told Adah about my decision it was clear that she had never for an instant entertained the thought that I might leave Jamaica without taking her with me. She has every right to feel this way, and I am ashamed to admit that I had even allowed myself to consider the possibility of going without her. Here we pass freely in society, apart from the occasional coarse comment from Gilmour and his ilk. In Scotland it will be quite different, I am sure. I laughed aloud the first time I imagined the likely reaction of Fisher, that miserable, bibulous old lecher, when he meets me walking down the main street in Mauchline with Adah on my arm! Or Daddie Auld, who, I am sure, has never seen a black-skinned person in his life and would probably regard Adah as some form of sooty Satanic Manifestation and perish of apoplexy on the spot. How the tongues shall wag! Reading Equiano's book has been a valuable lesson for me, and has only strengthened my resolve. Why should I be ashamed of her? She's got twenty times more gumption than most of the simpering Mauchline *belles* I could mention. I have a broad enough back for both of us. Think what a picture we shall make on the platform of some abolitionist meeting – proof positive! Perhaps I should rein in my ambition a little, for there is the question of Adah's excessively direct manner of speech that might give offence in polite society.

I have had to deal with a hundred eager speculations about my homeland.

'So when we gets to Scotlan', we's gwine be rich? Live in a *castle*?'

'It's not quite like that,' I said. 'I'll never be rich. But I'll get work and we shall be comfortable. We shall live on the farm at Mossgiel, or I'll get a house somewhere.'

'Like Massa Douglas 'ouse?'

'A little more modest than that, my dear.'

'Wid a *slave* fuh cleanin' an' do de cookin'?' From her expression she seemed to find this a delightful prospect.

'We don't have slaves. Well, some very rich people might have Negroes in their households. I believe they dress them up in livery and train them as servants, like Mr Douglas does. But it's quite uncommon.'

'Yuh don' 'ave no slaves in Scotlan'?'

'Not really. You only find slaves in places like Jamaica and the other islands where there is sugar to be produced.'

She thought about this for a moment. 'So dere's no negers in Scotlan'?'

'Very few. Before I came here I don't think I had ever seen a Negro.'

'So de white folks gwine see me, and dey's gwine t'ink *wow*, I ain't seen nuttin' lak *dat* befo'!'

'They can think what they like,' I said, and tried to reassure her. There is no doubt that it will be a challenge for us both. I must raise the manumission question with Mr Douglas, but I shall not do so until I have made enquiries and secured our passages.

July 18th. The Sabbath. I had met Adah's parents before, but today I was taken to visit them at home for the first time. They were nervous at having an overseer in their wee 'but and ben', and kept apologising constantly for the merest trifles, but I told them to be at their ease. The wooden walls were whitewashed outside, and inside had been painstakingly scoured until they had turned soft grey; the furniture was plain and scrubbed, and the floor had been swept clean. Some simple shelving held their few possessions. At first they would not sit in my presence, and it was only with some difficulty that I persuaded them to do so. Food was produced – they must have killed one of their chickens in honour of my visit, for that was what they served me. They apologised in anticipation that it might not be to my liking, but I assured them that it was delicious, which it was. They had never sat at table with a white man before, and seemed quite over-whelmed by the occasion. They would respond to questions that I put to them, though I sensed that they were worried in case their answers might seem unsatisfactory. Adah did most of the talking, and as the afternoon wore on the atmosphere grew more relaxed.

I spoke about Scotland, and how we lived there, to which they listened with great attention. In case they entertained any doubts on the matter, I told them that Adah was going as my companion, not as my slave, and that before our voyage I would procure her manumission. They nodded gravely and said that they were pleased to hear it.

We parted on very good terms, and I promised that I would call again. As I left, I could see that all of the neighbours were watching me, although they were pretending not to. One or two waved at me in a friendly fashion, and I believe my reputation with the plantation people stands pretty high, for they know that I treat Adah well.

August 3rd. For the first time in my life I have watched a man die – the
most dreadful spectacle imaginable. I wish I could blot the picture
from my mind, but I can think of little else. God help us all!

The accident happened at the mill. The machinery consists of
two massive cylinders, set vertically, and with only the very narrow-
est of gaps between them. These are set in motion by a sort of capstan
to which two or three oxen are hitched, and as they steadily walk
around in a wide circle, the cylinders are made to rotate slowly in
opposite directions so that the cane is drawn in between them and
crushed. The bagasse emerges at the other side and is carted away to
be dried, while the cane juice runs down into a channel that leads to
the boiling house.

The man engaged in feeding the cane into the mill was careless,
that is the long and the short of it. Somehow his hand became stuck
between two cane stems, and as they were drawn in, he found
himself unable to extricate it. He shouted out, but there was a great
deal of noise and bustle, and it was only when he began to scream
that we realised what was happening. I at once shouted out to the
man in charge of the oxen to bring them to a halt, but he did not hear.

Beside the mill there is always a sharp axe hanging on the wall. I
had never realised why it was there until today – its ghastly purpose
is to sever the limb of anyone whose hand is drawn between the
rollers. The man in charge took it up, but it was too late – the poor
fellow's whole arm had disappeared between the rollers with a
distinct crackling noise, and the juices in the channel beneath were
starting to run crimson with blood. His screams were terrible to
hear, all the more so because there was nothing we could do for him.
By the time someone managed to halt the team of oxen, his arm had
been wrenched from its socket, and lay crushed and mangled on the
other side. We reversed the motion of the rollers, and he fell clear,
huge jets of blood spurting from the gory mess on his shoulder
where his arm had once been. Within a minute he was dead.

Word of the accident spread rapidly around the plantation. The
victim's woman ran up, sobbing and beating at her head and face,
staring at the body in wide-eyed incomprehension. The rest of us
stood around feeling useless. The death was unnecessary: we knew
the machine was dangerous, and the phrase on everyone's lips was
'if only'. If only he had held the cane differently – if only he had
made himself heard sooner – if only the team of oxen could have
been halted at once – then there would not have been this tragic
outcome, and he would have been going about his work cheerfully
as usual, instead of lying lifeless on the ground.

This sorry business meant that we had to clean the mill and flush away every vestige of blood and torn flesh. It seemed difficult to believe that the work of the mill could possibly resume after such a shocking event, but there was nothing else for it but to set to work with brooms and buckets of water and wash the place down – a melancholy task indeed.

August 24th. I am unable to sleep properly for thinking of that poor man who was killed by the mill. His funeral was held the following day, but this time I absented myself. I am thinking too much about mortality at present.

I never knew that Mr Douglas considered himself to be a musician until today. I had gone to the Great House to fetch papers, and after we had concluded our business he produced a fiddle, and tucked it under his chin.

'Here's a wee Scottish air for you,' he said, and commenced a vigorous scraping, torturing the catgut to produce sounds that would have insulted the dying agonies of a sow under the hand of a butcher. I did not recognise the air, and hurried away before he had a chance to play any more. A few weeks ago I would have found the incident amusing, but I have sunk into a kind of melancholy that lies over me like a heavy cloud, and I merely found it irritating.

September 3rd. Appalling news – McLehose has a wife, and she will be in Jamaica early in the New Year, on board the *Roselle*! He came round and confided in me this morning, hoping for my sympathy. She is an Edinburgh woman by the name of Nancy, the daughter of a surgeon who died about eight years ago. Apparently her uncle is Lord Craig, a buffoon with literary pretensions, or so McLehose says. It seems that the reason for McLehose's emigration to Jamaica was an estrangement between the two of them.

'She *claims*,' he said, 'that I was cruel to her, and that I drank too much. But it's not true, I swear it. I'm not saying I didn't enjoy a glass or two, and I won't deny that we exchanged words on occasion, but that's just the way the woman is. Everything blown out of all proportion. I thought she'd have forgotten about me by this time.'

'I don't know what to say.'

'Don't tell old Douglas, for God's sake,' he said, pacing up and down on my balcony. 'I've upset him enough over Ann, and I don't want to lose my position here.'

'But why is she coming here?' I asked. 'If it's all over between you, why on earth is she doing this?'

'Oh, she's talking about a reconciliation,' he said. 'She sent me a letter. You know the kind of thing, despite all of my faults she feels duty bound to fulfil her matrimonial obligations, et cetera, et cetera. She thinks that perhaps we could make some sort of a fresh start, that kind of nonsense. Of course it's out of the question. Promise me you won't tell Douglas. And promise me you won't breathe a word of this to Ann. I don't know what she'd do to me if she found out.'

'I'll keep this to myself,' I said, 'but what will happen when she arrives here? Man, I don't envy you.'

He grunted. 'I'll have to go to Kingston and head her off in some way. I'll try to procure her a passage on the next boat back, even returning on the *Roselle*, if that's possible.'

'But what will you tell her? She will have been six weeks at sea, and if you are expecting her to get back on board to face the prospect of another six, then you will have to conjure up some convincing arguments to place before her.'

'I'll find a little room in Kingston. Something dirty and cramped. I'll tell her that I'm living there, unable to get work, that I'm no good to anyone, and explain to her that she is wasting her time with me.'

'If she's come all that way to reconcile with you, then I hardly think she'll be put off by that,' I said. 'Before you know where you are she'll have moved you into better quarters, bought you a new wardrobe of clothes, and she'll be marching you round Kingston looking for a job. Besides, you are known in Kingston. Any chance meeting with an acquaintance could give the game away. You'll have to think of a better plan.'

'I just don't know what to do,' he said miserably. 'Help me, Robert, for God's sake.'

'I'm equally at a loss,' I said. 'I'll think about it, of course. You know that I am planning to return to Scotland.'

'My God! When?'

'As soon as I can.'

'Alone? Or are you taking . . .?'

'My specimen? Aye, Adah will be coming with me.'

'That'll cause a stir!' he said, with a chuckle. 'But seriously, promise me you won't go until I have sorted out this business with Nancy. I need someone to confide in.'

'What about Currie?' I said.

He looked at me sharply. 'He's only a boy,' he said. 'To be honest, I am beginning to find him tiresome. You and I – well, we are men of the world, are we not?'

I promised that I shall delay my departure until such time as he has resolved his situation. He sat with my rum-jug and bemoaned his fate for the best part of an hour before leaving me. Poor wretch. The truth is the situation is entirely of his own making and he has no one to blame but himself, but I felt sorry for him all the same. I find myself wondering what kind of a woman embarks on a journey across the oceans of the world to win back the man who deserted her.

September 17th. Currie continues to be offensive and difficult. Adah and I were out in the plantation together early this morning, and when he saw us he was at pains to swagger up and accost us in an over-familiar manner.

'Well, well, Mr Burns, so this will be Adah?' he said, looking at her with a leer. 'Are you not going to introduce us?'

'I don't think that will be necessary,' I said. 'You ken perfectly well who she is.'

'Aye, she's a bonnie wee thing,' he said. 'What do you say to me, my dearie?' He leered at her again, showing a mouthful of bad teeth, and stretched out his hand to pat her shoulder.

'Don't dare touch her,' I said.

'What are you going to do about it?' he said, and made to fondle her neck. I clenched my fist, but Adah moved more quickly than I did and brought her knee up to connect with his private parts. She did so with such force that he fell to the ground and rolled around gasping, and clutching at his bandileers. To make matters worse for him, this public humiliation was greeted with a great roar of approving laughter from the other overseers.

'Sorry 'bout dat, Massa Currie,' said Adah, and we walked on.

'You can certainly look after yourself,' I said in admiration.

'He nuh trubble me nuh mo',' she said.

We learned later that Currie went to the Great House with some story of having been violently assaulted by an insolent slave, and had demanded that she be flogged, but Mr Douglas had already heard of what has happened, and gave him short shrift.

There is no doubt that today's little incident will deepen his dislike of me. There is a sly, sneaking side to him that I distrust.

September 26th. McLehose has been here almost every evening for a week. When he sees Adah he feigns a fearful expression, and covers his privates. She found this very amusing the first time it happened, but the joke has become rather threadbare.

We sit and drink rum together, and mostly discuss plans for dealing with Mrs McLehose when she arrives. His mood appears to swither – one day he is convinced that he will handle the situation perfectly, but then the doubts and fears creep back and he fears the worst.

'There's still plenty of time,' he insisted this evening. 'Four months at least.'

'The time will soon pass,' I said, 'and we have still not agreed on a course of action.'

'Yes, we must have a plan.'

'*You* must have a plan,' I said. 'It has nothing to do with me. She is your wife, after all. But I still think that honesty is the best policy. You must tell Ann everything.'

'Tell Ann?' he said, with a humourless laugh. 'You don't know what manner of woman she is! She will be enraged.'

'She strikes me as the kind of woman who will be even more enraged when she comes face-to-face with a Mrs McLehose she never even knew existed, only to discover that you have known for several months that she was coming here.'

'You're right,' he said. 'But how do I tell her?'

'Just tell her the truth. You have been estranged for many years; she comes here uninvited; you will be sending her home again directly.'

He nodded, and agreed to talk to her along the lines I had suggested. However I *know* that he will not be able to tell Ann. She is a very formidable character, and I tremble to think what she would do to him – it would certainly be far worse than the treatment meted out by Adah to Currie!

October 4th. Heavy rain, and field work has had to stop. There is little for me to do, so I have poured myself a nipperkin of rum. I was casting around for something to read, but could find nothing except *Pamela*. I looked at the first two or three pages, but soon lost interest. The book is perfectly hopeless. Perhaps I should lend it to McLehose as the basis of a *modus vivandi* with Ann!

October 14th. The Sabbath. The Reverend Caldwell left Jamaica recently, and his place has been taken by a fellow by the name of Grubb. Caldwell was effete and useless but a decent enough fellow at heart. At least he had the common sense to restrict his religion to sentimental platitudes, so that if he did no good then at least he did no harm. This Grubb is different, as we discovered when he came to the estate today as part of his 'pastoral duties'. There is a refectory where we take our meals sometimes – a great barn of a place next to the kitchen, and confoundedly hot – and Mr Douglas insisted that we all congregate there for an hour in order to participate in Divine Service. Some of the drivers and older Negroes who have been baptised were bidden to join us, taking up their places at the back.

After a few prayers the Reverend launched himself into a sermon that took, as its starting point, words of Noah from the Holy Book. As I write I have my Bible before me, and I shall copy the text: *And he said: Cursed be Caanan, a servant of servants shall he be to his brethren. And he said: Blessed be the Lord God of Shem; and Canaan shall be his servant. God shall enlarge Japheth, and he shall dwell in the tents of Shem, and Caanan shall be his servant.*[5] We were reminded that Caanan was the son of Ham, who had dishonoured his own father Noah by inadvertently catching sight of him when he was lying naked and drunk on his bed. I confess I was unsure as to why Canaan should have been punished rather than his father, or why Noah himself should not have been reprimanded for his insobriety, so I listened with interest to what he had to say.

'Ham and his descendants practised all manner of heathen abominations!' he declared. 'From their loins sprang the Negro race, just as we are descended from Shem and Japheth! An omniscient God knew that this moral degradation would occur, and that is why he so wisely ordained that slavery should be *a natural condition for the Negro!*'

Having proved his case, he cited evidence. He reminded us of Abraham, whose slaves numbered three hundred and eighteen. Moreover his wife had a slave called Hagar who ungratefully ran away, and was commanded by the angel of the Lord to return to her mistress – in other words, to know her rightful place. He went on to allude to the rules governing the hiring of slaves, and the ownership of their children, a matter of some interest to me. Not surprisingly, the text clearly states that the children shall be the property of the master.[6]

In short, the Bible provides ample justification for slavery in general, and a very perfect proof of the fact that, foreseeing their debased natures, God had ordained that Negroes should be slaves.

'Now, we are all Christians here,' he said, looking at us as if challenging anyone to deny it. 'Is there any one of us who can dispute these facts? In fact, *would it not be blasphemy to do so?* There are those who argue that it is a sin to enslave another. But if slavery is a sin now, then it must have been a sin at the time it was ordained by God. Can there by any blasphemy more disgraceful and unpardonable? Not only to deny the Word of God, but to declare it as sinful?'[7]

Grubb's proof of the biblical justification for slavery was brought to a close with a series of threats, describing, at great length and in the minutest detail, what horrible torments awaited blasphemers in the next world. I am weary of hearing of a gloomy heaven reserved for the nineteen thousandth part of the tithe of mankind, while Hell awaits the vast residue of Mortals, regardless of the good or ill they have done.

Mr Douglas turned to me and nodded in a kind of grim satisfaction. 'We need more of that kind of preaching around here!' he said. 'This is the sort of thing the Wilberforces of this world should be thinking about. Getting the facts straight, that's what we need.' I could have disputed the matter with him, but I saw little point in trying. Why is it that a religious turn of mind so often has a tendency to narrow and illiberalise the heart?

October 17th. I am nursing a painful and swollen set of knuckles this evening, but I cannot say I am sorry for it. That boy Currie finally went too far and he has learned what it is to cross me. The boiling house is a dangerous place and the process is a delicate one that has to be supervised carefully. Mindful of what happened to Scipio, I have been more vigilant than ever in ensuring that the work is done properly. Today I had my whole team at work when Currie walked in with that arrogant swagger of his. Ignoring me, he went over to one of my men, who was employed in stirring the cooling juice, and made a gesture towards the door that he had left open.

'There's a cart to be unloaded,' he said. 'Get outside there and lend a hand.' The man looked at him, and then at me. I told him to get on with his work. Still ignoring me, Currie went up to him with a most insolent expression.

'Didn't ye hear me?' he said. 'Get outside. I need ye.'

'Stay where you are,' I said, and motioned to Currie to follow me outside, which he did with bad grace.

'You can't do this,' I said, with as much patience as I could muster. 'He's needed here. Go and find someone else.'

'Ye canna tell me whit tae dae,' he said.

'Aye I can.'

'I'm an overseer as weel! Ye can gie orders tae yer vicious wee neger bitch, but no' tae me,' he said. At this point all my self-control deserted me, and I delivered him a blow to the face that sent him crashing to the ground. He lay there for a minute, then got to his feet, with blood streaming from his nose and mouth.

'Ye bastard, ye bastard!' he shouted, coming towards me with fists flying, at which I struck him to the ground again. Some of the others came running up and pulled us apart. I hope this has taught him a lesson. It seems a terrible to thing to admit, but in honesty I felt a Grubb-like righteousness as my fist smashed into his face.

November 2nd. I went to see Mr Douglas today to give him formal notice that I had decided to leave Jamaica early in the New Year in order to make a fresh start in life. I have to say that I had been dreading some form of confrontation, but he was reasonable about my request, as I have been here for four years now. When I asked about manumission for Adah he said that he'd been expecting something of the sort, and that he would be prepared to put matters in hand for forty pounds.

'I know it's more than you earn in a year, Burns,' he said, 'but she's ripe, and she would have been good for four or five healthy little ones. The price of slaves being what it is – well, I think it is a fair price.' I had been putting money aside, so we were able to conclude the bargain directly.

'You're taking Adah with you, are you?' he said. 'Is that wise?'

'I see no reason why she should not come with me,' I said.

'Don't you? What kind of life will she have in Scotland, may I ask?'

'I shall do everything in my power to ensure her well-being.'

'That's easy enough to say,' he said, focusing on me intently from beneath these vast eyebrows. 'But she will be an oddity.'

'What do you mean?'

'Please do not be disingenuous with me, Robert,' he said. 'You understand my meaning very well. You propose to take her back and treat her as your wife. She will be the subject of unwelcome and unwholesome gossip; heads will turn wherever she goes and every day she will have to suffer ridicule and worse. Is it not a cruelty to take her to live in Scotland?'

'Perhaps it is time that people realised that there is no reason why she should not occupy any position she pleases. She will be a free woman.'

He shook his head. 'Brave talk, Robert. But misguided all the same. She will never belong in Scotland.'

'She belongs with me,' I insisted, with some heat. 'And if I am to be in Scotland then she has every right to be there as well.'

'Mauchline is not Kingston,' he said. 'We are surrounded by Negroes here, and we think nothing of it. Liaisons such as yours occasion little comment. You know my views, and I regard myself as liberal-minded, with considerable knowledge of the matter. Believe me, in Scotland you will confront narrowness compounded by ignorance. Your lives will be made a misery.'

'If my countrymen are so narrow-minded,' I said, 'then it is time they faced the truth.'

He raised his eyebrows. 'Do you think you can accomplish that alone?' he said. 'Do you think a humble book-keeper, newly re-turned from the Indies with his manumitted Negro mistress, will be in any position to convince Scottish society at large that such a relationship is *natural and proper?'*

'People will draw their own conclusions.'

He sighed heavily. 'They will indeed, they will indeed. You have been away from Scotland for a long time. There is great debate, and much passion on both sides. I urge you to think carefully.'

These thoughts have passed through my head a thousand times. I'm sure I'm strong enough to cope with whatever happens, but all the same it's depressing to hear the argument laid out in such blunt terms. At any rate, Adah will soon be a free woman, and her joy at hearing this news, together with her excitement at the prospect of leaving Jamaica, have conspired to raise my spirits again. The way ahead will have its pitfalls, but I am confident that we can prevail.

I have sent a letter to Gilbert, advising him of my intentions – he should have it by the year's end. It was a surprisingly difficult letter to write: I started it a dozen times, only to find myself tossing the scored-out sheet on to the floor and having to start again, for I was unsure of how to tell him about Adah. In my heart of hearts I feel ashamed of my own cowardice in this regard, for although I scorn the censure of those foolish people who would point fingers at us, and for whom I have no respect, there is no doubt that Adah would present a shock to him if she were suddenly to appear with me at Mossgiel. I have told him that she will come to Scotland as a *former* slave, now a free woman; have made much of her good qualities as a housekeeper; praised her steadfastness, and declared my belief that he will find her in every respect delightful. I took the opportunity to ask after Jean, the twins, and my darling Bess, who will now be in her seventh year.

November 13th. Adah is free! I paid over the forty pounds to Mr Douglas, and he has drawn up the document of manumission. He has been to Kingston and entered it in the registry, returning this morning with a copy, which he handed to me.

'Keep it safe,' he said. 'And make sure that Adah understands how important it is. There are plenty of people outside this plantation who would take one look at Adah and assume her to be a runaway. I don't just mean in Jamaica either. If you are determined to take her back with you, make sure you look after her. If there is any doubt cast on her status, then that document is your only safeguard.'

The document itself expresses the absolute dominion that one man can claim over his fellow, though Mr Douglas has never abused his position in that regard. It runs as follows:

Jamaica – To all men unto whom these presents shall come: I, Charles Douglas, of the parish of Portland, in the said island, plantation proprietor, send greeting: Know ye, that I the aforesaid Charles Douglas, for, and in consideration of the sum of forty pounds current money of the said island, to me in hand paid, and to the intent that a Negro woman slave, named Adah Mawunyaga Adumensa, shall and may become free, have manumitted, emancipated, enfranchised, and set free, the aforesaid Negro woman slave, named Adah Mawunyaga Adumensa, for ever; hereby giving, granting, and releasing unto her, the said Adah Mawunyaga Adumensa, all right, title, dominion, sovereignty, and property, which, as lord and master over the aforesaid Adah Mawunyaga Adumensa, I have had, or which I now have, or by any means whatsoever I may or can hereafter possibly have over her, the aforesaid Negro, for ever. In witness whereof, I the abovesaid Charles Douglas, have unto these presents set my hand and seal, this tenth day of November, in the year of our Lord one thousand seven hundred and ninety.

Charles Douglas

Signed, sealed, and delivered in the Presence of Andrew McIntosh.

Kingston, Jamaica

Registered the within manumission, at full length, this eleventh day of November, 1790, in *liber* D. Andrew McIntosh, Register.

I showed it to Adah, and repeated what Mr Douglas had said. I do not think that she understood much of the lawyer's language of the document, but the salient fact that I stressed to her was that she had awakened that morning as a slave, and subject to control by another, now she was mistress of herself, and this sheet of paper proved it to the whole world.

'So me a free woman?' she said.

'Completely free,' I said. 'From now on you can go where you please and do what you please.'

'So Massa Douglas cyan't sell me? An' he cyan't ax me tuh do nuttin'?'

'No, he can't.'

She wrinkled her nose. 'Me nuh feel diff'rent. Anyway, I *likes* de plantation.'

'That's because of Mr Douglas, You are lucky. Imagine if you had belonged to Mr Thistlewood, or Mr MacPherson.'

'Mmm,' she said, coming close, and rubbing herself against me in a way calculated to provoke immediate ardour. 'Is I still yuh *specimen* even if I's free?' I told her that she was a very fine specimen: indeed, a perfectly delightful specimen. I shall draw a veil over how this little scene ended.

November 20th. In the light of my decision to take Adah to Scotland,
I have been considering the lot of white women on this island, and
I believe it is a poor one. Many are brought here with the expectation
of living the lives of fine ladies in careless indolence, but the
behaviour of their menfolk drives them instead into a lonely seclu-
sion. How quickly do these *grandes dames* discover that their hus-
bands have strayed from the nuptial bed? Not only are they relegated
to a cold and purely honorific marital role – when their sons are
born, they are suckled by some Negro wet nurse and soon grow to
emulate their fathers, so that husbands and sons alike *sont tous perdus*,
and all that is left is the emptiness of the Great House. Mr Douglas
is an honourable exception in this respect, for his behaviour towards
his wife is exemplary, but I fear there can be few like him. Mary is
dead, poor soul, and I have nothing to reproach myself for, but had
she still been alive, I wonder whether I would have been like Mr
Douglas? In any event, I have Adah, and could not be more content.

News came today that Effingham, our Lieutenant-Governor, is
to quit his post, for his health is very poor, and daily made worse by
the climate. I believe that he is returning to become Master of the
Mint. In the meantime, Major-General Williamson shall act in a
temporary capacity.

November 22nd. I feel compelled to take issue with Mr Hume in what
he asserts about the Negro people. Mr Douglas has lent me a book
of his essays and suggested that I read it with care, and there was
something smug about his countenance as he handed it to me that
put me *en garde.* Sure enough, it turns out to be plain and palpable
nonsense; a diatribe against a world of men whose sin is *not to be of
a white complexion,* and *not to be English.* My indignation is com-
pounded by a shamed regret that these views come from a distin-
guished compatriot. To be sure he has been dead these past fourteen
years, which circumstance mitigates the offence a little, but had he
been alive today, would he have compared Equiano to a parrot that
'speaks a few words plainly'?[8] Would he have dismissed the skills of
our coopers and distillers as 'slender accomplishments'? How easy
it is to disparage those of whom one understands nothing! His essay
reeks of the lamp in the cloistered study – the self-righteous
ramblings of a man who has seen nothing of the world but lays claim
to the most perfect understanding of it.

The tragedy is that good men like Mr Douglas find excuses in
such sanctimonious philosophy for their beliefs, though they stand
contrary to plain reason and clear evidence. Mr Hume would have

us believe that the Irish are by nature dishonest; that the Danes are dull-witted; that Jews are fraudsters; that the Greeks are cowards and drunkards, and that Negroes will gladly exchange their wives, children and mistresses for a cask of brandy – *voilà!* – all mankind dismissed with a wave of the quill but for the English who, he sagely opines, are the most remarkable of any people that ever were in this world. What he makes so bold as to postulate, as I understand it, is the notion that the further removed a nation finds itself from England, be it measured by distance or by the skin colour of its hapless inhabitants, then the more ignoble and debased its people must be.

I do not propose to discuss this with Mr Douglas – he will only wax indignant and tell me I have not read it correctly, or miscon-strued its meaning, and then there will ensue one of these endless lectures that leave me with an aching head. I have been prompted to scribble a few lines as follows:

To David Hume

Alas, poor Hume! All lost, you rove
Through Learning's lush and verdant grove;
From Academe's exalted portal
You scorn your worthy fellow-mortal!
False Certainties you do expound
While humble Truths crowd all around,
But, blind to these, you dare to preach
Of matters far beyond your reach.
Intoxicated with your fame,
You quite forget from whence you came:
A man – tho' rob'd in scholar's guise,
And, like me, born 'neath Scotia's skies –
With no more right than any other
To sit in judgement on his brother!

I had planned to make a copy and leave it in the volume for Mr Douglas to find, but on reflection I have abandoned this idea.

December 7th. I have been making enquiries about the passage home, and it should be possible to arrange this without difficulty. To think that within a few weeks I shall see my mother again, and Gilbert, and of course my little Bess! If old Armour has mellowed, perhaps I may even see Jean and the twins. I am feeling excited by this prospect, and my spirits grow lighter by the day. Adah is also looking forward to the voyage, though it lies beyond anything of her previous experience, and I sense that she is more apprehensive than she would care to admit. I long to be in Scotland with Adah – to take her to places that are dear to me; to walk with her in the woods around Alloway, and to share my country with her. For four years I have been a part of her world, soon she will be a part of mine.

December 26th. We spent our last Christmas in Jamaica very quietly. We exchanged a few little gifts and that was all. Tomorrow we propose to visit Adah's parents again, and this time I shall take some rum with me. We shall speak at greater length about Scotland and show them Adah's manumission. They will be sad to be losing a daughter, but I believe that they trust in my integrity, and I shall not fail them. A new year is almost upon us, and I sense that it will be a momentous one!

1791

January 2nd. The Sabbath. We hope that we shall be able to sail at the end of February. Adah still amuses me with her fanciful notions of what Scotland will be like, and plies me with questions constantly.

The weather is very clear today and we have been out and about. I have begun to take for granted the striking beauty of the landscape, and it is only on days like this, when I deliberately take the leisure to appreciate my surroundings, that I realise how blessed this island is. A few minutes walk brought us to the summit of a little hill from where we can look down over the town, with its two harbours, and Navy Island beyond. The East Harbour is particularly beautiful, being enclosed almost entirely like a lagoon by two narrow arms of land that seem to embrace the anchorage and its still waters. Under a cerulean heaven, the ocean stretches to the horizon – the water a marvellously dark blue, shading to pale sapphire or white over the sandy shallows. Cotton is produced on one of the plantations on the hillside nearby, and the crop has recently begun to ripen so that the pods are in full blossom and the bushes present a very beautiful appearance. The whiteness of their stalks, opposed to the greenness of their leaves, presents from a distance a scene not unlike an Ayrshire hillside in winter. Behind us are the precipitous slopes of the Blue Mountains, thickly wooded with verdant greenery stretching into hazy distance. From here we have a clear view of our plantation, an ordered and pleasing picture, in contrast to the wildness of nature that surrounds it. The mill, the boiling house and the distillery, with all of their ancillary buildings, cluster at the very centre, with neat roads and pathways radiating out from it. Half-hidden by trees to the left we can see the overseers' quarters, and the roof of the Great House. Over to the right are the slave villages. The cane fields, divided by the drainage ditches, make up a vast rectilinear patchwork extending to the foot of the hills on whose gentle slopes are the pens where the cattle are kept, and the provisions for the plantation are produced.

For me it was a moment almost of epiphany – a manifestation of what, to all outward appearances, is heaven on earth. With my arm around Adah's waist I felt as Adam and Eve must have felt in Eden.

However this is no Eden. Beyond the boundaries of this plantation lie nearly seven hundred other estates, on which nearly three hundred thousand Negroes toil in conditions too wretched to imagine; where starvation is commonplace; disease and sickness rampant, and vicious cruelty an everyday occurrence. The island is

like a powder keg with a fire beneath it. That is why I am glad that
Adah and I shall be leaving soon: we would both wish to remember
the Jamaica of our hillside view.

January 20th. Mrs McLehose will be here in about three weeks, and
James is quite beside himself with worry. We sat outside in the shade
of the mill house today in further discussion. The air was full of the
smell of bagasse, and all around us were sounds of activity – the
shouting of the men; the stamp of hooves and the thud of the
machinery. It was a brilliantly clear day, and there was a clear vista of
the bay beneath us. It was idyllic, but a more morose individual than
McLehose it would have been hard to imagine.

'Less than a month!' he kept saying. 'What am I going to do?'

'Listen,' I said. 'Make a clean breast of things. When the time
comes, go to Kingston, meet her, and find comfortable lodgings for
her. Then you have to explain to her that you regard the marriage as
over. Tell her that you had honestly believed that she felt the same
way, and that in the interim you've met someone else, and so cannot
possibly reconcile. Tell her that she's free to divorce you on her
return to Scotland. Make sure she's comfortable, and has enough
money to pay for a return voyage when it is convenient for her. Then
simply take your leave.'

He considered the matter and agreed that this was the only way to
proceed, though he looked very unhappy about it. For what seemed
like the hundredth time he moaned about what a narrow-minded and
foolish woman she was; how she had made his life a misery with her
petty criticisms; how her head was full of Calvinistic piety; how she
passed judgement on his worthy acquaintances; how she disapproved
of his innocent pleasures – in short, how his entire existence com-
prised being censured; rebuked; reproved; chidden; humiliated;
scolded; reproached; berated and blamed. He cited me a dozen
instances to prove how kind and generous he had been towards her,
and a dozen more to demonstrate how entirely unreasonable she had
been in return. Indeed I feel I know Mrs McLehose, and can already
envision the beetle-browed, peevish shrew approaching Jamaica,
nursing her wrath to keep it warm! I do not blame McLehose for
wanting nothing to do with a woman like that!

25th January. Thirty-two years ago a snell Ayrshire wind ushered a
squalling Robert Burns into this world, with the malevolent expec-
tation of freezing him to the marrow as he laboured in the frosty
fields as a miserable farmer and then blowing the dust of obscurity
over his grave after a wretched handful of illness-wracked years.

Today I feel the tropical sun on my back; I am blessed with the gentlest and kindest of female companions; my salary is accruing; I feel fit and well; that damned rheumatic fever has not returned, and my duties are straightforward. Although I am well into the middle years of my life, I feel young and full of *joie de vivre,* ideally prepared to return and make something of a name for myself in Scotland!

February 13th. The Sabbath. McLehose has gone missing. He was nowhere to be found on the plantation yesterday, which angered Douglas a good deal, and did not return home at night, which has made Ann furious, and consumed by all manner of speculations. By my reckoning the *Roselle* is due to dock at Kingston any day now so I assume that he has gone there to meet his wife. Of course I am sworn to secrecy and can say nothing that would alleviate the concerns of these good people.

As our departure draws closer, I enjoy a lightness of spirit that I have not experienced for many a day. I feel determined to return to Scotland with Adah and do all I can to assist the abolitionist cause. The qualms I felt when writing to Gilbert have disappeared. Despite all my blundering prose and convoluted justifications everything comes down to a brutally simple question – *are you ashamed of your union with Adah?* To which the unequivocal answer is – *no!* In my mind, this inevitably raises the question of marriage, though this is something we have never discussed. As with Mary, we would exchange Bibles. We cannot be married here, for the Reverend Grubb would never consent to conjoin a white man and a black woman in holy matrimony – doubtless on sound and unimpeachable Old Testament principles. As for Daddie Auld in Mauchline – no, no, no! – the very idea is unthinkable. However I feel it will help our cause if we were to be married. I also minded Adah's thoughts about marrying a white man and having light children, and although I thought little about it at the time, perhaps Mr Douglas is right, and she has had this ambition from the outset.

February 14th. St Valentine. Betrothed to Adah! I wrote a few feeble lines last evening, painfully aware of my poetic efforts some four years ago, when their recipient was Mary. I sat Adah down and told her that I had something very important to discuss with her. She did so obediently, and, kneeling at her feet, I delivered myself of the following:

A Proposal

Your skin is black as raven's breast
While mine's as pale's the snow:
And yet we two alike are bless'd
As hand in hand we go.

You are the mistress of my soul
Whose love I fondly craved:
For when my heart you gently stole,
I was the one enslaved!

I pray to thee on bended knee
To walk with me through life:
Oh! promise me that you will be,
My true, my wedded wife!

'Yuh wants tuh *marry* yuh specimen?' she exclaimed. 'Oh Lordy!'
'I should be honoured. I want to take you back to Scotland as my wife, and as a free woman there is no reason why we cannot marry.'
'Yuh wants me tuh be *Missiz Burns?*'
'Aye, I do. What do you say?'
'I says yes! Oh yes, Massa Rab!'
'Not *Massa* Rab,' I said. 'Rab will do just fine. You don't ever need to say 'Massa' again to anyone, remember?'
She flung herself at me and smothered me with kisses, then asked me to read the poem again, which I did several times, explaining some of the words she did not understand.
'I never 'ad no pome written fuh me befo',' she said. I explained about the exchange of Bibles, and proposed that we perform the ceremony on board ship in a few weeks' time, in the presence of the Captain, to which she readily agreed. In fact she was *toute boulversée* by this turn of events, and so hugely grateful for both 'pome' and proposal that she demonstrated her appreciation by pinning me to the bed and giving me a 'doing' that made my bones rattle.

February 16th. Still no sign of McLehose, and more's the pity. At about seven last evening Amos called on me, saying that the master required my attendance forthwith. I went to him directly and found him sitting grim-faced in his study.
'Have you seen McLehose yet?' he asked abruptly. I replied that I had not seen him for some days, but that perhaps he had gone to Kingston on business.
'Business? If there is any business to be done in Kingston I

would have known about it,' he said. 'It is really confoundedly inconvenient.'

'If there is anything I can do, then I shall be glad to oblige.'

'There isn't much *you* can do,' he replied with a snort. 'The man is married, apparently, and his wife is here. She arrived about half an hour ago, having endured a vile journey from Kingston on her own. She was not met at the quay when the *Roselle* docked, despite having written to her husband. You'd think that the man might at least have extended that small courtesy to his wife. Damn it, man, I had no idea that there *was* a Mrs McLehose! I would not have tolerated this Rivvere business otherwise. What in God's name is the man playing at? Did you know the man was married?'

I replied that I did know, and that I had earnestly counselled McLehose to be honest with both women.

'Well he hasn't been anything of the kind,' grumbled Douglas. 'So what in Heaven's name am I supposed to say to his wife?'

'Where is she?' I asked.

'Upstairs with Mrs Douglas. She needs a complete change of clothes and a sponging down. You know what the journey from Kingston is like. What am I to say to her when she asks for her husband? What will she think when she goes over to his house and finds Rivvere there, with their little Jamaican daughter? What kind of a situation is this?'

There was much more of the same, and I was thinking that he would have made a fine figure in a pulpit. We eventually agreed that she would be told that her husband had been unavoidably detained on business, but if he has not returned by tomorrow then the painful facts of the matter will have to be laid before her.

Damn the man!

February 17th. A battering at my door awoke me at an early hour, and when I opened it, there was Miss Rivvere in a towering passion – a Fury – a perfect Maenad! Someone, presumably a servant from the House, had apprised her of the arrival of Mrs McLehose to reclaim her errant husband.

'Where is he?' she shrieked, storming around and flinging doors wide. 'Where is he? He never told me he had a wife! I shall kill him, I swear it!'

'He's not here,' I said, grateful that he was not, for in all the ferocious legions of Hell no demoness could have been more terrifying than Miss Rivvere at that moment.

With difficulty I persuaded her to calm herself and take a seat, promising that I would give her the facts as I knew them, omitting nothing. I told her, *item.* that James had been married many years before coming to Jamaica; *item.* that the marriage had not been a happy one, and there had been a long separation before his voyage, during which no marital intimacies had occurred; *item.* that there had been four children by the marriage, though only one, a boy named Andrew, survived; and *item.* that I had no doubt as to the depth of his attachment to the lady in whose presence I had the privilege to be, or the sincerity of his paternal love for the perfectly delightful little Ann. I concluded by saying that the situation was a delicate one, and that until Mrs McLehose had been spoken to, it was hard to see which way to proceed.

'Don't call her Mrs McLehose!' yelled Miss Rivvere angrily, stamping her feet. 'What right does she have to such a title when her own neglect of her husband has driven him here? Who is this *woman?*' I have never heard the word uttered with such a degree of withering contempt. 'What more can she offer my James than I can?'

She continued in this vein for some time. Her anger, previously directed at the perfidious McLehose, was now focused on the new arrival, and within a few minutes she had convinced herself that Mrs McLehose had made the voyage to Jamaica for the express purpose of ruining their idyllic existence, concluding that she would eat that woman's liver out before she let her within a hundred yards of her precious, long-suffering James. I repeated that nothing could be decided until we had heard what that woman had to say for herself – I had almost said 'Mrs McLehose' but prevented myself just in time, being mindful of my health.

She eventually flounced off, and I betook myself with all possible haste to the House, telling Mr Douglas what had transpired.

'Has Mrs McLehose risen?' I asked.

'Yes. She is somewhat refreshed, but she has no idea about … about any of this. But she is speaking of going in search of her husband. She has to be told, Burns.'

'Granted, but by whom?' I replied, with the uncomfortable sensation of already knowing the answer.

'You know McLehose better than I do,' he said. 'You have already spoken with Miss Rivvere. Your powers of diplomacy must be impressive, Robert.' He looked at me with a twinkle in his eye, knowing that he had me on the hip.

Thus it was that I was presented to Mrs McLehose.

I am not sure what I had expected. Certainly I had entertained extremely unfavourable ideas about her. What I do know is that when I entered her room, there rose to meet me one of the most beautiful women I have ever seen, with a confident and assured manner – perfect poise – a veritable goddess! She was of middling stature, with large green eyes that looked straight into mine with complete candour. I was smitten in an instant.

'This is Mr Burns, Mrs McLehose,' Douglas was saying.

'I am very pleased to make your acquaintance, Mr Burns,' she said in a soft voice.

'And I yours,' I managed to say, with a bow.

'You will forgive me if I withdraw,' said Douglas. 'I have pressing matters to attend to.' With a nod to each of us he left the room. We seated ourselves. Mindful of the information I had to convey, I felt ill at ease and found it hard to imagine how McLehose, who had always struck me as a coarse individual in some ways, had contrived to wed such a fine woman.

'How was your journey, Mrs McLehose?' I asked.

'Excessively disagreeable, Mr Burns,' she replied. For a few moments there was silence, and I sensed her unspoken question hanging in the air between us.

'And how do you find our climate here in Jamaica?'

'Too hot and too humid,' she replied. 'And these flies – mosquitoes, I believe they are called – are quite insupportable.'

'Yes,' I said. 'They are particularly troublesome in the evenings. However if one takes the precaution of . . .'

'Where is my husband, Mr Burns?' she asked.

'To be perfectly candid, I do not know. However he frequently has to travel away from the plantation on business.'

'Obviously,' she said, 'otherwise he would have met me at Kingston. I had the greatest difficulty in procuring transportation to bring me here. Do you know when he is likely to return?' I said I did not know, but supposed that it would be no longer than a day or two.

'In that case I shall have my baggage moved to his house,' she replied. 'Mr Douglas and his wife were good enough to take me in last evening, but I would prefer to be in my husband's quarters when he returns. I have no doubt that his bachelor surroundings will require a woman's touch.' Dear God, I thought.

'Mrs McLehose,' I said. 'I think that you may have to prepare yourself for some alteration in your husband's circumstances.'

'What do you mean by that, Mr Burns?' she said, with a light laugh. I replied that I understood that she had been separated from her husband for some eleven years, to which she readily assented. I went on to say that it would be understandable, would it not, if he had formed the impression that the marriage was over, and had formed . . . er . . . other attachments.

'Other attachments?' she retorted. 'We are married, Mr Burns. Heaven knows I have had the opportunity to form 'other attachments', as you call them, but I have always put such temptations aside. Do you mean that he has been in the company of other women?' I nodded and she remained silent for a few moments.

'Mr Douglas tells me that there are only some half-dozen white women in the parish,' she continued, 'and that they are all married.' I remained silent, while a look of disbelief spread over her features. 'You cannot mean that my husband has been consorting with the Negro women!' she exclaimed. 'I had heard that such things happened, but I would never have dreamed he would have formed liaisons with slaves.'

'Not a slave,' I said. 'And not black either. A free woman – a mulatta.'

'Mulatta? What is that?' she cried.

I tried to explain it was a term used to describe the issue of a white person and a Negro, and that in Jamaica they shared most of the rights enjoyed by the white population. However, she did not seem to hear what I was saying.

'So my place has been taken by a Negress!' she exclaimed. 'He gave me four children, and now he takes his pleasure with a heathen savage!'

'Miss Rivvere is hardly a savage.'

'So that is her name?' she said with heat. 'And dignified with the title of 'Miss', I observe. And this *Miss* Rivvere holds her head high while I suffer sorrow and privation in Edinburgh, and have to tolerate the misery of an ocean voyage, to which was added the indignity of finding myself alone on a disgusting quayside without friends. This is a fine way to treat a respectable woman. Have you any other news for me, Mr Burns?'

'Er . . . there is a child,' I said wretchedly. From her demeanour on hearing these words I thought she was on the verge of swounding, and I offered to summon assistance, but she composed herself.

'So he has sired bastards,' she whispered, as if the words gave her physical pain in the uttering. 'I have buried three of my children – our children! – and he fills the world with . . .'

'There is but one child,' I said. 'Her name is Ann Lavinia. I know how you must feel, but she is a bonny wee bairn, and surely forms no part of your dispute.'

'God preserve me,' she said.

'You must not judge your husband too harshly,' I said. 'He has done no more than many white men do here, and I am sure that he meant no harm by it. He will, I know, be anxious to make amends.'

'Amends! What amends can he make for such betrayal?'

There was the sound of voices in the hallway, and a moment later McLehose burst through the door. He presented a shameful and sorry spectacle – he had not shaved for several days – his clothes were filthy – his hair was unkempt – he was greatly flushed and unsteady on his feet, clearly very much the worse for drink. He stood swaying on the threshold, staring at his wife. She rose and looked at him steadily, and although she said nothing, I saw a tear start down her cheek.

'Nancy!' he said thickly.

She made no reply. Mr Douglas and his wife came in and made a great fuss about seating McLehose, and asking for strong coffee to be brought. I made a bow and left. This has been a most distressing day for me, but as nothing compared to what the wretched McLehose must needs face in the next few days, now that the truth is finally out. I would not be in his shoes for all the rum in Jamaica.

I cannot put Mrs McLehose out of my mind. Her silly husband does not deserve her. How could he ever have turned his back on such a woman? I have this evening penned two verses that I would dearly love to send to her, but for the fear that such a move might appear too forward.

February 18th. McLehose came to see me this morning, and was highly offensive in his manner.

'What the devil were you were thinking of?' he cried, waving his finger in my face. 'You have made me look a complete fool before both Ann and Nancy!' I quite lost patience at this.

'Made you look a fool? Good God, man, you made a fool o' yourself. You didna require my assistance!'

'What?' he yelled. 'You told Ann about Nancy – our marriage – our children, damn it – and not twenty minutes later you have the temerity to give Nancy all the intimate details of . . .'

'Stop there, McLehose,' I shouted. 'I counselled you that nothing was to be gained by secrecy and concealment. We had agreed you would meet her in Kingston, remember? Instead your wife turned up here, and it would have only been a matter of time before she met up with Ann. Can you imagine the scene there would have been? And you were not in Kingston, and you were not here!' I fairly bellowed in his face. 'You were not man enough to do for yourself what had to be done, and I had to do it for you!'

'Not man enough? Not man enough?' he shrieked, and started towards me with a raised fist. But I was broader and fitter than he was, and he knew it.

'A man has to face up to his responsibilities,' I said, 'not run away. You have married one woman, and as good as married another, and had children by both. Each considers you to be her husband, and you do neither of them justice by failing to be honest with them.'

'You sound just like Nancy,' he muttered, somewhat subdued. 'She says the same. So does Ann. In fact I have heard little else for these twelve hours past. It fairly makes my head ache, man.'

'Then it is probably true,' I said. 'Women have a knack of viewing things from a different perspective. So what have you resolved to do? You surely cannot allow matters to continue in this way.'

He sat down and rested his chin in his hands. 'Mrs McLehose means to have no more to do with me,' he sighed. 'She will return to Edinburgh, and I have agreed to furnish her with an annuity. As for Ann, she has been beside herself with rage, and says she can easily find someone else who will treat her better, but little Ann Lavinia, bless her heart, means too much to us both, and I hope I may prevail upon her mother to forgive me, in time.'

'So it is to be Ann, and not Mrs McLehose?' I said. 'And is that how you would have wished it, had the choice been yours to make?'

'Aye, I believe so,' he said, after a pause. 'Nancy is a good enough woman, but she is strait-laced and allows me no scope. She is like Edinburgh itself – pretty enough to look at, but with little substance beneath the fine show. Damn it, she can't laugh, or loosen her stays for a moment. I would never have been so fond of a dram had she been able to have a glass or two with me, instead of tut-tutting and shaking her head at the merest mention of whisky. Anyway, you know all about that. But Ann knows how to enjoy life. She can drink me under the table. I never want to leave her side. Why should I? She's everything I want. Maybe it's the climate, Burns. I could have lived with Nancy if she could have shaken off this long-faced propriety and her damned Calvinistic decency, but it's bred too deeply in her, I fear. Now that's all over, and as far as I'm concerned it's all for the best.'

I listened to this denunciation of his wife with disbelief and a deal of contempt. He had thought enough of her to marry her and father four children on her when she was little more than a child, so it seemed to me callous of him now to disparage her in this way. Even if she was indeed as he described, which I misdoubted, these were not faults, but rather aspects of her character that he should have been aware of from the outset.

'So when does Mrs McLehose leave for Scotland?' I enquired, with ironic stress on the 'Mrs', though he did not appear to notice.

'It may be another two or three weeks,' he said. 'A month, possibly. Until then she remains at the Great House.'

We parted soon after, without any of our accustomed cordiality. In truth I am not sorry that Nancy (I may call her that in the privacy of these pages!) has repudiated him.

February 20th. I called at the Great House earlier this evening on a pretext to do with the accounts of the estate, but the true purpose of my visit was, I own, the hope that I might see Mrs McLehose again. I was not disappointed, for she was taking coffee with Mrs Douglas when I arrived, and I was invited to join their company. I cannot claim to recall very much of the conversation. I remember asking her if she was somewhat recovered after the difficult events of the previous few days, and she said that she felt much better. Her voice is soft, and those dark green eyes fevered my imagination to such an extent that I could only sit and luxuriate in a delicious reverie. Oh! fair, exquisite flower of Scottish womanhood, blossoming unexpectedly in the midst of a desert! – every cadence of her sweet voice a caress! – if I do not see her again I shall not rest in my grave for chagrin.

March 1st. My mind is no longer my own. I am finding it difficult to concentrate on anything but [M̶r̶s̶] Nancy. I have not spoken to her since I wrote last, but I have seen her several times walking in the gardens of the Great House: such a picture of elegance and grace, and looking so preoccupied and despondent. I long to spend time with her alone, but she is the guest of Mr Douglas, and it is not my place to intrude.

Adah asks me when we shall be making our preparations for the journey to Scotland, and I tell her that I shall take this in hand at the first available opportunity, but I find it all too easy to contrive procrastinatory pretexts.

Otherwise plantation life is pleasant enough. I have made a friend in Toby, an elderly man who has now retired from field work and devotes his time instead to fishing. Every few days he goes off, and returns with a basket containing his catch. He finds it easy enough to sell his wares, for salt fish, though plentiful, is greatly inferior to the fresh variety. He makes a point of coming to the house and offering me the pick of his catch in exchange for a sum so trifling that I feel ashamed to pay it – indeed I offer to give more, but he will not hear of it. We have had some feasts, Adah and I! Toby likes to stand and reminisce about the old days. Although his Creole is very difficult to follow, he loves to tell his stories, and I enjoy listening to them.

March 6th. The Sabbath. I have made enquiries about the passage to Scotland, and have ascertained that there are berths available on board the *Orange Grove* with Captain Langley, due to set sail for Liverpool in the middle of next month. I have placed a deposit with the agent, the balance being due on departure. So the die is cast!

Adah is wildly excited now that the date for our journey is fixed – I have tried very hard to share in her enthusiasm, but the eagerness with which I had contemplated my return home is, I confess, subdued of late by the knowledge that I shall see Nancy no more. Stern Reason, who should be the mistress of my turbulent passions, is being won over by foolish Sentiment. I cannot allow this to continue, and I have decided to put Nancy out of my mind once and for all. I have had many cruel disappointments and difficulties in my life thus far, and with a fair prospect finally before me, it would be folly to place it at risk.

March 22nd. I have spent the most agreeable day imaginable in the company of Nancy. The circumstances were not of my choosing; it was as if the Fates had decreed that it was to be so. I was about my plantation duties when Amos came to summon me to the presence of Mr Douglas. When I arrived he was standing with Nancy on the steps of the Great House and a carriage was waiting nearby.

'There you are, Burns,' he said. 'I wonder if you could oblige me?'

'I am at your disposal,' I said, though I was looking at Nancy and thinking how beautiful she looked, with her white dress and a dainty little parasol.

'Mrs McLehose wishes to visit Port Antonio,' he said. 'I would have taken her myself, but there are matters demanding my attention here today, and I wonder if you would escort her there instead.'

'I should be honoured,' I said very politely, though my heart was pounding at the thought of spending time alone with her. How sweet and light was her touch on my arm as we walked to the carriage, and how soft her voice when she spoke!

'This is very kind of you, Mr Burns,' she said. 'I am sorry that you should be inconvenienced on my account.'

'It is no inconvenience whatever,' I said. 'It will be a pleasure.' Ah, how little did she know how fervently I meant those words!

As we drove, I asked her how matters stood with James, and she said that his disloyalty had distressed her very deeply.

'We are still married, Mr Burns,' she said. 'I have always believed that marriage is a sacred bond, and I cannot understand how he could have taken up with that Rivvere woman.'

'I can understand your feelings,' I said, wondering for the hundredth time how any man could desert a woman such as this.

Time seemed to pass very quickly. We admired the bay, and took a drive through Port Antonio itself, but it is a very different place from Edinburgh, and I could see that she was made nervous by the dust and the proximity of all the loud voices and staring faces, so after an hour or so she asked to be driven back to the plantation.

'Mr Douglas and his wife are very kind,' she said, as the Great House came in sight. 'Yet I feel abandoned here. There is nothing for me in Jamaica, and I do not yet feel strong enough to undertake the voyage back to Scotland.'

'May I can call on you again at some time that is convenient to you?' I asked. 'I should be glad to hear news of Scotland.'

She flushed very prettily. 'That would be very good of you,' she said. I brought the carriage to a halt and helped her to alight. She thanked me for my courtesy, and extended her hand to me. 'I hope to see you again, Mr Burns,' she said, with a smile that melted my heart, and then she was gone.

My whole mind was whirling as I walked slowly home. I explained to Adah that I had been instructed to take Mrs McLehose to Port Antonio and presented it as rather a tiresome chore that I could well have done without. But I *must* see her again, even if it is only to exchange pleasantries – a minute in the company of such a perfect creature is worth an eternity spent with ordinary mortals!

April 5th. For the past little while I have been trying to put Nancy out of my mind. I shall call on her, of course, but I do not wish to appear overly precipitate. Her presence has an effect on me that I cannot explain. Perhaps I should wait for a week or so I, until my passions have subsided somewhat.

Since the visit to Port Antonio I have tried to be more attentive to Adah, for I know I have been moody and preoccupied, and she deserves better.

We shall not be able to travel on the *Orange Grove,* as she has been greatly delayed in the Bahamas. Adah is disappointed, as am I, for we would have been setting out for Kingston in the next few days.

More fish from Toby today. I have asked him if I may come fishing with him one day, and he has readily agreed. I am sure there is an art to it, and if anyone has mastered it, that man will be Toby.

April 16th. I walked with Nancy today in the garden of the Great

House for an hour. How can I describe my feelings? We understand each other so perfectly. We spoke of things of which no one on the plantation has any knowledge – our favourite Scots airs – the amazing exploits of Signor Lunardi[1] – the new buildings and streets presently being constructed in Edinburgh – she has even read Fergusson, and sometimes takes up the pen to compose poems of her own! I have never before met such a woman – what kind of ungenerous and narrow soul must McLehose have, to see imperfections in such a one? He drinks too much, and his manner can be boorish, so it does not surprise me that she has reproved him on occasion – I am sure that any trouble between them must have been his fault. Anyone who sees Nancy and does not love her deserves to be damned for his stupidity, and anyone who would injure her deserves double damnation for his villainy!

April 17th. Last evening, after completing my journal, I again found myself unable to think of anything but this goddess who has conquered me. My anguished feelings are not to be endured. For years I have not seen a Scottish woman, and now the embodiment of perfection is here on this plantation! I have only met her a few times since her arrival, and on these occasions her demeanour is of such solemnity that it quite makes my heart break. I cannot believe the calumnies that her brainless fool of a husband has so thoughtlessly heaped upon her. He is quite unworthy of her. My verses are ready, but the fair copy remains here between the pages of this book, where I am about to copy it out. In truth I cannot pluck up the courage to deliver it into her hands.

Alone on Neptune's Stormy Waste

Alone on Neptune's stormy waste
You braved the sea and thunder, O!
A victim, sorrowful and chaste,
O' mony a bygone blunder, O!
And as this mangrov'd isle grew nigh
You thought, in some spot lowly, O!
Wi' tremblin' heart again to tie
The bonds o' wedlock holy, O!

Alas! Thy pains are dearly bought!
Cast doon, thou'rt on thy lane, O!
Thy fondest dreams have come to nought;
Each tender thought in vain, O!
Dame Fortune is a fickle quean

> Wha twists and jouks and turns, O!
> But when you feel her spite grow keen:
> Count on a friend in BURNS, O!

April 20th. I can wait no longer, and have had my poem delivered to Mrs McLehose at the Great House. How will she receive it? I spend hours conjecturing her reaction – attempting to imagine the expression on her face as she peruses its contents and considers its sentiments. Have I been too bold?

April 21st. No word. I fear I have offended her. What on earth possessed me to write such a thing? She has suffered bitter humiliation from her husband – why should she feel anything but contempt for the effusions of a complete stranger?

April 23rd. When I returned home tonight I found that a note had been delivered to me. With a mingling of joy and trepidation I saw at once that it was from Nancy. To my delight she thanked me for my poem, which she was good enough to describe as 'very charming, and alas! how true', and hoping that we might meet again! To be sure it was couched in rather correct and formal terms, but it is not the rejection I had feared; indeed, my heart danced with rapture as I read it over. So I must consider it an invitation!

April 24th. I have made so bold as to pen another little poem for Nancy, and enclosed it together with a few lines, hinting that she has become the constant companion of my thoughts, and begging her not to reproach me for my presumption in making a sincere expression of my sentiments. Am I too hasty? My emotions are in such turmoil that I hardly know what I am doing. Reason tells me that this is utter folly – that we could never be together – that McLehose will regard any familiarity with the severest misgivings, to say nothing of Mr Douglas, whose Puritan soul would recoil in horror at the slightest hint of intimacy with a married woman living as a guest under his roof.

As for Adah, dear, good, kind soul – what of her? She has been as good to me as any wife, and I have been faithful and true to her all this while. I well recollect her jealous fit of chagrin on discovering that I had spent a few moments in formal conversation with that Josephine creature – what would she say if she knew of my sentiments for Nancy? She suspects nothing, I am sure of it. What an impulsive wretch I am, to risk all! Yet I cannot thwart the promptings of my heart: Nancy is of a different order of being, and, despite all the forebodings and fears that crowd my breast, she has captured my soul – I am hers!

To a Fair Newcomer

Fower thousand miles frae hame I'm sittin',
In search o' words baith fine and fittin':
For a' the nonsense ever written
    O' broken hearts,
Ah! fatally I fear I'm smitten
    By Cupid's darts!

Epitome of earthly grace;
Divinest princess of thy race:
Why should such loveliness embrace
    A heart of stone?
Oh, for a smile upon thy face
    For me alone!

April 25th. A letter by return of post, or rather by the hand of Amos! My little verses have been well received, indeed she praises them for their sensitivity, and hopes that I will not be offended if she opines that their delicacy is a tie which binds us, as two exiles in a foreign land. She invites me to call on her, trusting, she says, that I will not trespass against the letter of decorum's law. I have sent word back to request the honour of walking in the gardens of the Great House tomorrow afternoon, if the weather be fine.

Adah saw me with the letter, and was understandably curious about it. I thought it wisest to be as truthful as possible, and explained with feigned indifference that there were certain enquiries I desired Mrs McLehose to attend to on our behalf if she returned to Scotland before we did. To this end I would call on her at some point in the next few days, and that was all there was to it.

'Wha' matters?' asked Adah.

'Oh, just some letters to deliver; that kind of thing,' I said, hoping that I would not blush and occasion suspicion. To my relief she appeared to accept my explanation.

'Missiz McLehose a fine lady,' she said. 'Yuh friend Massa James done bad fuh she.'

'Aye well, he could have behaved better,' I said. 'But he has made his choice, and that's an end of it.'

'She a fine lady,' she repeated. Then she kissed me, and went off about her business, leaving me with a host of conflicting feelings. I am almost minded to make an immediate attempt to subjugate my turbulent emotions. Yet I may, without any fear of censure, spend some time in tender but innocent dalliance with Nancy, without doing anything to merit reproach. If what she says about *decorum* is true, then perhaps this is all I can wish for.

April 26th. I spent an hour with Nancy this afternoon. I am intoxicated! How sweet to be in the company of an unfortunate woman, amiable and young, deserted by one who was bound by every tie of duty, nature and gratitude to protect, comfort and cherish her! How sweet when she is among the first of lovely forms and noble minds! Oh! what a fool I am in love! How can all this have fallen to the lot of a poor harum-scarum poet and plantation-worker? Must I love, pine, mourn and adore in secret? Today I am quite *distrait*, and Adah, poor misguided soul, thinks I am ill. She treats me with the greatest kindness and most tender solicitude. Why am I so foolish?

April 28th. The qualities I most admire in Nancy are the very ones that Adah lacks. I have been in the colony for so long that I have grown accustomed to her Jamaica-bred ways and quite forgotten the intense pleasure to be gained from the interaction with a woman's mind so perfectly attuned to my own, particularly when that woman is such a divine creature as Nancy. Her mind hits my taste as the joys of heaven do a saint. She and I can discourse at length on so many topics – she is full of ideas about the process of poetic composition – whereas Art, Music and Poesy are, for Adah, denizens of a *terra incognita* that must remain forever unexplored. To be sure, we share the sensuous delights of Aaron's Rod, but imagine the overwhelming joy of being able to share these delicious pleasures with Nancy in addition to our intellectual communion – a perfect, two-fold conjunction of exalted minds and yearning bodies! – the marriage of *agape* and *eros!* I should not be thinking this way.

May 1st. The Sabbath. Heavy rain; very satisfying to a Presbyterian disposition, no doubt, but not to mine. I awoke with a dreadful headache, having spent a sleepless night listening to the roar of the downpour on the shingles, and the relentless dripping on the floor in those places where the roof leaks. Every time the rain eased a little, the frogs resumed their Aristophanean chorus with increased vigour. Outside was a dismal prospect – sodden grass; bedraggled bushes; ragged palms, mud everywhere. When we arose, the only piece of bread we had was soggy and inedible. Adah began to eat a mango, which is a messy business at the best of times, but she made such a slaistery show of it that I fell out of patience with her and told her to mind her manners, or words to that effect. I know that I should not have spoken sharply to her, and normally I would never have done so, but the a curt note from Nancy saying that she would not be able to see me today had put me out of humour. Adah complained that I had grown tired of her, and no longer cared for her. She demanded to know why I had been so preoccupied of late, and why I have been spending so much time at the Great House. I endeavoured to placate her, saying that I was tired, and overly busy with plantation business – and felt disgusted with myself. I am a fool, and like the proverbial fool I am drawn inexorably back to my folly.

May 16th. Today I kissed my Nancy for the first time, and remain dizzy with the memory of it. I seized my moment in the garden as we returned from our stroll. For a moment she made no resistance, but then she pushed me away and ran off to the Great House. I fear that she reproaches me for my forwardness, and have hastened to write to make my position clear. She has often allowed me the head to feel the influence of her female excellence: is it not blasphemy, then, against her own charms and against my own feelings, to presume that I could conceal my passion?

May 18th. A brief note from Nancy, saying she is neither well nor happy today, and that if she is to regain her peace, then we cannot meet again. At a distance, she believes, we could retain the affection we feel for each other's concerns, while absence would mellow and restrain these 'violent agitations' which threaten to render her unfit for the duties of life. She penned a few lines of verse, the concluding lines of which have pierced me to the quick:

> Why urge the odious, one request
> You know I must deny!

'Odious'! How could a single word inflict such pain? Yet I have forced myself to write, asking her to mark the line of conduct, and promising that I shall regard her wishes as the most sacred and inviolable of commands.

May 22nd. The Sabbath. I spent the afternoon with Nancy, walking in the gardens of the Great House. Our conversation turned to the verses we had exchanged. Had not our sentiments been sincerely and beautifully expressed? She assured me that they had been. And was this not evidence that we were drawn to each other by some Power greater than either of us? Blushing, she acknowledged that this was indeed the case. And were not these feelings more than the mere whims that excite the passing fancy of the Many? Were they not of an exalted and dignified nature, to be experienced by only a

privileged Few? A heavenly light, in short, rather than the sulphur-
ous flickerings that serve for lesser mortals?

'What of the light which leads astray?' she said. 'Everything you
have said has had a powerful effect, and our friendship is delightful to
me when under the check of Reason and Religion, but . . .'

'Reason?' I said. 'What is Reason? Bliss like ours is not attainable
through Reason! Did Dante find his Beatrice through an arid
exercise in metaphysics? Did Juliet's heart beat for her Romeo
through the operations of logic alone? My *heart* carries me farther
than boasted *Reason* ever did a philosopher! When we gaze in
wonderment at a glorious sunset, or marvel at a magnificent vista, is
it *Reason* that instructs our feelings? When we see some ancient
ruined church surrounded by fallen, mossy gravestones, is it *Reason*
that teaches us to feel melancholy?' I pounded on my breast with
these last words, and it was clear from her demeanour that I had
made an impression on her.

'What about Religion?' she said.

'What indeed?' I replied. 'Does Religion place you under the least
shadow of an obligation to bestow your love, tenderness, caresses,
heart and soul on one who has barbarously broken every tie of duty,
nature and gratitude to you?'

'He is my husband, Mr Burns,' she said, though with a sigh and
in a distinct tone of regret. 'I am a married woman, and therefore
constrained by the bonds of matrimony.'

'Bonds indeed!' I said. 'Go and visit the slave market if you want to
know about bonds, chains and shackles! Are you McLehose's slave?
Does he own you? Must you do the bidding of a man who does as he
pleases, and does not give you a second thought? You must cast off
these foolish fetters. You are under no obligation to him whatever.
You have noble and exalted feelings, Nancy, that you cannot indulge
except with a man such as myself who has a soul capable of appreci-
ating them, and reciprocating in kind. It is not in the slightest degree
hurtful to your duty to God, or to your children, or to society at large
if you bestow your affection on me rather than on James. I am sorry
to speak harshly, but you are effectively a widow – as far as your
matrimonial ties are concerned, James may as well be dead.'

I could see that she was swayed by the argument, and would have
pressed my advantage further, but the hour was late and we had to
part. Now that I am at home again, I can think of nothing but Nancy.
My head is in a kind of delirium. No rum can produce intoxication like
this! Such beauty and grace in the arms of truth and honour!

May 24th. On Sunday Mr and Mrs Douglas are going to Port Antonio for the day, setting out at first light and not expected back until the evening. I shall find a pretext for calling on Nancy, and then? *Qui sait?* I have written to her to request an audience, which she has granted.

Adah is cool with me these past few days. When I came in this evening she avoided my embrace and looked at me very steadily.

'Is all de wimmin in Scotland lak Missiz McLehose?' she asked.

'How do you mean?'

'I means *fine* ladies. I means *gran'* ladies wid fancy dresses – ladies dat speaks prap'ly.'

I tried to explain that I had never believed in the silly dictum that 'clothes maketh the man'. The most lowly woman, I assured her, can be a *lady* by virtue of a noble character alone, with no need for the assumption of silly airs and graces, while many of the most high-born women in the world are vain, foolish and worthless, and all the powder and silk in the world cannot conceal that fact. I never thought that Adah set any store by such trifles – she dresses herself in cotton shifts of the simplest kind and devotes little time to her appearance. I felt very sorry for her, and tomorrow I have determined to go into Port Antonio to buy her some of the clothing she lacks. If I am honest with myself, this fine intention stems from a guilty conscience as much as anything. It would be far better for me if I were to forget Mrs McLehose altogether, and concentrate on the one who – for all her shortcomings – is to be Mrs Burns.

There is word from the agent that the *Orange Grove* is now in Kingston, and we shall be leaving Jamaica on June 5th. That is when out new lives shall begin.

May 25th. Following Adah's expressions of concern yesterday I have been to Port Antonio to visit Mrs Tebbitt's pretentiously named Millinery Emporium – much patronised, I gather, by the sort of 'fine lady' Adah aspires to emulate. I found the place frequented mostly by haughty mulattas who derived much amusement from seeing a man in the establishment. The place is rather small and exceedingly cluttered with haberdashery; drapery; shoes; ornaments; wigs; jars of rouge and powder; ribbons; patch-boxes; knick-knacks, and assorted cheap jewellery – all newly imported from London, according to the proprietrix. She is a coarse, sweaty woman to whom I took an instant dislike as she boasted in a Cockneyish accent of being able to furnish everything that a lady could ask for in order to set off her beauty. Most of her merchandise was gaudy and completely impractical for a climate such as this. The place suffocated me – the cloying reek of perfume and pomanders mingled in a very disagreeable way with the fooshtie smell of cloth and the rank smell of Mrs Tebbitt herself.

At any rate, I purchased a fine linen petticoat; a pair of black shoes with silver buckles; a comb and a hairbrush; a pretty pomander; a dainty parasol; a lacy white bonnet and – *pièce de résistance!* – a silk dress in dark crimson. When I had done, Mrs Tebbitt asked me for four pounds – I offered her two, which she accepted with alacrity – and I bore the treasures home to Adah. She received them at first with incredulity, and then with delirious delight, bestowing a thousand kisses on me before rushing off to the bedchamber in order to try them on.

I waited patiently for a very considerable time. I dare say that when the Last Trump sounds there will be a *fortissimo* chorus of protest from the female moiety of the human population, demanding an hour or two more in order to ready themselves for so momentous an occasion. I was drifting into a reverie about a libretto on that subject to deliver to Herr Handel – *Delay thy Trump, Lord! Hear our prayer! Alas, we have no clothes to wear!* or words to that effect – when the door opened, and there Adah stood.

What can I say? She was utterly transformed – gone was the unassuming Adah I had once known, and in her place was a goddess! She had fastened her hair back with a ribbon; the dress accentuated every curve and contour of her body, and she had applied colour to her lips. I had always thought her pretty, but as she stood there, she presented a picture of complete loveliness. I rose and gawped at her in open-mouthed astonishment, unable to think of words to express my sentiments.

'Yuh like?' she said anxiously, mistaking my silence for disapproval. 'Is I a lady now? Or is I still yuh *specimen?*'

I went up to her and took her reverently and diffidently by the shoulders, for it seemed impossible that this radiant vision was really mine to embrace. 'Adah,' I said, 'you are beautiful – truly beautiful. There is not a grand lady in the whole of Scotland who could compare with you.' I meant what I said, and I felt a fierce resolve to be worthy of this young woman who has given herself to me – heart, body and soul – and who surely deserves my honest devotion in return.

May 28th. Tomorrow I shall pay my last visit to Mrs McLehose at the Great House, and bid her farewell. I shall thank her for the friendship she has shown me, and praise her many qualities; I shall tell her that I esteem her as a person of education and taste. I must then steel myself to acknowledge that I have been too forward with her, and for honesty's sake I must tell her that, like James, I have found a Jamaican wife with whom I am shortly returning to Scotland. I shall ask her most humbly to forgive me for any offence my words may have caused, then take my leave. I have my little speech all learned by rote, and I shall have nothing to do but deliver my lines.

Adah has found my trunk, and is busily packing everything that she thinks we shall need for our new life. I have tried to persuade her that she does not need to pack pots, knives and other cooking utensils as such items are very readily to be found in Scotland, but she is determined to leave nothing behind.

May 29th. I write in a mood of the most extreme uneasiness and trepidation. I do not know what is going to happen. I am full of misgivings and horrible fears. What should have been a dignified parting has turned to a nest of vipers in my bosom, and I shall have no rest until I find some way in which to resolve the predicament in which I find myself.

I went to the Great House with the intention of acknowledging Nancy's reservations about the future conduct of our friendship. God help me, that was truly what I intended. She received me in her *boudoir*, which I now realise was a mistake. There can be few things that arouse the amorous sentiments more than the intimate details of a woman's life laid out carelessly to the view – a garment draped over a chair; the little bottles of scent; the personal gewgaws dear to her heart – all conspire alike to foster a too-easy familiarity, and to militate against propriety and restraint. I should have known this, but like the fool I am, I allowed myself instead to be drawn into conversation about our feelings for each other.

'I have been thinking about what you said about my being effectively a widow,' she said. 'Jamaica is no place for us, but were we in Scotland then I do believe we could be together.' A few short weeks ago, these words would have raised me to transports of joy, but now they were not what I wanted to hear. I began to prevaricate, mumbling something about our needing more time to be sure of one another.

'Do you not love me, Robert?' she said. 'Did you raise these hopes in my heart only to dash them now?' She began to weep; I took her in my arms to comfort her; she raised her lips to mine; fool that I am, I pressed my advantage; she offered no resistance, and I was lost. At the height of her ardour she cried out that she had never experienced such pleasure before, and in a few moments *voilà* – the fateful deed was concluded. At that instant of conquest, I knew that it was a dreadful and irrevocable mistake. We lay together for a few moments in a guilty silence, and then without looking at me she abruptly rose and left the room.

When she returned, her whole bearing made it quite apparent that she felt the most intense repugnance about what had just taken place. She refused to meet my eyes, and only told me very coldly that I had better leave, which I did, muttering meaningless apologies. I returned here feeling profound disgust with myself – for my damned impetuosity; for my lack of consideration, and for my betrayal of Adah. My first act, before penning these lines, was to write a letter to Nancy offering the most abject of apologies for what had occurred, blaming myself in the most self-reproaching, contrite and penitent terms, and imploring her forgiveness. The best I can hope for is that she will acknowledge that the situation was not entirely of my making.

Adah was delighted to have me back home and has been making a great fuss of me, which only makes me feel worse. What kind of a man am I, to have behaved as I did? What is going to happen now?

May 30th. Back at work. Nothing from Nancy. A dozen times I have been on the point of calling on her, but I am afraid of what will happen if I do.

May 31st. No word. I was useless at work today. I am totally preoccupied with this constant worry. I spent the evening pacing up and down. I am on the verge of confessing my misdeed to Adah, and indeed only two things prevent me from doing so – my craven cowardice in the face of her likely response, and the equally pusil-lanimous hope that Nancy may find it in her heart to keep our secret so that Adah will never need to know.

June 1st. Still nothing. I met Mr Douglas today, anxiously scanning his demeanour for any trace of reproach, but he gave no indication that anything was amiss. I asked politely after Mrs McLehose, and he said that she was not feeling well, and had confined herself to her room.

'There's something on her mind, though,' he said. She's been badly treated, make no mistake about it. There's something you and I need to talk about, by the way.'

'What might that be?' I asked, feeling my heart starting to pound.

'It's that Adah of yours,' he said irascibly. 'She's been walking around the plantation in fancy clothes, haughty as you like. I know she's a free woman, but she might show a wee bit of restraint, and make less of a show of herself. It does not go down well.'

I said that I would have a word with her. As I walked away, I felt a keen sense of relief. What transpired between Nancy and me is still a secret to us both. It has been three days now. Time is a great healer – surely she will agree to put this business behind us! I shall write to her again this evening.

I have told Adah that we must be ready to leave for Kingston tomorrow. She came up and put her arms around me.

'I'se real 'appy we's leavin' dis place,' she said. 'Yuh's been sad, Rab. Dere's sump'n 'bout dis place givin' yuh bad grief, nuh?'

I did not know what to say, I just held her tightly and prayed for a resolution to this wretched situation. All I want is to leave this place behind me, and head off to Kingston with Adah by my side.

June 2nd. The last day of felicity and happiness for Robert Burns – all over!

Everything happened in an absurdly short space of time. I was on my way to the Great House early this morning with another letter for Nancy. There is a neatly tended grassy area in front of the House, and as I was crossing it I saw Nancy come out. When she saw me she hesitated for a moment and then came down the steps and began to walk towards me. I took the letter from my pocket, ready to hand it to her. That she had decided, however reluctantly, to speak to me gave me great hope, and in that instant I felt sure that she would accept my spoken and written expressions of contrition.

I was just collecting my thoughts when there was a cry of 'Rab!' and who should come parading by but Adah, resplendent in her new red dress and parasol. She came up to me and affectionately took my arm, just as we came face to face with Nancy. There was a slow silence as the two women looked at each other in dawning comprehension, and then at me. In that moment I knew my entire world had changed – I wished myself anywhere on the earth but there – I wished myself dead. Nancy's face turned chalk-white as she looked from Adah to me with an expression of revulsion. Adah slipped her arm from mine and looked at me with disbelief, then tears welled up in her eyes, and she ran off. I could not move. I thought of offering Nancy the letter, but was unable to do so.

The expression on her face was awful. I wanted to say something, but was incapable of speech. She finally broke the silence.

'All these fine words!' she said. 'Metaphysics and heavenly light. And all the time you were bedding a common Negress. Why are you

men so fond of black women? And I permitted you . . . dear God . . .'
Her voice broke, and she stumbled back, sobbing, to the Great
House. I came back here, sick to my heart with guilt and self-
loathing. I called Adah when I entered but there was no reply. When
I looked in the bedchamber I saw the crimson dress and parasol laid
out very neatly on the bed, together with all the other items I had
bought her. It is growing dark now, but there is still no sign of her.

It is all *en pleine vue* now. Mr Douglas will know. Then there is
McLehose, and the other overseers – the whole damned plantation.
My relationship with Adah was common knowledge, and I realise
now that it was naïve in the extreme to assume that Nancy would not
have discovered the truth sooner or later. If only she had done so
before we lay together, the affront would not be as mortal. I could
face Adah's tears or her fury, but her absence is infinitely more
painful. I have been incredibly foolish, utterly deceitful and dishon-
est with those who trusted me most. I should leave New Cumnock
now and return to Scotland on my own, for there is nothing here for
me now. But I cannot leave without Adah!

I do not know what to think. I cannot write any more. Some rum
may deaden this pain.

June 3rd. Evening. Oh what a damned fool I have been! I am
forbidden the Great House on account of the impropriety of my
conduct. I am beyond all forgiveness. Mr Douglas himself issued the
prohibition: he came banging on my door this morning before it was
properly light and awakened me. I staggered to the door and there
he was, with a wrathful expression on his face such as Moses might
have worn when confronting worshippers of graven images.

'You've been at the rum again, I see,' he said. 'Well, well. I am
sorry to inconvenience you. Please do not bother to explain your-
self,' he went on, seeing that I was about to speak. 'What I have to say
will not take long. Mrs McLehose has given me an account of what
you have done to her. You visited my home – in my absence! – upon
the Sabbath day! – and you did so for the express purpose of carrying
out a sinful act of fornication with a vulnerable, unhappy woman
who is my guest!'

'I feel nothing but contempt for myself,' I muttered.

'Not as much contempt as others feel for you. In the meantime
I want you nowhere near my house, and I absolutely forbid you to
make any contact with Mrs McLehose. The woman is completely
distraught. In the meantime I shall leave you to your rum. Good day.'

I debated whether to turn out for work or not, and I finally decided that I had better do so. George, the head driver, told me that I was to be in charge of the third gang – the most menial task on the plantation, supervising children weeding and collecting rubbish, if you please! When I protested he said that the orders came from Mr Douglas himself.

'I t'ink Massa Douglas real vex wid yuh 'bout sump'n,' he said.

'I spoke to him earlier,' I said. 'By the way, have you seen Adah this morning?'

'Adah?' He gave me an amused look and I realised that he must know the whole story. 'Nossuh, cyan't say I 'ave. She free now, nuh? She nuh need mix wid us slave folk.' He made to move away, then turned back. 'Massa McLehose want speak wid you. If I see'm I tell'm yuh wid de weedin' gang.'

The gang was already at work. They are a cheerful and industrious group of women and children, and require little supervision, so I sat down under a tree. The heat of the sun and the effects of the rum from yestreen conspired to make me drowsy, and I must have fallen asleep. I awoke to feel a damned hard kick on my shin, and sprang up at once to find McLehose there, accompanied by Currie.

'You besmirched my wife's honour, damn you!' said McLehose.

'I did nothing of the kind!'

'Ye had me locked up for daein' less tae *your* wife,' said Currie. 'It's your turn noo.'

'Mind your own business,' I said. 'Look, McLehose, you must let me tell my side of the story.'

'Your side of the story!' he said, sneering.

'I'm not proud of what happened,' I said, 'but I did not force myself upon Mrs McLehose. I regret what happened and so does she. I realise it was quite wrong. We were carried away. I take responsibility. I have apologised to her. What more can I say?'

'That's not the story I hear,' said McLehose.

'I hear yer neger bitch is lookin' for a new man,' Currie sniggered. 'Maybe I'll apply for the position! She's got a merry wee cunt, I'm shair, an' I'd bang her belly fu' nicht an' day!'

I stepped forward, and he must have seen murder in my face, because he recoiled from me and hid behind McLehose. 'If you ever go anywhere near Adah,' I said, 'or if you even mention her name again in my presence, then I promise you that I will seek you out, and with my bare hands I will throttle the life out of you.'

'Death threats in front of a witness!' said Currie, trying to sound brave but failing.

'It is not a threat,' I said, 'it is a solemn promise.'

'It's time you left New Cumnock,' said McLehose. 'Nobody wants you here.'

'I had already reached that conclusion,' I said. 'My arrangements are in hand.'

'Good. Just keep out of my way in the meantime,' he said.

'And keep out o' mine,' said Currie, with an attempt at swagger.

'Why would I want to go anywhere near you?' I said. 'I'd sooner seek out the company of a latrine bucket. Mind what I said to you.'

They went off, muttering to each other. I decided at that point to remove myself from the plantation as soon as I could. Today is Friday. I must find Adah – if I can persuade her, then we might still be able to embark on the *Orange Grove*.

Adah was not there when I returned. I went out again and scoured the plantation, but there was no sign of her, and nobody would admit to knowing her whereabouts. George thought she might be at the Great House, but of course that is one place I cannot go. Tomorrow I shall send word to Mr Douglas that I am leaving, and ask for my salary to be sent over so that I can be on my way. I have very few possessions, and it will take me but a few minutes to collect them together.

No Adah; no food in the house, but plenty of rum.

June 4th. Yesterday I had thought myself the most miserable of mortals – today I am in a black despair, and pen these lines feeling myself to be verily in the darkest regions of hell.

I was summoned to the Great House early this morning by Amos who seemed very strange with me. When I asked him what it was all about he refused to say. I did not know what to make of this turn of events, though I have to confess that I was hoping it might mean some kind of reconciliation with Nancy. When I arrived, Amos showed me into the drawing room where Mr Douglas stood awaiting me. I had hoped that Nancy would be there, but she was not. From the look on Mr Douglas's face it was evident that something was seriously wrong.

'There you are, Mr Burns,' he said. 'Well, this is a bad business. A bad business.'

'I have already told you of the contempt I feel for myself,' I said. 'I can only repeat my most profound apologies for abusing your hospitality.'

'That was yesterday. Things have happened since then.' I waited, but he seemed reluctant to proceed.

'What things have happened?'

He cleared his throat. 'Mrs McLehose – how can I put this? – she took her own life last night.'

At first the words made no sense to me. I heard them clearly enough, but they might as well have been spoken in a foreign tongue.

'What do you mean?' I said.

'She took her own life. Killed herself.'

I felt all the blood drain from my head, and I had to sit down or I would surely have fallen.

'Killed herself? What do you mean, she killed herself?'

'The servants found her this morning. There was an empty arsenic bottle by her bed. Her father was a surgeon as you probably know, and it looks as if she had – how can I say? – come to Jamaica prepared for this. There was a letter too: you had better read it.' He went to a table, picked up a sheet and handed it to me. I cannot recollect its contents word for word, I only remember the words 'betrayal' and 'shame'.

'You have to leave without delay,' he said. 'I shall see that you are conveyed to Kingston tomorrow; after that you are on your own. I suggest you go home and pack.'

'I do not know what to say.'

'Then do not try. Now you must excuse me, I have matters to attend to, as you will no doubt appreciate.'

I can remember returning home, feeling detached from the world. I was not conscious of walking or finding my way. Dear God, what have I done? Neither peace nor rest can approach me, and anguish is eternally awake in my breast, subjecting me to the most purgatorial tortures I have ever had to endure.

At about noon I walked in the plantation, but everywhere I went found only coldness or contemptuous scorn. The slaves are surly, and though they dare not give utterance to their feelings, I know they feel I have treated Adah most wickedly. I took her into my bed – reason enough for them to regard me with animosity – but for me to have behaved so dishonourably towards her has, I fear, been sufficient to earn me their deepest antipathy. Now Nancy's death, the blame for which lies unquestionably at my door, has rendered me a detestable pariah. Worst of all, I know I have to face McLehose, and in my heart I shrink quivering in abject cowardice from the prospect of that encounter. What can I offer in my own defence?

[Later] McLehose has been. I was prepared for wrath – for reproach – for anything but the coldness and deadly determination in his manner.

'I will not sit in your presence, Burns,' he said. 'I have nothing but contempt for you. There is only one matter remaining to be settled between us.'

'Contempt?' I said, with my head in my hands, ashamed to look him in the face. 'Can there be greater contempt than I feel for my own actions? Are there any words you can say which will make me feel worse than I do already? God knows I am beyond all forgiveness.'

'And you will answer to Him,' he said, glaring at me with a malevolence that made my blood run cold. 'There is no justice on this earth, I know that now, so there is only one course of action I can undertake; and that is to deliver you to the Judgment seat to face your Maker. If He has mercy on your soul, then Heaven help us both.'

'What do you mean by that?' I said, starting to my feet and looking around for a weapon, fully believing that he intended to kill me.

'Oh you need have no fears on that account,' he sneered. 'I am not the man to murder you without giving you the opportunity of defending yourself. But you will answer to me tomorrow at dawn. I believe it is customary for the injured party to give some token cause for offence, and so this will suffice for now.' With that he stepped up to me and struck me lightly on the cheek with his open hand, his eyes never leaving mine.

'Don't be a fool, McLehose,' I said, as calmly as I could. 'I would give anything – anything – to have my Nancy back . . .'

'*Your* Nancy? he screamed. 'My wife! How dare you sully her name by calling her your Nancy? What gives you that right?'

'The fact that you repudiated her, perhaps?' I said, suddenly finding my anger overcoming my guilt and apprehension. 'You were finished with her, remember? You were going to send her back to Scotland with a paltry allowance, and marry Miss Rivvere, remember? Or do you forget these things? I wish I had the hardness of conscience to permit such convenient lapses of memory. You had taken your fill of her, and were content to send her packing. What gives you the right to behave as if I had besmirched her honour?'

'She's dead, Burns!' he shouted. 'Can't you realise that? Dead! And all because of you!'

'Because of me?' I retorted, getting to my feet to face him. 'Yes, I can see my part in all of this, and I am man enough to admit it. But who left her waiting on the quayside in Kingston? Who hid himself away like a coward when she arrived on the plantation? Who confronted her with a mulatta mistress and a bastard child?'

'That's enough!' he shouted, but my dander was well and truly up, and I was unable to stop myself. 'Who married her?' I shouted back. 'Who husbanded her and gave her four children? Who grew tired of her, and ran away from his responsibilities? Who found a compliant mistress, and fucked her, and started another wee McLehose clan? What kind of loyalty was that to your wife, may I ask? In fact, how can you use the word 'wife' to describe Nancy? You were never man enough to be a proper husband to her.'

'I'll kill you, Burns, I'll kill you!' he roared, flushing with rage. I know now that I should have gone no further, but there was no restraining me. God forgive me for my temper: I knew I had already said too much; but now the Rubicon had been crossed.

'Do you know what she said to me when we lay together, McLehose? Eh? She said she had never experienced such ecstasy before. One thorough scalade from me gave her more pleasure than all your years of awkward connubial fumblings. Oh, you managed to sow your seed in her, McLehose, but that's all you managed! Any clumsy carthorse can mount a mare,' I went on, knowing I was goading him beyond endurance, yet unable to prevent myself, 'but it takes a man to deal with a woman properly – a knack you have obviously not mastered.'

I have never seen such fury in a human face. He went white; his jaw dropped; the pupils of his eyes grew smaller. I returned his hate-filled glare with all the defiance I could muster. For what seemed like an age he was silent. 'I'll see you at dawn tomorrow,' he said, with a trembling calmness. On the avenue at the back of the estate. I shall provide the pistols. Currie will second me. I shall ask Mr Douglas to attend, and see that fair play is done. Good afternoon.'

I cannot believe that he is serious. I am furious with myself for letting my heart over-rule my head. I must see Mr Douglas before this ridiculous business proceeds any further.

[Later] Well, I am in a pretty pickle, and no mistake – my damned star holds its place in my zenith, and its baleful influence never leaves me for a moment. McLehose has beaten me to it. I called on Mr Douglas, and found him in his office, where he received me with great coolness. I explained that McLehose had proposed a duel, and that I hoped that such an extreme course of action might be avoided. But to my astonishment, he said he was perfectly content to officiate tomorrow morning, and was quite unmoved by my entreaties.

'It'll clear the air, one way or another,' he said.

'But one of us could be killed!' I exclaimed. 'What's the point in that?'

He shrugged. 'You'd best find a second, Burns,' he said. 'That may be easier said than done. This horrible business with poor Mrs

McLehose has upset people badly, and to be frank, there isn't much sympathy for you on the plantation. In the meantime I am extremely busy, as you see, so I will bid you good day.'

I could barely believe what I had just heard. Here was a man I had looked up to, almost as a son looks up to his father, and now he snubbed me, and seemed content to see me struck down by a bullet. I felt my frailty most acutely. This time tomorrow, my stiffening corse may be resigned to the earth, with none to mourn me.

I have found a second. Toby, good fellow, has agreed to stand by me. It grows dark outside. As I write, I realise that this could be the last entry I ever make in this journal. If there is another life, it is only for the just, the benevolent and the humane, and not for wretches like myself. Oh, would to God there were a world to come!

To heap misery upon misery, I have seen Adah. She came to the house, but would not enter. I moved to embrace her but she pushed me away; I tried to speak to her, wanting more than anything to beg her forgiveness, but she would not listen.

'Lemme speak,' she said. 'Yuh gwine fight wid McLehose, de 'ole plantation knows dat. Maybe yuh git dead. I knows 'bout Missiz McLehose. She dead now, and cyan't suffer no' mo'. Yuh teach me one t'ing, Massa Burns. Cyan't trust no white man. A neger like me's only a *specimen* fuh de white massa. Anyway, I's come fuh tell yuh.'

'Tell me what?' I asked.

She patted her belly. I's git yuh pickney. Nice, nuh? I don' t'ink I's gon 'ave much trubble findin' a man tuh tek care of we both. A man who don't run 'roun' after gran' white lady.'

She turned and walked away, and I realised that I would never see her again, or my unborn child. I came back in the house, and for the first time since Mary died, I put my head in my hands and sobbed bitterly. A week ago I could and should have been the happiest of men – now I have nothing, and it is my own fault. God knows I am no saint, but if I could wipe away tears from all eyes, I would do so; I know myself to have a benevolent spirit, yet I have caused so much injury that I cannot conceive how matters could possibly be worse with me.

June 5th. God forgive me! I have killed McLehose. I must set down an account of what happened, if for no other reason than that I wish to have the facts clear for my own reference, now that Scandal and Rumour are doing their worst.

Toby called for me just as the sky was beginning to lighten in the east, and we walked to the back of the estate. I cannot say what was going through my mind: my recollection is that it seemed to be happening to someone else. I found myself noticing insignificant trifles, like the call of a frog, or a fallen leaf, with a preternatural clarity. On the way I went to the spot where Mary and my little son lie together, and stood there for several minutes in silent contemplation. There was a strong likelihood that I would be sharing that grave in a matter of hours, and indeed I felt that my life was already over. I almost welcomed the thought of being at peace.

'Yuh gwine be all right, Massa Burns?' said Toby, as we neared the avenue. I could see that Douglas was already there, with McLehose and Currie, and I had to ask Toby to repeat his question.

'God alone knows,' I replied.

'Yuh di'n't do nuttin' wrong,' he said. 'De lady was on she own, she lonely, yuh good tuh she. Some of us folks, we says de lady git shock seein' Massa McLehose wid Miss Rivvere an' she kill she self.' I appreciated his charitable diagnosis, but I had no time to debate the point, and instead gave him some instructions about the disposal of my effects in the event of my death.

Mr Douglas look at me very disapprovingly as we came up. His eyes flicked disdainfully from me to Toby and back again.

'You've found a second, I see,' he said dryly. 'Well, well.'

'Is that the best you could come up with, Burns?' said McLehose. 'A neger as a second? You've always been too fond of negers for your own good.'

'You deserted your wife for a mulatta,' I retorted. 'And it broke her heart.'

He flushed. 'Enough of this. Let's get on with it.'

'Mr Douglas,' I said, 'if things go badly for me, I trust you will see that I am buried alongside Mary?'

'Aye,' he said, 'I'll do that for you.'

'Thank you.'

'Let's get on with it,' said McLehose again.

'You may choose your weapon,' said Mr Douglas, indicating a small chest containing two ivory-handled pistols. 'I have loaded them, and they are ready to fire, so please be careful.' I remember thinking that it seemed an incongruous remark in the circumstances. I reached down, selected one, and McLehose took the other. 'Are you determined to go through with this?' Mr Douglas asked. 'I believe I am supposed to put that question to you both.'

'Yes,' said McLehose grimly.

'I seem to have no option in the matter,' I said in resignation. I looked at my opponent. 'All I would say is that I have no wish to harm you. I am truly sorry for what has happened, and I shall carry my sorrow and guilt to the grave. We were once friends. Will you not reconsider?'

'My mind is made up,' he said with a scowl. 'As for your fine talk of graves, you'll be in yours soon enough.'

'Very well,' said Douglas. 'Stand back to back, please, and listen carefully. You will take ten paces, on my count. When I reach ten, you will turn and fire. Are you ready?' Neither of us said anything as we positioned ourselves. The pistol seemed very heavy in my right hand and I wondered if I would ever muster the strength to raise it. Ahead of me I could see the sky lightening above the banks of cane.

'One,' said Douglas. Numbly I began to walk forward.

'Two. Three. Four. Five.' There seemed an eternity between the numbers. I remember seeing a John Crow soaring high above the estate, and wondered if it could see the drama being enacted far below: two insignificant figures approaching what might be, for one of them, the final scene in the bitter tragedy of his life.

'Six. Seven. Eight. Nine.' In a rush of recollection, I saw the faces of my mother, of Jean, of my little Bess, of Mary, of Nancy. Time stopped, and I could feel the cold Ayrshire wind in my face and the cold, dead weight of a plough on a November morning; I could see a mouse scuttling away in terror from the ruins of its nest; I could remember the bleak realisation that we were alike, and that nothing on this earth is certain.

'Ten.'

I turned in a daze. McLehose seemed very far away. I saw a puff of smoke, and heard the ball whistle past my head. Without thinking, I lifted the pistol: the trigger yielded beneath my finger and the piece jerked as it discharged. I was quite sure I had missed, for these weapons are notoriously inaccurate except at very close quarters, and I had not made any conscious effort to aim. To my horror, I saw McLehose stagger back, clutching his hands to his stomach. Currie ran to him, and lowered him to the ground. Toby came over to me.

'Lak I say, Massa Burns, yuh all right.'

'What have I done?' I said. 'I didn't mean to harm him. Oh God, I should have fired into the air!' I crossed over to where Douglas and Currie were kneeling beside McLehose. They were opening his shirt, which was rapidly reddening, and as I came up I saw to my dismay that my bullet had struck him in the stomach. He was pressing his hands to the wound, and blood was gushing between his fingers. On his face was a pitiful expression of shock and disbelief. Douglas motioned me to one side.

'He's done for,' he said in a low voice. 'No man takes a shot in the stomach and survives.'

'I didn't mean to harm him,' I declared. 'You heard me say as much before we began. I didn't even aim. The gun just went off. I never wanted such a thing to happen.'

'Maybe you didn't,' said Douglas, 'but he's finished.'

McLehose, who had been gasping and moaning, now began to cry out. It was a terrible sound, made all the worse by the fact that there was nothing to be done for him. To carry him away was out of the question, and we had nothing with which to alleviate his suffering. He lay on his side with his knees drawn up to his chest. After a few minutes the screaming gave way to moans again. Then he vomited a great gush of dark blood and exhaled a last, shuddering breath.

'Ye fired on the count of nine,' said Currie. 'He didna hae a chance.'

'What do you mean?' I said. 'He fired on the count of ten, and he fired first. I appeal to you, Mr Douglas.'

'It's a bad business,' said Douglas.

'What? His pistol is discharged. You saw what happened.'

'He pulled the trigger as he fell,' said Currie. 'I saw it clearly.'

'Massa Burns fire on ten,' said Toby indignantly.

'Well, ye would say that, wouldn't ye?' said Currie. 'But the word o' a plantation neger isna worth onythin' in court. Ye really were rather careless in yer choice o' a second, were ye no', Burns?'

'Massa Burns fire on ten,' repeated Toby stubbornly.

'Well, it doesna matter what ye think,' said Currie disdainfully. 'A duel is one thing – an affair o' honour and a' that – but shooting yer man doon afore he has had a chance to fire – that is quite different. I am shair the authorities'll be maist interested. A man can hardly expect much leniency in court when he seduces a woman so that she kills herself for the verra shame o' it, and then guns doon her grieving husband in cauld blood.'

I ignored him. 'Mr Douglas,' I pleaded, 'you know full well that none of this is true. I know that Toby can't testify, and so it's my word against Currie's. But you know what happened. I appeal to you now as a gentleman, whose probity and rectitude I've always respected and admired. For God's sake man, put an end to this nonsense.'

'Hmm,' he said. 'It is a difficult situation, to be sure.'

'Are you forgetting that it was McLehose who challenged me? Are you ignoring the fact that he was the one who wished to proceed, while I offered to forget the matter? Can you seriously deny that he fired first?'

'It's difficult when there are no reliable witnesses,' he said slowly. 'I refuse to be drawn into this. Toby is obviously partial, and in any case he cannot testify, as you are well aware. I allow that Currie here may also be considered partial, but his word will count for much in court. On balance, the evidence, though admittedly circumstantial, appears to weigh against you. What better way did you have of silencing McLehose, who was clearly distraught, than to provoke a duel and put an end to him, as you have undoubtedly done?'

'I must request an audience with you later, in private,' I said, and turned on my heel with Toby following in silence. And so here I am, making an account of this horrible business, knowing myself without a friend in the world, and with the mark of Cain on my brow. I am a murderer, whatever construal one places on the circumstances. I have killed a man, and am feel only a bitter disgust with myself.

[Later] I have spoken with Mr Douglas. He kept me waiting for a good ten minutes before he deigned to admit me into his presence.

'We must have this out, you and I,' I said, coming straight to the point. 'I am an honest man, not without faults, but honest. I regard that as one of my virtues, however few and far between they may be. I do not lie. And I did not fire on McLehose first. You know that, and I know that. Now I call upon you to repudiate what you said earlier.'

He played with the papers on his desk for a few moments before replying. 'I respect your honesty, Burns,' he said quietly. 'I propose to be equally honest in return, and I would ask you to listen carefully to what I am about to say. Firstly, McLehose. The man was unprincipled, and I cannot say I am sorry to see the back of him, though I deplore the manner of his passing. His affair with the Rivvere woman was a disgrace. I would not have minded so much if he had kept it to himself, but his insistence on flaunting it openly was completely unacceptable. The arrival of Mrs McLehose was the last straw. The slaves look for order and decorum from us, and this has unsettled them at a time when I would have wished for stability. You behaved abominably in my house. Now Mrs McLehose is dead, and you have killed McLehose, and there will be hell to pay. If the white man cannot set an example, what hope is there for the slaves? You must remember that running a plantation cannot be done without discipline. This must extend to all of us. McLehose transgressed and so did you.' I began to protest, but he raised his hand and silenced me.

'You have been a thorn in my flesh, Burns,' he continued. 'You are probably a good man, but too principled for your own good. In Jamaica that is not a virtue – it is not even a luxury you can allow

yourself. We have had many discussions about the position of Ne-
groes, and your views on the subject simply do not square with your
position here. I dare say that the abolitionists may well win the day, but
that day is yet to come, and in the meantime I have this plantation to
run.' He pounded the desk with his fist as he spoke the last words.

'You treat Negroes as your equal,' he said, more quietly. 'You
have taken Adah into your bed, and you brought along Toby today
as your second. I simply could not believe your *naïveté*. Currie hates
you, I know that. He says you have threatened to kill him. Now you
have given him the opportunity to crucify you. Can you not see that
he was hoping all along that you would kill McLehose? Can you not
see the position you have placed me in? If two blacks kill each other,
that is one thing, but the death of a white man is a huge issue here
in Jamaica, as you ought to know. The death of McLehose is bad
enough. But add to this Currie's suggestion that you may have fired
before the count of ten. Add to that the fact that we have the suicide
of a white woman on the plantation, which will require a full
accounting to Kingston, and to her family in Edinburgh. Add to that
the fact that she was the wife of the man you killed. Add to that the
fact that you are a known sympathiser with the slaves. It is a complete
mess, Burns, and I absolutely refuse to become involved with it. If
I support you in this, then I shall be viewed as condoning your
behaviour and attitude, and my position will become untenable both
with the slaves and with our own community.'

'So you are prepared to deliver me to the gallows for the sake of
a 'position'?' I said bitterly. 'You would lie under oath to preserve it?
What kind a man are you?'

'A fair one, I hope,' he said. 'I know that you did not shoot
McLehose down. He fired first: I saw that perfectly well. And no, I
do not believe that you intended to kill him. But this matter has
grown too big for me now, and we have to find another way out. It
will take Currie at least a day to reach Kingston, and at least a further
day for your arrest. You have to leave Jamaica for a place where there
is no jurisdiction in such cases.'

'Where would I go?' I exclaimed.

'To the Guianas,' he said, 'to Demerary.[2] I have an acquaintance
there – a man by the name of Allardyce, who runs a plantation at a
wee place called Goed Intent. Once you are in Demerary there can
be no question of legal proceedings against you, for it is a Dutch
colony, as you know, and I shall, for my part, do all I can to muddy
the waters until this business dies down. Allardyce owes me a favour.
All you have to do is arrive, mention my name, and you will be safe,

and assured of a position. I have written a letter of introduction for
you. Now to practicalities. There is a boat tomorrow departing from
Port Antonio that will take you to Trinidad, and I have already paid
your passage. From there you will have to arrange your crossing to
Demerary, but that should not be difficult.' He took an envelope and
a small bag from his desk drawer. 'I have twenty pounds here in
doubloons, together with all of the information you will require, and
the letter of introduction. Take it. That is my final offer and I believe
it is a fair and generous one. By the time anyone gets around to
instituting a search, you will be safely away from here. I give you my
word as a gentleman that I shall never reveal to a living soul what has
passed between us today. People may make whatever assumptions
they choose, but my lips will remain sealed. What do you say?'

'I have no alternative but to accept your terms,' I said. 'And I am
grateful to you for your magnanimity.'

'I am glad you see it that way,' he said. 'During the night you must
make your way to the port, and seek out a ship called the *Venus*. The
captain is a freed slave by the name of Benedict, and he is beholden
to me for a variety of reasons. He will take you on board, and expects
to set sail under cover of darkness. Your journey will take you to
Santo Domingo, to exchange cargo, then east to Antigua. From
there you travel south until you reach Trinidad. Once there, the rest
is up to you.' He stood and came over to face me. 'I bear no animosity
towards you, Burns,' he said kindly, 'and I wish you well. Goodbye
now, and may God be with you.'

He extended his hand and I grasped it, feeling tears prickling in
my eyes. 'Goodbye then, Mr Douglas,' I said. 'Thank you for your
many kindnesses. I only wish . . .'

'Now, now,' he said, patting me on the shoulder. 'No need for
that. Get along with you, now, man. You have preparations to make.'

I bowed and left the room. Here I am now, in my little room,
surrounded with my paltry possessions. This morning I left this same
room faced with the prospect of imminent death. Now I have a man's
blood upon my head, and am about to become, yet again, an exile, with
the pitiless hounds of the Law baying at my heels. Who knows what
I will have to report when I pen my next entry in these pages?

The carriage should be here for me at about four in the morning.

June 6th. On board; early morning. What an utterly wretched day. I
had gone to bed after finishing my journal last night – sleep was
impossible, and I was tossing restlessly when I heard someone in the
room outside. Hoping it might be Adah, I went to the door of the

room and opened it. There was no light except that of the moon, but it was sufficient for me to discern a figure standing there.

'Adah?' I said. The figure ran at me with a scream, and I realised it was Ann Rivvere.

'You killed James, you bastard!' she shrieked as she lunged at me. I felt a blow to my left shoulder and realised that she had a knife, and was intent on butchering me there and then. I managed to wrest it from her grasp. Fortunately for me, her yelling and cursing alerted Mr Garvie's household, and they soon burst in and managed to restrain her. Together with my belongings, I was removed to the Great House, where the wound was dressed. Fortunately it was not serious but it aches damnably.

Later Mr Douglas himself took me to Port Antonio where I met up with Benedict, a most unprepossessing, shifty-looking man, whose first words were a demand for money, and it was only Mr Douglas's stern intervention that compelled him to admit that he had been paid already. It was about five in the morning when I boarded, and already growing light as we cast off and set sail.

The boat – I will not dignify it by terming it a ship – is about twenty feet in length with no cabins, only sail canvas stretched over the deck for'ard of the mast. I am the only passenger. Apart from Benedict, there are four other members of crew, all Negroes, who look at me suspiciously. My box, in which I keep my journal, has already been the subject of much covert scrutiny, and when I finish this entry and replace the volume, I must take care to let them see that it contains no jewels, diamonds, or whatever they imagine it to hold. As for my money, I took good care to conceal it safely on my person.

We are carrying a cargo of allspice, which grows only in Jamaica and is much valued on the other islands, and indeed in Europe. The smell of it is very strong, but at least it masks that of the boat and the crew. Our journey to Santo Domingo will take us about four days if the winds are favourable.

We have now cleared the harbour, and the morning light is giving me a last view of Fort George and Woods Island. I remember the nostalgia I felt when I set sail from Greenock and saw the Ayrshire coast slipping away. Now I feel an equally sharp pang of loss as I look up over the port to where the plantation lies. I have spent the best part of five years of my life there. What is Adah doing now, I wonder?

The swell makes it difficult to write.

June 11th. Saturday, Santo Domingo. I had no further opportunity to write on Benedict's wretched and ridiculously named boat because of the motion of the craft, indeed I have had barely a moment's sleep since leaving Jamaica. The boat was exceedingly uncomfortable. The only place to rest or to sleep was on flea-ridden bags of straw. These quickly grew sodden, for the sea was rough and water was constantly splashing over the sides. To make matters worse, I was not prepared for the fact that the nights would be so cold, and when darkness fell I was compelled to huddle under a few filthy sacks, all of a shiver. The wound in my shoulder throbbed incessantly. At least we had a barrel of fresh water on board, but I had not brought any food with me, and Benedict and the others were not inclined to share theirs, so I have subsisted on a few bananas for the best part of a week.

These privations would have been disagreeable enough, but matters were rendered worse by the fact that I quickly realised that Benedict and his crew were entirely treacherous, and would cheerfully have thrown me overboard, given the opportunity, to lay their hands on my modest possessions. Fortunately I had a good knife with me – the one I used to carry in the cane fields – it has a blade about eight inches long, and is sharp enough to shave with.

The first night I was dozing when I felt a hand in my pocket and I started up to find that one of the crew was trying to rob me. Of course he scuttled away when he saw he had been discovered, but after that I made sure that my knife was very much in evidence. I decided at that point that I was going to find some other means of reaching Demerary, but I said nothing, reasoning that I would be safer if they believed that I would remain with them for the much longer voyage from Santo Domingo to Antigua. It may mean spending some or all of the money Mr Douglas gave me, but I feel a not unreasonable aversion to having my throat cut.

Neither Benedict nor the crew spoke more than a few words to me, and I could not understand much of their rapid Creole. I was not sorry for that, for it has given me time to reflect on the events of these last few days. That I am to blame is evident. I allowed my head to be turned by Nancy, and that was my undoing as well as her own. Life had bestowed many blessings upon me, and I threw them away. I have been the cause of an innocent woman's death, and that of a man I once liked; I have forfeited the opportunity of ever seeing Adah again, and the child she is carrying. I have nothing to offer in the way of exculpation and I stand condemned in the sight of those I once called my friends. Squatting in the heaving boat I felt I was enduring a justly deserved penance for my impetuosity and foolishness; suffering a richly merited punishment for a damned, impulsive hotheadedness that has ruined me. My worst enemy is *Moi-même*.

We arrived in Santo Domingo in mid morning. It presented very much the same scene as Kingston, though all of the shouting was in Spanish. When I left the *Venus*, Benedict said that he planned to set sail again early tomorrow morning, and I said I would return in good time although I have no intention of doing so. I had been worried about making myself understood until I discovered that my French was well fitted to the purpose. I have never been to France, nor have I ever spoken with a Frenchman, so it was gratifying to realise that my childhood book learning had been to good account. I managed to find a rum-shop near the quayside where I was able to obtain something to eat and secure a little room. It is dirty, and the whole area is full of clamour and raucous shouting, but I do not plan to be here any longer than I can help. From what I understand, Benedict had planned to sail to Trinidad by way of Antigua and the other islands, and while my knowledge of geography is poor, I believe that it must surely be quicker to seek passage on board a vessel headed directly for Trinidad.

I am very tired, which is hardly surprising. My shoulder aches very badly – it has swollen up, and the skin around the wound is red and very tender to the touch. I have bound it up as best I can.

I am feeling light-headed and confused, with no way of knowing what the morrow will hold. I shall try and rest.

June 12th. Santo Domingo. Late afternoon. Still in my room above the rum-shop where liquor, victuals and women are in constant demand day and night. All three are in abundant supply, and, I suspect, equally cheap. I went down to the quay this morning and found to my relief that the *Venus* has departed. I made enquiries about a passage to Trinidad, and, after wasting a good deal of time on false errands, eventually found myself in negotiations with a Captain Fernandez, master of a neat square-rigger called the *Santa Maria*. He is a tall, spare man of about my own age, courteous in manner, and amenable to my request. We settled on a sum in gold that I take to be equivalent to around four or five pounds in Jamaican money. I am to embark this evening, for we sail during the night with the tide.

My shoulder is no better, and I felt feverish when I returned. I have taken a little rum to help alleviate the pain and bathed the cut with cold water.

June 13th. I barely managed to drag myself onboard the *Santa Maria*– Captain Fernandez was most solicitous and sent one of his crew to tend me. At least I have a cabin that is clean and quiet, with fresh bed linen – a blessed relief, for I am decidedly poorly and my shoulder gives me constant anguish. The crewman was a wizened old man called, I think, Diego. He speaks neither English nor French, but there is little need for words as the problem is plain to see: there is mortification in the wound and already it exudes the foul smell of putrefaction. Diego went off and returned with a hot poultice of bread and milk on a clean cloth, and applied this after first rubbing an onion on the infected place. I fainted clean away during his ministration, and when I recovered consciousness it was already daylight, and from the movement of the vessel I could tell that we were at sea.

I have risen from my bed to write this, but it took several attempts to heave myself up. It is not cold, but I am shivering and trembling, and the sweat is running from me. All I want to do is *sleep*, but this accursed pain *[entry abandoned]*

June 28th. Tuesday. I have not been able to write for two weeks, and for most of that time I gather I have either been in a delirium or completely insensible. I have only the vaguest recollection of the passing of time. The terrible pain has gone from my shoulder, which is now covered with a simple bandage. Captain Fernandez tells me that the wound must have been badly infected since the application of the poultices caused the inflammation to suppurate to the extent that it had to be lanced, and that for a time they were fearful for my life. I am grateful that I was delirious throughout the procedure. Diego, it seems, has been my guardian angel all this while, fulfilling the duties both of nursemaid and of surgeon. I could not have had better care from Simpson. He brought me a tonic this morning that had an immediate effect, though exceedingly bitter in taste. Captain Fernandez has told me since that it is made from the bark of a tree found in Peru, notable for its restorative properties.[3]

We are expected to arrive in Trinidad on Saturday.

June 31st. These have been lazy days – Diego has slung a hammock for me on deck, so I have been drowsing in the heat of the sun in order to regain my strength. In the evenings I go below and am regaled by Captain Fernandez and his officers who ply me with food and wine until my head spins, whereupon I collapse into my berth and sleep more soundly than I have done for months. I feel much more vigorous, and my shoulder hardly troubles me at all. It is early evening as I write, and the light is beginning to fade, but from deck it is possible to make out the dark shape of Trinidad. We should be there by morning.

Now that I am restored to health, the last month seems like a nightmare from which I am only slowly awakening. Sitting here in my neat cabin, listening to the creak of ropes and the crackling of canvas I am reminded of the *Bell,* all these years ago, when Mary was alive and we had everything to look forward to. How much has happened since then! If only we had the power to change things! What if Nancy had never come to the plantation? I would never have taken leave of my senses in the way that I did, and Adah and I might still be together, sailing across the Atlantic, waiting in eager anticipation for the 'pickney' she wanted so much. But instead of resuming life in Scotland, here I am: alone and headed for a place called Demerary about which I know next to nothing except that it is a Dutch colony with sugar plantations.

I am filled with remorse each time I think of Nancy, and the part I had in driving her to take her own life. As for James, the memory of that duel is so horrible that I do not know what to think any more.

Diego has just brought me a jug of wine, so I shall close for now.

July 1st. Trinidad, Port-of-Spain. Yet another bustling harbour. I have taken my leave of the good Captain Fernandez and his men, and the faithful Diego, to whom I gave some money in order to thank him for his many kindnesses. He was loath to take it, but eventually did so, kissing me warmly on both cheeks.

I was most impressed by the courtesy with which I was treated aboard the *Santa Maria*. Relations between Britain and Spain have not always been cordial, but I was treated like a valued guest during the journey, and lacked for nothing. There are good people everywhere: indeed I incline to the view that, left to their own devices, ninety-nine hundredths of the human race would happily live as brothers. It is only the selfish rabble-rousing of pious priests, puerile politicians and pompous polemicists that turns nation against nation.

I am writing this in a little rum-shop overlooking the harbour. My next task shall be to secure a passage to Demerary.

July 2nd. I was surprised to be able to find a ship so quickly, but I am given to understand that the route is a very busy one, and the sole preserve of Dutch traders, so I now find myself on board the *Voorzichtigheid,* bound for the port of Stabroek.[4] Captain de Ruyter is in command, and he speaks excellent English, which makes life easier for me. I told him that I wished to go to Goed Intent; he says that it is on the opposite side of the river from Stabroek and some distance upstream, but has promised to take me there. The ship is solid rather than elegant, and designed to accommodate the heavy cargo of ironmongery to be offloaded in exchange for sugar and rum which will be brought back to Trinidad to be loaded into larger vessels bound for Europe. The accommodation is not capacious, but the journey should only take three or four days.

I asked the Captain if he had ever heard of Allardyce, but he said he had not. He explained that Demerary is the name of the colony, named after the river that runs through it, and that there are two other principal regions called Essequibo and Berbice, also named after their rivers. Together they form the United Colony under the control of a Governor. The current incumbent is called Albertus Backer. He gave quite a lecture on the political system, but I cannot remember much of it, and I hesitated to ask him to spell too many names so that I could enter them correctly in this journal. The name of his ship alone took me several attempts – he tells me it signifies 'caution'.

He asked me if I was English and I told him that I was Scottish, which seemed to please him. There were many Scots in Demerary, he said. I asked whether the presence of English and Scottish planters caused difficulties, given that the colony was Dutch. He told me that it posed no problems at all, and I have the impression that the governance is very tolerant.

I am writing this on the table in the main cabin where we have just had supper. The plates have been cleared away and I am enjoying a glass of schnapps, courtesy of the Captain. I had never tasted it before – it is completely clear, like water, and he says that no matter how much of it one drinks, there will be no ill effects the following day. It is fiery stuff, however, and I shall limit myself to this one glass before heading for my berth.

July 3rd. A day into our journey. There is a slight breeze, and in the shade it is almost tolerable. The sea is no longer blue, but brown and dirty looking. Although land is not in sight, I am told that the mighty rivers of the Guianas carry great quantities of silt in their prodigious waters, and that this may be observed many miles out to sea. The air smells different, and I remember how the Mr Galbraith, on board the *Bell*, had said that sailors could scent land. The air smells thicker, if such a thing is possible, with the faintest suggestion of vegetation.

The Captain has been telling me improbable tales about the United Colonies, and in particular the wild animals – snakes of immense size, man-eating fish and the like. I have been listening with polite interest, but believe none of it. Every countryman has exaggerated stories with which to frighten the incomer – Scotland has the kelpie, or water-horse that persuades the unwary traveller to mount before plunging into the depths of some benighted loch.

Only the most foolish give such a tale any credence, but it is a grand story to tell an Englishmen newly arrived in Scotland!

July 4th. Nearer to land. It is much warmer. Such land as I can see is low and flat, but little detail discernible as yet. Overhead are massive white clouds. The sea is choppy. The crew tell me we are passing the mouth of the Orinoco, one of the great rivers of this mysterious continent, stretching over a thousand miles into the forests of the interior. It carries so much water that when it reaches the sea there is not one mouth but many, each larger than any river-mouth found in Europe. I shall set down more impressions when I reach my destination, for the boat heaves so much that it is hard to write.

July 6th. I have arrived, and what a wretched place it is! This morning we entered the Demerary River, which is a seething mass of dun-coloured water about a mile wide. Even with the wind behind us, progress was slow against the current. To the left of the estuary mouth sprawls the Dutch settlement of Stabroek of which I could make out little through the driving rain. On the right hand side were fields of cane, separated from the river by what looked like a sea wall, punctu-ated at intervals by odd structures that I take to be connected in some way with irrigation channels. The horizon was very low – no hills to be seen anywhere – the sky oppressive, filled with heavy-looking grey clouds in which lightning flickered. The boat headed towards a miserable jetty with sagging timbers. We came in close, dropped anchor, and the crew took the strain on the ropes, allowing the current to swing us into the berth. There were two people there, a Negro and a white man, sheltering in a small open-sided thatched hut. When they saw me, they came forward to assist me from the boat.

'Well, well,' said the white man, shaking me by the hand. He was man of about five-and-forty years, with a white beard, and from the sound of his voice a fellow-Scot. 'Who have we here? We don't see many strangers around here, do we Ambrose?'

'Nossuh,' agreed the Negro politely.

'My name is Burns,' I said. 'Robert Burns.'

'I'm Forsyth. This is Ambrose, our head driver. Welcome to Demerary. What brings you here?'

'I have come from Jamaica,' I explained. 'I have a letter of introduction to a Mr Allardyce, whose plantation should be near here. Perhaps you could tell me where it is. The place is called Goed Intent, I believe.'

'You're standing on it,' said Forsyth. 'I work for Allardyce myself.'

We walked for about ten minutes through thick bushes that eventually thinned out to reveal a panorama of cane fields and a cluster of roughly constructed buildings. The rain had providentially ceased by this time. Forsyth excused himself, saying he had duties to attend to, and Ambrose led me towards what I took to be the overseers' quarters.

'Allardyce live dere,' said Ambrose, pointing to a thatched hut raised on massive wooden pillars, with a stairway leading to a veranda. The whole edifice, constructed out of rough-hewn timber, was devoid of any decoration. The other buildings were much the same.

'Will you let him know I have arrived?' I asked.

'Oh nossuh,' replied Ambrose emphatically. 'Yah bes' see Massa Allardyce yahself.'

I climbed the stairs to the veranda, and as I did the door opened and a man came out. I have never before encountered such an entirely unprepossessing individual. He was very tall: at least six feet and two inches. His hair was long, and had clearly not been washed or combed for many months. His thick beard was matted. His eyes were bleary and bloodshot, and to judge from the stench of rum, he had not been sober for weeks. But the general impression he gave was one of extraordinary physical strength, despite his evident dissipation. His shirt lay open, revealing a massive hairy chest, and his muscular arms were as thick as a man's thigh. To my embarrassment I saw that his breeches were open at the front, revealing his privates.

'Wha the hell are you?'

'I'm Burns. I come on the recommendation of Mr Douglas.'

'Wha?'

'Mr Douglas, of the New Cumnock estate in Jamaica. I have a letter from him.'

'Oh, thon Douglas. Aye. Ye'd better come in then.'

I followed him into a room containing a desk heaped with papers, and a few chairs. There was an overwhelming stench of rum-sodden sweat and unwashed linen. He bade me sit down.

'Whaur's the letter, then?' he said. I handed it to him, and he perused it without any enthusiasm.

'He says ye've had a wee bit o' bother.' He sniffed, throwing the letter on to the table. 'Weel, it's no ma business. I owe him a favour, an' forbye I could dae wi' the help. I'm doon tae fower men since MacDonald passed awa, damn the man.'

'What did he die of?' I asked.

'Rum,' he replied briefly. 'Ye can either handle it or ye canna. MacDonald couldna.'

He explained my duties, which are to keep the accounts of the plantation and generally to lend a hand as required – in other words, a factotum. In return I am to have the quarters of the late Mr McDonald, and a salary of forty pounds a year, though he was evasive when I enquired when it would be paid.

'Ye'll hae little need o' money here,' he said with a grin. 'Ye'll tak yer food wi' the ithers. Thomas is a braw cook when he sets his mind tae it. Mind ye, he needs a kick up the arse frae time tae time. If ye need tae cross the river tae Stabroek I'll gie ye an advance.'

He made a gesture for me to leave him, which I did, and I sought out my accommodation which is a hut situated nearby, of the same construction as that of Allardyce. The roof is thatched with the long leaves of some kind of palm-tree, woven together. Altogether it is very primitive, and infested with tiny red ants, which emanate from nests that resemble clumps of mud adhering to the walls. These get everywhere, and although their bite is not painful, it is irritating. Apart from the bed, a table and a chair there is nothing. The place is filthy, and I shall have to have the bed linen washed. There are mosquitoes everywhere. The hut is in a small clearing of rough grass, and the aspect is of a thick wall of dense greenery about fifty feet distant, hardly the panoramic vista one might have hoped for. It is damnably hot, and I stink.

July 10th. Besides Allardyce, there are four other white men on the plantation. William Forsyth is the most senior among them. He hails originally from Edinburgh, and is a very decent sort, though he defers constantly to Allardyce. He has been here since he was a young man, and speaks Dutch in addition to some of the languages of the local Indians. He has a 'wife' called Eliza, a cheerful young black woman, and two bonny children. I feel sure that he and I will get along very well together. I cannot say the same for George MacDuff, a Glasgow man, who strikes me as a most uncouth and surly individual. He is constantly complaining, and will snatch at any excuse to avoid work. He is a small man, grossly overweight and perspires constantly. I estimate him to be around thirty years of age. Our conversation, such as it is, is limited. David McLean is of about the same age, but slender in build and sunny in disposition. I have been here but a few days, and already he greets me like an acquaintance of many years' standing. Like myself he is an Ayrshire man, from Irvine, and so we have much to talk about. I mind well the few months I spent there ten years ago learning to spin flax, a dismal business if ever there was one, which concluded for ever when my house burned down. Anthony Smith is the youngest of us, barely twenty, and the only Englishman. He made the passage from Bristol to the Slave Coast, and from thence to Demerary on a slave ship. He is an unhappy young man who speaks but little, and I have not yet observed him smile. MacDuff taunts him constantly.

August 21st. The Sabbath. I have not written for some time, having had little leisure to do so. This plantation lacks the order and the humanity I was accustomed to in Jamaica. Allardyce is merely an agent of the owner, Lord Balcarres,[5] and runs the plantation with the same cruel disregard for dignity as that oaf McPherson in Savanna-la-Mar. It is impossible to go anywhere without hearing the lash of his whip, and his bellowed imprecations and obscenities. MacDuff is a very willing lieutenant; McLean and Forsyth, to their credit, far less so; Smith tries to act the tyrant, but his heart is clearly not in it. It is Ambrose, the head driver, who really runs the plantation, though Allardyce is either too foolish or too drunk to recognise the fact.

The mill house and the distillery are dilapidated affairs, in need of repairs that are always spoken of, but never carried out. The heat and humidity are debilitating. As I write, I have to place a rag over the page to prevent the sweat on my hand from turning the paper sodden. The whole place breeds a lethargy; the simplest task leaves me streaming in sweat.

The pleasantest place here is the benab, a round hut with low sides, and a thatched roof. It is the coolest place on the estate, and the overseers often gather together there of an evening.

September 23rd. Word has been received that there has been a massive uprising of slaves in Saint-Domingue; they have gone on the rampage and killed every white person they encountered. It is reported that these ruthless men carry before them a pike bearing the impaled body of a white baby, and are intent on taking over the whole country. Everything appertaining to the slaveholders has been put to the torch – factories; houses; whole fields of crops, and indeed entire plantations. The events in France have led to the issuing of a variety of edicts that no one seems inclined to accept, for it would mean all mulattoes being granted the same rights as white men, rather than the grudging privileges they currently enjoy. Revolution is afoot![6] Allardyce is adamant that this matter is not to be spoken of in front of the slaves, as it would only serve to fill their minds with mischief.

The Charter of the VWC has expired and is not to be renewed.[7] Quite what this means for us, nobody seems to know. We receive scant information from the outside world, and what we do hear reaches us at second or third hand. Just before I arrived here, someone tried to start a newspaper, but I gather the venture came to nothing.[8]

October 2nd. McLean has told me more about MacDonald, whom I replaced. Allardyce's mention of over-indulgence in rum, is but part of a rather horrible story. It seems that he had two small children by a plantation woman called Grizzel – one was a year or so old and the other a mere babe in arms. A few months before I arrived, the mother drowned while bathing in one of the creeks not far from here. MacDonald was distraught, and began drinking heavily, in consequence whereof he grew preoccupied with all kinds of morbid and bizarre notions. One day he was seen heading for the fatal spot with the children, muttering about reuniting them with their mother. The alarm was raised, but when the party caught up with them, he had already drowned the children, and was about to plunge in after them when he was restrained and brought back here. McLean says that he never spoke again, and was found dead in his bed a few days afterwards, surrounded by empty rum bottles.

Stated in these stark terms it seems a strange and unlikely story, but in this heat a man's head could easily be turned. The only tolerable part of the day is the early morning when it might almost be called cool, though in Scotland even that blessed coolness would be accounted warm!

October 15th. I am slowly becoming familiar with the workings of the plantation, but I feel out of place here. The Negroes are tougher and more muscular than any I have seen before. Everyone lives in fear of Allardyce, including the overseers. He is harsh and uncompromising, and the whip is never out of his hand. In Jamaica there was laughter and banter; here there is only a joyless application to the endless and repetitive task of tending the cane. On the Sabbath, the slaves are given leave to tend their gardens, but Allardyce will not allow them to sell their produce, and indeed they have few possessions to call their own. Their dress is drab, and of the cheapest quality.

I still have most of the money that Mr Douglas gave me, and I am giving thought to leaving here. The only reason for not doing so is my uncertainty about what proceedings, if any, have been taken against me in my absence. Forsyth and MacLean are the only ones that I feel I can talk to, and I have divulged nothing of my past to them. I have done my best to make my quarters comfortable, but without much success. The nearest market is at Vreed-en-Hoop, which means an excursion lasting the best part of a day, on a muddy track.

November 7th. I arose this morning just before dawn and took a walk down to the Demerary. For a long time I stood by its swiftly flowing brown waters and relished the blessed cool of the morning. Over the far bank the sky began to brighten, until the blazing disc of the sun slowly rose into view, banishing the fine morning mist and heralding the start of another day. In the distance I could hear the bell of our plantation sounding. Great buzzards wheeled silently overhead, sweeping down occasionally into the mangroves. It was a scene of astonishing beauty and tranquillity. In all directions there is only sugar cane stretching to the horizon – no hills in the distance to suggest a limit to an endless plain. In consequence the sky above appears incredibly vast, and I feel like an insignificant speck in the midst of this immensity. At such times one could almost be content with one's lot here.

Then I walked back to the plantation. Allardyce was cursing and yelling as usual.

I have brought out my table and chair, am now sitting on my balcony writing this, listening to the song of a bird, which frequents these parts and has a very haunting, distinctive call, accented on the final syllable, which accounts for its name of kiss-ka-dee. It is a fine-looking creature that flies busily around the trees, often in pairs. The crown of its head is black, the throat is white, but the rest of it is a delightful yellow. I suppose it must be a little larger than the common starling back home, and a very fine sight it is too.

November 26th. Went to Stabroek in the company of McLean, who had business there. We were rowed across at the turn of the tide, for at other times the current moves so swiftly that a boat would either be carried upstream, or swept out to the open sea. We arrived at the dock, which was constructed very solidly with massive greenheart timbers.

I was delighted and surprised with the appearance of the city, which was only begun some ten years ago. The streets are broad, and furnished with trees and neat irrigation canals. The buildings are without exception built of wood, but very expertly made; many have their balconies decorated with carved wood, and everything has been painted in white so that the impression is one of cleanness and order.

It is a long time since I saw so many white faces together at once! I believe that they were mostly Dutchmen, though I heard other languages spoken. The only Negroes I saw were in attendance on their masters, and dressed very finely – I even saw one with a wig.

We were walking in the street when we heard shouting and the tramp of marching feet coming closer. Everyone stopped to stare as a column of soldiers came past, escorting four or five Negroes all chained together.

'Runaways,' explained McLean. 'I do not envy their situation.'

'What will happen to them?' I asked.

'Oh, they will be hanged outside the jail. It isn't far – we could go and watch if you like.'

'I would prefer not to,' I said. They all bore signs of having been badly beaten, and there was on their faces a look of complete hopelessness, a pitiable air of wearied resignation as they shuffled towards their fate. And for what? Brought from Africa in a stinking ship; put to work in cane fields infested with rats and snakes; cursed at and lashed; compelled to tolerate the intolerable – they ran away. And for this they were now to suffer death.

'If they are to die anyway, why did the soldiers not just shoot them when they found them? I asked McLean. 'Why go to all the trouble of bringing them here?'

'There's a bounty of a hundred guilders for each runaway.'

So that is the price of a man's life – about ten English pounds.

We returned to the plantation in the late afternoon, very weary, myself despondent. I do not know how much longer I can last in this country.

December 13th. I find it difficult to summon up the energy to write, as I feel tired and listless all the time. Every action seems to demand an enormous effort, and even thought becomes laborious. I find I am increasingly forgetful. The other day I forgot my cutlass and had to go home for it, but by the time I returned home I had quite forgotten what it was I had come back for. Thomas, the cook, says that this enervation is best cured with karela, and he has been feeding it to me for the last day or two. It has a very strange, bitter taste and my first impulse was to spit it out, but I have persevered.

Ambrose has given me a macaw – a very fine bird indeed, with glossy feathers of crimson, yellow and blue. We see many of them flying by, but this one is tame, and sits very happily on my balcony, from where he can easily hop on to a branch of a nearby tree. He does not like to be petted as I discovered when I put out my hand to stroke the top of his head. He opened his black beak and would have bitten me for certain had I not pulled back. He gives off a very strange, pungent smell: I believe this comes from some substance secreted to keep the feathers groomed. He is good company for me, and indeed there are times when I feel like Robinson Crusoe as I sit here in my wooden shack, so I have christened him Poll.

December 31st. It is damnable to have no books apart from my Equiano! Next time I am in Stabroek I must seek out a library, although if there is such a thing it is likely all the books will be in Dutch, and of no use to me unless I teach myself that language. I have been reading this journal and trying to reflect on the events which have led me here. A year ago I wrote of myself as being in Eden, but where am I now? I think the karela diet is helping, for I feel less lethargic – I wish I could enjoy the taste of the medicine!

1792

January 5th. At table this evening MacDuff was very amusing, as he thought, at the expense of the unfortunate Smith. For my part, I am not in the slightest concerned about the poor lad's English origins, but MacDuff cannot let the matter alone. Thomas, the cook, had served us up a black, oily stew which he called pepper-pot, well-named because after a single mouthful I felt my eyes begin to water, and if someone had poured spirit of salts down my gullet it would have been a welcome relief. Smith's reaction was more violent, for he immediately spat his mouthful back on to his plate with an exclamation of disgust. MacDuff was on to him in an instant.

'Whit's the matter wi' ye, laddie?' he shouted. 'Whaur are yer manners? Or is this the wey the English behave at table – spittin' ower their neebours? Damn it man, ye'll be pissin' in ma rum next!'

'I'm sorry, I couldn't help it,' gasped Smith, flushing crimson. 'It's too highly seasoned for my taste, that's all.'

'Oh, it's too highly *seasoned,* is it?' scoffed MacDuff, affecting an English accent. 'Oh, how *frightfully* dreadful!'

'I couldn't help it,' insisted Smith. 'I can't be the only one. What do you think, Forsyth? Shouldn't we ask Thomas to put in a little less of whatever it is . . .?'

'Ye're no' fit tae kiss Thomas' arse!' roared MacDuff. 'I can eat this – nae bother!' He set to and began to shovel the stuff into his mouth.

'Leave him alone,' said Forsyth mildly. 'He has done you no harm.'

MacDuff made no reply. His face took on rather a peculiar expression, and rivulets of sweat began to trickle down his forehead. He sat still for fully a minute, and then suddenly leaned forward and vomited on the table.

'What were you saying about table manners?' I asked. This raised a roar of laughter, and MacDuff leapt to his feet and ran from the room. I went round to the kitchen and suggested to Thomas that he use less pepper in future.

'Ain't nuttin' bad wid de pepper-pot,' he said. 'He's good pepper-pot. Me mek he good, man.'

'Aye well, MacDuff's left his on the table,' I said. 'Unfortunately it's been in his stomach first. And none of the rest of us could eat it.'

'He's pig,' said Thomas, which I felt was fair comment, although of course I could not say so.

I managed to mollify his ruffled feelings, and he eventually assured me that the plantation *cuisine* (my word, not his) would be

less emetic in future. I could not be angry with him; the incident
made me recollect my own attempt to make a haggis – oh! poignant
memory! It seems an eternity since we sat round that table, McLehose,
Miss Rivvere, Adah and I, drinking rum and laughing about my poor
skills. How simple and easy life seemed then!

February 17th. I amused myself with the composition of some foolish
verses on the pepper-pot incident. I read them aloud to the company
this evening, and they were greeted with the utmost hilarity –

Lines on a bad cook

Thomas was a tireless cook;
His gifts, alas, were few.
For all the efforts that he took,
He made a 'fearful stew'.

He treats us a' wi' scant respect
Although we are his masters:
Nae purgative has half th'effect
As Thomas's disasters.

There's some resemble fricasee,
There's some ower sharp and tart:
There's some that mak us want tae dee,
And some just mak ye fart.

We shat and spewed frae morn till night,
Our wames were swall'd and sair:
Ours was a truly grievous plight:
We could 'stomach it' nae mair.

'It will not do!' MacDuff declared,
'He wouldna daur repeat it
If we served *him* what he'd prepared,
And damned well made him eat it!'

And as it chanced, the very next day
We looked at what we'd got;
And saw to our extreme dismay
A fiery pepper-pot!

We took it to the cookhouse door,
And Thomas 'gan tae squeal
When we bold four said wi' a roar
He had to share our meal!

Then wi' a snarl up spak MacDuff,
His patience ever sparse:
'If you serve pepper-pot again,
I'll shove it up your arse!'

We gied the cook a muckle spoon
And watched him as he ate,
Until he'd forced the hale lot doon
And fully cleared his plate.

He claspit at his bulgin' wame;
Saut tears poured frae his e'en:
His very innards were aflame:
His skin, tho' daurk, turned green.

But here my Muse maun tact display,
And draw a tactfu' veil:
Sufficeth it (I think) tae say
He went 'beyond the pale'.

Ye pow'rs! I beg ye, send a curse
On villain cooks wha dare
Tae serve us pepper-pot, or worse:
And send us better fare!

MacDuff was very pleased to find himself the subject of a poem, and urgently demanded a copy of it, declaring that the eighth verse, in particular, was the finest piece of rhyming he had ever heard; but although it is flattering to receive praise, I do not consider the verses to be of any quality.

February 18th. Today I was out on the dams, supervising the clearing of an irrigation canal that had become blocked with weeds. Some distance away I heard the sound of shouting and screaming. When I went to investigate its cause, I found that Allardyce had tied an old slave to a tree, ripped the shirt from his back, and was meting out a vigorous lashing with the cowhide whip which he carried with him at all times. Forsyth was looking on. The old man's entreaties were all but drowned out by Allardyce's bellowings. I was powerless to intervene, but asked Forsyth what the wretched man had done to occasion such a punishment.

'Slacking,' he said. 'He should have been weeding, but we found him sleeping over there.'

Allardyce put his whip down and untied the man, who fell to the ground moaning, his back a mass of bloody welts.

'Get up, you lazy piece o' black filth!' he cried, kicking at the old man's stomach. 'Get up, I tell ye! Flat on yer back, sleeping on the job, eh? My God, ye'll no' sleep sae easy the nicht! Get him up,' he continued, gesturing to the small group of children and elderly slaves who formed the weeding party, and who were crouched together some way off, watching in horror. They came forward as one, and silently dragged him away.

'Did he have to be treated so?' I said to Forsyth. 'Would you have flogged that old man?'

'Not I,' he said. 'I hate whips.'

'So do I,' I said. 'A sharp word would have been quite sufficient. No good can come of this kind of treatment.'

'Whit are you twa whispering aboot?' demanded Allardyce.

'About that,' I said, pointing to the whip. 'Was that really necessary?'

He came up to me at a half run, and I recoiled instinctively, putting up my hands to ward off the blow, which I felt certain was coming. His face twisted up into a rictus of pure rage.

'Are ye tellin' me how to treat ma slaves, Burns?' he shouted in my face. 'How daur ye, sir? How daur ye? *You* of a' people – *you*, wha shot doon a man in cauld blood – *you*, taking issue wi' *me* ower a few cuts wi' a whip on the back o' an idle neger?'

'I beg your pardon, Mr Allardyce,' I said, much taken aback. 'I have never killed a man in cold blood, as you well know. And yes, I do believe that these 'few cuts', as you put it, were unnecessary.'

'Unnecessary?' he sneered. 'What's *your* opeenion on this, Mr Forsyth?'

'Well sir . . . it's not really for me to say,' Forsyth stammered.

'Aye,' said Allardyce. 'It's no' for ye tae say. It's no' for Mr Burns here tae say. It's for me tae say!' He waved the whip in my face. 'So I wad thank ye tae keep yer fancifu' scruples tae yersel', Mr Burns. I hae enough tae contend wi'. I'll no' be surrounded by neger-lovers.' With that he stalked off, muttering to himself.

'My God, Burns,' said Forsyth, 'ye canna antagonise him like that!'

'Why not?' I retorted. 'He's a bully o' the worst kind, and he'll have a rebellion on his hands if he isn't careful. That would be the end of him – and both of us. He canna treat his slaves like this.'

'He can,' said Forsyth morosely. 'There's nothing we can do about it.'

'That remains to be seen,' I said.

'What do you mean?'

'Wait and see.'

Now that I have witnessed Allardyce's inhumanity at first hand, I am convinced the man must be stopped. If entreaty fails, then I must needs take other measures, and have resolved to write to Lord Balcarres to inform him of the iniquities being perpetrated, and the appalling consequences that this could have for his investment here. What bullies fear most is to be confronted. I have learned what Coffy unloosed in Berbice thirty years ago, and the thought of such a terrible thing happening here is too awful to contemplate.[1]

February 18th. This morning I determined to get it over with, and went to Allardyce's hut as soon as I heard him stirring. I was anxious to converse with him early, believing that he would be more amenable to reason when he was sober.

'What the hell d'ye want?' he snarled.

'I want to explain my attitude yesterday,' I replied.

'Come tae apologise, have ye?'

'I have come in the expectation of being able to discuss the matter,' I said. 'May I speak?'

'If ye must,' he grunted, with bad grace, and motioned me to sit.

'Mr Allardyce,' I began. 'I have no wish to question your authority. Yet I believe with all my heart that such treatment of the slaves will do more harm than good. The man you flogged yesterday won't be able to work for several days . . . no, hear me out,' I added, seeing that he was about to interrupt me. 'So you lose a labourer, which the plantation can ill afford. If flogging is commonplace, then there's no other way to maintain order, and we end up having to flog each and every one of them to secure even a grudging compliance. There is much talk of emancipation, and the slaves have learned of it. They're waiting, Mr Allardyce, and it will come. We must prepare for that day by treating them with fairness and kindness. If we do not, then they will at best desert the plantation, or at worst, exact a terrible revenge. Even when they are free, we will still need these people – we cannot run the plantation without them.'

'People?' he said with a snort. 'That's yer mistake, Burns. They arena people: they are savages. And the only way tae rule savages is through fear. They dinna understaun' onythin' else.'

'But they *are* people, despite what you say. They are different from us . . .'

'Different? They are brutes and animals and . . .'

'You see the mulatto children on the plantation. How do they come to be here? You know the answer. Do white men copulate with *animals*, Mr Allardyce?'

He laughed. 'The black lassies hae their charms, Mr Burns!'

'If they have charms, then they may also prove to have other qualities,' I said, 'given the opportunity.'

'It's the menfolk,' he said. 'Aye, the women are compliant. They'll gie themsel's tae ye because it brings them privileges. Their mulatto bairns are looked up to – ye ken that fine. But the menfolk! Shall I tell ye somethin'?' He dropped his voice and leaned forward confidentially, putting his face close to mine. A reek of stale rum was on his breath, which stank like a privy, and it was all I could do not to turn my own face away. 'I fear black men, Burns,' he said, with a desperate intensity. 'I fear their broad shoulders and their thick lips. I fear the shape o' their noses. I fear their gapin' mooths, fu' o' teeth, and their thick pintles hingin' doon their thighs. Nae argument o' yours, or o' Wilberforce, can change that, Burns. Maist o' a', I fear the thochts in their minds. I can beat them; I can flog them; I can whip them, but never a word escapes them, only 'Yessuh, Massa Allardyce'. Ye fuck their womenfolk, and what do they say? 'Yessuh, Massa Allardyce'. I see them lookin' at me and I am *afraid.* God man, whit goes on ahent their e'en? That is why I mak recourse tae the whip!'

He subsided. The candour of his outburst had surprised me. I recognised his fears, and was astonished that he had articulated them so clearly. For all my dislike of the man, I had to admire this honesty.

'Things could change, Mr Allardyce,' I said. 'You could do yourself much good by declaring that harsh punishments were to end. Perhaps by offering inducements . . .'

'Inducements? Ye havena been listenin' tae me, man! I canna change how I feel. I ken nae ither way but tae be strong – stronger than they. That is the way the plantation shall be run, as long as I hae the runnin' o't.'

'Despite the risks?'

'Risks?' he replied with a snort. 'This whole place is a risk, Burns. There's snakes that'll kill ye, an' fish that'll rip the flesh aff yer banes in twa meenits. Have ye no' seen the spiders? Great, ugsome things – I hate them! One o' the beasties bit me on the foot once, and I couldna walk for a week. There's yaws; mosquitoes; ants; marsh fever – and negers. This is hell on earth, sir! This is the maist inhospitable, miserable, terrifyin', disease-ridden place on earth! This isna a place for humans! We dinna belong here. We get sick. We die. But this is whaur the sugar grows. And I'll control the negers, just as I control the weeds an' the snakes. Ye dinna ask the snakes tae stop bitin' ye, or ask the weeds tae stop cloggin' up the channels. Ye beat them doon!'

'Very well. But I must tell you that I cannot condone this harsh treatment. It is my belief that unless you profess yourself willing to change, then your future here is a bleak one.'

'Condone?' he sneered, showing his great yellow teeth. 'So ye canna *condone* me, Mr Burns? Dear God, I'm feart o' yer fancy words!' He got up and went over to the rum-jar. 'I've listened tae ye, Burns,' he said quietly. 'I've listened wi' great patience. Now *you* listen tae *me*.' He poured out a mug of liquor, and drank deeply from it. 'If onybody needs floggin', I'll flog him. I'll even kill if I must. D'ye understaun'? I willna barter, or flatter, or cajole, or beg. If I went doon that road, the hale plantation wad go tae perdition. They hae places tae live, they hae food, and they hae each ither. In return they work. If they willna work, then they suffer the consequences. Now get oot.'

I went to the door. 'I still think you are mistaken, Mr Allardyce.'

'Tae hell wi' ye!' he bawled.

The man must be stopped before it is too late. I fear that my letter to Lord Balcarres will have to be written. In one respect Allardyce is perfectly correct – this is indeed hell on earth. It is fearfully hot and airless tonight, without even the slightest breeze to render it tolerable, and the creaking chorus of the frogs renders sleep impossible. I am running with sweat, but unable to strip off my clothes to keep cool because of the mosquitoes, which are everywhere. I am reminded of the plagues of Egypt, and am certain that even they, dreadful as they were, could not have been so miserable to endure.

February 27th. It has rained pretty well each day and each night for almost a week. The ominous, ragged clouds are dark, almost black, with a sulphurous tinge, and they hang very low, giving the appearance of drifting smoke. They arrive quickly – the onset of rain is prefaced by a violent wind, which sets all of the trees in noisy motion. A few drops fall at first, and then the heavens pour down their floods with such plenitude that one can hardly see twenty yards. The flashing of the lightning turns the clouds pink from within, and this is followed by the cacophonous thudding, rattling and crackling of the thunder. It can be hours before the clouds move away, giving us a little respite before the next downpour. Out in the fields we are almost deafened by the constant hiss and rattle of the rain on the leaves. The rain falls with such force that it hurts the shoulders and stings the eyes. Underfoot is a quagmire. Needless to say we are frequently soaked to the skin. I cannot sleep at night because of the maddening, incessant roaring of the rain on the roof. Every garment I own is sodden. The only consolation is that the mosquitoes are fewer in number. If this continues for much longer, I shall become as insane as any raving madman in Bedlam.

March 2nd. The water level is rising. I swear I never dreamed there was so much water in the world; and we are quite at its mercy. As far as the eye can see are cane fields built to the Dutch pattern – with a great criss-crossing maze of canals, all dug out and maintained by the slaves. When it rains it does not take long for these canals to fill. At low tide, we normally open the koker to allow the water to drain away. This is no longer possible, for the Demerary is so swollen that even at low tide its swift brown waters almost reach the top of the embankment and at high tide they threaten to pour over the topmost plank of the koker. We can only pray that the embankment holds, for once the river makes a breach there will be no holding it back, and we shall be engulfed in the torrent.

March 16th. Work has been impossible these last ten days. The rain has not abated, and Forsyth says that he has never seen the like. The plantation is inundated, and we have had to take refuge up in our huts, whose elevation on stilts is fortunate, though it is strange to look down through the gaps in the floor and see the brown water flowing beneath. The only way in which we can get about is by boats that were brought up from the stelling. The slaves have abandoned their houses and have taken refuge on the back dam where they have built shelters for themselves. They do not appear unduly perturbed, for they are spared labour, and they have nothing to lose. We, on the other hand, have a pervading sense of utter helplessness in the face of a malevolent Nature. Allardyce is blind drunk and in a terrible fury, raving at the water like a modern Canute, but even his cowhide whip cannot subdue the flood. If we lose the crop we are done for. Poor Poll hates the rain, and sits on the arm of my chair, the very picture of misery, calling out plaintively to others of his kind.

April 7th. The rains stopped about a week ago, and within a few days the level of the river had fallen sufficiently to permit the opening of the koker. The plantation has now drained. To my surprise the cane seems unaffected by its immersion, and appears to be thriving in the hot sunshine. The skies are a clear blue, and everywhere is steaming in the heat. The damned mosquitoes have returned – in the evenings we are followed around by great swirling clouds of the loathsome things. The slaves have now gone back to their plots, and we have – with great difficulty! – persuaded Allardyce to allow them a few days to effect necessary repairs to their houses.

April 10th. Work resumed. We have had to move prodigious quantities of mud from the mill and the boiling house, but apart from that there appears to be little damage. The mud is grey and slippery, and adheres to one's boots in great lumps; when it dries, it forms an exceedingly fine powder.

I am concerned about Smith. By reason of his youth he is less able to cope with the vicissitudes of life than we are, and has been looking very despondent. He takes his meals with us, but eats little, and when he is not about his duties on the plantation he keeps to himself, and speaks to no one. MacDuff's rough banter does nothing to improve matters. I found time today to speak to him, and asked what had brought him to Demerary.

'I was sent by my father,' he said. 'He's a merchant, and I worked in his offices for a time. I was never any good at it: I have no head for figures. He seemed to think that there was a good trade to be learned out here. He told me that there might be trouble in Jamaica soon, and that Demerary would be safe.'

'I am sure he had your interests at heart.'

He laughed. 'My interests? He wanted rid of me, that's all.'

'I am sure that's not true.'

'Of course it's true,' he said. 'My elder brother will inherit all the family estates in Scotland. My father has interests in sugar, tobacco and cotton – all he wants now is to become a Lord. He has no time for me, he's too busy parading around Bristol in his carriage, playing at being English. He seems to forget he was born in Kirkcaldy! Now I've been sent off to learn about the sugar trade and earn my fortune.' He gave a bitter little laugh. 'I do not know what he imagined Demerary would be like, and I doubt if he cared very much. Anyway, here I am. I hate this place.'

'You could always return home.'

'What is there for me at home?' he said. I offered him some rum, but he refused. 'I don't like the stuff,' he said. 'I'm sick of it, and I'm sick of the disgusting smell of it in the air. I can't imagine why anyone would want to drink it.'

I recounted some of my adventures in Jamaica, but he did not appear to be interested, so we sat in silence for a while. To be honest I could think of nothing else to say to him and eventually got up and wandered away. I'm going to have a word with Forsyth about him. To survive in this climate requires inner reserves of strength and determination and the boy lacks these. Once a man gives up on life here, he is done for.

May 2nd. Thomas is no longer serving us chicken on the grounds that his birds are being stolen by what he calls a 'salapenta'.[2] Sure enough, the coop is empty. I had no idea of what manner of beast this might be. Thomas describes it as a huge lizard, something like the iguanas we see every day, but very much larger, and exceedingly powerful and agile. He says that we must catch it, and together we have contrived a plan – we shall tether a chicken in an open space, and construct a simple trap with a net so that if the creature seizes the bait, then it can be ensnared and captured.

May 3rd. We have our 'salapenta', and what a monster it is! Thomas gave a great shout at first light, and we all came running to find him struggling with the net in which something of considerable size was entangled and from which it was desperately attempting to escape. It was hard to tell what kind of creature it was: all I could make out was a thick, lashing tail, a blunt head, and a gaping mouth with a scarlet forked tongue.

'Kill he! Kill he!' Thomas shouted. MacDuff seized a stick and began beating ineffectually at the animal in the net, which only served to enrage it still further; it was Allardyce with a cutlass that finally dispatched it. We pulled it free from the net and stretched it out on the ground – a hideous reptile a yard or more in length and of a greenish colour. Its body was as thick as a man's thigh, tapering to a long, powerful tail; its front legs were short and the hind ones exceedingly muscular; its head was huge and fearsome – it looked for all the world like the dragon of legend.

'I cook he fuh yah!' declared Thomas, highly elated.

'I'm no' eatin' that!' said MacDuff.

'It good fuh eat,' insisted Thomas.

'Lizards are perfectly edible,' said McLean. 'This one is certainly fat enough, and it seems a just end for stealing our chickens.'

'Well, ye can eat it if ye like,' said MacDuff in disgust. 'I'd rather hae pepper-pot than that.'

I must confess I felt a certain trepidation as Thomas served dinner that evening. He had skinned the animal and chopped it into small pieces before cooking it, so had we not known what it was we would have been none the wiser.

'Ye're a' mad,' said MacDuff, who had already procured some simple plantain and rice for himself. I looked at what was on my plate, and the texture did not seem very different from that of the chicken we have been served in the past.

'Ye'll a' be deid by the morn,' declared MacDuff.

I took a mouthful and then another. It was absolutely delicious, and the others were plainly of the same opinion.

'You really should try this, MacDuff,' said McLean. 'It's the best dinner we have had for months.' Even Smith was devouring his portion with obvious relish.

'It's very good,' said Forsyth. 'It tastes of chicken, only better.'

MacDuff picked unenthusiastically at his boiled plantain, clearly wavering.

'Are ye sure it's safe tae eat?' he said.

'Of course it is.'

'Are ye sure it's no' poisonous?'

'Don't be silly,' said Forsyth.

'I might just try a wee bit,' said MacDuff, and took a piece. Within a few moments he was reaching for another, then another.

'Good, isn't it?' said Forsyth.

'Man, it's braw!' said MacDuff, with his mouth full. We began to discuss the possibility of setting a trap to catch another one, for the taste was exquisite. I expect that project will come to nothing, for we are all far too busy; besides I do not know whether the 'salapenta' is a common creature or not – I rather doubt it. However the whole episode was a welcome relief from the tedium of our everyday lives.

May 22nd. The natal day of my beloved Bess – seven years old. I have just looked back in these pages to see what I wrote last year at this time, and I find, to my shame, that I did not mention her at all, being too preoccupied with Nancy, and debating foolishly with her about Reason and Religion. For my folly, I am here, condemned to these mosquito-ridden, foetid swamps – a sojourner in a strange land, harried by a growling pack of odious necessities and anxieties. I feel myself sink daily deeper beneath a galling load of regret, remorse and privation. Oh, to be in the bosom of my family once more! To walk hand in hand with my daughter on the banks of Ayr! I can recollect a day, many years ago, when the sun flamed over the distant western hills, and I stood in rapture, listening to the feathered warblers pouring their harmony on every hand – a golden moment for the poetic heart! What would I not give to revisit such scenes, and return afterwards to Mossgiel, to see my mother sitting by the ingle!

I have poured myself a glass of rum, and have drunk a solemn pledge to them that *I shall return!* A few days ago one of the Negroes referred to me as 'de big massa'. I was quite flattered for a while, but when I told Forsyth he laughed and said that in Creole 'big' means 'old'. A mere three and thirty years!

June 5th. The six o'clock beetle has commenced his raucous grating somewhere in the nearby undergrowth. The last few days have dawned pleasantly enough, but by mid afternoon heavy rain has swept down, and it has been hard to keep the slaves at work. Allardyce's answer, as always, has been to resort to the lash, but to my mind there is a feeling of rebellion in the air. The Negroes have been congregating in animated groups, and after work we have seen them moving covertly from house to house, as if spreading some message. They avert their eyes when they see us, and break off conversations. Ambrose has been invaluable – he never raises a hand to anyone, but when he speaks it is with such a tone of persuasive authority that somehow a crisis is averted, and work is able to proceed.

I have sounded out Allardyce about my salary. I have been here the best part of a year, and I was anxious to know how I stood, but he was very evasive about it, saying that the plantation would settle with me in due course. He made all manner of excuses about not keeping cash on the estate, but his prevarications make me apprehensive. Forsyth says that he and the others are in very much the same situation, though Allardyce keeps a reckoning of what is due. If I am to return home, then I need the money in my pocket, rather than in the coffers of some agent or other in Stabroek.

June 20th. I have finally written to Lord Balcarres, placing before him the facts as I see them. The slaves on this plantation are treated like brutes. Are they more useful by being thus humbled than they would be if permitted to enjoy humane treatment? As for Allardyce, he possesses a mind debauched, and has become hardened to every feeling of humanity. His Lordship's estate stands in grave danger and unless he takes measures to remove his agent, then it may be lost altogether, together with all its produce and the lives of his loyal overseers. Can I look tamely on and see the plantation brought to ruin? These are my sentiments, but in my letter I voiced my concerns more circumspectly. The problem lies in how to ensure that it reaches the addressee safely and without interference. I believe that all letters bound for England have to be handed in at the office of the Secretary[3] in Stabroek, and are liable to be opened in case they contain anything untoward concerning the activities of the Company.

Dark, rainy days are upon us. My feet are in a bad way, because my boots leak. I never seem to be dry these days, and everything is covered in mould. Ambrose says I should try walking barefoot for a while; Forsyth advises me to rub rum on the soles of my feet. Maybe I shall try both.

July 7th. By my reckoning I have been here for a year now, and there is still no sign of my salary. I sought out Allardyce this morning and asked him about it. Despite the early hour he had already started on his rum, but he was not as belligerent as usual.

'So ye've come tae pay me a wee social call?' he said.

'There was something I wanted to discuss with you,' I said.

'Aye, well come in an' tak a seat. Ye'll hae a dram?'

'No thank you.'

'Please yersel', he said. 'Whit wis it ye wanted tae discuss?'

'It is the matter of my salary,' I said. 'I arrived here a year ago, and I believe I am entitled to it.'

'Aye, ye're entitled tae it.'

'So when shall I have it?'

He scratched his head. 'Dae ye need money?'

'My boots are falling to pieces; I require new ones.'

'Man, dinna fash yersel' ower that. The plantation'll provide these. Ye dinna need money here.'

'I just wanted to be sure that there was a proper accounting.'

'Dinna concern yersel'. Ye've earned a year. The agent at Stabroek keeps a reckonin'. If ye need money, tell me how much ye require an' I'll advance it tae ye.'

'Can I not receive all of my salary now?'

'All o' it? Whaur wad ye keep it? Whit wad ye dae wi' it?'

I had to admit that he was right. We do not have the security of a Great House here, and there is nowhere in my quarters where I could be sure that a large sum of money would be safe. No doubt if I told Allardyce that I wished to resign my position, and required the money to finance my passage out of Demerary, then he would have no option but to let me have it. But I do not altogether trust him.

Word came today that France has declared war on Austria and Prussia. Details are scant, but one thing is certain – more bloodshed, and more chaos for the people!

I have still not been able to send the letter to Lord Balcarres. I have determined to go to Stabroek myself and deliver the letter into the hands of someone I can trust. I can make enquiries about a passage home at the same time.

On a less serious note, there is a slave girl called Prudence who works with the weeding gang. She is aged about eighteen years or thereby, and when her time permits, she follows me around making foolish eyes at me. It is has not escaped the attention of the others that she is interested in me.

'There's yer chance.' said MacDuff this morning, seeing her

looking in my direction. 'Whit are ye waitin' for? Ye havena had a woman tae bide wi' ye since ye came, man!' I made some dismissive comment, for he is not a man with whom I care to discuss such matters. But he is right in one respect – I have not lain with a woman since those dreadful days last June. Love should be the alpha and omega of human enjoyment – the spark of celestial fire that would make these cheerless quarters warm and comfortable: for the want of it, life seems a poor gift indeed. But my impetuous ways have invariably been my undoing, and I have vowed not to repeat the mistakes of the past.

Smith grows worse daily. He performs his work in a desultory manner, as if his mind is elsewhere, and he is losing weight. Forsyth agrees that the lad is in a bad way, but when we speak to him he shrugs off any suggestion that he might be ailing.

July 18th. Prudence came to where I live this evening, as bold as you like, and leaned against the wall, staring at me.

'What are you doing here?' I asked.

'Massa MacDuff say.'

'Said what?'

'He say yah need comp'ny.' She came across the room and started to unfasten her clothing. I cannot truthfully say that I was not tempted at that moment – she is a strapping, sonsie lass, and plainly very willing. Nobody on earth would have blamed me if I had seized that moment to achieve an easy conquest, and yet I could not bring myself to do so. In the first place, I think it was a damned cheek of MacDuff to send her to me, and if I had yielded he would have been quite insufferable about taking the credit for putting the girl my way. In the second place, I hope I have achieved something of a reputation as a fair-dealing man among the Negroes, and if I had taken advantage of her, then Lord knows what the consequences might have been.

'Yah want me?' she said, pulling loose her coarse chemise to reveal very attractive breasts. I picked up the garment from the floor.

'Get dressed,' I said curtly. 'If I want company I shall ask for it. Get along with you now and let us have no more of this. I shall speak to MacDuff.'

She did as I ordered. I stood at the door, and watched as she went off in the direction of the slave village. I knew that I had done the right thing. In the moment she revealed herself, I had an overwhelming memory of that first time with Adah, when my *proper doin'* became a delicious, shared consummation, long deferred, and all the sweeter for that. I remembered her humour, her devotion and her tenderness.

I could not have lain with Prudence – it would have been like animals coupling, nothing more.

Several members of the great gang felt the lash of Allardyce's whip today, although mercifully the man was so drunk that his blows seldom met their target. Jacob, one of the drivers, caught my eye today in what was clearly a plea for intervention, but there was nothing I could do save remonstrate, which drew down the usual torrent of abuse on my head.

July 29th. The Sabbath. Smith is giving everyone cause for concern. His eyes are sunken and his skin has an unhealthy, yellowish hue. He still maintains that he is perfectly well, but he seems very weak, and I noticed him stumbling today, as if his legs lacked the strength to support his weight. Even Allardyce has shown some solicitude – which amazed me – and offered to take the lad to Stabroek to see a doctor. But the boy refuses help, and just asks to be left alone.

Despite my rebuff, Prudence continues to make eyes at me, and smiles as she does so, as if we have some shared secret. After her visit I told MacDuff that I did not appreciate the fact that he had sent her to my quarters, and have asked him not to do it again. He told me that I was a mad fool not to take advantage of the opportunity.

This afternoon she came again, but this time she behaved very properly, and knocked politely at my door. When I opened it, she held out a coconut shell filled with cooked rice.

'I cook fuh yah,' she said. I had no wish to be beholden in any way to this girl, but it would have been churlish to refuse, so I took it and thanked her. I had a little, but could not finish it – it had an unusual taste, though I have only eaten Thomas's cooking since I came here, and am not accustomed to new flavours.

Two weeks from now I shall travel to Stabroek and hand over the letter for delivery.

August 12th. I have been to Stabroek today, and given the letter over to the Secretary of the VWC. I had been worried in case it would be opened, but nothing of the kind happened, and I watched with my own eyes as it was placed in a great bundle of letters bound for England. I feel a great sense of relief now that the deed is done. I made haste to return while the tide was still favourable. I have made some enquiries about passages, and their likely cost.

Forsyth met me when I came back, telling me that Smith has not risen from his bed today. I went to see him, and sure enough he was lying there, staring at the ceiling. I was concerned to see that his body was covered with small white spots, resembling tiny blisters.

'How are you?' I asked in a jocular voice. 'Time to get up, surely. I've been to Stabroek and back.'

'I don't want to get up,' he said. 'It's the Sabbath.'

'It would do you good to take the air,' I said.

'I don't wish to,' he said.

'What about something to eat?'

'Thomas can send something for me later if he likes.'

'Is there anything I can bring for you? Some water?'

'Just leave me.' His voice had a great weariness in it. In this climate it is essential to eat and drink regularly. Short of dragging him bodily from his bed there is nothing to be done for him.

When I reached my own quarters I found that Prudence had been, leaving another coconut shell filled with her rice dish. I was hungry after the trip across the river, and ate it eagerly. Perhaps I have judged her too harshly and these little offerings of rice represent a wish to make amends for her conduct.

August 14th. Tuesday. Smith has not been at work this week so far. He remains in bed, and cannot be persuaded out of it. I offered to let him borrow Poll, as macaws can be attentive company, but he was not interested. Finally a doctor has been fetched from Vreed-en-Hoop, and has spent some time examining him. He concludes that the boy is suffering from a miliary fever,[4] exacerbated by damp conditions and want of proper food – he also suspects that the condition is further aggravated by a rooted melancholia.

'Whit can we dae for him?' said Allardyce. 'I canna afford tae lose a man.'

'Plenty of water and fruit,' said the doctor, who had the brisk, unemotional manner of having seen all this before. 'Get your cook to make him some chicken gruel. Don't give him any meat for a while. Avoid peppers and spices.'

'Whit are his chances?'

He scratched his head. 'You have to get him out of bed. If he lies there and broods, then there's less hope for him. A little gentle exercise will greatly help his case.'

When the doctor had gone we went in to see the patient.

'Richt,' said Allardyce grimly, 'it's tae be plenty o' fruit and water, and Thomas is gaun tae mak soup for ye.'

'I don't want any,' said Smith.

'It's for yer ain good.'

'I'm just tired.'

'Damn it man!' shouted Allardyce suddenly. 'Ye'll dae whit I tell ye! Ye're no' lyin' in bed wastin' ma time, ye lazy English slughan! I *need* ye, so ye'll damned weel tak the soup! If ye dinna, I'll bloody weel pour it doon yer thrapple masel'! Now *sit up* or by God I'll drag ye oot o' bed an' kick yer shilpit wee arse a' roon the plantation!'

Smith did as he was told with greatest of alacrity and took a few pieces of mango and a little water. I did not recollect that the doctor had prescribed the threat of physical violence as part of the cure, but it seemed to work. In a few days, when he is a little stronger, we will encourage him to leave the house and walk a little.

August 20th. Smith is, I think, at death's door. We have discovered that unless he is carefully watched he throws away the food we bring and pours Thomas's soup out of the window. He is sick constantly, and we suspect that he puts his fingers down his throat to induce vomiting. He is starving himself to death. I went to see him this morning and was shocked by the change – he is little more than a skeleton now, and I do not think he will ever leave his bed again. When I entered he did not appear to know me, but I spoke to him and he turned his head towards me.

'Is that you, Burns?' he said, in a voice that was only just a whisper.

'Yes,' I said in a cheerful voice. 'I just came to see how you are.'

'Tired,' he said. 'Very tired.'

'Can I fetch anything for you?'

'No, thank you.' There was a long pause during which he stared at the ceiling intently, almost as if he could see something there that I could not.

'Robert?' he said at last.

'Yes?'

'What happens to us when we die, do you think?'

'You shouldn't be having such thoughts. You'll be better soon.'

'I don't think so. What happens to us, do you think?'

Before Mary died, I had believed that there was some state of existence beyond the grave where the worthies of this life would meet again with those they had loved and lost – this time to part no more. But after her death the dogmas of reasoning philosophy threw in their doubts. Smith's question is one I have addressed many times to the departed sons and daughters of men in the hope of a reply, but not one of them has ever thought fit to answer.

'There is one thing I do know for certain,' I said. 'We will be at peace.' He nodded, and was silent for a moment, then looked at me again.

'Will we be punished, do you think, if we have done wrong?'

'I do not believe that. If there is a God, then He loves us. If there is not, then there can be no reward or punishment, only peace.'

'Like being asleep?'

'Yes.'

'So there is nothing to fear?'

'No.'

He turned his head to stare at the ceiling again. It was strange to sit in that room, with the cloud of death hanging over it, and hear the bustle outside – the bark of dogs, the sound of the men calling to each other.

'Thank you,' he said at last. 'Will you come again?'

'Of course.'

'Thank you.'

I went off in a very pensive frame of mind. If only I could discover why the boy is doing this to himself! I suspect it has to do with being sent away from home. Perhaps I should send Prudence round to take his mind away from these gloomy thoughts.

On the subject of Prudence, I returned here to discover that she had left more rice for me. I believe I have misjudged the girl, and perhaps I rebuffed her in too rude a fashion that evening. There will never be another Adah, of course, but Prudence is comely enough, and a man needs comfort.

August 23rd. God help me, I think I am going down with that fever again. It must be four years since I was last afflicted with it, but today I can hardly walk and my joints pain me. I am all [fevr] of a shiver – my appetite is quite gone – I can b***ly [barely?] write [*entry abandoned.*]

September 17th. I have been very ill – in a delirium – and am still very weak, but for the first time strong enough to stumble over to my table and take up my quill. I need a stick to walk about. If ever I suffer another bout of this fever then I am convinced it will be my last. I am to resume my duties in a week; in the meantime Thomas supplies me with strong gruel that he says will help me recover my strength.

Smith is dead, poor soul. I was too ill at the time to be aware of it, but apparently he passed away a few days after I last spoke to him. Thomas found him on his bed, facing the wall. What was he thinking of in these last moments, as he felt his life ebbing away? I am glad now that I did not try to fill his mind with religious platitudes, but told him what I sincerely believe – but to die all alone!

September 24th. Back to work today. I still need my stick, but I hope that I will be able to discard it soon. Ambrose was pleased to see me on my feet once more.

'Hey, it's Massa Burns!' he said. 'Yah betta, suh?'

'Much better, thank you.'

'Good, good, ' he said with a chuckle. 'We's worry 'bout yah.'

'Thank you,' I said. 'Anyway, I am improving, I think.'

'Hope so, Massa.'

Later I saw Prudence who appeared very relieved, and gave me a look that would have melted the stoniest of hearts. I did not speak to her, but I feel sure that I am due another of her culinary offerings. She is a very attractive creature, and once I am strong enough, I must ensure that our acquaintance improves still further!

I am tired after the exertions of the day and writing is an effort.

October 4th. Prudence has indeed been bringing more of her offerings, and each time that she does I find that my attitude towards her softens a little more. I was eating some of it today when Ambrose came past my balcony and saw me.

'Yah eat rice?' he asked, and I told him that I did.

'Yah cook de rice?'

'No, Prudence cooks it. She brings it to me sometimes.'

'Prudence? De girl in de weedin' gang?'

'Yes.'

He came to where I was sitting and held out his hand. 'Please Massa Burns, lemme see dat,' he said. I handed him the shell, and he sniffed at the contents carefully, then tasted a little.

'What's the matter?' I said.

'Massa Burns, I tell yah sump'n,' he said, putting the shell to one side. 'Yah nah eat dis rice no mo'. He nah good fuh yah.'

'You don't think the girl has poisoned it, do you?'

He shook his head. 'Listen tah Ambrose, Massa Burns. I's a big man, an' dere's t'ings I *knows*. Y'un'erstan' me? I *knows*. Dis rice nah good fuh yah.'

'What's wrong with it?' I asked, perplexed.

'I *knows*,' he said, but he would not explain what it was that he knew. He has made me promise not to eat the rice she brings, and I have agreed, without too much reluctance. The taste is not entirely to my liking, and I assume that Ambrose has identified some ingredient that might prove injurious to the health of a white man like myself.

October 31st. My almanac tells me it is Hallowe'en, and in far-off Scotland the folks will be entertaining each other with tales of bogles lurking by old thorn trees, or kelpies haunting some lonely ford on a starry night, mixing their yells with the roar of the flood and the cries of the doomed man on the foundering horse. Ah, the tales of ghosts I have heard from my mother – how they flit in the shadows of time-worn churches, and in between the silent, ghastly dwellings of the dead! No such clishmaclaiver here today, just work as usual.

I feel very much better, and the pain in my joints has almost gone. I have converted my walking stick into a perch for Poll.

November 10th. I am sure that Lord Balcarres must have my letter by now. Allardyce is, if anything, worse. Ambrose is clearly concerned, and I know he spends much time with the slaves, endeavouring to keep the peace. I sleep with my cutlass beside my bed, and Poll is an excellent watchman, for if anyone approaches he lets out such a screeching that the whole place is aroused. If trouble happens, it will happen by night – of that I am certain.

November 23rd. We have heard that the French have declared a republic, and that Louis has been condemned to death. I have no sympathy with the man, for he oppressed his people most cruelly, but I fear for what must now follow. I fervently believe in republican sentiments, but to what extent can I believe in a new golden age, spotless with despotic purity? That corrupt and vile monarchy is gone, and I shed no tears for it, but the ignorant multitude remains, doomed perhaps to be led by the nose and goaded by the backside. *Le roi est mort* – but 'will a worse come in his place'?[5] No one could have had purer principles than Brutus, yet when Julius was slain, it was the man of honour who was compelled to run on his sword, leaving the Roman world riven by civil strife and discord. War between Britain and France is now inevitable.

December 13th. The year draws towards its close, and I fear I have been a poor chronicler. I do not have the energy to describe mundane details as I did when I was in Jamaica – oh, happy times! Life is brutish and unpleasant.

I had once entertained thoughts of allowing Prudence to live with me, and for a time I had felt quite drawn to that prospect, but in the last two or three weeks I have changed my mind. I have told her that I can no longer accept the rice, and she now appears quite dejected when we meet. It is odd, but I no longer find her attractive. I do not know what has changed, but the idea of lying with her no longer appears the delightful prospect I once thought it to be. Perhaps it is the wretched fever that has changed me.

December 23rd. The most damnable thing about this place is the noise. There is never any silence, just a constant cacophony of chirruping, screeching, barking and croaking, together with the noises made by a million insects that fill the air with their incessant, sibilant hissing. There is a blessed respite just before dawn, and then it all starts again. What a place for insects! A great moth has entered my room – it is the size of my hand with a loathsome fat body, and is fluttering and flapping around my lamp, seemingly bent on self-immolation. When it settles, I can see that the markings on its wings resemble the head of a snake, with its eyes and markings correct in every detail – no doubt this is how it preserves itself from attack. In a way it is perversely beautiful, and I imagine that such a thing would drive any natural historian into raptures, but for me it is just another irritation. The mosquitoes are worst of all: great clouds of them lurk in the shadows and sally forth to attack any part of me that I make so bold as to expose. I have a bite on my eyelid that itches horribly so that I cannot forbear from scratching and rubbing at it: now it is so swollen that I can hardly see from that eye.

It is very hot and humid. In two days it will be Christmas, but I do not suppose that the festival will be marked in any way. I always found Mr Douglas's sermonising tiresome at the time, but at least it was *civilised,* and marked the passage of the year. Time here is meaningless, and unless I have recourse to the almanac I can easily forget what day it is. As for *civilisation,* it has not reached these parts.

1793

January 1st. According to the almanac this is the first day of the New Year, but it was not the occasion for much rejoicing on the plantation. We had to bury a cow today – the beast must have been dead two days or more, and in the prevailing heat the carcass had begun to decay, sending a waft of horrid putrescence into our nostrils every time the breeze came. When we found the animal a great cloud of black flies already surrounded it; its stomach was bloated, and its legs were sticking out, stiff and straight, from its body. Forsyth and I had to supervise the operation otherwise the men would just have tipped the body into a canal to rot, or covered it with a little soil, which would have amounted to the same thing. The first thing was to make a deep hole to hold the body, the men using a leaning motion to bring their weight to bear on the long shafts of their turskil-like spades, slowly digging down into the heavy, sticky clay. The head was hacked off with axes and cutlasses, attracting still more flies. The legs also had to be removed, as they would not have fitted into the hole. Of course we left the most unpleasant task until the last possible moment – the belly was chopped so that first there was a hiss of escaping gases – whose smell I cannot begin to describe – and then great loops of distended guts and swollen intestines burst forth and slopped on to the ground in a revolting, stinking, bloody heap. The eviscerated body was then tipped into the grave, and the guts shovelled in after it, followed by the head and the legs. I have been scrubbing myself in an endeavour to rid myself of the smell. Unsurprisingly, none of us has much appetite for food this evening.

Allardyce missed all of this, as he is off with MacDuff to Stabroek to fetch supplies and to make the necessary returns to the authorities.

January 6th. Sabbath Day. No work today, and an opportunity to write a little. Allardyce has had a great deal of trouble with the big slave called Simon who is the focus of some unrest on the plantation since he was purchased last week. His previous owner kept a farm somewhere on the Essequibo coast, and apparently told Allardyce that he was cutting back on production and no longer needed so many workers. The asking price of twenty pounds seemed more than reasonable, for he is very large and powerfully built, with huge muscles on his chest and arms.

However he was sullen and difficult from the outset, and it has quickly become clear that he is a troublemaker, which is why his price

was so low. When Allardyce and MacDuff returned with him he was
fettered; his hands were fastened behind his back; he was bleeding
from the mouth, and there were livid welts on his back

'He'll no' be givin' *me* trouble, at any rate,' said Allardyce with an
boastful laugh, slapping his whip against his leg. 'On the boat across
the river he had the impudence to sit there glowerin' at me; lookin'
richt into ma e'en, damn it!'

'We showed him the error o' his ways,' said MacDuff. He was
flushed and animated, for I believe that violence excites him. 'Did
we no'?' he shouted in Simon's face. It was a ghastly yet comic
spectacle to see this fat, sweaty little man prancing around in front
of the huge Negro who, despite his degrading circumstances,
presented a dignified appearance of lost nobility. He gave MacDuff
a malevolent look that I would not care to have received. For the
thousandth time I find myself sick with the inhumanity of it all. I
await the reply of Lord Balcarres with increasing impatience.

January 7th. In the cane fields all day. Simon has been put to work,
still bearing the marks of the lash. He is a powerful chap, and he can
cut cane almost as fast as two men. While others chatter and
sometimes sing together, he keeps to himself. When he saw me he
glanced quickly at me with detestation before looking away; for my
part, I was conscious of the sharp cutlass he was holding and, not for
the first time since I have been here, I felt a strong sense of danger.

January 15th. I believe that Simon would in any case have caused
trouble, but his harsh treatment on arrival meant that it happened
sooner than we had anticipated. He was increasingly reluctant to
work last week, and the sting of the lash seemed to have little effect
other than to increase his demeanour of resentment. When one of
the Negro drivers, growing impatient, raised his whip to him, he was
picked up for his pains and thrown bodily into the trench. For that,
Allardyce and MacDuff tied him to a tree and flogged him until he
was all but senseless. I absented myself: I cannot be a party to
brutality of this kind; it sickens me. I am told that he never uttered
a sound, only fixed his eyes on his tormentors with that terrible glare
of his. Of course Allardyce has taunted me about what he calls my
'cowardice', accusing me of weakness and fanciful ideas. When he
asked me directly what I would do to keep order, I confess to my
shame that I had no answer for him. The slaves have been brought
here against their will; they receive no recompense for their labours;
to work is death, and not to work is death – how can we expect to
have order and compliance?

Simon has begun to associate more with others, speaking to them quietly but animatedly in a language they understand, always breaking off the conversation when he sees he has been noticed. This is a very unwelcome development, and even Allardyce is worried.

'I ken this is how rebellions start. We'll hae tae get rid o' him.'

'Has anyone tried talking to him?' I said. He looked at me pityingly.

'Are ye thinkin' o' *reasonin'* wi' him?' he said sarcastically. 'Or were ye thinkin' o' *lashin'* him – wi' yer tongue, o' course?'

'I don't think any white man could reason with him,' I said. 'Not after what he's been through. I meant Ambrose.'

'Aye, Ambrose *might* make an impression,' he agreed, though without enthusiasm. Forsyth will ask him to intervene.

January 16th. Ambrose has handled the situation with Simon. He drew him to one side this morning and spent some time talking to him. Now, though he continues to wear a threatening expression, he works well enough. I mentioned this to Forsyth.

'Oh, he's quite a remarkable man,' he said. 'Simon is a Yoruba, and Ambrose speaks enough of the language to make himself understood. There's no point trying to speak to him in English.'

'What did Ambrose say to him?'

'I have no idea, but it seems to have had the desired effect.'

'He has a natural authority over the others. He never fails to surprise me.'

Forsyth looked at me with a smile. 'Ambrose may have more surprises in store for you.'

'What do you mean?'

'Oh, you'll find out, I dare say,' he said, and walked off, leaving me intrigued to know what he knew about Ambrose that I did not.

February 3rd. Allardyce has put me in charge of the boiling house, which is a great relief, as I do not find field work conducive and I am tired of hearing the cursing and whipping all day. In the factory, I can organise the men as I please, and I am confident that the work can be done efficiently and harmoniously. I observed the men while they were about their work today, and I have noted several changes that will have to be made. The first will be to get rid of the rats. They are filthy brutes, and have no place in the boiling house, where cleanliness should be of paramount importance. McLean has a dog called Muffy who is a formidable ratter, and I shall ask to borrow him. He is very small, but utterly fearless, and able to squeeze himself into the smallest of places.

February 28th. I have had a reply to my letter to Lord Balcarres, and am exceedingly dissatisfied with it. His Lordship did not even deign to reply in person, and all I have for my trouble is a brace of curt lines penned by his secretary in which I am thanked for my letter and haughtily informed that His Lordship has taken note of the matters raised therein. I find the letter arrogant, dismissive, as well as displaying a marked lack of gratitude, particularly since I had the man's best interests at heart. I am now at a loss as to how to proceed, for there is no higher authority to whom I can appeal. At any rate, now that I have the boiling house to myself, life is a little more agreeable .

Muffy has done his job well: there are no more rats and the place has been thoroughly cleaned out. The men are working cheerfully, and Allardyce is pleased because production is much more efficient and very little of the cane now goes to waste. But the prevailing mood on the plantation is still tense, and I am bitterly disappointed that no steps are to be taken to rectify matters.

March 5th. Simon is causing trouble, despite the best efforts of Ambrose. He knows better than to display outright defiance towards us, but he works grudgingly, and I suspect that he is responsible for inciting others to voice the endless litany of grievances and complaints that we have had to tolerate recently. Whenever a dispute arises, he is always there, ready with unhelpful remarks in his own language. Allardyce's response to this is to have him repeatedly flogged. I have argued a hundred times that this only makes the man worse.

The work of the great gang is very difficult when it rains. Because of the canals, the cane has to be loaded on to rafts and floated down to the mill with a team of men pulling from the bank – it is impossible to get an ox cart into the fields. But the rain makes everything slippery with mud, and the banks of the canals quickly become treacherous at the places where the rafts are loaded. I have suggested to Allardyce that the work would proceed more quickly if we made a simple paal-off at such places. He agrees that it would be a good idea, but I doubt if he will do anything about it.

March 31st. The colony has a new governor in the person of van Grovestins following the return of Albertus Backer to Holland.[1] The Baron has been here for some time, charged with the task of reorganising the administration. He is only three-and-twenty years of age, but is accounted one of the shrewdest minds in the colony. His appointment is not likely to have any effect on us here – we are left very much to our own devices; indeed, it is hard to believe that this is a Dutch colony.

Many of the slaves are poorly clad, and such apparel as they possess is very ragged. I have suggested to Allardyce that they should have better clothes, but he shrugs off the idea.

April 16th. We appear to have acquired yet another dog, a lithe, sandy-coloured beast with a proud, curving tail that arches over his back like an arrogant question-mark. No one has the slightest idea where he has come from. He appears friendly and well nourished, and I imagine he has been kept as a pet and either abandoned by his owners or strayed. Today as I set off on my rounds of the plantation he trotted along at my heels, which was companionable enough. On the way I had occasion to stop and speak to Ambrose, and as I was doing so, I felt a warm wetness on my leg. Looking down, I saw that the wretched creature was in the act of pissing on my breeches. I gave it a damned good kick in the bandileers, which are in constant view, due to the jaunty elevation of its tail, and it fled, yelping and howling. I did not see it again until later in the day, when it came up the stairs of my hut, as bold as you please, greeting me with the most fulsome expressions of canine cordiality before lifting its leg and pissing against my bed. I chased it down the stairs with a broom.

April 17th. We were at breakfast today when the new dog trotted into the hut and sat beside the table, looking expectantly at us. MacDuff got up to chase it out, and it ran off, but not before it had pissed against the leg of the table.

'That dog of yours is a menace,' said Forsyth.

'It's not my dog,' I replied crossly.

'Well, it seems to follow you around all the time,' he said.

'I do not give it any encouragement,' I said, 'unless you consider a kick in the balls to be a friendly gesture.'

'The bloody animal pisses everywhere,' grumbled MacDuff.

Simon is still as sullen as ever, but he does as he is told. The only time he displays any animation is in the presence of Ambrose, whom he regards with deference and, to my thinking, something approaching fear. *[End of volume two.]*

May 2nd. That blasted dog continues to cause embarrassment. Today I was supervising a weeding party when up it came, friendly as ever. It sniffed around us for a while, and then pissed all over Jacob's leg. He eyed the beast malevolently, but did nothing, obviously under the impression that it was my dog, and that I would punish him severely if he dared to maltreat it in any way.

'It's not my dog,' I insisted for what seemed the hundredth time.

'You can do what you like with it.' Jacob gave a loud yell, and ran furiously at the animal, brandishing his cutlass. It fled at once into the safety of the cane, and I did not see it again for the rest of the day. Upon my return home, however, the damned brute was sitting at the foot of the stairs waiting for me. I threw a stick at it, but it thought this excellent sport, and picked it up and brought it back to me. The more I castigate the animal, the more devoted it appears to become!

Sunday, May 12th. Close to the plantation there is a large open space that is given over to general use, and the slaves foregather there, during such leisure time as they have. Today there was a larger exodus from the plantation than is normal and, sensing an air of excitement, I followed some of their number. At the open space in question, I saw that a large crowd had assembled and were listening intently to someone speaking to them from a raised platform at the far end of the field. As I drew closer I saw that it was a white man, dressed in the garb of a priest – one of these platitude-mongers who wander around the region, spreading their nonsense to the gullible and the vulnerable. I was reminded of Grubb in Port Antonio.

'My little brothers and sisters in Christ!' he was shouting, as I came to the back of the gathering. 'Truly you are blessèd in the eyes of the Lord! Praise be unto Him! Render thanks unto Him, who hath delivered you from evil. Hallelujah! Thank you, Lord!'

There were a few mumbled hallelujahs and amens, but for the most part the listeners were silent.

'Who can understand God's greater purposes?' he went on. 'For His own reasons He sent down the Lord Jesus Christ to live among you, my little brothers and sisters. He could, in His divine omnipotence, have showered His only begotten son with gifts and grace, and caused him to live in joy and contentment. Oh yes! But we know the story of Jesus Christ, do we not?'

I could see him more clearly by this time: a thin, mean-faced man of forty years or so, with the glittering eyes of the fanatic.

'Yes, we do!' he cried, when there was no response. 'We know the story of the Lord Jesus Christ! Jesus lived a humble life! He truly knew the meaning of suffering! In the end, God permitted him to be crucified – to be hung up on a cross to die! Pierced through the hands and feet; pierced through the side; beaten; scourged; humiliated and scorned! And did Almighty God send down His angels to rescue him? No, my brothers and sisters, He did not! He left him hanging there to die? Has anyone present in this congregation known as much fear and pain?

There was a mumbling in the crowd. Suddenly someone shouted out, 'Praise de Lawd!'

'Yes!' yelled the priest, waving his arms in the air. He was perspiring very greatly in the heat, and the sweat was pouring from a face turning scarlet with passion. 'Yes! Oh, yes! He died for our sins! He suffered to save us! He suffered so that we would understand that even though God loved His son, He loved us more! What suffering on earth can compare with that?'

I could see that the crowd was becoming interested in the notion that the Son of God had suffered much more than they had.

'Now God's plan touches each and every one of us,' he went on, rather more quietly now, pointing his finger here and there towards the press of faces. 'I myself have to travel spreading the Word of God. And I suffer for it, my brothers and sisters! The heat; the flies; the privations of a solitary life – these are all the rewards I can hope for in this world. But with the example of Christ the Saviour before me – I can endure! I welcome my sufferings, brothers and sisters!' His voice began to rise again. 'When the mosquitoes bite me, I fall to my knees and I give thanks to the Lord that He has sent me this suffering! When the hard road blisters my feet, I give thanks to the Lord!'

He picked up a large Bible and began to brandish it. 'Do you remember the tribulations of Job – the sufferings he had to undergo?'

I doubted whether anyone in the crowd knew the word 'tribulation' or who Job was, but the idea of overcoming suffering still interested them.

'The Lord plagued him with *boils* – the most terrible boils you can imagine.' He uttered the word with intense relish. 'It says here in the Good Book that he was smitten with boils from the soles of his feet to the crown of his head! Can you imagine that?'

There was another murmur, this time of sympathy. Few of us here in Demerary are free from these egregious eruptions, these foul little volcanoes.

He leaned forward, eyes gleaming. 'Can you imagine having a boil – on the sole of your foot? Imagine the pain when you walked! Can you imagine . . .' – again the dramatic pause – 'having boils on *both feet?* Can you imagine having a really large boil – in your armpit?' The moans were louder this time, mingled with shouts of 'Oh nossuh!' and 'Lawd have mercy!' and suchlike. With a sort of malevolent glee, he leaned forward again. 'And can you imagine what it would be like to have boils on your nose? On your *private parts?*'

At this there was a chorus of shrieks and wails, at which he seized his opportunity to pursue the theme still further. 'Can you imagine the *pain*,' he yelled, 'when these boils *burst*? Or when they are *cut open* to release the festering poison inside?' The preacher allowed the hubbub to die down, before raising up the Bible in one hand and stretching out the other in an imperious command for silence.

'But did Job curse his God?' he said. 'He did not. He bore his infirmity with fortitude, and in the end he was cured, and God rewarded him. God gave him fourteen thousand sheep!'

There was a great cry of 'Hallelujah!' at this.

'And a thousand oxen!'

'A thousan'? Praise de Lawd!'

'And six thousand camels!'

No one in the throng had the faintest idea of what manner of beast a camel might be, but the cries and shouts of approbation lasted for several minutes.

'You see, when Job suffered, and when Jesus Christ died for us, there was a reason for it. My little brothers and sisters in Christ, the reason is that God's will must be done.'

'Amen,' went the congregation.

'For just as Job accepted the will of God, so must we all bow down before His holy will. And for you, my dear brothers and sisters in Christ, this means working hard in this life and obeying your masters.'

At first I had thought that this man was inebriated, or mad, or both, but I quickly realised that he had most probably been hired by the authorities in order to help stave off any rebellious inclinations the slaves may have been harbouring. I remember such preaching regularly took place in Jamaica where some slaves like Toby, bless his heart, had seemed to believe in this absurd perversion of the word of God and, in consequence, to accept their servile status as being divinely ordained.

'God has given us all a place, and your place is in the fields! I know that it is a burden to bear, but remember how Job bore *his* burden! Remember the boils! For your true reward is not in this world, brothers and sisters, but in the world to come!'

'What 'bout de sheep and de oxen?' someone shouted. 'Don' we git no reward in dis world, like de man wid de boils? Don' we git set free?'

'If it is the Lord's will that you should be set free then the Lord's will shall be done! But there is no man among us who can tell the day or the hour of our emancipation.'

'So yah t'ink 'mancipation comin' soon?' someone called from the crowd. From the murmur of agreement that greeted the remark, it was obviously a popular question. The pastor licked his lips nervously.

'The day of freedom will come,' he said, and quickly raised his hand to halt the rush of excited comment in the crowd. 'Oh yes, my little brothers and sisters in Christ, that day must surely be at hand! But do not thrust away the cup of happiness from your parched lips just as it is about to be delivered unto you! As freedom approaches you must be doubly patient! Any revolt or insurgence at this time would merely serve to delay that glorious day when the doors of the plantations shall be opened wide, and you shall step outside as free men and women.'

'What 'bout de sheep and de oxen?' someone repeated querulously.

'God has many gifts to give,' said the pastor, in a tone of slight exasperation. 'And although emancipation will be a wonderful gift, it will be as nothing as compared with the greatest gifts of all, which are His gift of love and His gift of grace. Let us pray together now,' he added hastily, sensing more difficult questions. 'Dear Father in Heaven, be with us this day, we pray Thee. Help us to endure the hard times with courage and fortitude, firm in the knowledge and belief that we shall be rewarded when the time comes. Those of us who have been chosen by God to labour in the cane fields, and to serve their earthly masters, let them rejoice in that labour and that service! Give us the strength, we pray, to bear smilingly the weight of Thy divine yoke until Thou choose to lift it!'

There was more of the same sanctimony, but I would deem it a waste of paper to set it down. When he finally prepared to leave, I observed that he did so in a tidy carriage in which there sat a pretty black child, smartly attired in the English fashion with a little bonnet and a parasol. I jaloosed that she would have been about ten years of age. It was not difficult to guess what use this fine upstanding churchman made of this particular little infant sister in Christ behind the closed doors of his bedchamber. In a land such as this the white man can avail himself of any means of carnal gratification he desires.

22nd May. Bess will be eight years old today. I try to imagine what she must look like now, but I find it difficult – all I can manage is that memory of seeing her on the floor, playing with her dolls, and her cry of Da-da when she saw me and came running to embrace me. She will have changed so much during these intervening years. I have a thousand reveries and schemes about her, and her future destiny. To turn these into reality – that is my dream.

May 30th. Lemons are the answer! After seven years in the tropics, a sovereign remedy against the pestilential brigade of mosquitoes! The green, lumpy, unprepossessing fruit grows in abundance, and it is a simple matter to squeeze out the juice, with which one anoints oneself liberally. The blessed result is that the bothersome insects leave off their unwelcome ministrations! It was McLean who told me, and he seemed surprised that I had not known already.

Our koker man has gone missing. We did not realise that anything was amiss until mid-morning, when the level of water in the canals did not fall as expected. Allardyce was furious. At first he thought the fellow had simply forgotten his duty, and went storming and cursing to find him, lash in hand, ready to make an example of the wretch. However he was assured that the man had set out during the night and had never returned. Investigations were made at the koker, where the lamp was still burning, but of the man himself there was no sign. It seems most probable that he has simply absconded. He will not get far without being noticed, and I feel confident that he will be brought back and doubtless flogged. In the meantime another koker man has been appointed and trained in his duty.

We heard today that, to the sound of tumultuous drums, Louis of France had his head removed in January, and that of his prostitute Marie Antoinette is very likely to be removed also, a circumstance that places Britain at war with France. There will be a few fine Lords and Ladies trembling in England, I daresay! It would not do to express one's anti-monarchical sentiments too freely, but privately I have to admit to rejoicing at the news. In Ayr once, I remember being obliged to leap into a ditch lest the rattling equipage of a gaping patrician blockhead – some contemptible noble puppy – some detestable aristocratic scoundrel – should mangle me in the mire. I always wonder what merit these wretches have had, or what demerit I have had, in some state of pre-existence, that they were ushered into this scene of being with sceptre of rule and the key of riches in their puny fists; and I was kicked into the world, the sport of their folly, or the victim of their pride. For all their condescension, disdainful sneers, vain pride, and lip-curling contemptuousness of lesser ranks, they are not *men.* So, *adieu,* Louis! and safe passage to whatever brimstone depths that await you! Your whore will soon follow, I am sure!

June 6th. The second koker man has now disappeared in exactly the same circumstances as the first. I was sent down to the koker to investigate. There are two on this plantation, a mile or so apart. The one nearest the plantation stands in open ground next to the river with only a few bushes around, and in full view of the estate buildings. But the other is a gloomy place at the head of an inlet, some way back from the river, and deeply overshadowed by mangroves and tall trees. If one looks carefully in the undergrowth, one can find the remains of an old gibbet that still bears a few rusty chains. Also, by a sad coincidence, it is the spot where Grizzel drowned. Altogether it is a dismal spot, and one from whence it would be a simple matter to slip unnoticed into the bush and make good one's escape.

When I arrived I saw that the lantern was still burning but there was no sign of anyone. I was about to turn back when I noticed a cutlass on the ground. It had clearly belonged to the deserter, but why, I wondered, would anyone take flight into the bush without his cutlass? Allardyce was predictably incensed, and has vowed to hang the fellow by his heels and strip the skin from his back when he catches up with him. He presents a terrible sight when angry, and when he is drunk at the same time then he looks like a madman. Another one of the slaves was sent on koker duty.

June 19th. There is bad news today – the third koker man has disappeared. There is now deep unrest amongst the slaves, who do not believe that the men have run away, but have been carried off by a jumbie, which is their local equivalent of a duppy, as far as I can tell. There was a great outcry when a fourth man, William, was ordered on koker duty, and it was only when Allardyce threatened to hang the fellow on the spot that he went off in a state of pure terror, for they are very superstitious. Frankly I do not know what to make of this. To judge by their mood, it would not take much to push the slaves to open rebellion, and if indeed the post of koker man were being used as an opportunity for escape, then this reluctance to go anywhere near the koker is hard to understand. Forsyth and I attempted to convince Allardyce of this, but he was not receptive to our argument. I offered to accompany the new koker man for the first night, on the grounds that he would not dare to run away.

'Ye can dae as ye please,' he said. 'Just make sure ye're fit for yer duties in the mornin'.'

'May I take a musket with me?'

'Aye, if ye feel ye need it,' he said. 'If ye come across a jumbie it'll no' get far wi' its brains blawn oot.' He laughed and went off. I do not believe in jumbies, but neither do I give any credence to the notion that the men have simply run away, so I am inclined to the view that it would be as well to be armed.

June 20th. The night passed without incident and we have returned safely. Our lanterns gave us a good light, and we arrived at the koker at about midnight. It is an eerie place, and in honesty not one that I would care to visit on my own during the hours of darkness. The night is never silent and there were all manner of sounds in the forest that were no doubt innocent enough in origin, but sufficient to keep us constantly glancing nervously into the darkness beyond the pool of light cast by the lanterns. Of course I was obliged to conceal any qualms I may have felt, and pretended a matter-of-fact insouciance about the whole business.

On either side of the sluice gate there is a pole with the depth of the water marked off in feet, and when the tide began to recede, I explained this to the man and instructed him to raise the sluice. This is done by means of a handle attached to gears that draw the rope through a series of large pulleys, thereby lifting the heavy wooden gate that holds the water in or out, depending on the state of the tide. It is a laborious and slow process, punctuated only by the clink-clink-clink of the ratchet as the handle is turned. When the job was done we sat in silence, I with the musket over my knees, he crouched on his haunches looking into the stygian darkness. Bats fluttered around our heads, and great moths flapped around the lanterns. The air was full of the chirr of crickets and the rasping and croaking of frogs.

'Massa Burns, yah t'ink de jumbie come?' he asked.

'There is no such thing as a jumbie,' I said reassuringly, but he was not convinced.

'Me t'ink de jumbie watchin' we. Me t'ink Grizzel come back.'

'I don't think so, William. Anyway, I have this musket, remember?'

'Dat musket nah work wid a jumbie,' he said, shaking his head. 'Jumbie dead a'ready.'

The conversation continued in this disheartening and depressing vein until it was time to lower the gate again and make our way back. I remain none the wiser about where the other men have gone, but there is clearly no supernatural reason for their disappearance.

June 29th. Koker being operated without further incident – no jumbie. That damned dog still pisses on me whenever it can. I had a tarantula in my room last night – everyone says their bite is no worse than that of a marabunta[2] but I am taking no chances, and besides I have always harboured a distinct dislike of the unfortunate descendants of Arachne. It was on the wall of my room, about four or five inches across, and perversely fascinating to look at when motionless; covered in very fine black hairs with a tiny yellow spot at the tip of each of its eight legs. They normally move slowly, but I have seen them run with amazing speed, and the prospect of having the creature make a sudden, scuttling foray on to my hair or inside my shirt makes me shudder. I knocked it from the wall with a stick and squashed it with the sole of my boot.

July 7th. The mystery of the koker is solved, and a ghastly business it was. Poor William is dead, and the manner of his passing was so terrible that it will haunt my dreams for the remainder of my life. Had I been more alert, I might have been able to save him, but I was taken completely off guard and it was too late.

Last night we had completed our work, and were preparing to return home. I had picked up my lantern, and had begun to lead the way back along the path. I had only taken a few paces when I heard William utter a kind of gasp. As I turned around I observed that his lantern had fallen to the ground and gone out. From the dim light cast by my own, I could see he was standing stock still with his mouth open. At first I could not determine what was wrong with him. His eyes were bulging in terror and agony and suddenly blood began to pour from his mouth. Then I realised that a huge camoodie had seized him, winding its dark coils around the wretched fellow's body. There was a cracking sound, caused by his ribs breaking, as the creature squeezed the life from him. I hurriedly set down the lantern, cocked the musket and tried to take aim but the light was so poor that no easy target presented itself. I eventually let off a shot that must have missed – there was no time to reload, so I dropped the gun and advanced with my cutlass only to see that the snake had the lower part of its body anchored around the top of the koker and was lifting William off the ground and out of my reach. For a few seconds his legs kicked in a final death-throe and then he was pulled out of sight. There was nothing I could do for him, so I ran back to the plantation and summoned help.

When we arrived at the scene of this dreadful event we thought at first that the creature had taken to the water and gone off, but then we saw that it was still on top of the koker, which has a platform above the pulleys, allowing access to the other side of the trench. It raised its head, but did not move, so we began to fire our muskets at it and hit it several times. It fell into the trench with a great splash, and began to lash about, flailing and writhing in the brown water. We thought it would never die, but eventually its struggles slowed, and the current moved it to a place where we were able to pull it to the bank. It took six of us all of our strength to drag it from the water and

stretch it out on the path. We had no means at the time of determin-
ing its length with any degree of exactitude, but from head to tail
measured some ten paces, so I estimate it to have been about thirty
feet in length.[3] The creature's body was dark green in colour, as
thick as a man's waist, tapering towards the tail, but in the middle –
horrible to see – was a great, distended bulge. We chopped the beast
open with our cutlasses, and pulled out the crushed remains of
William, coated with a vile-smelling slime. What a way to die! and
what a howling and wailing amongst the terrified slaves when we
returned with the lifeless body!

What kind of country is this that harbours such terrible creatures?
I am trembling as I write. It could so easily have been me, caught up
like some modern Laocoon in the toils of that most hideous serpent!
Even Allardyce is aghast, and has ordered that in future two of the
overseers must offer armed protection to the koker man at all times.

July 15th. For some days I have had a tune in my head that would not
leave me alone – like a persistent mosquito – and at last I hit upon the
expedient of manufacturing a lyric, which I completed this evening.

The Banks of Demerary

> The firstling rays o' comin' dawn
> Shone on the Demerary, O!
> As I stepped out wi' staff in haun
> Tae meet my bonnie Mary, O!
>
> As to the koker I came nigh
> My heart was licht and airy, O!
> When I my true love did espy
> Doon by the Demerary, O!
>
> I laid her doon and lo'ed her weel –
> I trow she'll ne'er be sairy, O! –
> And vowed to be forever leal
> Unto my bonnie Mary, O!
>
> What lies ahead we canna know,
> And Fate may prove contrary, O!
> But I'll treasure aye thon hour, my Jo,
> Doon by the Demerary, O!

The incident I describe did not, of course, take place. Writing the
verses has made me recall my *own* Mary once more – the high hopes

with which we set out for Jamaica; her goodness and sweetness of nature, and the cruelty of a pitiless Fate that snatched her from me.

More floggings on the plantation today. The punishments are being meted out for the smallest offences – theft of a cup of rum from the still house: forty lashes. Theft of an egg: thirty lashes. Insolence towards overseer: fifty lashes. Slacking: ten lashes. I have remonstrated with Allardyce a hundred times, but he simply ignores me or calls me a neger-lover. I dare not intervene physically – the appeal to Balcarres has come to nothing – what more can I do?

July 30th. I have been here for two years now, and the matter of my salary has never been resolved. Today I was frank with Allardyce and told him that I wished to leave, and so would require to have the monies in hand.

'So ye're thinkin' o' leavin'?' he said in surprise. 'And why, may I ask?'

'I wish to return to Scotland.'

'I see. Well, I'm no' sure I can spare ye. I'm a man short as it is.'

'I would not leave immediately,' I said.

'That's verra guid o' ye,' he said sardonically. 'I'll see whit I can dae. But damn it man, it's hellish inconvenient. Ye ken the workin' o' the boilin' hoose and the mill better than onybody else. Ye'll be a great loss tae the plantation.'

I was taken aback by this, because in all the time I have known him he has never uttered a single compliment to me, or to anyone else for that matter, so this was either high praise or shameless flattery.

'That's very good of you, Mr Allardyce. I shall not leave until you have someone else in place, and working to your satisfaction.'

'It may take a wee while,' he said. 'Leave it wi' me. I'll see whit I can dae.'

'And you will see to it that my salary is paid to me?'

'I said I'd deal wi' it,' he said impatiently, and waved me away.

I do not feel confident that I shall receive my salary soon, and I shall have to prompt him regularly, I am sure. I know that I am very useful to the plantation, particularly in the factory, so there is little incentive for him to find a replacement.

August 3rd. I reminded Allardyce today about my salary, but he just growled at me and told me to be patient.

'I havena got money here. I'll hae tae go tae Stabroek for it.'

'When will that be?'

'Damn it man, stop pesterin' me! There's ower mickle tae dae!'

With that he walked off in an ill temper. It is not pleasant dealing with the man, but I have no option but to continue raising the matter until he does something about it.

August 17th. Today Allardyce summoned us all to the benab, clearly very aggrieved about something. We had no clue as to what it might be until he produced a letter, which he waved accusingly.

'Which one of ye did this?' he shouted.

'Did what, Mr Allardyce?' said Forsyth.

'Wrote letters aboot me! Complained aboot me!' There was, I realised, no point in trying to play the innocent, for he either knew already or had formed a pretty accurate conjecture.

'I wrote a letter to Lord Balcarres,' I said.

'So ye're the clype!' he yelled. 'Aye, I could hae guessed! Ye're aye scribblin' nonsense, and ye're ower keen tae tell the rest o' us how tae run the plantation. Well damn ye, Burns, ye've gone ower far this time!' He was in a real rage, and I felt a qualm of fear. I am not a weakling, but if Allardyce had attacked me at that moment, then I would have stood little chance. The only course of action was to remain calm: I was also reassured by the presence of the others.

'Mr Allardyce, I expressed my concerns to you on many occasions. My letter was a last resort – and it was not motivated by personal animosity, but out of concern for the safety of all of us.'

'Concern? Concern? Anither o' yer fine fancy words!' he sneered.

'You can't pretend that the situation here is a happy one,' I said.

'We're no' here tae be happy! As for the slaves, I dinna care if they're happy or no'. They're here tae work!'

'If they are ill-treated, then they will not work – they'll rise up against us. It has happened before.'

'Why dae ye persist in arguin' wi' me?' he bellowed.

'Because I believe myself to be in the right,' I shouted back. 'You know the problems we face here. Ambrose is doing all he can, but without him we'd be finished. All this flogging is making it worse by the day.'

'I dae whit I consider best!'

'It may not *be* best.'

'Wha are *you* tae judge?'

'I spent five years on a plantation where we had no trouble.'

'That was Jamaica! This isna Jamaica!'

'Maybe,' I said. 'But the same principles apply.'

'Principles!' He spat the word out as if it was something dirty.

'Maybe Mr Burns has a point, sir,' said Forsyth. He had not

spoken before, and frankly I was surprised to hear him speak up now.

'Weel, weel, Mr Forsyth,' said Allardyce scornfully. 'Ye've found yer tongue, have ye?'

'All I'm saying is that Burns may have a point.'

'I agree with Forsyth,' said McLean. 'We canna go on as we're doing.'

'Whit does the letter say? Is it frae Balcarres?' said MacDuff.

'Aye, it is.'

'Ye've no' been relieved o' yer post, hae ye?'

'Naw. His Lordship has been *apprised* o' the *concerns* o' Mr Burns here, an' he instructs me tae introduce *measures* tae alleviate the conditions o' the slaves.'

'Is that a'?' asked MacDuff.

'Oh, there's a whole dictionary o' fancy words. Mr Burns'll be able tae explain them tae ye, nae doot.'

'So ye're still in chairge?'

'Aye.'

'Nobody disputes that you are in charge, Mr Allardyce,' I said. 'We all want to work with you to improve the situation.'

'So ye want tae work wi' me, dae ye? I thocht ye were verra anxious to leave the plantation, Mr Burns,' said Allardyce. 'Ye've been girnin' aboot yer wages for the last twa weeks.'

'You never told us you were leaving,' said Forsyth.

'I haven't made up my mind yet,' I said.

'If there are changes tae be made,' said Allardyce, 'then I expect ye tae bide here an' play yer part. Ye canna persuade Balcarres tae order *measures*, and then rin awa' when it's time tae implement them. It's bad enough losin' Smith, but I *need* ye, much as I wish I didna.'

I was compelled to agree with him on that point, which mollified him slightly. I have revised my low opinion of Lord Balcarres a little. There was a good deal more discussion during which I took care to humour Allardyce as much as possible. Forsyth and McLean took my part, which made it easier to decide on the reforms that are needed. The upshot of it was that by the evening we had agreed to four measures – *item*. that no slave shall be flogged except by one of the Negro drivers, and then only for serious offences; *item*. that, save for the periods when cane is being cut, slaves shall have Saturday as well as Sunday at leisure, to occupy their time as they see fit; *item*. that slaves shall be permitted to sell any food they produce, and keep any proceeds arising from that sale as their own; and *item*. that the plantation will provide an immediate issue of new clothing.

Allardyce did not like any of this, and of course MacDuff argued in support of his superior, but the three of us finally carried the day. An end to indiscriminate flogging will surely be welcomed by everyone; all necessary work can be carried out as well in five days as in six, and there is no reason why they should not profit from pursuing their own modest commerce. The provision of new clothes, though expensive, can be set against a hoped for increase in plantation income. There are several additional measures I would have liked to see introduced, but gaining this modest concession from Allardyce is progress enough for the moment. He has given me a few baleful looks during the course of this day, and I recognise that his pride has been hurt. However he retains his position, and he has nothing to lose.

August 18th. The Sabbath. We asked Ambrose to come to the benab, and outlined our proposals, although of course we did not tell him about the letter from Balcarres. He listened with his usual intentness, his face impassive, nodding carefully as each point was made.

'So there ye are,' said Allardyce. 'What d'ye think?'

'I t'ink it could work,' he said. 'Dey nah un'erstan' why dey is git de lash all de time. Dis way betta, Massa Allardyce.'

'It puts a lot of responsibility on you for keeping order,' I said.

'I un'erstan' dat, Massa Burns.'

'Any questions, Ambrose?' asked Allardyce.

'Yessuh. When we git de clothes?'

'As soon as they can be procured,' said Allardyce. 'I'm sending MacDuff tae Stabroek tomorrow tae order them.'

'Yessuh. Nex' Sat'day we nah work?'

'That's right. I'll expect good work during the week, mind!'

'Yessuh. Yah want I tell dem?'

'Aye. Tell them today. Tell them now.'

'Yessuh,' said Ambrose, and strode off.

'I hope for God's sake that we're daein' the right thing,' said Allardyce, giving me a bad-tempered look.

'A lot depends on Ambrose,' I said, 'but then, it always did. He seems to think it's a good idea. At any rate, I do not see what harm it can possibly do.'

'Gie them a little an' they'll be wantin' mair,' grumbled MacDuff.

'Treat them reasonably, and they'll be less intractable,' I said.

'Intractable!' scoffed Allardyce. 'Anither fine word!'

There is nothing for it now but to wait and see for ourselves how things develop. As in Port Antonio, I am convinced that the policy of placing our head driver in charge of discipline will prove effective in lessening any resentment felt towards ourselves, and I know that Ambrose will use the lash sparingly. The other measures must surely be welcome ones and will serve to thaw the sullen frost of resentment that blights our days here in Goed Intent.

September 2nd. In two weeks the character of the estate has changed considerably, and I feel entirely vindicated. Ambrose has organised the drivers to supervise all aspects of the plantation except the mill, where McLean is in charge. Allardyce has been astonished to find that the work of the estate progresses perfectly well without his constant intervention. The clothing has been ordered from Stabroek and its delivery is expected daily.

Ambrose tells me that Simon is rather at a loss, for many of the issues that aroused his anger and resentment have now been re-solved, and he is finding a less ready audience for his attempts to incite discord. None the less, he remains a problem. Ambrose said today that I should take him to work for me in the boiling house. At first I thought this was an odd suggestion but the more I consider it, the better it appeals to me. Firstly, such a move will serve to keep him out of the fields – which should please him! – and, more impor-tantly, will prevent him from associating as freely with other work-ers. Secondly, it can be presented to him as an advancement from which he may profit in future, for skills in sugar-boiling are greatly valued, and always will be for as long as sugar is grown in Demerary. Finally, I am hopeful I may be able to befriend him through the expedient of demonstrating that not all white men are like Allardyce.

September 18th. Progress maintained. Simon has come to the boiling house to work for me. I am not sure what to make of him. He responds immediately to any request I make – and I take the greatest pains to ensure that I always make requests and never issue orders. He is an attentive listener and is proving an adept pupil. He is polite in his manner, but he never speaks to me, which I attribute to the fact that he has either not yet mastered Creole, or does not yet choose to communicate with me – I suspect the latter, since he appears to have a perfect understanding of what I say to him. Be that as it may, I can now leave him in charge of the boiling house for extended periods.

The new clothes arrived ten days ago. Ambrose sent two mule carts to the stelling to unload the bundles, and busied himself all day with distributing the contents. It is many months since I have seen such a host of smiling faces! Such heartfelt gratitude! Such shouts of joy! And for what? They deserved nothing less than what was being given to them! These are fine, proud, handsome people who should be able to walk with dignity – it saddened my heart to see the duddies they wore until recently, and makes me ashamed to think that it is only now that we have had the decency to clothe them properly.

Allardyce has been muttering gloomily that with the cessation of work on Saturdays, the work of the estate will never be completed, and everything will fall into wrack and ruin. We have had four such Saturdays so far, and everything runs very much as usual – under Ambrose's supervision, people are actually working harder. I have noticed some people singing as they go about their work, something that I had not heard recently. I have no idea what the words mean, but it does not sound like the angry, warlike chant of the disaffected, and we do not feel threatened by it.

October 1st. I had a very revealing conversation with Simon this morning – the first I have ever had – and it has given me a great deal to think about. I feel he is now more relaxed in my presence, and this prompted me to question him directly.

'You can hear me when I speak to you, Simon, can you not?' I said. He looked at me sharply, then gave a nod. 'Do you understand what I am saying to you?' Again he nodded. 'There is something I find surprising,' I said. 'I hear you speaking to the other workers, but you never speak to me. Why not?'

He looked at me for a long time, seemingly struggling with some strong emotion within, before finally speaking.

'I cyan't say de word,' he said, in a deep voice. 'Dat's why I nah speak.'

'What word?'

'De word.'

'I don't know what you mean.'

He sighed. 'I cyan't say de word "massa". So I says nuttin'.'

'So what would you call me?' I said.

'I knows yah name is Burns,' he said. 'But yah nah me massa. Allardyce buy me fuh twenty pound, but he nah me massa. Nobody me massa. So I says nuttin'.'

'So what would you call me?' I said again. He looked at me for a long time.

'A white man,' he said at last – not in the least rudely or contemptuously. 'A white man wid de name Burns.'

I really did not know what to say to him. I have been called Massa Burns for so long that I rarely think about it, and I had almost forgotten what it means.

October 18th. How long is it now since I even thought of poesy? To think that I was once well known in my neighbourhood as a maker of rhymes! I once wrote some verses that I believed to be of merit, but, to prevent the worst, gave a copy to a friend who was very fond of these things, and told him I could not guess who was the author of it. How sweet the roar of applause! How my verses alarmed the kirk session so much that they held meetings to look over their artillery, to see what they could point at profane rhymers! It all seems so long ago. It is not that I am lacking for subject matter, however – there is a poem in my mind now, and I have been feeling once again the gentle promptings of my Muse.

I have said to Simon that he may address me as Mr Burns if he wishes to. He thinks that 'mister' and 'master' are much the same thing, but I have assured him that they are not. If we were truly on equal terms, then he would call me Robert, but I cannot permit this familiarity, since there has to be a distance between us, just as there must be between any employer and his workers. I feel that we now understand each other tolerably well – he is mannerly towards me, and he is now able to operate the boiling house as expertly as I.

November 8th. Today I finished a little verse – my antipathy to the notion of slavery never leaves me – my dealings with Simon have acted on my mind like an inspiration, and I have not been able to resist rhyming on the impulse. I fear that my stanzas do poor justice to the subject, but they are sincerely felt –

A Man's a Man for a' that

> What man deserves to live in dread,
> To cower and cringe, and a' that?
> Why should he learn to bow his head
> And call me 'Sir', and a' that?
> For a' that and a' that,
> Their manacles and a' that:
> You canna brand the human soul –
> A man's a man for a' that.
>
> What right have we to bind the free
> And call them 'slaves', and a' that?
> Force them to toil and bend the knee
> If we but nod, and a' that?
> For a' that and a' that,

> Our sov'reign powers, and a' that:
> Man's inhumanity to man
> Is rank offence, for a' that.
>
> Yon overseer, wi' haughty scowl,
> Wha waves his whip, and a' that –
> His skin is white, his soul is foul:
> He'll roast in hell, for a' that!
> For a' that and a' that,
> His strutting gait and a' that:
> The meanest slave he spurns aside
> Is twice his worth, for a' that.
>
> So let us pray that come it may,
> As come it will, for a' that,
> That slavery shall pass away
> An' be no more, for a' that.
> For a' that, and a' that,
> It's plain to see, for a' that,
> Beneath the skin, the man within
> Deserves respect, for a' that.

This is not a poem to be shared with anyone else. However, the exercise of setting it down has acted a sovereign cathartic for my mind!

November 23rd. I am convinced that the changes in the plantation have been beneficial for everyone. Even Allardyce and MacDuff admit – grudgingly – that the grumbles, grievances, complaints and protests that we used to be plagued with have now largely ceased.

December 4th. Prudence has been round to my house again on four or five occasions, bearing her inevitable bowls of rice, for all the world like a reverential priestess bringing her offerings to the high altar of some pagan deity. I am still mindful of Ambrose's advice, and when I take the coconut shell from her I set it aside with the promise that I shall eat it later, which I never do. Although I do not entertain the same warm thoughts towards her as I used to, the promptings of nature's fleshly thorn can be insistent at times – I know that she would not refuse me [and I still recall her shapely brea].

Allardyce has been true to his word, and another overseer has been appointed. He arrived three days ago – a big, clumsy fellow called Jock McClure, with the same sulky look about him as Currie used to have. He must be about thirty – black haired, black-bearded and taciturn. We have helped him move his few belongings into Smith's quarters, which have been swept out and washed down with vinegar. He has little to offer in the way of conversation, but he is strong and healthy, and very willingly does as he is told.

'How d'ye get on wi' McClure?' asked Allardyce this morning.

'It is hard to tell. He seems dependable enough.'

'Mmph. D'ye think ye could teach him the sugar boilin'?'

'I could try.'

'How are ye gettin' on wi' Simon?'

'He works well for me,' I said. 'I think he has considerable talents. He has mastered everything I have taught him.'

'I didna mean his work. Does he gie ye trouble?'

'I have had no problems with him,' I said.

'Aye, weel, watch yer back. There's trouble comin' – I can feel it.'

'What kind of trouble?'

'Wha kens? I dinna trust Simon. An' there's some o' the big laddies on the second gang I'm worried aboot.'

'I thought the plantation was running very well,' I said.

'Aye, nae doot.'

He is still angry with me for writing to Balcarres, but I cannot share his suspicion that there is trouble in store. He has been compelled to change his ways, and now he is unable to admit graciously that he has been in the wrong.

December 13th. I wonder whether Allardyce tries to be provocative on purpose, or whether there is a perverse demon lurking deep in his nature so that he cannot help his aggressive approach to everything and everybody. I once saw him try to drive in a nail that twisted a little before it was fully hammered home. Rather than pull it out and start over again, he grew more and more impatient with it, striking at it this way and that, growing scarlet in the face and cursing at it all the while until it was bent sideways and hammered flat – an ugly, botched mess of a job. In his dealing with the plantation people he behaves in exactly the same way. He cannot give a simple instruction – he pushes, he provokes, he goads, he taunts, and finally reaches for his whip. He cannot understand the reason for the ill feeling that is the inevitable consequence of this wilful obduracy.

The new *régime* has meant that he has lost the opportunity of bullying, and as a result his natural inclination to cruelty, lacking an outlet, has been pent up. He had no reason to come to the boiling house today, no reason to engage with Simon, and as I consider the matter now, I can only conclude that he came seeking confrontation.

He was drunk when he arrived, and carrying his whip and a set of shackles, which made matters worse. He acknowledged me with a nod and a grunt, and made an unconvincing pretence of checking the simmering vessels and the various implements the men were using. Simon was about his business stoking the fires, and to anyone else I am sure we would have presented a picture of purposeful industry, but it was not enough for Allardyce.

'Whit are ye up tae, boy?' he said to Simon.

'He's in charge of the fires,' I said. 'He does a good job.'

'I wisna askin' *you*, Mr Burns,' he said. 'I wis askin' Simon here. Whit are ye up tae, Simon? Eh?' He spoke quietly, but began tapping his whip against the side of his leg. Simon looked at him, and then at me, but said nothing.

'Ye havena answered ma question.' He raised his voice a little. 'I asked ye whit ye were daein'?'

'He fetches bagasse and makes sure that the fires are hot enough.'

'Keep oot o' this, Burns,' he said. 'It's Simon I'm speakin' tae. Whit are ye daein', Simon?'

Simon looked at him. 'I fetch de bagasse. I mek de fire.'

'So ye fetch bagasse and make the fire. Dae ye enjoy yer work?' Ambrose said nothing. 'I said – dae ye enjoy yer work, Simon?'

'He's a good worker,' I said. This conversation was going to hell and I wanted to stop it. But Allardyce had the bit between his teeth.

'Ye can keep yer damned mouth shut, Burns!' he shouted, and prodded Simon in the chest with his finger. 'I'll ask ye again, boy. Dae ye enjoy yer work? Answer me now – yes or no?' I could see Simon's jaws clenching convulsively, and his nostrils flared as Allardyce poked him again and again, but still he said nothing.

'Are ye deaf, boy?' shouted Allardyce.

'No,' said Simon.

'Oh, ye can speak! That's verra guid! Let's hae a proper answer now – let's hear ye say "No, Massa Allardyce". Come on now!' Simon shook his head, and Allardyce prodded him again.

'You don't need to make him do this,' I said.

'Mind yer ain damned business! He'll treat me wi' respect or he'll suffer the consequences!' He prodded Simon again. 'Come on, boy, let's hear it! "No, Massa Allardyce". I'm waitin', boy!'

'Yah nah me massa.'

Allardyce stepped back, astonished. 'Whit did ye say?' he said.

'Yah nah me massa.'

Allardyce gave a malevolent leer. 'Wha is yer maister, then? Mr Burns here, maybe?'

'Me nah have a massa.'

'Ye dinna hae a maister?'

'No.'

'So when did ye procure yer manumission?' said Allardyce. Simon made no reply, but I could see the muscles of his cheek moving as he clenched his teeth.

'Nae manumission,' sneered Allardyce. 'So I am yer maister after a', *an' I will be addressed as such.* Will I no'?'

'He intends no disrespect,' I said.

'God, Burns, why are ye forever takin' the side o' the negers?' he barked. 'This slave here disna acknowledge me as his maister, an' yet ye say he intends nae disrespect. Man, I dinna understaun' ye!'

'He has worked well enough for me,' I said.

'I'll tell ye whit I think,' he said, coming over to me and sticking his face close to mine. 'I think ye're ower fond o' Negroes.'

'I think it does no harm to treat them with respect,' I said.

'Respect?' he scoffed. 'Respect on this estate is for me, no' for the slaves! They are here tae work, like the beasts that drive the mill.'

'If you want a beast to work for you, you do not starve it, beat it and curse it,' I said. 'You treat it with care and consideration, and it will give you faithful service. I know – I was a farmer. I do not imagine that people are any different.'

'These are slaves, not people,' he said. 'It's time ye went back tae Scotland richt enough,' he said. He turned and went outside, returning a moment later with MacDuff and McClure who must have been waiting there all the while.

'Is there some problem, Mr Allardyce?' said MacDuff.

'Aye. Simon here says he disna hae a maister. He refuses tae ca' me Massa Allardyce. I ca' it barefaced disrespect!'

'There's ways o' dealin' wi' *that!*' declared MacDuff.

'Aye. Pit the shackles on him!'

All this time, Simon had been standing still and silent, his eyes fixed in the distance. He made no resistance as the shackles were applied, and he allowed himself to be led away. I felt revolted by the whole episode – it was entirely unnecessary, and it has undone all I have accomplished with Simon these three months.

Later I discovered that Simon had been flogged by one of the overseers, but not before Allardyce, MacDuff and McClure had taken him to a secluded spot and given him a cruel beating. Throughout all of this, Simon refused to utter the word 'massa'.

December 16th. Simon not at work today – hardly surprising after the punishment to which he was subjected yestreen. McClure has been sent to learn the sugar boiling, though I fear he has little aptitude for anything requiring more than brute effort. He will do as he is told, but shows no initiative or interest whatsoever. So we have lost Simon, who understood the whole process very thoroughly, and gained in his stead a great, hulking booby – a daft gowk who understands nothing – all for the sake of Allardyce's damned *amour propre.*

December 23rd. Monday. We have had a bad time of it the last two days, and no mistake. On Saturday Simon went around stirring up more discord, and, because of his bleeding stripes, gained a good deal of sympathy, especially among some of the bigger boys in the second gang. They are about fourteen years of age, a time when all lads are restive and rebellious, and they look up to Simon as a champion – regarding him perhaps as the Israelites did David, believing that he might step forward to smite the Philistine Goliath of slavery. The drivers usually keep these youngsters in their place, but of late they have adopted rather an insolent manner.

On Saturday afternoon, Ambrose went to Allardyce and told him he feared that there was serious trouble afoot, and advised caution. We were all issued with pistols and a supply of powder and shot. As it began to grow dark we could hear shouting from the villagers, so instead of going to our own quarters we remained together in the benab. Night fell – our little lamps cast no light beyond the benab itself – in the heavy darkness beyond we could see nothing.

'What did Ambrose say to you?' asked McLean nervously. 'What's happening?'

'He wisna specific,' said Allardyce. 'He thinks Simon's plannin' somethin'.'

'He can't do much on his own,' said Forsyth.

'He's been whippin' up the second gang,' said MacDuff.

'Keep yer eyes peeled,' said Allardyce. We did, but there was nothing to see – not a glimmer. The shouting in the village died down suddenly, and apart from the frogs and crickets there was nothing to be heard.

'We should cover our lights,' I said. 'If anyone comes, they will be able to see us before we see them.' This was done, and very gradually our eyes grew accustomed to the darkness. There was a tiny sliver of a moon, and by its pale light we could see the grassy area in front of the benab, and the shadowy, looming shapes of our huts. Beyond that lay a dark wall of standing cane. We reasoned that any attack would have to come from that direction, for there are dense bushes on the other sides.

We waited for what seemed like hours. I do not know what we expected – I suppose we feared a sudden, frontal attack by some sizeable force. Every innocent sound of the night sounded ominous: the rustle of an animal in the cane presented itself to our minds as the stealthy approach of the foe. For a long time nothing happened, and I had almost determined to return to my quarters when Forsyth suddenly pointed over towards Allardyce's hut.

'Look!' he hissed. 'Can you see them?' Two or three shadowy shapes had emerged from the cane, and were cautiously approaching the hut stairs.

'They think I'm in ma hut,' said Allardyce, cocking his pistol.

'Who are they? Does anyone recognise them?' said Forsyth.

'It's too dark, and they're too far away,' said McLean. 'But I don't think Simon's one of them. I think these are just boys.'

'Boys or no',' said Allardyce grimly, 'they shouldna be there.'

'What are we going to do?' I asked. 'They don't seem to know we are here. We could take them by surprise.'

'Wait till we see whit they're up tae,' said Allardyce. All our attention was now fixed on the space between the benab and Allardyce's hut, so none of us was prepared for what happened next.

With a terrible scream Simon leapt over the wall of the benab behind us, cutlass in hand, and made directly for Allardyce. There was utter confusion as everyone tumbled to the ground in a heap, and the flailing cutlass was kicked from the hand that held it. Then there was the muffled report of a pistol, followed by a cry of pain.

'Let's have a light, for God's sake,' shouted Allardyce. 'Is anyone hurt?'

A lamp was uncovered, revealing Simon lying on the floor with a ball through his shoulder, grimacing in pain. Allardyce had a gash on his arm, but miraculously there were no other injuries.

'Where are the others?' gasped Forsyth. 'They may be coming next!' McClure, McLean and I took our lamps and pistols and began a thorough search, but we could find no sign of anyone – they must have run off on hearing the shot. When we finally returned to the benab we found that Allardyce and MacDuff had trussed Simon up and tied him to the central pillar of the benab.

'He'll hang for this,' said Allardyce. 'I'll go tomorrow an' fetch the militia.' He looked at me, and a self-satisfied smirk came over his face. 'Ye see whaur these neger-lovin' *measures* lead, Mr Burns? Rebellion! I telt ye this wad happen!'

'One slave hardly makes a rebellion,' I said. 'If you hadn't provoked him, he would never have attacked you.'

'I provoke wha I please!' he said. 'And whit aboot the ithers, eh? Wha were they? Aye man, there's revolution in the air. The negers hae ower mickle time on their hauns, an' we've been ower lenient wi' them. I'll see to it that Lord Balcarres is *apprised* that Mr Burns' fine liberal ideas dinna work.'

There was nothing to say at that moment. We were all exhausted, and went to our quarters, making sure to lock the doors and to take our pistols with us. MacDuff and McClure remained in the benab with Simon.

On Sunday morning, Allardyce went to the plantation village in search of whoever had approached the huts on the previous night. Of course no one admitted to knowing anything about it, so he had everyone in the second gang lined up and questioned individually. There was not one of them, boy or girl, who did not feel the whip that morning.

In the afternoon he summoned Ambrose and very curtly said to him that the plantation people might keep their clothes, but from now on they would work on Saturdays as usual, and must regard all of their produce as being estate property. As for the lash, this would once again be wielded as the overseers saw fit. Ambrose went away very stony-faced, saying nothing.

December 30th. Life here has returned to the way it was before the reforms. Allardyce is convinced that the 'rebellion' – as he terms it – was my fault, and cannot be argued with. He relishes the fact that he can use the lash again, and he loses no opportunity of doing so. Nobody, it seems, has learned anything. Simon – silent as ever, and looking at no one – has been taken away by the militia.

In France, I hear, the whore Marie Antoinette has gone the way of her husband – all her plotting has come to light, and for all her remonstrations and pleadings she has had her empty head removed from her pampered body. For the crime of refusing to call a man his master, Simon is now doomed to the hangman, and shall likewise be sent to perdition, which is precisely where I fear we are all headed. We are told by very respectable authority that 'the righteous perish and no man layeth it to heart'[4] – where is the justice in this world?

1794

January 10th. A sour, sneering poem has been in my mind for some time. I am low in spirits these days, and avoid speaking to people. Simon has been hanged in Stabroek. Allardyce has reverted to acting like a vicious animal, and if it were not for Ambrose then this plantation would be finished. When I think of what we accomplished last year, I am quite in despair. I cannot allow myself to participate in brutality, and this has made me an object of derision among the others. Even Forsyth has suggested that I should at least carry a whip, even if I do not intend to use it. Once my passions are lighted up they rage like so many devils until they get vent in rhyme. Surely some irate Muse stood at my shoulder as I penned the following –

The Happy Negro

Behold the joy that fills the happy Negro's breast
As red-hot branding irons are applied with zest!
See how he laughs to feel the cowhide lash,
As white men scream that he is nothing more than trash.
How pleasant are the festering wounds upon his back,
Inflicted for the heinous crime of being black!
Good fortune smiles upon him in this happy land
Where blessings, rich and full, abound on every hand:
The gag; the whip; the goad; the merry hangman's noose,
Are daily boons, each put to wholesome Christian use:
Fine precepts for the savage man to contemplate,
And make him realise the joys of his estate.
Freed from the deadly dangers of his native soil,
He spends each day engaged in blissful, careless toil:
Freed from the fearsome peril of distant Africk shores,
He smiles to see his daughters made the white man's whores.
And when he dies, he knows a white man's doom awaits,
With overseers to bar his path to heaven's gates.

I shall not bother to show it to the others – it would be wasted on them. I dare say if I had found some way to include the word 'arse' in the lines, then I should have been adjudged the best of poets, by MacDuff at least, but I shall keep this to myself. For the last few days I have been debating whether to continue this journal, but have concluded that for someone of a solitary disposition it is a salutary exercise – besides, I often read through it in order to remind myself of times past.

Adah has been much in my mind. There have been times of late when I have awakened in the night and imagined that she was lying by my side, only to realise that she is gone forever. She gave herself to me without reserve, and had it not been for my silly infatuation with Nancy, we might still be together. It is strange to think that I now have a little son or a little daughter growing up amidst the scenes I remember so well. It sometimes makes me weep to read through my account of those carefree times. One day, perhaps, I shall have happier events to record, but at the moment it seems unlikely.

January 15th. Ever since my arrival here three years ago, I have been increasingly impressed with Ambrose. He seems to possess an intuitive grasp of what needs to be done; he never has to be reminded of anything; he is polite without appearing obsequious, and he has the knack of resolving potentially difficult situations. I recall that Forsyth once told me that he would 'surprise me yet', or words to that effect, but until today I had no inkling of what he meant.

I was standing with him watching the gangs hacking at the cane with their cutlasses, and I was making some remarks about how well the work was progressing. 'Allardyce will be pleased,' I said, expecting the usual 'Yessuh'.

'It is a matter of supreme indifference to me how Allardyce feels,' came the reply. At first I thought that a third party was present, and looked around in astonishment. Of course there was no one else there but Ambrose, who was looking at directly me with a somewhat mischievous expression. This in itself was unusual, since Negroes have been well taught to avoid meeting the eye of white people, as an intimacy tantamount to insolence.

'I beg your pardon?' I said.

'Allardyce's feelings are a matter of complete indifference to me,' continued Ambrose, in cultured tones that would have done credit to any Milord. I gawped at him, unable to think of anything to say.

'What is the matter with you, Mr Burns?' he went on. 'Are you surprised to discover that I speak English?'

'Yes . . . no, but I have never heard you do so until now. I had always assumed you only spoke Creole. Why do you hide your talents . . .'

'. . . under a bushel?' He laughed, clearly enjoying my lack of composure. 'A little learning is a dangerous thing, at least so Mr Pope tells us. But for a black man like me, any learning is dangerous. You see, white men are afraid of educated black men. An erudite Negro may get ideas above his station. He may actually be able to find the words with which to articulate his grievances. Heaven forfend, he might even win an argument.'

'Who else knows this?' I asked.

'Only Forsyth. I told him some time ago, when I realised I could trust him. I am now placing the same trust in you.'

'You may rely upon me absolutely,' I declared. We parted soon after, both of us aware that any lengthened conversation might appear suspicious, but I am determined to discover where Ambrose acquired his learning.

January 16th. What a life that man has had! Ambrose I mean. He was born in Saint-Domingue some eight-and-thirty years ago, which means he is fully three years my senior. From a tender age he laboured on a French plantation until, at the age of ten, he was taken to France where he was cultivated as a servant boy in the household of some Marquis or other. The affairs of this noble Lord having declined, he was sold in his fifteenth year to attorney-general Lord M[ansfield?], in whose household he seems to have been well enough treated. Then he was captured in broad daylight on the streets of London, and returned to Saint-Domingue where he was sold to another plantation owner. He escaped and made his way here as a fugitive, much as I did myself. Whether he made his way on to this plantation willingly I have not yet ascertained. He must be a human chameleon, adapting himself to those around him. How difficult it must be to conceal so much knowledge and learning! I would willingly talk to him more than I do, but to do so would arouse suspicion, so we must be circumspect.

February 1st. We have made a good friend in Mijnheer Bos, a Dutchman whose business it is to keep revenue records of the estates on this side of the Demerary. He is a small, portly individual with a round, sonsie face that always seems to be wreathed in smiles. It is difficult to imagine him other than cheerful. He wears spectacles that add to this benign and jovial demeanour. We often sit in the benab and talk after matters of business have been concluded. Fortunately his command of English is perfect, for I had always thought Dutch to be entirely incomprehensible, though he chided me on that point.

'Listen more carefully. What do you call a church in Scotland?'

'We use the word "kirk" for that,' I said. 'An Englishman wouldn't understand.'

'But I would,' he said, beaming. 'The Dutch word is *kerk*. And if I say *kom hier?*'

'Come here?'

'Exactly! What about *goedemorgen?*

'Good morning?'

'Ah, you are learning quickly,' he said, delighted. 'Our languages are not so different after all, especially the variety you speak in Scotland.'

'What about "potato"?' I said.

'Ah, yes. We say *aardappel.'*

'You mean because it is like an apple, only harder?'

'No, no – *aarde* means "earth". It is the apple of the earth.'

'We have a word "yird" meaning earth,' I said.

'Doubtless they are connected in some way,' he said, nodding and smiling, with the sun glinting cheerfully from his eyeglasses.

I found this a most interesting conversation. Mr Bos is like a window through which I can see something of a world beyond these cane fields. I have resolved in future to greet him with a hearty *goedemorgen,* and to wish him a fond *vaarwel* when he departs. I almost forgot to add that he reads widely, and has access to *books!* – for that alone I must cherish his friendship!

February 7th. I was foolish today. I went for a walk into the forest, and on setting out on my return journey, must have chosen the wrong path. I attempted to retrace my steps, but within a few minutes realised that I was hopelessly lost. I had never realised until that moment how terrifying the forest can be. The terror arises, I believe, from its complete *indifference* to any human being foolish enough to stray into its toils. One has a dreadful sense of not belonging there. The forest is not particularly hostile, it simply does not care. Plants which appear harmless turn out to have thin, terrifying barbs on the underside of their leaves, carefully angled so that the more one struggles to extricate oneself, the more deeply they become embedded. I have heard of bushes whose leaves only have to brush your skin to induce instant paralysis, and another whose sap will quickly eat away iron. No white man like myself could possibly know which was which, and so each tentative step in this wilderness is a hazard, while all around the vegetation proceeds about its determined business of *growing* with a hot, steamy aloofness, in a green, stifling detachment, oblivious to the terrors of an insignificant, sweating mortal who has been so foolish as to stray there.

I called out several times, but there was no reply. I had visions of perishing miserably, to have my flesh consumed by ants, and I must confess that I panicked completely and began to run foolishly to and fro until I was quite exhausted and pouring with sweat. When I finally regained some composure I realised that this was no way to proceed, but for the life of me I had no idea what to do next. I was standing, irresolute, when I felt my leg turn warm and wet. A horror filled my soul, for I honestly believed that I had gashed myself, and was about to bleed to death. When I looked down, I saw that the dog was there, pissing copiously and enthusiastically on my leg. What can say of my emotions at that moment? Relief at finding him there was mingled with exasperation, and a realisation of the ridiculous humour of the situation. Having relieved himself, he trotted off, and I followed eagerly. After ten minutes or so, we emerged on to a path that I knew, and we were soon back in *terra cognita*, to my infinite relief. Tonight, despite his idiosyncratic predilections in the matter of the bladder, he is now *chez soi* in my room, and shall have well deserved the kindnesses I intend to bestow on him in future. In tribute to his heroism I have christened him *Piss-on-me* – not the most flattering of sobriquets, to be sure, but it suits us well. Did he sense that I was lost, and seek me out? No matter, from today forth we shall be bosom friends, and henceforth I shall be proud to acknowledge him as *my dog*.

February 14th. I found myself alone with Ambrose today, and I took the opportunity to ask him directly what he thought of Allardyce. He looked at me quizzically.

'He is responsible for the running of the estate,' he said. 'He is my master. He is your employer. What more can I say?'

'You must have an opinion about him.'

'It is not for me to have an opinion,' he said. 'I am the head driver, and I simply carry out my duties.'

'I carry out my duties too,' I said, 'but that does not prevent me from having an impression of the man.'

'And what is your impression of him? Is it favourable?'

'You know that it is not.'

He laughed. 'I know no such thing. He is a white man, after all.'

'Do you imagine that I would condone his behaviour just because he was white?'

'Surely it is wrong to speak ill of one's employer,' he said.

'You are being evasive, Ambrose,' I said.

'Not at all. I am being cautious, which is quite a different matter.'

'You know you can trust me.'

'True. You must remember that my situation is more precarious than yours. Anyway, I imagine that our opinions of Allardyce are very much the same.'

'He is a savage.'

'An interesting choice of word,' he said. 'He considers the plantation people to be savages, does he not?'

'Yes, and he is worse than any of them.'

'And why is that?'

'It is in his nature, I imagine.'

'I disagree. No one has it in his nature to behave as Allardyce does. I believe the man is desperately afraid, and his condition is made worse by the fact that he does not really know what he is afraid of. He is driven by a compulsion to maintain the highest possible degree of control.'

'He admitted as much to me once,' I said.

'Did he? That interests me. I assume he was drunk at the time?'

'Yes, he was.'

'*In vino veritas*, then,' sighed Ambrose. 'I believe that one day he shall perish, face to face with one of his fears.'

'As he came close to doing with Simon?'

'Something like that. That little incident only confirmed him in his ways.'

'But it was his own fault, Ambrose!' I said.

'No doubt.'

'I wrote to Lord Balcarres, you know. That was why the clothing was issued and Saturdays were made free.'

'So that was your doing, was it?' said Ambrose. 'That was good of you. But now we have returned to the *ancien régime*, and, as you Scots are so fond of saying, we have to *thole* it.'

At this point we saw MacDuff and McClure approaching, so had to stop speaking. I began to talk about the progress of the cane, and Ambrose went back to his deferential 'Yessuh' and 'Nossuh'. I shall find the opportunity to sound Ambrose out more fully about ways in which Allardyce might be persuaded to soften his stance.

February 26th. Mr Bos has told me a very diverting tale about a Dutchman called Jan van Leyden who once lived here in Goed Intent. He was an inveterate drunkard, spending most of his time in rum shops, and more than once he was almost drowned after falling headlong into ditches and canals when trying to make his way home in the dark. His wife was a freed slave, and by all accounts very intolerant of her husband's behaviour. One night he had gone off rather further than usual, in the Vreed-en-Hoop direction, and in consequence the return journey was more difficult, for the path was unfamiliar and it was raining very heavily. When he eventually reached home he told his wife of how he had come across a place where there were old graves, and had been chased by what he insisted were evil spirits, determined to end his miserable existence. Only by the expedient of leaping over a narrow canal had he saved himself, for jumbies cannot cross water. Everyone mocked him, but it seems that from that day on he never touched strong drink again, and to his dying day insisted on the veracity of his story.

'I can show you the graves, if you wish,' said Mr Bos.

'You must do so,' I said. 'We may even find our own jumbie.'

'We are more likely to find a *spook*[1] than a jumbie,' he said.

'What's that?'

'It's our word for a ghost. I think jumbies are supposed to be actual dead persons who have come out of their graves. I find it hard to believe in such things. But spirits – who knows? They say that the graves are haunted.'

'I cannot believe that,' I said, and related to him how my grannie often told me of how ghosts and devils were constantly looking over my elbow, but that despite all the tales and legends of fairies, haunted castles, dead-lights, warlocks and suchlike trumpery that abounded in Ayrshire, I had never come across any that could stand up to the light of cold reason.

'This is not Scotland,' he said, very seriously, and I laughed.

'Do not laugh,' he said. 'There are things here of which we know little.'

'What sort of things?'

'We have been in Demerary for a long time,' he said. 'Nearly two hundred years – since the time of your Shakespeare. You can find Dutch ruins here that are older than many of your Scottish ones. But even when we arrived there were spirits. We had a settlement on the Disseekeeb – that's the Essequibo – and everyone was convinced that it was haunted, even though the area had never been inhabited.'

'Haunted by what?' I said.

'Who knows? They say that the forest is haunted, and that every tree has its own spirit. Who are we to say that it is not so?'

I wanted to find out more, but the boat was waiting and he had to go. I have a natural inclination towards the belief that in certain wild and desolate surroundings the mysterious forces of nature conspire to create a *spiritus loci* whose ethereal presence can make itself felt to the visitor. I must speak more with Mr Bos about this.

March 2nd. I had some time with Ambrose today. We were talking when Prudence walked by – as she passed she gave me her usual bashful smile. When she had gone, Ambrose asked me if she was continuing to trouble me.

'I have not seen her for some time.'

'And you do not find yourself thinking about her?'

'No.'

'Ah. Then she is casting her spells on someone else.'

'What do you mean? What spells?'

'Forgive me, but there was a time, was there not, when you had given thought to taking her as a concubine?'

'If I ever entertained such a thought,' I said, 'then I'm sure I never shared it with anyone else.'

'Of course not. But it was obvious to me.'

'Obvious? How?'

'You remember the rice she brought you?'

'Yes. You warned me against it.'

'I did, and with good reason.'

'Why? Do you think she had poisoned it in some way?'

'Oh no,' he said with a laugh. 'She didn't want to do away with you. She wanted to make herself desirable in your eyes – hence the rice.'

'I still don't follow you,' I said. 'Are you trying to tell me that there was something in the rice?'

'Yes.'

'What?'

'It's a delicate matter,' he said. 'Let's say that there was something of herself in it. The women call it 'steamed rice' – it has the reputation for bringing errant husbands back to their wives and rendering them faithful ever after. It can also be employed as a means of attracting a reluctant man, which is what Prudence was engaged in doing. That is why one should never accept rice from a woman unless you are sure that she has no ulterior motives.'

'What do you mean, there was something of herself in it?'

'As I said, it's a delicate matter.'

'Just tell me, Ambrose.'

'Very well. She pissed in it.'

'Good God!' I exclaimed in disgust. 'And to think that I ate the stuff! Why on earth would anyone do such a thing?'

'I do not know,' he said, 'but the womenfolk swear by it.'

'It's the most revolting thing I've ever heard. I refuse to believe it!'

'Perhaps it imparts something of the bodily essence of the woman to the food so that the woman herself appears more attractive. Why do you think that dog of yours pisses everywhere? It is all to do with scent and ownership. All women smell differently, and so does their . . .'

'Stop it, Ambrose! This conversation is turning my stomach.'

'So you agree that I was right to advise you as I did?'

'If what you say is true, then I can't thank you enough.' I meant that sincerely. Imagine being in thrall to a woman by virtue of so indelicate and horrid a process!

Poll continues to be an excellent companion, although he – or she, for I would not know how to determine the issue – makes a habit of pecking at every piece of wood in the house. Sometimes he perches quietly in the tree outside, until suddenly, for no reason at all, he gives vent to a series of deafening screeches. At other times he's content to remain on my balcony with his head under his wing. He likes me to scratch the top of his head, although when others try to do the same he pecks at them furiously.

March 20th. I'm sitting on my balcony watching the afternoon turn to evening. After the unforgiving glare of the day there's a soft, golden quality to the light at this time that I find very soothing, and a glass of rum induces a mellowness of spirit that almost persuades me that I am content. I like to watch the parrots crossing the sky, and I know that soon the bats will begin to swoop silently around.

I was telling Ambrose about the Douglas plantation today, and remarking on how differently its people were treated. He was interested in what I had to say, and questioned me very minutely about it. There was, however, a sense of hopelessness in our discussion, for to introduce such measures here would take months or indeed years; there is no will for it among those who would be able to bring it about, and I cannot do it on my own.

April 7th. Allardyce is worse then ever, and I am sorry to see that MacDuff is following his poor example. My three years will be up this summer, and this time I am determined to go. McClure is making a little progress in the boiling house, and I dare say that given a decade or two he will be moderately competent. He *believes* himself to be perfectly capable of handling production on his own, but every time I have left him in charge there have been problems for me to rectify afterwards. He invariably attributes these to mistakes by others, or to circumstances beyond his control, but the real reason is that his head is thicker than a block of granite, and it is only with the greatest of difficulty that the simplest idea can be forced into it.

At any rate, I shall tell Allardyce that McClure has mastered his craft, so there will be no excuse for detaining me here any longer.

April 24th. I hear that van Grovestins received word yesterday from States-General to regard the French as allies, and this was agreed unanimously in the Court of Policy. I have only a very imperfect idea of what is happening at home, and I cannot imagine what lies behind this decision. I had thought that Holland was at war with France and it is infuriating to have no information. It does not bode well for us.

May 1st. MacDuff's house has been invaded by wood ants, and they have damaged the structure so severely that it will probably have to be pulled down. He has only himself to blame, for there's an enormous nest on his wall, and snaking trails everywhere to show where they have been about their destructive business. All he had to do was get rid of it. I have already been successful in removing a smaller nest on my own house by means of an expedient that Ambrose described to me. Although wood ants are fairly large, they are not as aggressive as their tiny red cousins – unless of course one has a wooden leg. Ambrose instructed me to mix sugar and water together and pour it into the wood ant nest. Red ants are inordinately fond of sugar, and they will attack the nest in huge numbers, either driving the offending ants away or devouring them. I have told MacDuff about this, but he only grunts in his ill-tempered way. I suspect he is too lazy to undertake the job.

May 22nd. Bess is nine today. I believe there is nothing that would make me happier than to see her again, but what can I do? I've been considering asking Mr Bos if he can enquire about a passage to Holland, from whence I could make my way back to Scotland. I've been lax about this journal, and weeks go by without my being aware of the passage of time. I have grown slovenly and careless of my appearance – earlier this year I stopped shaving out of pure indolence, and I now have a thick beard shot through with grey. It's strange to think that I'm no longer young – the signs of age steal upon one so gradually. I suffer a lassitude that hitherto I had put down to the heaviness and humidity of the climate, but perhaps I'm just growing old. The effort of writing in this journal is becoming excessive – I can sit for many vexatious minutes bent over it; my head askew; my pendulous feather loaded with ink; my eye insensible to my surroundings, and still produce little but trite, foolish observations.

June 2nd. The floor of MacDuff's house gave way this morning. The ants have made the planks so rotten that they cannot suffer any weight at all, and MacDuff is the heaviest man on the plantation. We heard him shouting, and discovered that he had gone through the floor so that his feet were dangling in the space beneath, while his bulky paunch had jammed in the gap. He was quite unable to extricate himself, and had to be pulled out by four or five of the plantation people, while Forsyth and I pushed upwards from below. He was excessively ill-tempered about it. The Negroes showed no emotion as they effected the rescue, but we could hear them roaring with laughter as they went away, which did nothing to improve his mood.

He is talking of making a grander structure in a patch of land nearby that commands a far better prospect than any of ours but which, for some reason, is completely vacant. He found a lot of old bricks when he was clearing the site, so there may have been a plantation building there many years ago.

June 6th. Some of the plantation people have been eating mud, a practice that must be halted at once, as they quickly grow sickly and die. I believe that this is a common habit amongst those who have lost the desire to live through a sense of despair and despondency. Forsyth and I have been to see Allardyce about it, arguing that even a modest amelioration of the slaves' conditions would do much to improve matters. However we met with the usual dismissive reaction. He is in a bad temper today as he tripped while crossing a little stream down by the koker this morning, and fell in. He was not injured, but it happened in the view of the weeding gang, and his pride has been wounded. There is much sickness on the plantation: some of it cannot be avoided, and arises from the climate, but we see many cases of yaws, and I suspect that sometimes people infect each other deliberately in order to avoid work. There is one woman, a young, healthy lass, who habitually cuts herself with packthread for the same reason. This spirit of disaffection is almost as worrying as open revolt would be – indeed, it is mutiny of a kind.

July 12th. My criminal indolence reproaches me – I have not lifted a pen for over a month. I have been unwell with a malignant squinancy[2] that has tormented me for two weeks and more: it has been difficult to speak and painful to eat, but it has improved in the last few days. An unlucky fall last week has bruised my knee so badly that I can hardly mark my leg to the ground. Why is that indispositions that might be tolerable in Scotland make one fearful for one's very life in this climate?

July 20th. I had it out with Allardyce today, and at last I have a definite commitment to having my salary paid. He has asked me to work until the end of the year, and in return will arrange for me to be paid a full four years' salary, a sum amounting to around two hundred pounds. I am amazed by this generosity, but he does not have to find it out of his own pocket, and I suppose he can do as he pleases. I still have some of the money that Mr Douglas gave me, and so I shall very easily be able to afford the journey home.

It is still my intention to resume farming with Gilbert, but if this fails then I shall have recourse to another shift and, if I can effectuate it, be admitted an Officer of Excise. I have friends able to petition the commissioners on my behalf, and the emolument of thirty-five or forty pounds per annum will cover my expenses and give me a decent living.

September 3rd. MacDuff's house is almost finished, and very fine it is too. The other one is little more than a ruin now, and fit only for burning, as the ants have rendered every piece of wood useless. The air has been filled with the sour, sickly smell of newly sawn greenheart as the last few floorboards are cut and laid.

September 10th. All being well, MacDuff will move into his new house tomorrow. The thatching of the roof is almost complete, and the structure looks imposing. He has been carrying over his possessions, and has had the plantation carpenter make new furniture.

Piss-on-me has disappeared. He has been a very faithful companion, and never strayed far from the house, but he did not come when I called him two days ago, and no one has seen him since. Despite his unusual habit I had grown very fond of him, and I am concerned in case he has come to harm.

September 11th. I was sitting this evening, working at some verses, when I heard MacDuff calling up to me, asking if he might come in. When he entered he looked uncharacteristically nervous, and kept glancing around as if he thought there might be someone else in the room. He was sweating, which was not unusual, but he looked pale. I asked him what the matter was.

'It's ma hoose,' he said. 'There's somethin' no' richt aboot it.'

'How d' you mean?' I said. 'It looks solid enough to me.'

'I dinna mean that,' he said. 'I canna explain it. It feels strange.'

'It's a new house,' I said. 'It's bound to seem unfamiliar at first.'

He shook his head, and I could see that he was trembling. I fetched him some rum, and he downed it in an instant and motioned for more.

'Ye'll be thinkin' I'm daft,' he said, 'but it feels like I'm bein' watched a' the time. An' it's cauld.'

'Cold?' I said. 'How can it be cold?'

'I ken, I ken. But it is. Can ye come an' see for yersel'?'

We lit another lamp, and went to his house, which was at no very great distance. I was convinced that MacDuff was imagining things, and that we would find nothing amiss. As we drew close, I noticed that the usual raucous sound of the frogs and crickets died away, leaving an uncanny silence. As we climbed the stairs, I could feel gooseflesh on my arms, and as we entered it grew deathly cold. Even with MacDuff present, I felt extremely uneasy, for I had the distinct impression that there was a third person in the room – someone staring at us with loathing and the utmost malevolence. It made the hairs on my neck bristle, and I began to feel very afraid, although there was nothing to see or to hear. It was a sensation quite outwith anything of my previous experience, and it was so unpleasant that I could remain no longer. We ran out into the hot night in a panic.

'D'ye see whit I mean?' he said. 'It's no' right. D'ye think it's *haunted?*' His eyes opened wide as he forced himself to utter the word. Ten minutes earlier I would have dismissed the notion as ludicrous, but I was no longer so sure, for there seemed to be no other explanation for what we had both experienced.

'I don't know,' I said, but I cannot have sounded very confident. MacDuff has come back to spend the remainder of the night in my quarters. He is having more rum while I complete this journal entry. For the first time since arriving here, I look through my window into the darkness and feel apprehensive about what may be out there.

September 12th. MacDuff kept me awake all night with his confounded snoring. While he was still asleep, I went over to his house, but was unable to climb beyond the first two or three stairs before the onset of that awful sensation of dread. I told Ambrose about MacDuff's house and he seemed unsurprised; in fact, he said that the whole thing was more or less to be expected.

'Why is that?' I asked.

'Did you find any bricks when you were clearing the land?'

'I think MacDuff did mention that,' I said.

'Well, there's your reason.'

'Why should that be a reason?' I said. 'All it shows that there was a house there at some time in the past.'

'Not a house. A grave. It is very bad luck to disturb a grave in any way. The dead take exception to it.'[3]

'I am surprised that you, of all people, should believe such a thing.'

'I am surprised that you do not take these things more seriously,' he said, very solemnly. 'You told me yourself how the house affected you. How else do you account for your experience?'

He was right, of course, and even though it was broad daylight, I felt a little quiver of fear as I remembered last night, and the feeling I had in that room. I also know, with a deep certainty, that I would not wish to enter that room again. Perhaps there is a world of spirits – the Bible declares as much, after all. Remembering that Our Lord cast out evil spirits, I asked if the spirit in MacDuff's house could be exorcised.

'Oh yes,' he said.

'We would need to find a priest, would we not?'

'No need,' he said. 'I could do it for you.'

'How?'

'There are ways,' he said, smiling. 'We ignorant savages have all kinds of pagan beliefs and observances. White people consider them foolish, but they are mistaken. Anyway, I hardly think MacDuff will ask me. After all, he does not believe in our black mumbo-jumbo.'

'If you explained the method, could I do it?'

'No.'

'Would you do it if he asked you to?'

'I might,' he said.

'Ambrose,' I said, 'did you know there was a grave on that site?'

'Of course.'

'Why did you say nothing to prevent MacDuff from building his house there?'

'Because he's an unpleasant little man, and it's satisfying to see him suffer a little. Besides, he would have disregarded my advice and mocked me for being a stupid neger.'

'May I speak to him about this?'

'By all means. Tell him I need a bottle of rum.'

'What? As payment?'

He laughed. 'No, for the casting-out.'

He seemed to be amused by the whole matter. I saw MacDuff a little later and suggested to him that perhaps Ambrose could help. I took care to stress that although it involved some kind of pagan ritual there was probably no harm in trying, and although I thought he would reject the proposal he agreed immediately, and asked me to bring Ambrose around as soon as possible.

As it happened, his duties did not permit him to come until after dark. MacDuff had flatly refused to enter the house, and I was of the same mind, so we were standing outside when he arrived.

'Massa Burns say yah gat trubble wid yah house,' he said.

'Aye. Can you sort it?'

'I kin try.'

'For God's sake get on with it.'

'Yes Massa. Yah gat de rum?'

MacDuff handed him the rum and we went up the steps. As we entered, we felt the same heavy oppression and apprehension that we experienced last night. I could see that Ambrose shared our feelings.

'Yah gat a spirit,' he said, taking the stopper from the rum. 'We drive he out.'

What followed was truly extraordinary. Ambrose walked around the room, sprinkling rum on the ground as he did so, and speaking softly in a language I did not understand; then moved into the other room where he repeated the process. Next, from his pocket, he produced a little bundle of what looked like dry grass and lit it at the lamp. It took fire, and he walked through the rooms again, waving it above his head so that the pungent smoke filled the place with a thin haze. Then – suddenly; unaccountably; amazingly – what can I say? – that horrible, crawling sensation of being observed simply disappeared, and the room felt like any other!

'My God,' said MacDuff. 'It's gone, whatever it was.'

'Yessuh,' said Ambrose. 'He gone.'

'How in God's name did you do that?' said MacDuff.

Ambrose shrugged and said nothing. MacDuff was very effusive in his thanks, and shook Ambrose by the hand repeatedly and told him he was a splendid fellow, which he is, of course. I simply do not know what to make of this. Was it indeed some supernatural manifestation, or is there some rational explanation that depends on some natural law that we have not yet discovered?

September 23rd. The affair of MacDuff's house is the subject of much talk at the moment. For the last few days I have been jotting down some couplets on any old scrap of paper that comes my way, and maybe it will come to something.

There is news that in Jamaica the Maroons have risen up, and that there is open war between them and the authorities. The militia have been mobilised, and there has already been loss of life. All of this comes by word of mouth from Stabroek, and I can discover no further details – I pray that my Jamaican friends are safe.

October 1st. All this talk of jumbies and 'spooks' has at last led me to produce some finished verses. I have always felt disinclined to believe in superstitious nonsense, but this strange business of MacDuff's house has given me food for thought. I have therefore related the story of the late lamented Mijnheer van Leyden, somewhat embellished, with a judicious admixture of jumbies, rum and a *soupçon* of pious moralising. I have always held that when we find ourselves apprehensive in the face of matters we do not comprehend, then the best medicine for it is a hearty dose of scurrilous ribaldry. The devil himself holds fewer terrors for us if we can clap him on the back and call him *Auld Clootie*. This is what I wrote –

Jan van Leyden: A Tale

As evening licht begins to wane,
And workers trudge back frae the cane;
While we sit bousin', and succumb
To a' the warm delights o' rum,
We think na on the rotted paals,
The kokers, ditches and canals,
The pools o' rank and festerin' water,
That lie in wait as hame we totter;
Where, in a line, the pickneys gather,
To greet with joyous cries their father!

This truth fand honest Jan van Leyden,
A chiel in Goed Intent residin'.
Ah, Goed Intent! There's nane surpasses,
Thy fragrant rum and sweet molasses!

O Jan, had'st thou but been sae wise,
As ta'en thy dotin' mither's advice.
She tauld thee weel thou was a randy;
A lad ower fond o' gin an' brandy.
She prophesied that, bein' unwary,
Thou wouldst be drown'd in Demerary,
Or catch'd wi' jumbies in the gloom,
By some auld, haunted Dutchman's tomb.

Ah, gentle dame, Lord kens, thou tried,
To be a fond maternal guide!
Alas! thy tender, wayward lamb,
Becomes the talk of Amsterdam!
Wi' tearfu' e'en and heartfelt sighs,
Thou offer'st precepts sage and wise;
Deliver sermons lastin' days,
Upon the error of his ways.
Ah! drunkards never listen much:
Thou micht as well speak Double Dutch.[4]

But to our tale. Ae stormy nicht,
Jan had got planted unco richt,
In Jacob's howff in Vreed-en-Hoop,
Enjoyin' mony a blissfu' stoup.
He drain'd each tae its final draps –
The local rum, the Hollands schnapps –
The rum-jug passed the table round,
And bumper measures did abound.
Blessèd elixir of the cane!
Sweet antidote to grief and pain!
A balm for care and worldly strife;
 cure for a' the ills o' life!

The nicht drave on wi' sangs and laughin',
And every kind o' mirth and gaffin'.
The storm without grew worse and worse –
Jan didna gie a tinker's curse.

But pleasures we should never trust:
Their sweetest joys shall turn to dust;
Our expectations they betray,
Destined for sure to fade away.
For a' his boasts and tipsy talk,
The hour approaches Jan maun walk:
A hellish nicht – beyond a' doubt,
The very worst to venture out.
The thunder roar'd like cannonades,
The lichtnin' lanced its fiery blades;
The rain drave doon, a fearsome flood,
That turned the pathways intae mud;
The Demerary surg'd in spate,
An' tore its banks wi' fury great –
Sic omens clearly did portend,
The Deil some mischief did intend!

Wi' mutters, oaths and curses dire,
Jan stagger'd on thro' glaur and mire.
The tempest ever harder blew,
The lashin' downpour soaked him through;
The lichtnin' show'd the way ahead,
But threatened aye to strike him dead!

By this time he was past the dyke
Where Allardyce fell in the syke;

And near the rusty gibbet airns,
Where Mad MacDonald killed his bairns;
And by the koker on the dam
Where Grizzel perished as she swam.

The Dutchmen's graves were drawin' near,
An eldritch place o' dread an' fear –
Brick tombs, whaur lurk the restless dead;
And, e'en by daylight, few daur tread;
Whaur deadly serpents mak their home,
And ghoulish jumbies nightly roam.

Before him, Demerary roars;
From inky skies a torrent pours;
When, glimmerin' thro' the lashin' trees,
An unexpected gleam he sees:
The place o' tombs is brichtly lit,
And wow, Jan sees an unco sicht!

A dozen jumbies in a jig –
Each wi' his powder'd periwig;
Each wi' a face as white as chalk,
And ev'ry one a foul warlock!
The Deil himsel' stood in the centre,
In guise o' scaly salapenta,
Beatin' a drum whose furious strokes,
Lent vigour to the jumbie folks,
Who lowpit high and birled aroon',
And scurried up an' scuttled doon.

Jan thocht this was a brawly sicht,
And clapp'd his hands wi' a' his micht,
And, reckless through inebriation,
Yelled out some old Dutch imprecation.
And added, wi' a fine conceit,
'Spoken! U kunt me vangen niet!' [5]
But in an instant fraught with terror,
He realised his fateful error –
The jumbies, haltin' in their revels,
Screamed out in rage, like damnèd devils,
And as bold Jan took to his heels,
They gave pursuit, wi' yells and squeals.

As ants swarm out in urgent quest,
When careless boots disturb their nest;
As plump mosquitoes whine an' swarm,
To suck the blood sae sweet an' warm:
So poor Jan runs, the ghouls give chase,
Gainin' on him wi' every pace.

Ah Jan! Ah Jan! Thou'll get thy fairin'!
Hard on thy heels the pack is bearin'!
In vain thy bairns seek thy return –
In brunstane pits thou'lt surely burn!

But every child and woman knows,
They canna cross whaur water flows;
Jan saw the ditch he maun cross ower,
An' raced for it wi' a' his power,
An' wi' one final, forcefu' stride,
He lowpit to the ither side,
An' stood there, safe at last, an' proud,
An' turned to mock the jumbie crowd:
Enraged that Jan had 'scaped away.
And cheated o' their promised prey!

But this was not enough for Jan,
A crownin' insult was his plan.
His pintle frae his breeks he drew,
And wav'd it at the jumbie crew,
And cried aloud, 'Thou'st met thy match!
A Hollander thou canna catch!'

Ah, reckless Jan! Thou'll learn too late,
The foolishness o' temptin' Fate.
That hasty act thou soon shalt rue:
Bringin' thy pintle into view.
A cayman, lurkin' in its lair,
Look'd up and saw it brandish'd there;
Wi' ae snap o' its fearsome jaw,
It ripped his pintle clean awa' –
A silly stump alone was left:
Thus Jan o' manhood was bereft!

So when to rum we are inclin'd,
To deadly dangers we grow blind:
We heed not that our reckless splore,

> May harm our dignity, and more!
> Lord save us from a vice sae heinous –
> Remember Jan van Leyden's penis!

October 2nd. I read my poem to the assembled company at dinner tonight, and it was received with very gratifying approbation. MacDuff, unsurprisingly, was delighted with the last line, which he declared was the funniest thing he ever heard. Even Allardyce roared with merriment, and did not appear to take exception to my allusion to his unfortunate accident. Everyone was very convivial afterwards – my modest powers of poesy have softened attitudes towards me. I think that if they have been cool to me at times it is because none of them, with the possible exception of Forsyth, has any notion of what kind of person I am. They are simple people who live from day to day and think of nothing beyond the present. I call them the gin-horse class – what enviable dogs they are! – round and round and round they go, driving the mill, stupid and contented, while here I sit, my skull a confounded *mélange* of fretfulness and melancholy. I have a mind at times morbidly inclined to philosophy – my damned cerebellum does not stop for a moment – it will not let me alone!

October 16th. Today I have written to Gilbert announcing my intention of returning to Mossgiel and asking him to let me know the state of the farm. It will be hard work to follow the plough once more, but I have no fear of honest toil, and I can derive no pride from a harvest garnered by the sweat of brows other than my own. I did not mention my thoughts about the Excise, though my knowledge of distillation, gained here and in Jamaica, should be of some value when seeking a commission. I do not propose to mention my departure to the others until the date is certain.

I find it sad to have to reconcile myself to the loss of Piss-on-me. MacDuff has been very jocular about it, saying that the dog probably pissed on a cayman and had its pintle bitten off for its pains.

November 5th. We had a mishap in the boiling house today, thanks to that idiot McClure. He made the fire far too hot and some sugar boiled over and caught fire. The smoke was dense and choking, and we all had to rush outside. McClure seized a bucket of water and announced his intention of throwing it into the copper to douse the flames and seemed bemused when I warned him to do no such thing.

'But it'll put the fire out,' he said.

'No it won't.' I said. 'The sugar's too hot, and if water is poured on to it then we'll have flames and boiling juice spitting everywhere.'

'How will we put the fire out?'

'It'll go out by itself.'

'I'm not so sure. I think we should put water on it.'

'Have you ever seen someone who has been burned by sugar?' I said, and told him about the unfortunate Scipio, omitting no detail of the way in which the man's hand was cut off. This was sufficient to make him see sense – we fetched long rakes and pulled the bagasse from under the flaming copper. The fire eventually died out, but the copper will be too hot to handle until tomorrow at least, and it will be the devil of a job to clean it. We have no spare, and so there can be no production until the job is done.

Allardyce is very angry about it, and blames me for failing to ensure that McClure carries out his duties correctly. I have told him that it was an accident, but of course the fault lies entirely with McClure, whose skull is so impervious to sense that I must explain even the simplest idea a dozen times before I see a glimmer of comprehension on his vacuous features.

November 23rd. Mr Bos was here today and we enjoyed an hour together in the benab. I have been practising a little Dutch, and he says that I pronounce the words very correctly.

I was anxious to ask him more about the interior of this continent. He says that it extends further than any white man has ever ventured. There are some mountains with curious flat summits, one of which rears up thousands of feet with sides so precipitous that in all probability it will never be climbed. There are vast tracts of dense forest, nearly all of it unexplored, and beyond are high plains called savannas. What lies beyond them, nobody knows. The country is inhabited by nine tribes – I had heard of the Arawaks and Caribs, but there are also Warrau, Makushi, Wapishana, Akawaio, Patamona and Arecuna – I made Mr Bos spell out their names for me so that I could record them accurately. There is another tribe, the Wai Wai, of whose existence we know only through the accounts given by members of other tribes, for they live in the most extreme isolation.

What an adventure it would be, to explore this place? Who knows what may lie deep in the forests? I feel the hairs on my neck rise in a *frisson* of mingled trepidation and excitement when I contemplate the prospect of stepping where no man has stepped before!

December 3rd. At last I have been paid my salary, and now I am a rich man, with two hundred pounds in rix-dollars delivered to me in a bag by Allardyce.[6]

'There's yer pay,' he said. 'Tak care o' it.'

'I shall,' I said. 'Thank you very much, Mr Allardyce.'

He grunted. 'So when are ye leavin' us?'

'I have to work until the year's end,' I said, 'but with your permission I shall go to Stabroek in a week or two in order to enquire about a passage early next year.'

'Please yerself,' he said. 'How's McClure shapin' up?'

'He is making steady progress,' I said. This was perfectly true, though the same could be said of a snail making its laborious way across the floor.

'Aye. He's a wee bit slow tae learn.'

'He is willing,' I said.

'Maybe. Anyway, ye've got yer wages. I ken we dinna see eye tae eye, but ye've earned yer money. I'll grant ye that.'

I considered that to be high praise indeed! I have hidden my cash by burying it underneath my house, and covering the place with a stack of wood. At last – at last – home again!

December 21st. The Sabbath. I went to Stabroek yesterday and booked my passage to Trinidad on the *Vergelijking*, under the command of Captain Ter Heide. The vessel is in Barbados at present, and not due here until the middle of February, so I must be patient until then. Now that my departure is certain, I go about my duties with a light heart. The others know that I am going, and all of them have expressed their regret in their own way – even MacDuff, who has made me promise that we must have a good carouse before I leave.

The aspects of this place that have irritated me, like the discomfort and the mosquitoes, seem almost tolerable now that I am about to leave them behind. I cannot say with perfect candour that I shall *miss* the estate, but the sights and sounds of it are firmly fixed in my mind, and I know that I shall never forget them. I went down to the river today and stood there for many minutes, absorbing the scene, and realising that in a few weeks I shall leave, never to see its waters again.

I shall miss Ambrose very much. We have become friends, and I do not like to think of him here with Allardyce.

'I have no fear of Allardyce,' he said.

'I have money,' I said. 'I could procure your manumission.'

'Thank you, but I cannot take your money,' he said. 'Anyway, Allardyce would never let me go.'

'My offer remains,' I said. 'Please consider it.'

'I shall,' he said. 'Now, what of you? What will you do when you return to your country?'

'I shall go to my brother's farm and help him with it,' I said. 'Then

I wish to return to rhyming – I am all out of practice, for it is too difficult to write here. And of course I shall add my voice to those already raised against slavery. I can make a difference, Ambrose. Wilberforce has never lived on a plantation as I have – I am sure I could speak most eloquently against the trade.'

'I am sure you could,' he said. 'I wish you well.' There was a slightly sceptical tone to his voice.

'You do not seem to have high hopes of my success,' I said.

'You are a very good man,' he said. 'I am sure you would be a formidable orator – I do not doubt you in that respect. However those who would retain the slave trade are powerful, and they will not give it up lightly. There will be endless delays, reverses and disappointments. I fear that you may become impatient and disillusioned.'

'I shall certainly be impatient,' I agreed. 'As far as disillusionment is concerned, I can never forget what I have seen, and I shall never give up the fight to banish this evil for ever.'

I mean what I say. It is impossible to change the monstrous fact of slavery when one is so much a part of it. Once returned to Scotland I can become at last an effective advocate. Like Mr Equiano, I shall be able to speak from long experience – my voice will be heard in the world!

1795

January 1st. Mr Bos here again. He says that the number of estates in Demerara and Essequibo has now grown to four hundred, and with every ship from Trinidad a great influx of my countrymen anxious to make their fortunes. More and more slaves have also been brought here – we can see the ships making their slow way into Stabroek almost every week, and I am sure if the wind were to blow in the correct direction we would be able to *smell* them – the foul stink of a foul trade.

Many plantations have given up sugar and are growing cotton instead. It thrives in this climate, and there is a ready market for it; moreover there are none of the expenses, complications, dangers and inconveniences of crushing, boiling and distilling.

I only have a few possessions, and I am ready to go as soon as I hear that the *Vergelijking* has arrived in port. Forsyth has agreed to take Poll – I would have liked to take him with me, but I have no cage, and a ship's cabin is no place for a macaw. Also I fear that Scotland's climate would rapidly prove fatal to a creature so accustomed to tropical climes.

January 6th. Mr Bos was in the plantation today, and I had the opportunity of a long talk with him. We were discussing Gravesande, who was the governor here until about twenty years ago, and who is still spoken of in terms of reverence by virtue of the wisdom of his policies and the fair way in which he managed the colony. There is an account of his governorship, a copy of which Mr Bos has in his possession and has promised to lend me.

I have been in Demerary for four years now, and it is a curious business that just as I am about to leave, I grow fascinated by what might lie in the interior of this country. Mr Bos has taught me something of the geography and I knew that the Dutch had trading outposts on some of the great waterways like the Essequibo, and a fort at Kyk-over-al, on the Massaruny,[1] though I gather that is little more than a ruin these days. Today Mr Bos recounted some of the expeditions that have been made into the interior. One colonist by the name of Pijpersberg had penetrated further up the Massaruny than anyone before him, where he encountered natives who had never seen a white man. He returned with a tale of a huge pyramid on the left bank of the river as he made his way upstream. I am quite lost in wonder at this, as I have never heard of any civilisation in antiquity besides that of Egypt to have fashioned such constructions, and it is impossible to suppose that any of their colonists could have found their way to these shores. But Mr Bos tells me that there are places not far from here where it is possible to find fragments of fashioned tiles, iron-work, and instruments of an entirely different make and composition from those of today, the use of which is unknown even to the Indians who inhabit these parts. In the Portuguese colony of Brazil he says that evidence has been found to suggest a Phoenician presence at some time in the very distant past. As for the pyramid, the Indians refuse to go near it, claiming it is the abode of *a yawahü*, which is their word for 'devil'. They say that to approach it means certain death. In 1740 Gravesande sent a mulatto called Pieter Tollenaer to make a sketch of it, which he did, but died very shortly thereafter, which naturally gave further support to the superstitions surrounding this strange edifice.[2]

How can such things be? In Auld Scotia there are ruined castles aplenty, and I remember well how the Auld Kirk at Alloway was reputed to be the haunt of witches and warlocks, but Scotland is a nation where every inch of the soil is suffused with history, and trodden by many generations: here there seems nothing but wilderness. And yet in some past age, an unknown race of men erected a vast monument to their own civilisation, and then vanished without trace, leaving it to moss and creeping plants! What language did they speak? What manner of people were they, and how did they hew their building blocks from the forest floor? Until today, I had thought of the Guianas as a blank page in the history books – a vast tract of land unknown to man since the beginning of time. Today I realise that deep in these eternal tracts of lonely desolation there may lie secrets older than Europe; older than the Pharaohs; older than history itself. Mr Bos informed me that El Dorado, which I had always considered entirely a fable, was sought here by Ralegh. What strange things might there be, hidden in these terrible, dark, dripping forests?

Mr Bos says that I may be able to take part in an expedition that is setting out later this year to explore the upper reaches of the River Potaro. I immediately asked him to make enquiries on my behalf! How willingly I would delay my departure for a few months if, in return, I had the opportunity to explore these regions of mystery and primeval remoteness! What discoveries are to be made there? My poet's imagination is fired!

January 17th. A newcomer to the plantation today: a young woman of a most strikingly beautiful appearance. She was brought to us by Ambrose who was at a loss what to do, because she spoke no English.

Allardyce tried a little Dutch, and I addressed her in French, but to no avail. She just sat on the ground looking at us with a melancholy expression.

'Let me try,' said Fordyce, and squatted beside her. '*Hama biri?*'

'*Yinta,*' she replied, looking at him in surprise.

'Her name's Yinta. *B'ajia koma Loko ajiañ?*'

'*Ehei.*'

'That's it. She's Arawak. Or she understands it anyhow.'

'*Abareñ hamushia de,*' she said, putting her fingers to her mouth.

'She says she needs food,' said Forsyth.

'Anither mooth tae feed, then,' observed Allardyce glumly. 'As if we havena enough tae contend wi' already.'

'*Da'mekhebo tika – haha mekhebo b'amunka da'nishia ma?*' said the girl to Forsyth. He laughed.

'What did she say?' we asked.

'She says she wants to work, and asks if she may stay,' said Forsyth. 'So that solves your problem, Mr Allardyce. Why don't we set her to work in the kitchen? We can't put her out to labour in the fields if she's a native, but I'm sure Thomas could do with a hand.'

Allardyce nodded, and Forsyth took her off. About ten minutes later Thomas arrived, belligerently waving a ladle.

'What's the matter?' I asked.

'I nah want,' he shouted. 'I nah want she in de kitchen.'

'But think of all the work she will do,' I said. 'She'll fetch vegetables, and chop them up, and get firewood for you. You're aye complaining about how much you have to do.'

'I nah want she,' he repeated stubbornly.

'But you'll still be in charge of the kitchen,' I pointed out. 'And just think, you will have someone to work for you, just as I work for Massa Allardyce. You'll be *Massa* Thomas in the kitchen.'

He had not thought of that, and paused in his grumbling while the idea sank in.

'A slave o' yer ain,' said MacDuff. 'Man, ye'll be an overseer next.'

Later I asked Forsyth to write down the Arawak so that I could set down this account of the girl's arrival in camp. It bears no relationship to any language I have ever heard. Forsyth is not even sure how to spell it correctly, so I have done my best to write down the sound of it.[3]

January 18th. Yinta is installed in the kitchen, and has succeeded in charming even Thomas. As for the effect of her presence on me, I can say with truth that I never met with a person I more anxiously wished to have for my own, for she is the most exquisite creature on earth. I would conjecture her age as being around two- or three-and-twenty. Her skin, though somewhat dark, is not like that of the Negro; her lips are fine, like those of a European; her hair is long and straight, and of such an intensity of blackness that in certain lights there appears to be a tinge of blue in it. But it is her eyes that are the most striking facial feature – wide and dark, and in cast reminiscent of those of a Chinee, as is common among the natives of this part of the world, though why this should be the case I do not know. Her breasts are delectable; her waist is slender; her hips are rounded to perfection, and she walks with an artless grace, such as Eve might have done in Paradise – innocent of the world; uncorrupted; magnificent! I do not think she is conscious of the effect she has on others – she is pure and remote. I cannot take my eyes from her! I am captivated! However she does not understand a single word I speak to her.

I have just finished removing my beard – I am once again clean-shaven, and feeling much the better for it!

February 14th. The *Vergelijking* is in port. I have sent word to Stabroek with Mr Bos that I shall not be taking up my berth after all. I can endure the estate a little longer if there is at least a likelihood that I can join the forthcoming expedition he spoke of.

Yinta has quite turned my head. Daily I live in the hope of a smile from her, but she seems oblivious to my presence and unaware of these passions raging in my breast. On many occasions I have spoken to her, but she offers me no response whatever. Yet I am reluctant to abandon her to the coarse attentions of the others, who make no secret of their interest in her. I cannot allow that to happen – what an insipid, unfeeling blockhead I would be!

February 20th. If I am to win Yinta, then I must be able to *talk with her*. Even the most modest exchange of pleasantries would be sufficient to establish a *rapport* on which to build. Today I asked Forsyth if he would teach me Arawak.

'Why on earth would you want to learn it?' Then he laughed. 'Oh, it's Yinta you have in mind, is it? I wouldn't waste your time.'

'Why would I be wasting my time?' I asked, rather irritated that he had divined my purpose so easily.

'She has a mind of her own,' he said. 'She's not like Prudence, who would be yours for the asking.'

'I only want to speak to her in her own language,' I said.

'Aye, no doubt,' he laughed. She's a bonnie lass. Her charms are not lost on the others, I've noticed. But it is a most difficult language – I have only an imperfect grasp of it myself, and I'm no dominie. It would take a lot of study, and I don't have much time to spare.'

I asked him how she had ended up here in Demerary, so far from her own people, but he did not seem very sure.

'She said something about being abducted from her village, running away, getting lost and finally making her way north where she knew she would be safe and could not be forced to work in the fields. I only got the gist of it, I'm afraid.'

'I wish I had your proficiency,' I said. 'Surely you can teach me a little of her language?'

In the end he has agreed that he will teach me a few phrases and I am all impatient to begin. This wild, ardent venture may founder on the cruel rock of refusal, but at least I shall know that I have tried!

Mr Bos has sent me word that he has placed my name before the authorities in charge of the expedition to the Potaro – he promises to let me know if my application is successful.

March 6th. I have learned *'moroko'*, which is a common greeting, and a few other simple words, and have lost no time in contriving encounters with her and addressing her in a friendly fashion. However my best efforts have not been attended with any success whatever: she does not reply, and does not even deign to look at me, but placidly continues about her business as if I were not present. How I envy Thomas, with whom she shares the kitchen! I *must* declare myself her friend – her lover! – my mind is set on it! In *les affaires du coeur* I am not accustomed to failure, but I have never yet met with such an implacable obstacle as this want of a common language between us.

My only comfort in this exasperating business is that McLean's bungled efforts to ingratiate himself with her have been equally futile. *I am the man!* and must convince her of this somehow!

March 22nd. Ambrose is pleased that I have remained; he had guessed why even before I told him.

'She is a fine-looking young woman. You will do well with her.'

'She wants nothing to do with me,' I complained. 'But she occupies my thoughts constantly.'

'Maybe she has been feeding you steamed rice,' he said.

'Don't be ridiculous,' I said.

'It's not ridiculous. She works in the kitchen, does she not? It would be a simple matter for her to do that.'

'If she were interested then she would surely give some sign of it.'

'Strange are the ways of women. Maybe she is more interested than she appears to be.'

'I wish I could believe that.'

'Don't despair,' he said. 'White men don't have a particularly high reputation amongst the tribes – they are regarded as untrustworthy, and not without good reason. Yinta is not going to fall into the arms of the first white man who is kind to her.'

'I suppose you're right,' I said. He counselled me to continue to behave pleasantly towards her, to demonstrate that I am a man of principle. Perhaps she is observing me and putting me to some test.

April 8th. Today Yinta spoke to me for the first time. I went to the kitchen while Thomas was absent, and greeted her with my usual *'moroko'.* I then began to speak to her in English, knowing that she would not understand it but hoping that she would gather from my tone that my intentions were friendly. After a while she looked at me and said *'bakhoro'* very clearly. At that moment Thomas returned, and so I went off to find Forsyth in search of a translation.

'What does *'bakhoro'* mean?' I asked.

'Hmm. It just means 'no'. You don't seem to be making a very good impression, do you?'

He is right – I am making no impression at all. Yet when I see her, I cannot – must not – admit defeat. Oh! the magic of these inscrutable eyes and the knowledge that she represents a whole world to explore – like the country itself, with all its potential for discovery.

April 15th. I am excited today, because Mr Bos has told me that I am to be part of the Potaro expedition. It is expected to depart in August, in order to take advantage of the dry season.

April 30th. A curious event took place today. Thomas has a cage in which he keeps a labba.[4] It has a door fitted with bars to prevent the creature from escaping, not that it is in the slightest dangerous, but because it is kept for its flesh which, when cooked, is quite delicious; not unlike chicken, but darker in colour and denser, with many small bones. Just before dinner, it was discovered that the door had fallen open. When the matter was brought to the attention of the cook, he rushed out in great consternation, convinced that the beast would have run away. To his astonishment it had remained in the cage, and showed no interest in venturing forth.

'Dis an'mal stupid,' muttered Thomas, fastening the cage. 'He nah know de door open.'

'Oh he knew all right,' I said. 'He just likes it better where he is.'

'But why he nah run 'way?'

'Because he doesn't want to have to hunt for food, and protect himself from danger, and find himself a place to live,' I said.

'But we eat he!'

'Yes, but he doesn't know that, does he? That is no worse a fate than being snapped up by a tiger is it?'[5]

'S'pose.'

I thought about this for much of the day, thinking that the incident held a moral of some sort. This afternoon I have written a short poem on the subject. It took me some considerable time to work over the verses, and I must own that I was rather pleased with it.

To a Labba

Pair twitchy-whiskers! what's the matter?
Mak haste and flee wi' squeakin' chatter!
We'll only keep you till you're fatter,
   Wi' sonsie hams,
Tae serve ye up upon a platter,
    Wi' rice and yams!

Your cage lies open to the skies,
See! where the path of Freedom lies!
So save yourself, poor beast: arise!
   'Tis no disgrace,
To run away and colonise
   Some other place.

And tho' the warld is broad and wide,
And tho' you hear this bardie chide,
Still fast within your cell ye bide;
   Sair feart, I judge!
Faith man, ye even cower and hide,
   Ower scared tae budge!

Incarceration taks its toll
And lends a deadness tae the soul:
Emancipation is our goal,
   Each weary minute;
But what privations must we thole
   The day we win it?

When Ambrose came round this evening I showed it to him, and he merely laughed.

'Emancipation for labbas!' he scoffed. 'That's a fine notion!' And he guffawed again, with tremendous heartiness.

I was offended by his flippant response, and said so. He immediately sobered. 'I'm sorry,' he said, 'but it seemed amusing. Maybe I did not appreciate how serious you were when you wrote it. Let me see it again.'

He read it over and over, nodding gravely as he did so. Finally he handed the sheet back to me, with a thoughtful expression. 'I am sorry I misjudged you,' he said. 'There is more truth in this than you know. In any event, it is remarkable.'

May 22nd. I was sitting in the benab today with Forsyth and MacDuff when Yinta came in to clear away some plates. As always it gave me delicious pleasure merely to watch her walk across the floor – she is lithe and sinuous and moves slowly but with exquisite grace, unstained by affectation – an angelic creature!

MacDuff evidently entertained similar sentiments to my own, but went about expressing them in a manner that was entirely inappropriate. He seized her by the waist as she passed, and made to fondle her *derrière*, making some ribald comment or other. The next instant all her languorous softness was gone, and she fetched him such a slap on the side of his head that he fell out of his chair and landed with a crash on the floor. Forsyth and I roared with laughter. Poor MacDuff is too mean a mortal ever to aspire to such an exalted rank of female excellence!

What beauty, and what spirit! If there is a God of Love, he must have fashioned her to be bestowed on *somebody* – what can I do to make *myself* that fortunate man?

I am ashamed to admit that it had almost escaped my mind that this is the day when I think most fondly of Bess, who attains her eleventh year today. Sometimes in the evenings I sit out on my balcony and look up at the night sky – there is one star that is particularly bright, although I am no astronomer and could not name it. In my foolish fancy I call it Bess's star – its bright, steady light is always there in the sky, just as she is always present in my heart – and yet both are immeasurably distant!

May 24th. I have shown Ambrose my Equiano book that came with me from Jamaica, hoping to convince him that that a black man can indeed prosper in a white man's world, and gain universal respect. He leafed through it for a few moments, frowning deeply.

'You may borrow it if you wish,' I said. 'I think you will find it has many interesting points to make.'

'Borrow it?' he replied, with a meaningful look. 'What are you thinking of? I am not supposed to be able to read, Robert. Possession of *any* book would be dangerous for me; but if Allardyce found me with *this*, I fear the consequences for both of us! How could I come by a book? I am glad that this man escaped his bonds, but this is not England. Here, a book of this nature could only be regarded as blatant sedition! If it were ever discovered that you had lent it to me, you would be accused of inciting the slaves to rebellion, filling their heads with fanciful notions of dressing in fine clothes, and riding around in a carriage like a lord. My advice to you is to burn it, for your own sake.'

He is correct, of course. Planters and their agents live with the spectre of emancipation haunting their every waking moment, like the ghost of Banquo at the feast, threatening the prospect of a collapse of their fortunes at the very least, or bloody insurrection at the worst.

June 8th. Another unpleasant day. One of the oxen has a bad case of the maggot-fly on its neck, and cannot be yoked to work the mill.[5] Paul is in charge of the beasts, and is full of silly excuses about it, claiming that it is not his fault that they are afflicted. But he has made no effort to organise replacements, and I was quite out of patience with him. In consequence, little progress has been made with the grinding of the cane, and whole cartloads were awaiting the resumption of normal working. McLean and I fetched another beast, and work resumed before the cane began to spoil.

I felt it incumbent upon me to notify Allardyce of what had happened, and went round to his quarters at about mid-day. I found him in a stupor from which I was unable to arouse him, and left him lying on the floor in a stinking pool of his own vomit, snoring like a hog. If the slaves were to see him in such a state, then we would have trouble on our hands. I am as fond of a dram as anyone, but this is damnable. I have written some lines this evening, which has served to make me calmer. What angers me most is the shameful fact that such a worthless brute should be in charge here at all.

On a drunken manager

Ye powers of natural justice, come
And see the vile effects of rum!
And share with me my sour disgust;
My loathing; my profound distrust
Of one who sprawls uncouth, besotted:
His mouth a sewer, his stomach rotted.
If this is Man, and God's creation,
We're truly headed for damnation.

June 20th. Two of the men have run away: Paul, who was in charge of the oxen, and Augustus, his cousin. They have been fractious of late, complaining constantly about their working conditions, and wilfully making all kinds of difficulties concerning their duties. When they did not appear this morning, MacDuff informed Allardyce, who has gone after them in a foul temper, taking McLean and Forsyth with him. There is an unpleasant atmosphere on the plantation, like the tense heaviness that precedes a thunderstorm.

June 21st. Still no sign of Allardyce. The men are working under protest. Even the women and children, who are normally well disposed towards me, are dour and unwilling to speak. Old Moses, who is normally the soul of cheerfulness, turned his back today when he saw me approach. I have a prickling sense of foreboding, and I have taken to sleeping with a pistol by me.

June 22nd. A letter today from Gavin Hamilton, in which he presents his compliments and tells me that the family is well and thriving. As for the vexed question of McLehose, he informs me that he has made the enquiries I asked, and that he knows of no reason why I should not return. It seems that the authorities in Jamaica are very lax in their pursuit of malefactors who have fled the colony, having insufficient resources to undertake such matters, and that unless there is a warrant for their arrest, or they return and draw attention to themselves, they have little to fear. The deaths of Mr and Mrs McLehose seem to have occasioned little if any comment, and he had not been aware of the situation until I wrote.

I saw Yinta earlier this morning, and called out '*moroko*' very pleasantly by way of greeting, but she did not respond.

June 23rd. Ambrose came to see me this morning. I voiced my alarm about the prevalent mood, and he replied that frankly he was not surprised at it.

'Who knows what Allardyce will do to them if he catches them?' he said. 'On other estates, slaves have been tortured and hung for running away. The people have nothing against you, but unless someone takes a stand against Allardyce, I fear for your position here. This is the stuff of rebellion.'

'I am as powerless as you are,' I said. 'What can I do?'

'There is something that you could do,' he replied. I enquired as to what he wished of me, and by way of a response he produced a strange object from under his shirt, and placed it on the table between us. It was a crude effigy of a human figure about two inches long. A grey, hairy, stick-like object had been attached to it with a length of cotton – it gave off a faintly unpleasant odour, and there was something repellant about the very appearance of the thing.

He told me that he desired me to enter Allardyce's quarters, and conceal the object near where the man was wont to sleep. I several times demanded the purpose of this odd business, but he was most reluctant to answer me. 'This will deal with Allardyce,' he said, and would vouchsafe no further.

'It is only a carving of a man,' I said. He nodded, as if that was the end of the matter. 'You must take me into your confidence,' I went on. 'I hate Allardyce as thoroughly as yourself, but I cannot agree unless you tell me what you mean to accomplish.' He demurred yet again, but when I remained insistent he leaned towards me and told me that it was a 'wanga' – a term with which I was not familiar. 'And what is this tied to the figure?' I asked. He told me that it was part of the leg of a species of spider, found hereabouts, and which reputedly attain great size. They live in burrows in the ground, emerging at night to prey on mice, lizards and insects.

'And what is the purpose of placing such an object in Allardyce's bed chamber?'

'It will solve our problem,' he repeated stubbornly. I began to realise that the figurine was most probably connected in some way with African magic, which I had often heard mocked by white men as nothing but the foolish superstition of ignorant savages. Like the steamed rice, I was not inclined to believe in it. I have no faith at all in talismans and the like, be they the reputed bones of saints or fragments of the True Cross. Yet I must allow that I experienced a most disagreeable sensation of unease as I looked at the unpleasant object on the table. Crude though it was, it displayed every sign of having been fashioned with some care. I expressed my misgivings about the venture, but Ambrose dismissed these, repeating that it would deal with Allardyce.

In the end, I decided that there could be no harm in falling in with Ambrose's wishes. I could not envisage any circumstances in which such an object could harm anybody, so there was therefore nothing to be lost by doing as I was bidden; and the goodwill of Ambrose was important to me. I told him that I believed his case to be just, and that I would do it. He seemed mightily relieved, and urged me not to delay, as Allardyce might return at any moment.

I pushed the 'wanga' on to a piece of paper with a stick, for despite my rational disbelief in its powers, I shuddered at the thought of touching it. I was able to enter the man's hut without occasioning any remark, and went quickly to his inner chamber, a sty, littered with empty rum-bottles, and mounds of unwashed clothing strewn upon the floor. His bed was a squalid, foetid mess. Grimacing at the stench, I looked beneath it, and discovered a loose board, which I was able to prise up to reveal a small cavity into which I dropped the object, feeling not a little foolish as I did so.

I am now writing up this diary in my own quarters. Allardyce has not returned. I pray to God that he may fail in his quest, though I fear the effect that such failure will have upon his temper in the days to come. I am still wrestling with misgivings over what I have done. The more I revolve the matter in my mind, the more I convince myself that no harm can come of it.

June 23rd, early morning. Ten minutes ago I was aroused from sleep by the sound of shouting and profanity in the darkness outside, and realised that Allardyce was back, and seemingly intent on rousing the whole plantation. McLean and Forsyth, both decent men at heart, seemed subdued, but the manager was the very Devil incarnate. To my dismay I saw that they had tracked down the fugitives and brought them back in leg-irons. They were squatted on the ground, looking about them in the most abject fear, the whites of their eyes bright in the lamplight. Both of them were bleeding around the mouth. He ordered them locked up, and screamed that in the morning he would personally flog them until they were close to death, and then hang them as a warning to any other slave who might contemplate a similar course of action. I attempted to remonstrate with him, and suggested as calmly as I could that we should discuss the matter before taking such extreme measures, but he called me a damned interfering neger-lover, and stormed into his quarters in a furious rage, slamming the door behind him. I have no doubt that he shall even now be feeding the flames of his frenzy by recourse to the rum-bottle. There was nothing to do but return to my room and write down an account of what has taken place. It is three in the morning, and I doubt that I shall have much sleep tonight. This is a terrible place.

June 24th. A day has passed since I penned the last lines. My hand is trembling, and I do not know how to write down what has happened in the interim. Several times I have picked up my pen only to lay it down again, pacing to and fro across the floor. I know that it cannot help matters, but I have broached a bottle of rum in the hope of steadying my nerves. All I can do is write the events down: I *dare not* think about what they *mean*.

Just as it was growing light, I was awakened from a restless slumber by a terrible, protracted scream. My first thought was that the slaves, hearing of the capture of their fellows, had indeed rebelled, and were exacting their violent revenge upon their oppressors, and notwithstanding the fair repute in which I believed myself to be held, I was mightily afraid for my own safety, and took care to load my pistol before unlocking my door and cautiously issuing forth. Far from the press of black bodies, which I had feared, there was nothing to be seen. Within a few seconds Forsyth appeared with a lamp, followed a few moments later by McLean and MacDuff. As we stood irresolute, dreading a repetition of that awful sound, McClure came along, fastening his clothing. We stared at each other.

'What in God's name was that?' said Forsyth.

'It was Allardyce,' replied McLean. We all looked towards the manager's quarters, where we saw that a light was burning. Armed as we were, we felt no inclination to enter, fearful of what we might find, but in the end there was nothing for it but to venture in. The outer office, where a lamp was lit, was deserted.

'He must be in his room,' I said. For a moment we listened carefully, but there was no sound from within. We called his name; there was no response. Summoning my courage, I pushed open the door of his bedroom.

As the light fell upon the bed I cried out in horror, and heard Forsyth draw in his breath and exclaim, 'Dear sweet Jesus!' The others entered and cried out aloud. McClure very nearly swounded away, so that McLean had to support him. I could not take my eyes away from the hideous sight on the bed, and I felt the hairs on the back of my neck bristle up and stand erect.

Allardyce lay upon his back, quite naked. His face was almost black; his eyes glared horribly; and from his mouth, which was working convulsively, a bloody froth was issuing. He had bitten deeply into his tongue, which protruded from his mouth. But it was not this, revolting though it was, which so appalled us.

Squatting on his chest was the largest spider I have ever seen. Its head was on Allardyce's neck, just above the Adam's apple, and its hairy, egg-shaped abdomen covered much of the upper part of his body. Its eight legs were spread wide over his chest and stomach, the front ones on the wretched man's neck and shoulders, and the rearmost ones reaching almost to his navel. The whole nightmarish creature was covered with thick, stiff hairs of a dirty grey colour. Its legs, the thickness of a finger, were segmented, with black bristles at the joints. I never wish to see such an odious and loathsome thing again.[7] For the space of a second or two we stood rooted, and then, with a speed which I would not have believed possible, it scuttled away with a ghastly rustling sound and dropped with a palpable thud on to the floor on the side of the bed furthest from us.

With a scream, McLean made a dash for the door, almost knocking McClure over in his haste, and the rest of us rushed in headlong panic after him. Forsyth slammed the door shut behind us. The whole incident can only have taken a few moments, but the impression it made upon me shall remain until my dying day. McClure lurched outside and vomited copiously. Forsyth kept repeating 'Jesus, sweet Jesus!' over and over again in a shocked whisper. The rest of us stood breathing heavily, the sweat starting from our foreheads. I felt my heart pounding like a blacksmith's hammer in my breast.

'For the love of God,' exclaimed McLean, 'what are we to do? What in the Devil's name *was* that?' Not one of us had the stomach to enter the room again. The creature might have been anywhere in the shadows, waiting for its next victim. However there was no doubt that we had to take some action, for whatever our feelings for Allardyce, he was still a human being, in the gravest distress, and it was incumbent upon us to render assistance to him in his extremity.

More lights were fetched; we armed ourselves with long sticks, and Forsyth took up a long-handled broom. We pushed the door open very slowly, peering around carefully before daring to move over the threshold. Allardyce lay in the same position, breathing stertorously, and twitching slightly. The garments and bottles were gently pushed back with the broom, but of the spider there was no sign. The space between the bed and the wall, where the monstrosity had fallen, was only a foot or so wide. After checking carefully beneath the bed to ensure that there was nothing there, we pulled it, together with its wretched occupant, a few inches towards the middle of the room, so that we could open up the gap and shine the light in.

'It's on the floor,' said Forsyth unsteadily. 'It isn't moving. It's on its back. I believe it's dead. Pray God it's dead.' With the broom he painstakingly scraped the spider into the middle of the room where we could examine it, taking care not to approach too closely in case it was merely feigning death, as I have read some animals are wont to do when threatened with danger. McClure jabbed at its under-belly with the point of his stick, but it made no movement. McLean was all for treading it to a pulp beneath his feet, but I insisted that its body be preserved in case there were any questions asked at a later stage. Forsyth, shuddering, pushed it into an empty water bucket with a broom. Once a heavy lid had been placed on the bucket we all felt much relief, and we were able at last to turn our attention to the victim.

He was still alive, but clearly had but a short time to live. His face was black. On his collarbone were two puncture marks made by the bite of the spider, much inflamed round about the edges, and issuing a watery, pus-like fluid. The veins of his neck stood out like cords, and were unnaturally dark, as if they had been suffused with ink. His mouth was moving, but the only sound that issued from him was a gargling noise which was horrible to hear. His eyes were bulging as if there was some great pressure inside the cranium forcing them forth. They stared fixedly, as if he were seeing something horrid beyond belief – as well they might, for when I think what it would be like to feel a movement on my chest, to open my eyes and see what he must have seen, my blood runs cold. His body was drenched with sweat, and jerked and twitched like some pathetic marionette. McLean fetched some water and wiped him down, but he made no sign of being aware of our ministrations.

The nearest man of religion – a Dutch pastor by the name of Frans Heyn – lives many miles off, at Vreed-en-Hoop, and there was no question of fetching him in less than a day. I misdoubted whether Allardyce, the greatest atheist on earth, would have received the slightest benefit or succour from religion in his present state. As for a doctor, the nearest was in Stabroek across the river, and we sent McClure to organise a boat to fetch him, though it seemed unlikely that more than a few moments could elapse before death put a merciful end to his plight. It was agreed that the others would take it in turns to watch over him, and I was able to return here to my room. As I have been writing, I have been expecting to be summoned with the news that the miserable man has given up the ghost, but as yet there is no word. I cannot write more for now. The rain has started again, and the rum has made me light-headed.

June 25th. At daybreak, although I did not feel like it, I arose, made my ablutions, and went to see what I could do to assist with the arrangements for Allardyce's burial. To my amazement he was not yet dead, though his condition, which had seemed insupportable, had worsened. The convulsive shaking of the limbs had grown so great that they had been forced to lash him to the bed. His head was whipping from side to side; his eyes looked ready to start from their sockets, and his mouth gaped wide. He was making guttural sounds, although I could discern nothing intelligible. At about ten o'clock in the morning he began to cry out – wordless howls at first, and then continuous screams which were terrible to hear.

'What can we do, Burns?' asked Forsyth in despair. 'If he were a dog, I would take my pistol and put him out of his misery.' I had been thinking along the same lines, but I remembered the last time I'd had occasion to fire a gun, and had no wish to repeat the experience. A curious thought struck me. Normally a commotion like this would have brought the slaves running to discover the cause of it, but none made an appearance, not even to enquire whether the runaways had been apprehended. For all they knew, the dreadful sounds might have been the cries of their brothers undergoing torture at Allardyce's hands, and it ought to have occasioned curiosity at the very least.

When the rain eased I went to find Ambrose. He greeted me with his usual courtesy, but made no enquiries otherwise, and began to speak of drainage problems in one of the irrigation canals. I told him that the fugitives had been brought back, and were under lock and key. 'And what will happen now, Mr Burns?' he said, looking at me very directly. I explained that Allardyce was very sick and not likely to recover. 'And what sickness is that?' he asked. I told him of the events of the night, and he nodded. There were such spiders, he said thoughtfully. They did not commonly enter houses, but such things had been known. They did not usually attack humans, but if disturbed or cornered could bite very badly. I asked him about the 'wanga', but he seemed not to understand. I reminded him of our agreement as regards the placing of the things beneath Allardyce's bed, but he said he could recollect nothing of any such conversation.

I grew impatient, but before I could proceed further, McClure arrived all out of breath, entreating me to come quickly. We hastened to Allardyce's quarters to find that he had at last given up the ghost. His body presented a lamentable spectacle, for the man's face was set in such an expression of horror that it was impossible to look upon it without shuddering. Forsyth had tried to close those terrible staring eyes, but without success. We covered him with a sheet. Three or four slaves were sent to dig a grave, for putrefaction sets in very quickly in this climate, and we hoped that McClure would not be long returning with the doctor, who would have to fill out the necessary documents. When everyone had gone, I looked under the bed and lifted the board that had concealed the 'wanga'. It was not there. The spider was still in the bucket, however.

The whole business of the 'wanga' has unsettled me greatly. Is it possible that this malign talisman – bringing together a likeness of Allardyce, a fragment of a venomous creature and, in bounteous measure, the ill-feeling of whoever constructed it – could have been responsible for what happened? Could the malice of the perpetrator have been, as it were, made tangible purely by an effort of *will*, supported by nothing more than a token carving? And what of MacDuff's house? If such things can indeed happen, then we must have no more condescending talk of 'primitive superstition', for we are dealing here with something of a sophisticated order, which sets our comfortable notions on their heads. Yet I dare not speak of it to anyone. No one knows of the 'wanga' except Ambrose and I; it is nowhere to be found, and he now denies all knowledge of it. Who made the thing? If it was not Ambrose, then I shall never know. *In fine,* there is no evidence to connect anyone with Allardyce's death. Although I would not have wished such a fate on a fellow mortal, it would be hypocrisy on my part to deny that I am relieved the man is gone.

Much business to be undertaken. The company has to be notified, and until a replacement can be found, there is the pressing question of the running of the plantation. Nature abhors a vacuum, as Aristotle said – someone must be in charge. I have found myself issuing instructions and making decisions – the other overseers seem happy to accept this. I have returned the runaways to their hut. They have suffered enough.

July 7th. Some time since I have had the leisure to write. There was no problem with Allardyce. The doctor looked at the body, and examined the dead creature in the bucket. He wrote out a death certificate, giving poisoning of the blood as the cause of death, opining that the victim's predilection for alcohol had seriously weakened his constitution, rendering him unable to resist the venom. Since he had been bitten close to the heart, this would have hastened his death. We did not trouble Pastor Heyn. Forsyth simply said a few words over the grave, to which we responded with a muttered chorus of 'Amen', and that was that. I composed an epitaph that is without doubt very uncharitable – I shall perhaps not share it with the others.

Epitaph

> John Allardyce? We knew him well:
> A drunkard, brute and knave.
> Oh! save him from the flames of hell
> By pissing on his grave.

Despite the tenor of this epitaph, I was oddly moved today while I was clearing out Allardyce's quarters. Ah, the inexpressible poignancy and pathos of *small things* – personal effects that now count for nothing and will never again be needed. There was a letter that I made so bold as to read – it was from his mother – a barely literate scrawl hoping that he was in good health; expressing a maternal concern for his well-being, and concluding with the simple expression of a mother's love. It was dog-eared and ragged from having been read so many times. How often must he have turned to it in a rum-sodden haze, to glean some comfort from its sentiments? Did he shed a tear, this flawed and brutal man, to realise that there was one person, at least, in this bitter world who loved him – who had borne him; suckled him at her breast, and followed his first faltering steps with a mother's tender solicitude? Now it was just a useless scrap of paper, to be thrown away together with stinking clothes, soiled bed linen, and the other detritus of this wearisome life. I do not know why it should have moved me as deeply as it did. It was the same when Mary died – it was her copy of *Pamela* that affected me the most, I think – so much so that I could not bring myself to record the fact at the time. To think how she had perused those pages with so much pleasure! – how her dear hands had turned each leaf! – how it had lain nightly by our bedside!

July 17th. The agent in Stabroek has sent word to say that a replacement manager has been appointed – a man called Henry Jennings – but he is unable to undertake any journey to the Indies until September, and that in the interim I should manage the plantation, knowing best the operations thereof, and being already responsible for the accounts. My salary of forty pounds a year has been raised to £60 for the duration. Five pounds per month! However, the arrival of the letter merely set the seal on the *status quo*. We had already discussed the matter exhaustively. Only Forsyth had any claim to the post, and he was perfectly adamant that he possessed neither the ability nor the inclination to undertake such an office, and in short all were agreed that I should take charge. The duties of the overseers are clear enough, but I have to establish myself with the slaves as their new master. This is not an undertaking that I approach lightly, and I am determined to discuss the matter with Ambrose before I proceed with it. I feel like the steersman of a boat entering uncharted and hazardous waters, and I am fearful of hidden reefs and shoals.

I cannot now join the expedition into the wilderness until Mr Jennings arrives, and I shall write to Mr Bos tomorrow to apprise him of the situation.

July 29th. I have not yet spoken at any length with Ambrose, and have spent today away from the plantation, sitting by the koker, watching the Demerary flow past and considering the difficult situation in which I find myself. I have come from being a humble ploughman on a miserable Ayrshire farm, with a mere brace of lads at my disposal, to the manager of a mighty estate with absolute command over two hundred souls. Many would consider this to be good fortune indeed, but like the notorious tyrant (whom I hope I do not resemble in any other particulars), my heart is 'filled with scorpions', for I must confront MYSELF.

All of my life I have regarded with the utmost abhorrence the assumption of superiority by mere virtue of rank or station, as if the possession of a title somehow conferred these qualities that demand – nay, *require* – our respect. I do not just mean aristocrats such as those m'lords and m'ladies who have of late perished most deservedly in France, but also 'elders' like these rascals Fisher and Lambie: I mean that whole contemptible race of posturing, empty-headed birkies who set themselves above us mere mortals because of a title bestowed upon them by a Providence blind to their demerits. I always burned with the injustice of it. Here was a chinless idiot who had never read a book in his life; who could write little more than his name; who was lamentably ignorant of the world around him. A buffoon who would perish in the midst of plenty without a servant-nurse to feed him, and wipe his arse for him, and help him into his breeches. And yet I must believe that this abject creature is a better man, and deserves my *veneration* because an accident of birth made him *My Lord*, and made me plain Robert Burns.

Here is a liquorish lecher, an inveterate tippler and incorrigible satyr, whose mind encompasses but two thoughts: strong drink and a pair of well-rounded legs. And yet he purses his mouth like a hen's fundament if I enter a tavern; and cries fornication to the rooftops if I succumb to Cupid's darts. Yet he is an elder of the Kirk and I must do penance while he looks smirkingly on; and as Auld thunders like Jove about the washed sow returning to wallow in the mire, holds up his head, the picture of superior innocence!

A man is either honest or he is not – as Pope observed: 'An honest man's the noblest work of God', a line I have used myself, for it is a sentiment in which I believe with all my heart. Yet I do not know if I am an honest or even a good man. I think of Bess and her mother; I think of Jean; I think of poor McLehose; I think of Allardyce – I am tormented with shame, and feel the burden of many sins lie heavily upon my wretched soul. But now I am to become 'master' because Fate has decreed it so, and because I have white skin I shall be entitled to unquestioning obedience and respect. I am sickened by all the sniggering disparagement of the 'useless negers' that I have been compelled to listen to. Had I been dragged bodily to Africa – beaten, humiliated, forced to labour, mocked for my stumbling attempts to speak the language of the oppressor, denied instruction and then cynically derided for my ignorance – then what *respect* would I have had for the black man who declared himself my 'master'? And so why should the slaves respect me? If I am to have respect, it must be as a man. It must be earned. If I am to be a 'master' it must be as a loving husband and father is 'master' in his own home. There can be no more of the iniquities perpetrated by Allardyce. It will be easy enough to put a stop to these, but I fear that even as I resolve on a course of action I am already guilty of presumption and *naïveté*.

August 1st. Today I took the opportunity of speaking to Ambrose at length – our first private conversation since I assumed my new position. To be truthful, the affair of the 'wanga' continues to disturb me, as does his odd reticence, and I feel this has placed a distance between us. That was why I had not sought him out before. However, I was most anxious to restore our previous intimacy, and felt it essential to discuss with him my views on running the estate now that I am in charge of it.

'So how does it feel to be manager?' he said. 'There are many who would find your new situation an enviable one. You are to be congratulated.' I felt a little annoyed by this, because he knows very well my views on slavery.

'I didn't seek this position, Ambrose.'

'To be sure.'

'Someone has to run the plantation.'

'Indeed.'

'Look,' I said, 'You know perfectly well how I feel about the system. You know my opinion of Allardyce, and why I wrote to Balcarres. Do you believe that I *relish* being in charge?'

'No.'

'I didn't choose to be white, and I don't believe the colour of my skin makes me any better than anyone else. I didn't set out from Scotland to become a slave-driver – it just happened. God, man, you *know* that! Do you think I haven't thought about my position? All I want to do is to make the best of a bad situation!'

He smiled and patted my shoulder. 'I believe you.'

'I can put an end to barbarous practices, but I can't alter the fact that we're here; there's cane to be cut; mouths to be fed, and a world beyond this plantation that I am powerless to change.'

'I understand that,' he said. 'I don't impugn your motives. You're respected on the plantation, and I'm sure you'll be a fair master.'

'I will, Ambrose, I will.'

'But not a weak one.'

'What d'you mean?'

'My people have been accustomed to cruelty and brutality for years,' he said. 'They'll be overjoyed to learn that these days are over. But their happiness will be accompanied by some confusion, and they'll need a firm hand. Only in that way can you be a fair master. As time goes by you can allow yourself to become more relaxed.'

'That's sound advice,' I said. 'I shall be sure to follow it.'

'Good. It is all you can do. I shall help you in any way I can.'

'Thank you, Ambrose,' I said in relief.

We spent some time discussing the changes I proposed, and when we parted I felt that our old cordiality had been restored. I did not raise the issue of the 'wanga' – that can wait for another time.

Afterwards I called the overseers together to apprise them of my intentions. I told them that I intended to reinstate the earlier reforms, that materials would be provided for the slaves to improve their houses, and these would become their own heritable property. All children would be taught to read and to write as soon as the services of a schoolmaster could be procured. Baptised slaves would be permitted to marry if they wished. The number of working hours would be limited, and business enterprise would be encouraged.

I made it clear that I would not have violence used against the slaves, and none would be flogged. The abuse of Negro women would no longer be tolerated, and I would deal very severely with anyone who exploited them for sexual gratification. Many of the overseers looked pretty discomfited, most having taken their pleasure with the plantation women at some time, though some of these liaisons are of long standing, as in Forsyth's case, and it was he who spoke up at this point.

'Damn it, Burns,' he said sharply, 'what of Eliza? She has lived with me these seven years, and given me two bonnie bairns. I know we can never be man and wife because the law forbids it, but frankly I care nothing about that. I have no intention of returning to Edinburgh with her and trying to introduce her to polite society. We're here, and we're together, and I'm damned if I'm going to turn her out of doors just because you say so.'

I told him that all I meant was that no slave woman should be lain with against her will, and that I had no objection to concubinage provided that the woman was treated decently and the issue of such a union properly cared for. At this all seemed relieved and said that they were happy to proceed along the lines I had set down.

August 15th. A most difficult conversation with Ambrose yesterday. I challenged him again about the business with the 'wanga', but he only laughed.

'I'm from Saint-Domingue,' he said, but would elaborate no further. We were sitting by the creek, where we knew ourselves safe from intrusion. In the dark water we could see the reflection of two men, but it would have been impossible to say which was black and which was white.

'Ambrose,' I said, 'what d' you think will happen when emancipation comes?'

'I wish I knew,' he said, with a sigh.

'Men should be brothers.'

'A fine sentiment,' he said, 'but a naïve one. Foolish, even. The memory of slavery won't be eradicated in a generation, or even two generations. The harm done to masters and slaves alike has been too great. You assume that because you and I are friends, then such friendship can become universal. But you're attempting to draw a general rule from a single friendship. I trust you, Robert, but you cannot expect all black men to have trust. If there comes a day when Negroes and white men live in freedom together, then some will do so harmoniously. But mostly I believe they will merely tolerate each other. For many, black or white, the old assumptions and resentments will remain – there will always be men like Allardyce and Simon.'

'There will always be wicked people, regardless of the colour of their skin,' I protested. 'But that need not prevent the rest of us from trying to make something better of the world.'

'White men will never relinquish their power,' he said. 'They own the land; the factories; the ships and the warehouses. They legislate; administer justice; write the history books; own the newspapers and the printing presses. The best we can hope for is the freedom to live without fear: without power, equality is beyond our reach.'

'You take a gloomy view, Ambrose. You could excel in any field you chose.'

'Perhaps. Who knows? If I were free, and had the leisure, I might indeed achieve some office hitherto the preserve of white men. I might indeed excel. But in their hearts these white men would still think of me as a neger.'

'By setting an example, you could strike a blow for your people.'

'How? By being one black face among a thousand white ones? Ah, well . . . ' His voiced trailed away.

'If you and I can be as equals,' I said, 'then so can others.'

'We are not equals,' he said. 'I am a slave, and you are my master.'

'You're misrepresenting me, Ambrose.'

'Yes, I know. You do not regard me as inferior.'

'I also value you as an intelligent human being.'

'But I lack a formal education.'

'So do I.'

'*Touché.* But you could get an education more easily than I, and even if I succeeded in that respect, I would still be patronised, ostracised, and called 'boy' by passers-by. I'm just a neger, after all. No better than an animal.'

'Don't say that,' I protested.

'But it's true, for the white man at least. And remember that the acceptability of an animal increases if it proves itself obedient and compliant. If a horse does not bolt and a dog does not bite, then its owner considers himself to be a 'good master'. If the slaves work, and do not rebel, then our plantation owners flatter themselves with the same assumption.'

'But men are not animals.'

'No, but it suits the white man's purposes to regard us as akin to the apes. In dressing us in their clothes; making us use their language; converting us to Christianity, and binding us to their laws, they do little more than patronise us. You assume, though you may not perhaps realise it, that *equality* means black people resembling white ones so closely that no difference remains, except for the colour of their skin. We must become like *them*. But does this not also beg the question that the ways of the white man are superior? Does it not deny us the dignity of a culture and an identity to call our own? Would I ask you to adopt the habits of Negroes?'

'I had not thought of that.'

'Of course not. You assumed it without thinking. And consider this – the more we became like you, the more you would fear us.'

'I do not agree with you,' I argued. 'If a job is to be done, then the colour of a man's skin should have no bearing on the matter.'

'It should not, but it does. It goes much further than that, Robert.' He moved closer and lowered his voice. 'You fear us because you are in awe of our physical strength and our virility. That's why such careful steps are taken to chaperone your women when they encounter our men, and why one of your women who willingly surrenders her honour to a Negro is regarded with an outrage that conceals a great deal of curiosity and envy. You fear that our men, with their supposed animal appetites, can offer experiences which your men cannot.'

'And yet we have few scruples about lusting after your women,' I added. 'It's hardly consistent, is it?'

'No, because our women tend to submit readily, for a variety of reasons. How many of your women are raped by our men?'

'Very few,' I said. 'I have only heard of two cases, and they both ended in a hanging.'

'Quite. But how many of our women are violated? Thousands. And how many yield only because of the consequences if they refuse? Or because they are offered inducements? Or because of the prospect of manumission? Or because they know that the offspring of the union will be favoured and privileged? It is all violation of a kind, I fancy.'

'If that is so, then any man who has ever lain with a woman who has the expectation of some advantage, whatever her colour or race, is guilty. Which is worse, a white man who entices a woman of his own race into bed with the expectation of a title and a fortune, or a white man who does the same for one of your women with the inducement of manumission? You heard what I had to say about concubinage. I myself have lived with a Negro woman, and although I realised at the time that I was favoured by being white, I did not coerce her in any way. I did not gain her by bribery or threats; I did not seek to exploit her; and I did truly care for her, Ambrose. I also secured her manumission.'

'Oh, I am sure you did. I am sure she gained much from her time with you. There are exceptions everywhere, and there always will be. But many of my women feel they have no option. It's a matter of power.'

He moved away, and his deep voice fell silent, and he stared into the distance, lost in his thoughts. For a long time we sat, surrounded by the sounds of the forest and the rippling of the water at our feet. I could think of nothing to say, for my principal emotion was a sense of shame in belonging to a race that had so utterly alienated another. Until this moment I had thought myself absolved from guilt by virtue of the fact that I genuinely hated slavery, treated Negroes with courtesy and respect, and in Ambrose had found a true and valued friend. But I had wronged Adah, and now, it seemed, I had to face up to the culpability within myself – like original sin – unforgiven and ineradicable.

'There is hope,' I said. 'People like Wilberforce are doing their best.'

He grunted. 'It will take more than a Wilberforce to effect any real change.'

'You must admire the stance he is taking,' I said.

'Oh, I do,' he said. 'But it is a very English stance, so it will take decades to achieve anything. Besides, the worst traders are the Africans themselves, who have been buying and selling slaves for generations.'

'Mr Douglas told me that once. I did not know whether to believe him or not.'

'It is true enough. We need heroes as well as lawmakers. Do you know who I admire, Robert? Toussaint.[7] *There's* a leader who believes in the rights of man! There are no slaves on Saint-Domingue now. In four years the entire institution has been swept away! Ah, if only I had remained.'

'Do you want to return to your native land one day?' I asked.

'Where is my native land?' he said wearily. 'Saint-Domingue? France? England? This benighted colony? Or perhaps a place in Africa where I have never been and whose name I do not even know? I have been a stranger in every land I have ever lived in. Where can I call home? Who are my people? In Saint-Domingue I could have been someone, certainly. But now I am just one black man amongst countless thousands who are everywhere and who belong nowhere. We are your slaves for now – mere possessions – but your children shall inherit us and our unmet desires, Robert.'

August 28th. Mr Bos has gifted me a book of Horace that has given me much pleasure. How uplifting it is to commune with one who, although long departed this world, clearly thought much the same as I do! The other day I was about my business when I saw one of the slaves approach. He did not observe me, and passed on singing softly to himself, the very picture of contentment despite his sorry situation. I had thought to write about it, but could not conceive of a way to begin, but earlier today I found that I had been anticipated by the Latin muse. After some thought I have rendered him into English as follows:

A Translation of Horace

Happy the man who, free from worldly care,
Goes forth with mattock or with oxen-train;
Who tills the soil, and breathes the pleasant air,
And dreams of neither profit nor of gain.[9]

September 3rd. Everyone is hard at work at the cane, which is now ready for harvesting. The crop is late this year, but we are achieving a good yield nonetheless, and the mill is working day and night. I have let it be known that when the harvest is gathered in, and the sugar and rum safely taken care of, then there will be a holiday for all. During this time, everyone will be at liberty to attend to their own gardens, or simply to relax at their leisure. Allardyce grudgingly permitted the slaves to sell vegetables or chickens, but he insisted on keeping the proceeds, so there was no incentive for people to fend for themselves. I have made it clear that from now on those who choose to work may retain what they earn, and use it for whatever purpose they so desire. My new *régime* has had the effect of greatly reducing tension. Where there have been difficulties, it has only been necessary to invoke the memory of Allardyce to produce an instant change of attitude.

I have had paal-offs constructed at regular intervals along the canals. Instead of having people splashing about in the water, this allows the rafts to come to the edge of the banks, so the loading is much easier.

September 10th. Everyone hard at work. The smoke from the cane drifts over the whole plantation bringing with it a fine ash that settles everywhere,[10] and there is the heavy sweet smell from the mill that lends its honeyed fragrance to the warm air. It is about four in the afternoon, and the sun is already dipping towards the palm trees. A kiss-ka-dee has just settled on my window ledge, regarding me quizzically with its black bead of an eye before flying off to rejoin its mate. At times likes these, this plantation is tolerable; it could easily be idyllic were it not for the blight of slavery that demeans everything.

Despite weeks and months of effort, my attempts to befriend Yinta have met with no success. I have been trying to learn a little more of her language from Forsyth, and when I speak to her she listens civilly enough, but makes no response other than to smile, as if my clumsy efforts amuse her. She exchanges a few words with Forsyth on occasion, but ignores the other overseers completely.

September 20th. Monday. What a carouse yestreen! I own that I have seldom experienced such conviviality – and for the moment it seemed that the division between master and slave was quite forgotten, though there is not a man on the plantation who is not nursing a confounded headache today! My Muse was with me when I awoke – perhaps I was still intoxicated – who knows? – but the following was the result –

A Summer's Night

The summer night was rich as gold,
The busy crickets bickered:
Nearby the mighty river rolled,

And myriad fireflies flickered.
In dwellings snug as any nest,
Faint lights, with starlight vying,
Showed where the workers took their rest
From hoe and mattock plying,
                At home that night.

A footstep sounded close at hand:
Forsyth it was, I reckoned:
Wi' Jock McClure, wha raised his hand,
And to me quickly beckoned.
'And will ye hae a guidly dram,
Tae celebrate the croppin'?
We havena ale that's worth a damn,
But rum'll set us hoppin'
                Wi' joy this night.

The honeyed nectar o' the cane!
Sweet essence o' molasses!
We downed our drams, then once again
Recharged our willin' tassies!
'Guid sakes,' quo Jock, 'this rum is fine,
And this estate supplied it:
It's grander than the choicest wine!'
And nane o' us denied it
                At a' that night.

Like speedy darts the minutes flew,
The banter was uproarious:
Forsyth and Jock gat roarin' fu'
And I was feelin' glorious!
'Now lads, now lads!' quo bold McLean,
Whose brow wi' sweat was beadin':
'My pipes shall gie a rare refrain –
It's music that we're needin'
                For mirth this night!'

'Your pipes? Your pipes?' we cried aloud,
'Brocht a' the way frae Scotland?
A quick Strathspey will do us proud
Within this steamy, hot land!'
He screwed the pipes and made a din
That would hae scared the Devil:

The slavers dribbled doon his chin,
While we commenced to revel
                              And dance that night.

We pranced aroon, as fu' as eggs;
The pipes screeched like a cat, man!
'Hey massa, what's dat t'ing wid legs
Yah blowin' t'roo lak dat, man?'
Quo Moses, who'd surprised us quite,
And gazed richt weel astounded,
Unable to believe the sight
O' sic-like joy unbounded,
                              That merry night.

'Come on!' quo Jock, 'and join the dance,
And kick yer heels wi' pleasure.'
So Moses 'gan tae leap and prance
In time to Scotia's measure.
'And tak a dram,' roared out MacDuff,
'My God, we'll teach ye well, man!
If any man cries out 'Enough'
Then he can go to hell, man,
                              This verra nicht!'

Wi' leapt, wi' mettle in our heels,
And danced, like men demented,
All kinds o' jigs and rowdy reels –
And some we just invented.
Now by this time the bagpipe's tune
Had roused the hale plantation,
And there assembled very soon
    A mighty congregation
                              Tae share that night.

Wi' clappin' hauns and beatin' drums
Loups each and ev'ry cotter –
The young, the old, the sick – each comes;
The strang rum flowed like water!
As Davie's pipes did skirl and squeal,
It was a sicht tae see, man!
Twa hunner in an eightsome reel
Imbued wi' dev'lish glee, man,
                              Tae dance that night.

But pleasures are like blossoms spread,
Where summer breezes waft;
Too soon the fragile blooms are shed
By zephyrs borne aloft.
When rum flows free, we seldom think
Of coming tribulation:
We soon forget the joys of drink
Are but of brief duration:
                    A single night!

Poor Davie's mou gied up the ghost:
Wi' sweat the pair man's pourin'!
And wee MacDuff, for a' his boast,
Falls ower, and lies there snorin'!
The revel ower, we went tae bed,
And ne'er a body tarried:
Tho' some, well fu', had tae be led,
And some had tae be carried
                    Back hame that night.

Dawn tip-toed in wi' tim'rous tread,
The village was awakenin'–
And mony an ee was blear and red,
And mony a head was achin'.
The arduous labour o' the cane
Leaves little space for leisure:
Yet all resolved to meet again
To seek once more our pleasure:
                    Some other night.

On sober reflection we probably put ourselves in danger by taking part in such a rowdy gathering, but I do not think that any harm has been done. There is nothing like a right guid-willie waught to make us forget the tribulations of life!

September 27th. Major von Bouchenroeder, the eminent Dutch cartographer, is in the colony engaged in surveying it. Mr Bos is greatly excited by this, for all existing maps are unreliable and constantly require revision.

The other news he had to impart was that the arrival of Jennings is imminent, and we must prepare ourselves. I knew that this day would come eventually, and yet it has given me a heavy heart. I have almost enjoyed being in charge; the slaves have welcomed my reforms, and I shall be truly sorry to relinquish my authority. I have asked Mr Bos if he knows what manner of man Mr Jennings is, but he has heard no reports of him. If he shares my views, then I am sure we will be able to work well together to improve the plantation.

October 2nd. Jennings arrived two days ago. I wish I could say that I was pleased to see him, but that is most emphatically not the case. In honesty, I felt that I had been carrying out my duties with perfect diligence, and so his arrival, even in the very best of circumstances, would have been something of a blow to my *amour propre.* But the circumstances were very far from being of the best. Once again the plantation has a bad manager, and I am fearful of what may now happen here.

I confess I took a dislike to the man the instant I set eyes on him. I was on the stelling with Forsyth and Ambrose as his boat approached. When he was yet some way off, I could see him sitting in the bow of the vessel staring at us. We waved to him, but he made no move to return our salutation. As the men made the boat fast, he remained immobile, gazing into the distance, and then climbed out, brushing aside any offer of assistance, and without a word of acknowledgement or thanks to the boatmen. He was a small man – not much over five foot, by my reckoning – and of a wiry build. I guessed his age to be about fifty. He had some gingery hair, but the top of his head was bald, and covered in large freckles. His eyes were blue, set rather close together, and I noticed that the eyelashes were so pale as to appear almost invisible. He had very thin lips, set in a humourless grimace. The muscles in his cheeks were taut. All in all, he gave the impression of being in a most disagreeable frame of mind.

We moved forward to greet him, and he fixed us all in turn with a cold eye.

'Which of you is Burns?' he said in a clipped, rather high-pitched voice. I stepped forward and introduced myself, extending my hand with a cordiality that I did not feel, and said that I hoped that his journey had been a comfortable one. He ignored my hand and stared directly at me for several seconds in a most searching fashion.

'I am in charge now, Burns,' he said. 'I hope you will not forget that.' He looked at Ambrose, and then again at me. 'Get your neger to see to my belongings. And if anything is damaged then I promise you he will regret it.' I was too embarrassed to look Ambrose in the eye, but he climbed down into the boat and started to unload its contents with studious solicitude.

Without another word to any of us, Jennings walked down the stelling and on to the pathway leading to the compound. Forsyth danced a sort of obsequious attendance on him, telling him to mind his feet at places where there was water, or pulling small branches out of his way. The man ignored him. I followed some paces behind, saying nothing, but with a heart filled with misgivings. The other overseers were waiting to meet him. He said nothing to them, and spoke only to enquire which was the manager's house. I explained that when Allardyce died, I had taken over his accommodation, leaving my own, which was the same in every particular and which had been made ready for his arrival. He looked at me quizzically.

'I am sure,' I went on, 'that once you are rested we will be able to organise things as you wish them.' He looked at me for a long time with narrowed eyes. His head was sweating, and there was a slight tic at the corner of his mouth.

'You have an hour to remove your belongings to their rightful place,' he said at last. 'I propose to make a tour of inspection, and I expect my quarters to be ready on my return. *My quarters*, Mr Burns.' I was too taken aback to remonstrate with him, and indeed had no opportunity to do so, for he abruptly turned away, signalling Forsyth to go with him.

With the help of others, I made short work of removing my possessions, for they are but few in number, and Ambrose, who had supervised the unloading of the boat, fetched in Jennings' luggage and began to sweep the floor. The other overseers went off rather sheepishly, having expressed their opinion that it was a damned shame the way the man had treated me, and MacDuff said with some bravado that he would not have stood for it; but their voices lacked conviction.

'This man is no good,' said Ambrose, when they had gone. They were the first words he had spoken since Jennings' arrival. 'He thinks he is God. Allardyce was a devil, but a man who believes he is God is worse than a devil.' I told him that I agreed, but hoped that the man was affecting the martinet in order to make an impression, and that in time he would behave in a different fashion. Ambrose said nothing, but gave me a sceptical look. We were sitting in silence in the inner room when a shadow fell across the door. Jennings stood there. He looked first at Ambrose and then at me.

'Mr Burns, do you permit a neger to sit in my quarters?' Ambrose looked at me, but made no move to stand.

'This is Ambrose,' I replied, fighting back a desire to express the anger I felt. 'He is your head driver, and the best man on the plantation. He has brought your belongings from the boat and, as you see, has made everything ready for you.' Jennings made no reply, but curtly ordered Ambrose to stand, which he did, his face assuming once more an expression of unconcern.

'I find your attitude towards this neger difficult to understand,' snapped Jennings, breathing heavily, and with a flush in his cheek. 'You are in a position of trust here, and *that* is a slave!' He gestured contemptuously towards Ambrose. 'He exists only to carry out our instructions. Yet I observe you have been exchanging social commonplaces as if you were equals, and you have even given him leave to sit *in my chair!* I do not understand, Mr Burns.' He turned to Ambrose. 'Get out of here!' he hissed. 'The next time I see you sitting in a white man's presence, I will have you flogged senseless.'

Ambrose did as he was bidden, and Jennings approached me, wagging his finger in my face and coming so close that I could feel his spittle on my face as he spoke.

'I have scarcely been here an hour,' he yelped, 'and already I have heard some of the things you have been up to. I cannot conceive you, sir! Cavorting like a savage with the negers! You have been lax, Mr Burns! More than lax! This is the stuff of insurrection! I shall bring you to heel, sir, I promise you! *I will not have neger-lovers on my plantation!* I will not have it, sir!' He spoke with such vehemence that he was almost choking for breath with the very passion of it.

I asked his permission to take my leave, to which he made no reply but simply turned his back on me. I returned to my duties in a daze of disbelief. Two days have passed, and I remain unable to come to terms with the man's insufferable arrogance. He does not improve on acquaintance. He neither drinks alcohol nor smokes, and makes no secret of his contempt for those who indulge these heinous vices. He will not eat with us, having his meals brought to his quarters, and spends no more time in our presence than he has to. Forsyth and the rest, for all their fawning, have met with the same lack of courtesy.

I have resolved to keep out of his way as much as possible.

October 3rd. I fear I have got on the wrong side of Jennings. Earlier this evening I took him the day's tallies for his perusal and signature – a simple enough transaction that I have hitherto been able to carry out without the need to indulge in conversation. I was somewhat later than usual, and he was being served dinner by Yinta. She was using a little ladle to dish up stew from a cooking pot on to his plate, and in a moment of nervousness allowed some of the hot gravy to drop on his leg. With an oath he sprang to his feet and struck the lassie across the side of the head, causing her to cry out and fall to the floor, and he continued to strike at her, calling her a neger whore and a black bitch, and accusing her of having done it deliberately.

I could not tolerate this. I seized hold of his arm, and told him that if he did not stop, then I would thrash him, manager or not. Yinta picked herself up and rushed from the room as I pushed him back into his chair. He was too taken aback to speak and I shouted in his face that the girl had intended no harm, and that any man who lifted his hand against a defenceless woman – whatever her colour or rank – was a despicable coward, and that I would not stand idly by if it ever happened again. He stared at me and said nothing, so I turned on my heel and left him. I know that I have done the right thing, but Jennings strikes me as the vengeful sort, and I must be on my guard.

October 4th. I told the cook today that in future he would have to take the meals to Jennings himself. He grumbled dreadfully, but I was adamant, and he finally agreed. Yinta was in the kitchen at the time: she said nothing, but instead of haughtily ignoring me, as she has been wont to do since her arrival, she nodded at me shyly. I wish there was some way I could communicate with her. As for Jennings, he has not referred to the matter, but there was no mistaking the malevolence in his face when I saw him earlier.

October 15th. Nothing further has been said about the incident with Yinta. Jennings says little to me beyond what is strictly necessary for the conduct of plantation business, and I am quite content with this. If anything, I detect a grudging respect. I am inclined to think that I have made my point, and that is an end of it.

October 30th. The way to Yinta's heart is through verse, I am sure. It is, *après tout,* a stratagem that has been successful for me in the past. But any poetic expression of my tender sentiments shall have to be made in the Arawak tongue, and although I have striven to come to terms with it, it is a task made diabolically difficult by the fact that nowhere can I discover how the language is written down, so that all I can give is a wretched approximation. I even doubt if the language has ever *been* written! So I have had to fashion something, and, like an actor, must needs employ it as a script for an amorous *performance* when I adjudge the moment to be right and the stage to be propitiously set. As for the fair and solitary member of the *audience* of this drama, who knows? Shall I appear the *villain* or the *hero* of the piece? These are my lines: their merit I cannot yet judge!

Da Lee-keeng [11]

A-koo-ee! Da an-shi-shi jee-ang ko-ray to-ko-ro
Bo-hoy-a o-lo-ko ma-kir-a-lee-ka:
A-koo-ee! Da an-shi-shi jee-ang ye-nee se-mee
Hi-yen-too-a ma-ooch-a.

Boo-ee hee-bee, da lee-keeng,
Ke-na dan-shi-shi hee:
Ke-na dan-shi-shi-fa hee, lee-keeng
Ba-ri-ko-ma Ma-la-li sa-kang.

Ba-ri-ko-ma Malali sakang, lee-keeng
Ke-no ko-no-ko-be n'ma-ka-wa-do-wa-fang:
Dan-shi-shi-fa kee-doo-a-ha
Da beth-eth-o, da lee-keeng.

November 1st. Let this day be blessèd forever in the calendar! And
blessèd, also, be my Arawak Muse, whatever her name may be! *Yinta
is mine!* – not grudgingly, but with a passionate willingness which
astonishes me. Verily, verily, the power of poesy! – *adieu* to celibacy!
– hail to the dawn!

I followed her to the well when she went to fetch water this
afternoon. When she espied me she smiled prettily and went about
her business. I showed her the sheet of paper on which I had written
down my little piece, and she looked at it in some bewilderment,
frowning and shaking her head.

'*B'kanaba,*' I said. 'Listen.' Then, nervously conscious of the
occasion, and fearful that what I had written might be incomprehen-
sible or distasteful to her, I read it to her slowly and with all the
feeling I could muster. By the time I finished she was staring at me
with her great dark eyes – whether in astonishment or horror I could
not at first determine. For a moment there was complete silence.

'*Toraha b'ajiasjia,*' she said at last, in a kind of whisper.

I was not familiar with this phrase – Forsyth has since enlightened
me – but her meaning was perfectly clear to me, for she pointed
repeatedly at my paper, and made it obvious in sign language that she
eagerly desired me to perform an *encore* of my little recitation, which
I duly did; and, divining that she was not displeased with me, made
so bold as to reach out and stroke her hair while I was about my
rendition, to which she made no resistance. When I had concluded,
she snatched the paper from me and gazed at it, rapt; then, thrusting
it in her bosom, flew into my arms with a cry of '*Ehei! Ehei! Ehei!*'
which, even with my miserable knowledge of the language, I knew

to be an assent. What followed in the next few minutes I shall cherish forever in my memory. I have never known such astonishing passion! And so, in brief, we are as one, and she is sleeping in my bed as I write.

November 2nd. Oh, radiant dawn of happiness! Oh, the glorious effulgence as the dazzling sun of domestic harmony illuminates Robert Burns with its joyful, warming rays! After years of monkish seclusion from the fair sex, I find myself a husband in all but name – I had quite forgotten that life could hold such delirious pleasures!

Yinta is continuing with her duties in the kitchen as before. I have told Ambrose what happened yesterday, and he said that he knew all along that she would allow herself to be won over. I have not mentioned anything to the others, but it will become common knowledge soon enough, and I do not feel inclined to comment on it.

November 30th. Yinta teaches me her language, and I strive to teach her mine. It is a slow business for me, but she is a very apt pupil and improving constantly. We have a game of naming things: I will point to my nose, for example, and she will say *shiri*, to which I reply *nose*, and so on. She takes endless pleasure in this, and laughs when I fail to pronounce the words correctly – hardly surprising when so many of them sound the same. When I attempted to pronounce the word for 'head', which is *üshí*, I made the error of stressing the word on its first syllable and saying *íshi* instead. I was pointing at my head at the time and could not understand her immoderate merriment, and it took her quite some time to regain sufficient control of herself to explain that *íshi* is the word used to describe a woman's private parts.

She is wholly herself, and entirely at home in this country. Now that I consider the matter, everyone I have known since leaving Scotland has been an *exile:* Mary and I from our native soil; Adah – Jamaican by birth but with parents taken from Africa, and of course the slaves on every plantation, and their overseers. Each and every one of them *displaced*, either forcibly, or by necessity, or in the vain hope of finding a fortune. Yinta alone belongs in this land and is content here, and possesses thereby a freedom and security that even the most privileged of white men lack. We may rule the Guianas, but we can never properly belong here. Eventually the climate and the forces of nature will kill us or drive us out.

A day or two ago I was walking, as is my wont, along one of the paths in the bush in the vicinity of the plantation. I had not been in this particular direction for some months. Along the way I chanced upon a clearing in which I remembered having seen a rude kind of hut or shelter, most probably used recently by workers clearing the forest. To my astonishment, the structure had all but disappeared beneath a profusion of creepers and climbing plants, and the clearing itself was now choked with undergrowth too dense and prickly to permit my passage. Certainly the paths rapidly disappear if we do not send men out with cutlasses to clear them regularly. There is a tiny bud-like plant that appears spontaneously on walls and window-ledges, presumably growing from a seed borne thence by the air, and too small to be seen. I know how assiduous we must be with the weeding of the cane. If we ever abandon this place, it will be but a short time until Nature has erased all sign of our presence.

December 7th. I am making slow progress with Arawak – I can remember the names of things, but I am sure that my attempts to form coherent sentences must be very wide of the mark. Yinta is much abler than I and has already acquired a good vocabulary. By making signs we find that we can understand each other surprisingly well.

How wonderful it is to bask in the love of such a woman – there can be no sporting with her happiness – I am committed forever!

December 25th. Today we shared the best Christmas imaginable – Yinta believes herself to be with child! – she patted her belly today and made me place my hand on it, saying *iloni* over and over, which in her language signifies a child as yet unborn. I shall have to give serious thought to our future. The slaves still hold me in high regard, but Jennings has applied himself most assiduously to undoing all that I achieved, and there is nothing more here for me. I still have my rix-dollars, and at the first opportunity I shall enquire about a passage home, taking Yinta with me. I must first find a way of explaining my plan to her – even the most eloquent mime cannot explain an Atlantic voyage, and a home on a different continent!

1796

January 5th. The general enthusiasm for the Batavian Republic has diminished greatly in the last few days. The reason for this has to do with Victor Hughes, the French Revolutionary, who has had much to say on the subject of slavery. I know that he was instrumental in driving the English from Guadeloupe a couple of years ago, and now he has put forward the proposition that all slaves in this colony should be provided with arms in order to slay their masters, and emancipate themselves! I would dearly love to see the slaves freed, but the means advocated by Monsieur Hughes would only serve to bring the entire colony to ruination and chaos. Mr Bos says that everyone in Stabroek now questions the wisdom of the revolutionary principles that once seemed so attractive. In the place of an old tyranny, Gaul has gained a new one! The Court of Policy, says Mr Bos, would require but little persuasion to throw in its lot with Britain, for if the hotheads have their way, then we shall be thrown into anarchy and bedlam.

January 16th. Jennings sickens me; by way of comparison, his predecessor now appears almost a decent man. That Allardyce was brutal cannot be denied, but there was a measure of predictability about his brutality – any man slacking, or committing a misdemeanour knew for certain what the consequences would be. Jennings, on the other hand, appears to relish the exercise of violence for its own sake, gaining a considerable degree of satisfaction from using his whip on those who have done nothing to deserve it. In short, he is not driven by a mad, rum-inflamed passion for control, but by the sheer pleasure derived from inflicting pain. I would write to Lord Balcarres if I felt that it would accomplish anything.

My domestic life is my sole consolation. Our joy in each other has no need of being set down in this journal. Where there is such perfect intimacy, few words are required, and none could do justice to the bond that daily grows stronger between us.

February 1st. McClure has been taken from the boiling house and Jennings has made him one of his lieutenants. It is almost comical to watch as the big, brainless oaf lumbers after his diminutive, dapper master, imagining himself very much the fine fellow with his whip. Jennings has chosen him because he has no brains, and will do exactly as he is told without question. He possesses an unthinking, cur-like loyalty, together with that voracious appetite for power often found in worthless, vicious, ignorant people who find themselves unexpectedly placed in a position of authority.

February 16th. My Arawak studies make but poor progress, but in English Yinta does very well. It is very agreeable to discover more about each other! I have been trying to explain my origins to her, and she now understands that I come from beyond the seas and a place called Scotland. My dearest wish is to take her back there, but we do not yet have the words with which to debate the matter! She has the sweetest, smiling disposition when we are together, though when she is about the plantation she retains the haughty, remote demeanour that was once all I knew of her.

There is as yet no outward sign of *our child* – what a joy to write these words! I have told her she must not exert herself and take as much rest as possible.

Within our little home all is harmonious, but the plantation grows worse and worse. Ambrose is looking strained and unhappy. MacDuff has taken advantage of the new *régime* to behave in a boorish fashion towards the slaves, and as for McClure, the less said the better. McLean and Forsyth seem uneasy, but they behave with deference towards Jennings, just as they did with Allardyce. I know they have their positions to consider, but I am disappointed in their moral cowardice.

March 3rd. I cannot remain here with Yinta – it is not safe. I have a very dangerous enemy in Jennings, and I believe he hates me so much that he might prove capable of anything. This week he has turned his vindictive attentions on the weeding gang, which is composed of women and children. He has got it into his head that they do not work quickly enough, and we are now accustomed to hearing his shrill, yapping voice exhorting them to ever greater efforts. He does not appear to care about the effect it has on the men of the plantation to hear their loved ones abused in this manner. Today I made the mistake of openly remonstrating with him – for a moment I thought he was going to set McClure on me.

'You dare to challenge me?' he seethed. 'You, who brought this estate to the brink of ruin? My God, you'll rue the day you crossed me!' He stamped off with McClure following as usual.

I still have the rix-dollars buried beneath the house. Stabroek is on the other side of the river – from thence we could be away from the colony in a matter of days. Perhaps this is the best course of action. I have spoken to Ambrose, and he says that I would be wisest to leave.

'What about you?' I said. 'How will you fare with such a man in charge?'

'You need not worry about me,' he said.

'But you are in danger. What if there is an insurrection?'

'No one will harm me.'

'But if the militia come, then there will be a general slaughter.'

'I do not think it will come to that. At any rate, I am prepared. You are in far more danger.' I know that Ambrose is far too intelligent to place himself at the forefront of a slave rising, but I have grown very fond of him, and I wish he would reconsider my offer of manumission.

March 19th. Outright confrontation with Jennings today. I heard cries, and when I went to discover what was happening I found him engaged in whipping one of the girls on the weeding gang, a buxom lass of about seventeen. This kind of thing always enrages me, and I asked him to stop.

'Are you giving me orders again, Mr Burns?' he snapped.

'The girl is doing her best! For God's sake, man, why are you doing this?' I knew the answer, of course, for it was perfectly clear by his demeanour – he enjoyed it.

'She was slacking.'

'She was not. She has been at work since first light; it is hot; you do not permit any rest, and she is tired.'

'I refuse to debate the matter in front of slaves. I shall grant you an audience in my quarters in five minutes.' With that, he stalked off, leaving the wretched girl weeping on the ground. I followed him, seething with indignation. I went into his room where he was sitting waiting for me, his mouth a thin, pale line, and the muscles in his jaw taut. I could see that he was in a cold fury – his pale eyes were watery and his freckled face was flushed.

'I intend to write to Lord Balcarres about this,' I said. 'We have already had a correspondence regarding brutality on this plantation.'

'Have you indeed?' he said. 'Well, well. Are you trying to intimidate me, Mr Burns?'

'No,' I said, although I had hoped that the mention of the owner's name would have had some effect.

'That is as may be,' he went on, with an unpleasant little smile. 'However, I know all about your correspondence, as you call it. And I have already written to His Lordship about *you*. Oh yes. You have offered violence against my person. You make a habit of undermining my authority. You have presented estate property to the slaves, and you have even talked about teaching them to read and write. You consort with them in a familiar and inappropriate manner. On the eve of my arrival you took part in a disgusting, drunken orgy with them! So what exactly will you say when you write to His Lordship?'

'That is a complete misrepresentation of everything I have done.'

'Is it indeed? Well, write your letter anyway, Burns. Oh, and be sure to direct it to the correct address.'

'What do you mean?'

'Lord Balcarres was appointed Lieutenant-Governor of Jamaica a few months ago,' he said with a grin. 'You spent some time in Jamaica, did you not? I have asked him to make enquiries about you, Burns. So go ahead and write your letter – I am sure he will be pleased to hear from a drunken, rabble-rousing neger-lover with ideas above his station.'

For once in my life, I was completely lost for words. To hear the wicked calumnies he has secretly conveyed to Lord Balcarres was a devious, underhand attack against which I had no defence prepared. Moreover, I had no wish for *anyone* – let alone my employer, now the Lieutenant-Governor – to make enquiries about the circumstances which led my fleeing Jamaica! Did Jennings know already?

'You can go to hell!' I shouted.

'I shall make a note of what you have just said to me,' he said, with a tight humourless smile , 'just as I have made a note of all your other acts of insubordination. Now will there be anything else?'

'I am giving you my notice,' I said.

'You may leave at the end of April,' he said. 'I have no use for you. You are not a practical man, Burns. You have all these fanciful notions about the benevolent management of slaves, and you do not seem to understand that the world simply does not work that way.'

'I shall be very glad to leave,' I said. 'If you continue as you are doing, then within six months this plantation will rise up. You will be torn to pieces, and my only regret is that I shall not be here to applaud.'

He narrowed his eyes. 'So you support rebellion, do you? I must make a note of *that*.'

'I do not support rebellion,' I said. 'All I am saying is that *your conduct* is rendering it an inevitability rather than a possibility.'

'I do what I have to do,' he said. 'Now get out.'

As soon as I returned here, I sat down with Yinta and tried to explain that we would have to leave soon. I told her that Jennings is *'wakhaia'* – wicked – and that he could harm us. She has understood most of what I had to say, I think. Now that I am responsible for Yinta as well as our unborn child I must be sure that I do nothing to jeopardise our safe departure.

April 3rd. I am even more uneasy now than before. I keep away from Jennings, and he carefully avoids me – all for the best. Forsyth knows what is going on between us, and he understands my concerns. He took me to one side today at about two o'clock and told me something that made me feel very anxious indeed, and actually fearful.

'Did you know that Jennings has been in your quarters?'

'When was this?' I asked.

'About an hour ago. You were at the mill, and Yinta was in the kitchen with Thomas. I saw him go in, and he stayed there for ten minutes or so. He didn't think he had been observed.'

'What would he want in my quarters?'

'You keep a diary, don't you?' he said.

'You know I do.'

'Aye, well, I hope you keep it under lock and key. A man's diary is his own business.'

I hastened back to find this volume lying open on the table. I could have sworn that it had been in its box when I left. My legs felt weak, and I had to sit down. The only person other than myself who has been permitted to read my journal was Mary. I have written *everything* here – all my foolish musings; my scurrilous little observations; my poems; the most delicate details of my private life; my impressions of people – *everything!* The last person on earth I would want to be reading it would be Jennings! I have no proof that he has done any such thing, but I must assume the worst – he is a sly weasel, well able to take harmless facts and place the worst possible construction on them. I can only console myself with the thought that in a little over three weeks we shall be gone, and his malice will no longer be able to touch us. I am tempted to leave before then – he will not expect me to do so before my wages are paid. We could go on the twenty-fourth, which is the Sabbath, for there is plenty of traffic across the Demerary.

It is the uncertainty – did he read the journal or not? – if so, which pages? Surely he would not have been able to glean much in ten minutes? I am sickened just by the fact that he may have *touched* the page on which I am writing – this journal is *mine* – it is my *life* – I want no bastard like Jennings anywhere near it!

April 20th. Huge consternation on the plantation, and for a time all work suspended. A veritable flotilla of ships lies at anchor at the mouth of the Demerary, and they are flying British colours! There was much excited talk among the slaves, several vociferously expressing the opinion that the ships had come to emancipate them. This is dangerous talk, and we had to exercise all of our powers of persuasion in calming them down, promising that when we had exact intelligence, we would inform them fully. There has been no word by this evening, and we shall have to wait and see what tomorrow brings. None of us knows what to make of this.

April 21st. Still no word, only silly rumours. Thomas has been at the rum, and when he brought in our dinner, it was not worth the eating. As if that were not enough he proceeded to deliver a solemn lecture on the subject of the ships, saying that King George was on board in person, together with Mr Wilberforce, and that liberation was at hand. MacDuff got up with a curse and kicked the foolish fellow out of the door. I went down to the koker earlier with a glass, and was able to make out some sort of activity. There are ten ships: four of them frigates, and six smaller vessels. They were attempting to land, but had misjudged the tide, and at least one ship was stuck fast in the mud. A number of small oarboats were plying between the frigates and the shore. If this is a military operation then it does not appear to be enjoying an auspicious start. The Dutch could have blown them out of the water, or raked them with musket-fire, but nothing of the kind appeared to be happening, as far as I could see.

[*Later*] We have heard from Mr Bos that it is indeed an English frigate, *Zebra*, which lies here at anchor. He came here today with remarkable news. Admiral Caldwell has brought a circular from the Prince of Orange, denouncing the edict of the States-General, and proclaiming that Britain is willing to protect the colony against attack from a perfidious and predatory Gaul! Caldwell has promised to bring 600 troops from Barbados to form a garrison. Van Grovestins now considers his position to be untenable, for as a firm supporter of the Prince he is embarrassed to have proclaimed himself so hastily an ally of the French. He has gone on board *Zebra*, which is due to set sail for Martinique within a few hours.

'Who is governor now?' asked Forsyth.

'Who knows? Van Well is in command of the militia: that is all I can gather. The Court is hopelessly divided. Dr Beaujon would be my obvious choice for governor, but he has declined to take up office.[1] Some of the Court have taken to wearing a tricolore cockade, others are wearing orange, and no one can agree about anything. Stabroek is a madhouse.'

'Which way will it go?' I asked.

He shrugged. 'My hope lies with the British, and not just because we live together amicably here. Sooner or later Britain will go to war

with this Batavian Republic, and I prefer to be on the winning side.[2]
France is overstretched, and she will lose in the end.'

April 23rd. What a life we lead – *semper mutabilis* – now up, now down!
The colony has been taken by the English! The capitulation was
obtained without a drop of blood being shed. Yesterday I was on
Dutch soil – today, without stirring from the spot, I am in one of His
Majesty's colonies! The fleet is under the command of Commodore
Parr, and he has with him a corps of some 1300 men under
Lieutenant-Colonels Tilson, Hislop and Gammell.

A hastily published broadsheet was handed out to all of the
plantations late today, describing how Sir Ralph Abercrombie and
General White went to the Court of Policy to request the surrender
of the colony and were courteously and graciously received. Dr
Beaujon offered to tender his resignation but this was not consid-
ered necessary. Rumour has it that Stabroek is to be renamed, and
Georgetown would appear to be the most likely choice. There is an
absolute guarantee of the security of personal liberty, and the free
exercise of religious worship. No one will lose private property
unless he be French. All Dutch citizens shall enjoy the same rights
and privileges as other British subjects in the West Indies; the militia
shall swear allegiance to King George, and be paid by the British
authorities. Even the civil officials are at liberty to retain their
appointments if they wish.

This is all very sudden and confusing, and I hope that Mr Bos will
come soon and tell us more – of course, as a member of the Court
he will no doubt have much to do over the next few days.

The first thought that flew into my mind was that I should now be
in a more advantageous position to obtain a passage home to Scotland.
It is now five years since that terrible business with McLehose, and
when Hamilton last wrote, he knew of no reason not to return. Surely
the matter must have been forgotten by now.

April 23rd. Jennings is off to Stabroek today on some business or other.
It is a relief to have him out of the way.

April 24th. Mr Bos sought me out early today while I was down at
the koker, waiting for a boat to take me across the river. For once he
was not smiling: he appeared agitated, and drew me to one side,
saying that he had something important to tell me. I thought he was
about to describe the arrival of the English, but I quickly realised that
he had come on more personal business.

'*Het is slecht nieuws,*' he said. 'Bad news. Your Mr Jennings has been very busy. We have received a petition from him which concerns you.'

A cold grue grasped my stomach.

'A petition?' I said. 'To what effect?'

He looked at the ground in embarrassment. 'You know that since the colony capitulated to the British, the Court now recognises and acknowledges the sovereignty of King George. Mr Jennings claims to have evidence that you killed a man in Jamaica some years ago, and has asked the Court to undertake proceedings against you. He is asking that you be turned over to Lieutenant-Colonel Hislop and placed under military arrest as a fugitive. If his petition is successful, you would be returned to Jamaica to face trial. There is also mention of sedition. *Ik ben droevig.*'

A blackness of spirit settled on my heart like a funeral shroud.

'I killed a man in a duel,' I said wearily. 'And as for sedition, all I've ever done is to treat Negroes fairly. It's all a conspiracy against me.'

'I never thought you the criminal type, Burns,' he said. 'I would not be speaking to you otherwise. But it is a bad business.'

'What can I do? Surely I have the right to speak in my defence?'

He shrugged. 'The Court of Policy is not a court of law. You know that. You also know that you cannot be tried under Dutch law for an offence committed outside our jurisdiction. All we are being petitioned to do is to hand you over to the British authorities. It will be argued that your defence will be best heard in the High Court in Kingston. Of course, if the matter of sedition is pursued, you could be arraigned here. It's a more serious charge.'

'When will the petition be heard?'

'At our next meeting in six days' time. I've brought you a copy.' He handed me a slip of paper that I took as if it was my death warrant. I already felt the cold manacles on my wrists. The thought of being transported in chains to Jamaica on a capital charge numbed me, as did the prospect of being flung into the stinking jail in Stabroek, and facing the gallows for encouraging the slaves to revolt.

'I ought not to be speaking to you at all, Burns,' he said. 'The proceedings of the Court are confidential and I have no right to be telling you any of this. I could even be imprisoned for divulging the contents of the petition to you. But you have been a good friend, and you can count on me to speak out on your behalf next week.'

'But what if the petition is granted?' I said. 'What on earth can I do?'

'You will have to leave the colonies. You could cross the Courantyne – you would be beyond the reach of British law there.

I will render any assistance I can, but my own position is a delicate one, as you will appreciate.'

'I realise that,' I said. 'Thank you for telling me this. I am much beholden to you.'

He patted my arm. 'There's always hope. In the meantime I suggest you make preparations against an unfavourable outcome, for there will be very little time to lose if the petition is granted. If it goes against you, I will arrange to have word sent to you about the result. Obviously I would be unable to bring it in person.'

'I understand.'

'I hope I shall meet you again, Burns,' he said, taking my hand in his. 'But if the fates decree that this is to be our last meeting, then allow me to say that it has been a pleasure to know you, and that I wish you well. *Vaarwel*, Mr Burns.'

'*Vaarwel*, Mr Bos,' I said, and we parted.

I returned to my hut in a leaden despond. The petition describes me not only as a common murderer fleeing from justice, but states that I am over-familiar with the slaves, and habitually engage in seditious debate with them, with a view to inciting rebellion. Even if the Court were inclined to leniency in the matter of McLehose, the second charge alone would be enough to send me to the gallows. Taken together they are utterly damning. I need time to think. At all costs I must not let Jennings know that I am aware of his machinations. I have sent word that I am suffering from a bad bout of malaria, and unable to fulfil my duties for a day or two. I have to leave here very soon, for I know there's little possibility that the Court of Policy will find in my favour. I have decided that the only persons I can take into my confidence are Yinta and Ambrose. Much as I esteem Forsyth, I cannot speak to him, because I desire him to be absolutely innocent about the circumstances of my departure. As for Ambrose, he will take refuge as ever behind his *façade* of Creole *naïveté*. Wherever I go, Yinta will be with me.

[*Later*] Jennings came round to see me, the damned hypocrite. I barely had time to conceal this journal before he entered, all seeming solicitude and concern, with his gingery face set in an expression which was, for him, as close as possible to pleasant. Given the turbulence of my emotions, it was not difficult to feign illness.

'I'm sorry to hear that you are indisposed, Mr Burns. Is there anything I can do for you?' He stood there smiling pleasantly, for all the world the very image of the caring employer. I could have risen from my seat and strangled him on the spot.

'I trust I shall be better in a day or two,' I said.

'Of course, of course,' he agreed, no doubt inwardly relishing the coming pleasure of seeing Hislop's men dragging me away in irons. 'Take your time, Mr Burns. We're not too hard pressed at the moment, and your health is the important thing, eh?

'Yes. Thank you very much, Mr Jennings.'

'Not at all, not at all. We've had our differences, Mr Burns, but I wouldn't wish you to think of me as an unreasonable man. If there's anything I can do to assist with your recuperation, you only have to ask.'

'Thank you, Mr Jennings. There is one thing – I have some plantation matters to discuss with Ambrose. Could you have him sent to me?' I fancy I saw a flicker of annoyance cross his face, but he rapidly controlled it.

'Of course. I do appreciate the way in which you place your duties first, Mr Burns. I shall have him sent here directly. Now I shall say good night.' He gave a bow and withdrew. A few minutes later Ambrose came in and stood rather awkwardly in the doorway.

'Yessuh?' he said.

'I need to speak with you, Ambrose.'

'Speak wid me, Massah Burns? What yah want, suh?'

I was surprised. Ambrose put a finger to his lips and crossed to my desk, where he picked up my quill and scribbled a few words on a scrap of paper, which he handed to me. It said: *Jennings is downstairs listening.* I nodded at him.

'Now Ambrose,' I said. 'I want you to stand guard in the still house tonight. Someone's been helping themselves, and we can't have that. Come tomorrow and let me know what you find.'

'Yessuh,' he said, with a grin. 'If dere be a tief, I catch he, suh.'

'Very good Ambrose,' I said, smiling in return. 'That will be all.'

'Yessuh,' he said, and went out. From the window I watched his burly figure hurrying away through the bushes without a backward glance. I remained where I was, and in a few moments I saw Jennings come out from under my hut, and walk silently in the direction of his own. I see that I shall have to conduct my affairs with the utmost circumspection. First I am traduced, and now I am spied upon!

April 26th. I have told Ambrose of my predicament. He listened in silence, shaking his head occasionally.

'It is a wretched business,' he said. 'I wish that I could be more hopeful, but we have to face facts. The references to rebellion are sufficient to condemn you: the authorities dare not ignore them.'

'I will not be taken back to Jamaica,' I told him.

'Of course not. This leaves us with the question of how you are to escape to a place of safety, and where such a place may be. I take it Yinta will be going with you?'

'Yes, she will. I haven't broached the subject with her as yet. Mr Bos suggested crossing the Courantyne, where the British have no jurisdiction.'

'Not a good idea,' said Ambrose. 'It's not far, but how would you get there? You could cross the Demerary and head east overland through Berbice, but you'd have to get over the river on your own, and that would be a problem. Even if you did, where would you go? It's just forest. The other way would be to go to Stabroek and then head down the coast road to New Amsterdam – you could be taken across there. But you'd be seen. How much money do you have?'

'I have sufficient. There is also four months' salary owing to me. But . . .'

'But you can hardly go to Jennings and ask for it without arousing suspicion.'

'No. So what alternatives are left?'

'Little Venice is impossible: it's a Spanish colony.[3] There's Trinidad, but again you would have to go into Stabroek to arrange a passage, and that would be very dangerous indeed. No, your best hope – your only hope – is to make your way into the interior here.'

'But there's nothing in the interior but the great woods.'

'Not at all. You know very well that there are many tribes of Indians there: where do you think Yinta came from? You have some smattering of the language, and of course you would have Yinta with you.'

'Hislop would send out troops to find me.'

'Perhaps. But he has many other concerns, and the costs of mounting an expeditionary force are considerable. Let me think for a moment.' He rested his head in his hands, and sat immobile while I stood up and paced restlessly to and fro. I confess that I had concluded my situation was hopeless.

'Listen to me,' said Ambrose slowly, lifting his head at last. 'If you and Yinta simply disappear into the forest, or head off up-river, then you are right: there is a risk that you will be pursued. In fact if the two of you disappear together, then it is certain to arouse suspicion, and to increase the likelihood that Hislop will come after you. But there is one way in which you can leave without any danger of being followed.'

'What is that?'

'By taking your own life,' he said. 'Then there will be no talk of escape, and no need for pursuit.' I stared at him in bafflement.

'Are you seriously suggesting that I commit suicide?'

'Certainly not. But you must give the appearance of having done so. You will write a letter, and leave it in your room, saying that you have heard of the action being taken against you, and that you have decided to do away with yourself rather than face the disgrace and humiliation of capture. It will be easy to leave some of your clothes on the bank of the river, and the only possible conclusion will be that you drowned yourself. In the meantime you only need to conceal yourself in the woods some distance away. Yinta will play the grieving widow for a day or two, and then announce her intention of going back to her people. After all, there will be nothing for her here. She will join you, and you can escape together.'

'You're a marvel, Ambrose!' I exclaimed. 'I could never have conceived such a strategy.'

'We'll have to plan the details carefully,' he said. 'When it's time to make your move, you'll have to behave in a way that will lend credence to the suicide theory. You should feign drunkenness, and announce your intention of going down to the Demarary to ponder some weighty matter. Make sure that plenty of people see you. I can easily arrange for word to be sent that someone has been seen struggling in the water. A search will be mounted and your clothes will be found. The letter will then be discovered.'

We spent the best part of an hour refining the scheme, which I am now convinced is the only one which offers a way forward. I then continued with my duties, with my head in a spin, and the first stirrings of hope in my heart.

On my return home I took the earliest opportunity of taking Yinta into my confidence. I sat her down, and explained that I had something important to tell her.

'*B'kanaba, bébe,*' I said. 'We shall have to go away together in the next few days.'

'*Haloñ?*'

'*Yaharia,*' I told her. 'Away from here. Into the forest – *orako konoko.*'

'*Hamadoma?*' she asked in puzzlement. 'Why we go *konoko?*'

I explained the situation as well as I could, and between my elementary Arawak and her improving English, we eventually managed to come to an understanding of what would need to be done. I impressed upon her the need to talk of the matter to no one except Ambrose, and to behave as normally as possible.

April 28th. I have used my leisure time as a supposed invalid to compose a poem for Ambrose. He has been a staunch ally, and I am conscious that I have nothing to leave him when I go. The words have been in my mind for some time, for they had originally been conceived in response to the death of Charles Edward Stuart, but set to one side in favour of a Scots verse. Looking at their sentiments I believe they apply equally well to Ambrose, and possibly even to myself! We are all exiles. It took only a few hours to set the words down:

Illustrious Exile

Illustrious exile on a foreign strand,
Bereft of honour or acclaim;
No refuge from his dark despair:
As one who should taste freedom fair
Is ground to servitude and shame –
A wretched menial in a foreign land.

Far distant are the fond and faithful few
Who would his anguish'd sorrows share
As, languishing, he weeps alone,
No homeland dear to call his own.
Oppressed by memories and care,
Each dawn brings miseries anew.

Fools' tongues may prate of glories vast
In commerce where the white men thrive:
Yet here, beneath an alien sky
He hears his suffering children cry
And prays that they, at least, survive
To hear the shout of 'Free at last!'

When he came round late this afternoon, I handed these verses to him, saying that they were intended as my parting gift, and he read them over with great care. As he did so, tears welled up in the corners on his eyes; then, putting the sheet to one side, he advanced towards me and embraced me firmly, patting me on the back as he did so.

'It is beautiful, Robert,' he said, 'truly beautiful. I shall always treasure these lines.'

'They will give you something to remember me by, at any rate,' I said, moved by the warmth of his response.

'Remember you?' he said. 'Do you imagine that I could ever forget you? You and Forsyth are the only white men who have ever treated me as a human being, and you are the only one who could have given utterance to thoughts such as these. Little do you know how well you have hit the mark. No, that is unfair – I'm sure that you did know. Ah, Robert! What can I say?'

'I am glad to have pleased you, Ambrose.'

'That is hardly the word,' he replied. 'These give me more than pleasure; they give me hope. If one white man can write such things and mean them, then perhaps one day . . .'

'One day,' I said.

He embraced me again; took up the paper, and folded it with the greatest of care before placing it inside his shirt. We sat for a time in silence. It was drawing towards twilight, and in the distance we could hear the singing of the men coming back from the cane. Bats flitted among the trees, and everything was bathed in the golden, gentle light that I love so much at this time of day. It was a moment of enormous tranquillity and great sadness. I shall miss him. As it grew dark I returned home, and carefully dug up my bag of rix-dollars. Everything is in readiness.

April 30th. I'm sitting down to write out of sheer habit, but my head is filled with nothing except that damned petition and what it means. I am cursing myself for being such a fool – I could have taken Yinta and gone to Stabroek last week – why did I not do so? Mr Bos said that the petition would be heard in six days' time, so by my reckoning, it will be considered today. Perhaps they are debating my fate even as I write? Surely I will hear from Mr Bos soon!

May 2nd. Still no word from Mr Bos. I can only think that the six days did not include the Sabbath – either that, or he has somehow been prevented from informing me of the outcome. What if our friendship has been discovered, and he has been thrown in jail? Hislop's men might be on their way at this very moment! I am very nervous indeed – I am inclined to flee into the forest, though I realise that flight would be a sure admission of guilt. I must force myself to be patient until I hear news, and then no time must be lost in putting Ambrose's plan into action.

May 3rd. A death sentence on the luckless Robert Burns, guiltless of any crime save stupidity! I have received an envelope that contained the following lines, hastily scrawled in Bos's spidery handwriting on a blank page evidently torn from a ledger:

'Read a Petition of Henry Jennings, planter of Goed Intent, Demerary, agent of Lord Balcarres, begging that the Secretary might be empowered to instruct the authorities to hand over Robert Burns of the same plantation to the custodianship of

Lieutenant-Colonel Hislop, military commander of these colo-
nies, in the light of evidence annexed to this Petition in the matter
of a charge of murder of James McLehose at Port Antonio,
Jamaica, in 1791, a warrant for his arrest remaining in force, and
in addition on the grounds that the aforesaid Robert Burns
habitually engages in seditious debate with the slaves on the said
plantation with the intention of inciting them to indiscipline and
rebellion. Resolved that the following answer be returned to this
Petition. The Court doth authorise the Secretary to the effect
requested in the Petition.'

To this had been added: *Tuesday. Hislop is in Berbice, but will return
tomorrow or the next day. Save yourself. Goed fortuin, mijn vriend.*

It is now time to put my plan into action. Tomorrow shall be my
last day on earth so far as the jackal Jennings is concerned! Yinta
knows what to do, and I know I can rely on Ambrose absolutely. I
have cleared out a great bundle of my rough scribblings and jottings
and made a bonfire of them, as I do not care to think of Jennings
picking through them in search of evidence of sedition. I have
packed a few essentials in a small canvas bag – an ink bottle, some
powdered ink, a few quills, my penknife, a tinderbox, and of course
my rix-dollars – also my almanac, so I can keep a tally of the days.

May 4th. In the forest, around noon. A curious sensation, being a dead
man. It will be tomorrow or the next day before Ambrose comes, and
in the meantime I have leisure aplenty in which to reflect on all that
has happened. Indeed it seems incredible to find myself here, on the
other side of the Rubicon, when only a few hours ago I was in my own
house. At any rate, I must set down my account of the day.

I awoke early this morning and penned a short letter, explaining
that I had learned that proceedings of a legal nature had been instituted
against me, and that I could not face the prospect of deportation. In
consequence I had decided to terminate my miserable existence by
throwing myself into the Demerary. I concluded by expressing the
hope that Yinta would be taken care of.

Having set the letter down on my writing table, I took a mouthful
of rum and poured the rest liberally over my clothes. Taking up my
bag and my journals in their box, I then went out, affecting a
drunken lurch, and clutching at my forehead, giving a very good
impression of a man in the throes of the most abject misery
imaginable. MacDuff was by the cookhouse, and when he saw me,
he came over to enquire what the matter was.

'Man, ye've had a few drams, I see. Whit's the matter wi' ye?'

'Nothing,' I said. 'I just need to be on my ain, damn it. I hae tae think. Lea' me alane, for Christ's sake.'

'It canna be that bad, laddie,' he said. 'Ye can tell me aboot it.' It was the first time I had ever known the man to express any form of solicitude towards anyone, and I was oddly touched by his approach, although of course this was no time to show it.

'No,' I said roughly, shaking my head, and moving away. 'Lea' me alane. I'm goin' doon tae the river.'

'Please yersel',' he shrugged. 'Mind ye dinna fa' in.' He nodded towards my box. 'Whit's that?'

'Never min',' I snapped, and staggered off. I encountered at least three or four weeding parties along the quarter mile to the river. They greeted me in their usual friendly way, and I took pains to ignore them, feeling their eyes on me as I passed, and hearing their expressions of surprise and conjecture as I continued in my unsteady progress. When I got to the dam, I looked around carefully to see if I had been followed before making my way to the spot where I had arranged to meet Ambrose. I found him waiting where we had agreed.

'Well?' he enquired anxiously.

I explained that everything had gone as planned, and quickly stripped off my shirt and breeches, donning the stiff cotton slave garments which he gave me.

'We must be quick,' he said. 'Put your clothes on the bank here. I'm going to find someone to act as a witness. When you hear me call your name, give a shout, and heave that log into the river. Then hide in the bushes there. Leave the rest to me. When we've gone, make your way upstream along the riverbank. You won't need to go far, but be careful not to leave any tracks. Here's a cutlass. Don't use it at first – it will be obvious that someone has been that way if you do. I've brought everything that you will need, and there's food enough for a day or two, until I can bring Yinta to you. Are you ready?'

'Yes.'

'Very well.'

He turned and slipped away. I placed my clothes on the river-bank, and made ready with the log, which was about four feet long and as thick as my thigh. After about ten minutes there came the sound of people approaching, and I heard him in conversation close by.

'Yah say Massa Burns come by here?' he was saying.

'Yeah, man. He look bad. De rum mek he walk funny.' I could not identify the speaker, but I assume he was a member of one of the weeding parties I had passed earlier.

'I wonder where he go?' said Ambrose. Then, raising his voice, he called out: 'Massa Burns! Massa Burns! Yah there, Massa?'

This was my cue, and, lifting the log like a caber, I hefted it into the Demerary, simultaneously giving a cry of exertion. There was a mighty splash, and I scuttled away into the bushes, from where I could peer out and see my bundle of clothes lying on the bank.

'What's dat, man?' I heard Ambrose exclaim. There was a crashing sound as the two men burst through the undergrowth.

'I don' see nuttin' . . . hey, wait, man! Dere's some clothes on de bank!' I could see now that the other man was George, an amiable old soul.

'Clothes? What clothes?' shouted Ambrose, deliberately starting out in the wrong direction.

'Not dere! Over here! Yah blin', man?'

'Dem be Massa Burns' clothes,' said Ambrose. 'He t'row heself in de water fuh sho'!'

'Oh Lord, Oh Lord,' wailed George in distress. 'Wha' we gonna do, Ambrose?'

'I dunno. We bes' go git Massa Forsyth an' de odders. Come on, man.'

They ran off, and I waited for a few moments. Taking up my box, the bundle and the cutlass, I made for the track that Ambrose had described. I took pains not to use the cutlass at first, ducking as well as I could around branches and creepers, and taking care to return the undergrowth to its former position behind me. After about half an hour of this I was able to use the cutlass to make quicker progress, and before long I had located a place to set up camp. It was situated well back from the river, so there was no risk of being seen by anyone passing in a boat.

I sat for a while, enjoying a curious sense of lightness and freedom. Here I was, a dead man, yet more alive in that moment, I think, than I have ever been. I have no idea what privations lie ahead, and I little care.

May 6th. A day of solitude and reflection – the first time for many years that I have been truly on my own, and at complete *liberty*. In a sense, I have been emancipated: the miserable shackles of my previous life have been cast aside and I am *free at last!* I was once a slave of sorts, labouring early and late to feed the rapacity of titled knaves and fat merchants, now I am a man again. Towns are raised; ships are built; the land is tilled; the cane is cut; slaves are bought and sold; everywhere is a sweaty scene of frantic industry and struggle –

but to what end? Human dignity and happiness are not advanced; decency and honesty are trodden scornfully beneath the selfish heel of commerce, and the good men who toil in obscurity – on whom all of this prosperity depends! – are valued at nothing, and can look to no comfort other than that which lies beyond the grave! Does the toper, besotted with rum, ever pause in his bibulous excesses to wonder, in his maudlin way, how many men toiled and died so that he could drink himself into oblivion? Does the fine gentleman, carelessly lacing his coffee with sugar as he discusses the latest gossip, ever realise the drudgery and suffering inherent in every spoonful? As for those who profit from all of this commerce – do they pause for one moment in their lives of luxury and opulence to reflect that their prosperity has been purchased in blood? I am ashamed to have been a part of it.

I have been watching the Demerary roll past, indifferent to the foolishness of the world. When Yinta comes we shall strike inland – one day soon we shall find a clearing where I can build a place for us – we shall fish in the river; cultivate a few simple crops; raise our child, and trouble no one – far from these scenes of ignoble strife we too shall keep the noiseless tenor of our ways.[4]

I have made a shelter with some branches and leaves, just sufficient to protect me if it rains. I am hopeful that Ambrose will bring Yinta tomorrow. Then, and only then, will I be able to surrender myself fully to the feeling of utter relief that I have felt today.

May 7th. I heard sounds today at about noon, and took care to conceal myself until I could be certain who was coming. To my relief it was Ambrose, and with him Yinta who ran to embrace me.

'Is everything well with you?' said Ambrose.

'Yes. What is the word at the plantation?'

'Jennings believes that you threw yourself into the river. He has been very irritable about it, for some reason.'

'I can imagine why,' I said. 'He was looking forward to seeing me hanged, and I have denied him the pleasure.'

'Quite so. Forsyth is very upset, and so is McLean. As for my people on the plantation, many of them are inconsolable. You were greatly respected.'

'I wish I could tell them the truth.'

'I know, but that's impossible. Yinta here played her part to perfection. She was with Jennings when he went to examine your clothes on the river bank. What a yelling and screaming! I am sure her performance went a long way towards convincing Jennings that you are indeed a dead man. Afterwards she went back to your quarters and howled all night. This morning she told Forsyth that she was leaving, and she headed into the forest. I met up with her, and here we are.'

'Well done, Ambrose,' I said. 'We could not have done this without you.'

'I have brought you some supplies,' he said, indicating some bundles that he had brought with him. 'There is food, and some other necessities that will come in useful.'

'I do not know how to thank you.'

He smiled. 'You do not need to thank me. Now I must be on my way back – my absence will be commented on otherwise.'

'I am sorry that I am abandoning you to Jennings,' I said.

'I shall deal with Jennings.' He uttered these words in a very careless tone, as a man might speak of removing some trifling obstacle from his path, and there was a look in his eyes almost of amusement. It set me to thinking of the events of last year and that strange business of the 'wanga'.

'Tell me something, Ambrose,' I said. 'What really did happen to Allardyce?'

He looked at me for a moment. 'Do you know what a 'hungan' is?'

'I've no idea,' I said. 'I've never heard the word before. What is it?'

He thought for a long time, and finally shook his head. 'You do not need to know. It is better that you do not. As Hamlet said, "There are more things in heaven and earth . . ." you know the quotation well enough. And as Mr Pope so perspicaciously pointed out, "A little knowledge is a dangerous thing". Now I must leave you both. I shall think of you every day.'

He embraced Yinta wordlessly, then turned to me. For a moment we looked at each other, knowing that we would never meet again. I could have wept bitterly at that moment, and so, I suspect, could he.

'Goodbye then, Robert,' he said finally, extending his hand.

'Goodbye, Ambrose,' I said, seizing it and gripping it tightly. I made to say more, but he shook his head and smiled sadly.

'I know,' he said gently. 'We both know.'

He went off, and was quickly lost to our sight. We took up our belongings and headed up the riverbank. There are a few settlements hereabouts, and we took pains to avoid being seen. Yinta would not have attracted any attention on her own, but a white man would have occasioned comment, and that would have been dangerous in the extreme. For several hours we made good progress, always keeping close to the river on our left. It is now the middle of the day, and I am writing this in the knowledge that I may not have the leisure to do so later.

May 8th. Yesterday as light began to fade, we came to a spot where a wide creek joins the Demerary. Unable to cross over, we turned to our right and followed the path upstream. As it grew dark, we saw a native village ahead. In what remained of the light, I strung up our hammocks in a little clearing while Yinta went off, returning after a short time with some cassava bread. We ate our meagre supper in darkness, and clambered into our hammocks, where, greatly to my surprise, I enjoyed the soundest sleep I have had for many a day.

This evening we have encamped by the creek again. We shall not seek to cross it after all, but continue on our present heading until we reach the Essequibo, of which I have often heard, but never seen.

We are crossing a flat plain where great woods alternate with wide savanna, much of it so damnably swampy that we are obliged to make lengthy detours that hinder our progress. Yinta has a natural eye for the lie of the land, and without her as a guide we would have made poor progress. At the last village she obtained a good supply of provisions, and we keep our calabashes filled with rainwater that collects in the concave leaves of a certain type of palm tree, where they meet the trunk. She is a strong lass, and carries her share of our baggage without complaint. Assuredly she is as much in her element here as I am out it.

May 9th. Good progress today, and no problems except that the sun has burned my cheekbones and my nose. Yinta has concocted a kind of paste that she has smeared liberally over my tender proboscis, and by her gestures indicates that I present a very comical spectacle.

May 10th. The Essequibo at last! We came out on to its banks at about midday. At first I thought it to be about the same size as the Demerary, but what I took for the opposite shore proves to be an island, and so I reckon its true width to be several miles. I have asked Yinta where we are going, and she says that we must head upstream to the point opposite the confluence of the Massaruny and the Essequibo, and cross over in order to ascend that tributary. For this we shall have to procure a *kanoa* and a boatman, which we should be able to do easily as I have my bag of rix-dollars.

It is too late to travel any further today, so we have made ourselves comfortable here by the river's edge and have enjoyed the last of the food we brought with us.

May 11th. We are finally safe on shore after a crossing that was long and difficult. We were able to persuade a boatman to ferry us across in a *koriaka*, which is a vessel with high sides, able to withstand rough water. Seeing my white skin, he immediately demanded six rix-dollars for himself and his two crew members, and although I suspect that this was excessive, I had little option but to pay him what he asked. We sat in the middle of the boat with our belongings, and set off into a vast expanse of water. The river flows swiftly so we could not paddle directly across to the other shore – instead the crew had to paddle the boat upstream. Any failure to maintain progress would have resulted in our being carried helplessly down the river and lost forever. Above us, in a massive sky that arched from horizon to horizon, we saw great looming clouds sweeping towards us. We could see the dark threads of rain falling from them, coming ever closer and resembling a wall of dense mist as it neared us. First there were a few heavy raindrops, then more and more, until very quickly it was a thorough-going downpour that drenched us to the skin. The boatmen knew their craft, for they continued to paddle and adjust their course, even though it was impossible to see more than a yard or two ahead. When the rain finally cleared, we were measurably closer to shore, and still on course for the settlement towards which we were headed. It was a journey that might have been exhilarating had it not been so dangerous and uncomfortable.

We are in the town of Bartica, a busy little trading post where, it is said, one can find everything necessary for a journey into the interior. It is not a pretty place, comprising a maze of untidy wooden shacks around a large stelling, and there is great bustle everywhere. No one gave us a second glance when we arrived, and I assume that they must be accustomed to seeing European faces. We sought out a place to stay, and found a room in the upper floor of a rum shop where we were able to change our clothes and take some rest. It is dirty and noisy, but at least we have our privacy.

Later we went out and bought some bread, mangoes and salt fish, returning here to enjoy a very pleasant supper. After that we walked around the town, such as it is, and saw that almost every building in it was a shop of some kind – here we can buy all that we require for our journey. This will have to wait until tomorrow.

May 12th. Bartica. Today we have been employed in gathering together provisions and supplies for at least a week, and we have brought these back to our room here. We have also obtained the services of two men with a large *kanoa*, and they have contracted to take us up the Massaruny to a place called Issano where they assure us there is a trading post. We have settled on a price of two rix-dollars per day, and a further five payable in advance for their own provisions and supplies.

We set out tomorrow at first light. As I write, it is about five o'clock in the afternoon, to judge from the light, and I am looking out over the stelling and the river. Yinta is asleep, and I want her to rest as much as possible. I do not know how frequently I shall be able to write in this journal during the days to come. I was able to obtain more ink powder today and I have a few quills on hand, but my main fear is that water may get into the box in which I keep these journals, and I shall only be able to write when my surroundings are perfectly dry.

May 13th. Our first day's journey was without incident. We loaded the *kanoa* and set out early, holding close to the left bank and entering the mouth of the Massaruny. This river, though still very wide, is considerably narrower than the Essequibo. The *kanoa* sits very low in the water, and at first I was fearful that we would be swamped by the slightest motion of the boat, but I was reassured by Yinta that this was unlikely to happen. It is much smaller and faster than the *koriaka* and our two boatmen are both powerful men, so we made excellent progress. In the middle of the afternoon we were able to make out an island in the far distance with some ruins standing on it – this is Kyk-over-al,[5] an ancient Dutch stronghold that was once, I believe, the seat of the Commandeur of Essequibo. All day we had been keeping close to the left bank, but now the boatmen headed across the open river towards the little settlement where I am writing this. It is called Skull Point – Yinta says it gained its gloomy name because there are dangerous rapids further up the Massaruny, and many poor souls have perished while attempting to negotiate them. Because of the flow of the current, the bodies of the drowned usually fetch up here.

The people of the settlement are Arawak natives, and Yinta can converse with them very freely, and at such a rate that I cannot make out more than one word in twenty! She has paid them a token sum and in exchange we have been given some food and shown to a rough sort of benab where we have been able to set up our hammocks. I am making haste to write this before darkness falls. I have done nothing today but sit in a boat, yet I am very tired: I expect it has to do with travelling on the water.

May 14th. This morning when I awoke there was a dense mist, so that I could hardly see to the other side of the benab. For the first time since I arrived in Demerary, it almost felt cold! I arose and went down to the river where we had dragged the *kanoa* high on the sandy bank. There is a stelling here, which projects some way out into the river, but I could see little of it, although a general lightening of the sky overhead showed that the sun had risen.

I reached the stelling, made my way down to its end, and stood there staring out into a white, ghostly nothingness. In front of me, I knew, stretched the wide expanse of the river, and although I could hear its hiss and ripple as it flowed though the supporting timbers of the stelling, I could see nothing of it at all. But the day grew brighter and the sun began to show as a small white disc low on the horizon. Overhead the white gradually gave way to blue – soon I could see the tops of the trees on the far bank – and it seemed as though the water was covered with a white, downy mantle – then, in the space of a few moments, *voilà* – it cleared, and there was the Massaruny, broad and magnificent, flowing sedately past in the brilliant sun of early morning!

By the time I returned, everyone else was up, and within an hour we had packed the boat and set off. Skull Point stands at the place where another river, the Cuyuni, joins the Massaruny, and at their junction, just a short distance from shore, is the island of Kyk-over-al that we saw from a distance yesterday. I asked Yinta to order the boatmen to pass close by. It is much smaller that I had imagined it, and almost entirely overgrown. Such buildings as I could see appeared to be in a very ruinous state. For all that, I was fascinated – it is the first stone building I have seen since I came to this colony, and there was something about its silent isolation that struck a chord in my heart, as invariably happens when I contemplate the remains of a once-proud edifice. I could not help but recollect the castle in my dreams – it invoked the same feeling of remoteness and mystery. I would dearly have loved to land, but we had not the time, and besides the undergrowth was so thick that it would have been futile.

We spent the remainder of the day making our way up the Massaruny. The waters are dark brown, almost black, save for where rocks jut above the surface, when a creamy foam is cast up. It is easier and safer to paddle against the current whilst remaining close to the bank, for the river is narrower here and there are many obstacles in the water. Sometimes great logs lurk beneath the surface. I know that if the *kanoa* were to capsize, flinging us into the water, then it would be fatal for us – not only would we lose all our belongings, but even if we made it to the river bank, then we would never be able to find our way out of the forest. On this river our lives are literally in the hands of our boatmen!

Towards mid afternoon we came to the foot of a huge, thundering cascade barring the way forward.[6] At its base was a broad pool that at first sight appeared placid, but was actually in constant and turbulent motion. The boatmen did not venture near it, but pulled in towards the bank, pointing at the pool and saying '*kayamü*' – Yinta tried to explain: I believe the word must mean 'whirlpool', for she made an eloquent mime of a boat swirling round and then being drawn down.

We went ashore and pulled the *kanoa* out of the water. The men lifted it and carried it through a path among the trees and Yinta and I followed with our bundles. We emerged at a point above the falls. The men would have launched the boat and gone on, but I was keen for Yinta to rest. She and I set up a simple camp and made a fire. The *kanoa* men went off with their spears, and soon returned in high spirits with three good-sized fish they had caught in a pool above the falls. We roasted them over the fire, and they made an excellent meal for us all. Now I am completing this day's entry. The sound of the falls shall be our lullaby tonight!

May 22nd. We have been making laborious progress upstream these last fifteen days. It has been a slow business because there are very many islands in the river, some small and some very extensive, and on more than one occasion we have spent hours battling against the current only to find the river impassable, so that we have had to go back and seek out another way. There have been innumerable rapids to negotiate, and each time the *kanoa* has had to be carried around them before we've been able to proceed. The boatmen think that we should reach Issano tomorrow or the next day. I have been taking my turn with the paddle – this has made me so fatigued by the end of each day that once we have established camp I have either been too tired to write or the light has begun to wane, making it impossible.

Although we are travelling through what appears to be a wilderness, we have been passing many little settlements on the banks of the river where trees have been cleared and a little cluster of stilted huts erected, each with its thatch of dry palm leaves. As we went by, little groups of children would rush down to the water's edge, greeting us as we passed. Every day we encountered several little *kanoas*, laden with coconuts or vegetables, so the area is more populous than I would have thought.

By my reckoning Bess is twelve today, and I have been very melancholy at the thought. She is so impossibly far away, and here I am, in the midst of a dark, wild continent where few white men have been – a fugitive from justice! But I have my Yinta, with whom I share an intimate communion that I never thought I would find with a woman. She is my loving wife – she is my dearest companion – she guides my uncertain feet when I leave the boat and step to shore – the touch of her hand and the warmth of her smile lift my spirits when I feel despondent – verily my cup runneth over!

It is late afternoon now; we are in a good-sized village of about forty or fifty souls where we have been given hammocks in which to rest our weary limbs. The womenfolk are busying themselves with pounding cassava root, which they put in long woven baskets they call *matapees*. These are ingeniously constructed so that they can be twisted to drive out the juice, which is unwholesome unless boiled. This squeezed cassava is cooked on heated stones to make bread.

Some naked little children are clustered round the benab as I write, gazing at me in giggling curiosity. A party of men has just returned from fishing with a fine catch – they are small of stature but possessed of a wiry strength and endurance that makes them well adapted to life here in the forest. The living huts and this benab are neatly thatched and of elegant construction, everything bound together with strips of vine that they also use to make their mats and baskets. Many of my countrymen would pity them as unfortunate savages, but what do they lack that we could give them?

May 30th. Issano. We arrived this afternoon, drawing into a rude stelling on the left bank. The river is a mere twenty yards across, and great trees come down to the water's edge. We stepped out and walked up a path into a clearing with many huts. Our arrival quickly attracted the attention of the village children. Soon an elderly man came to greet us, identifying himself as the village captain. Yinta spoke to him, and asked his permission to stay for a few days. As is customary, a few rix-dollars changed hands, and we have been shown to a simple shelter that will be our home meantime. The boatmen have been paid and they are to remain here tonight before setting off downstream tomorrow.

Bartica is a busy metropolis compared with Issano! However there is a store, and a plentiful supply of foodstuffs, all of it brought in from the surrounding region. Items such as cloth, rope, cutlasses, cooking utensils and clothes have to be fetched up from Bartica, and in consequence are both expensive and in short supply. We have been able to procure all that we shall require, but I feel it best to remain here for a few days to rest. It is now plain to see that Yinta is with child, and although she is very strong and healthy, the journey up river has wearied her. As for me, I must present a strange sight indeed, for the sun has burned my face so badly that the skin is peeling off. Yinta, on the other hand, is looking healthier and more beautiful with the passage of each day. The sun has made her skin dark and smooth; her belly swells softly, and she responds to my endless expressions of solicitude with a smile, saying *sakoada bariñ*, signifying that she is perfectly well.

Much of the trade here is barter – fishermen arrive at the stelling with their catch, and leave with great cargoes of plantain and sweet potato without any money changing hands.

We slept a good part of the afternoon – oh, the luxury of a hammock and a roof over our heads! I love to lie with her, stroking her hair and breathing in its mysterious, haunting perfume. When she caresses me, and speaks to me softly in her own language, calling me *bébe* or *lól*, I feel a deeper contentment than I have ever known.

June 1st. Our boatmen have departed. Before they left, they went to the store and, with the rix-marks I had given them, purchased a great volume of goods, loading the *kanoa* until I was fearful it would sink. As they go down river, they will be able to sell their cargo at the little settlements along the way.

In the evening I went to a nearby creek, intending to take a dip in order to wash away the sweat and grime of the day. I had barely entered the water when a group of people came rushing towards me, shouting something I could not understand, but clearly indicating that I should return to the bank immediately. Alarmed by the disturbance, Yinta was on the scene in a few moments. They spoke to her very animatedly for some time. It appears that this part of the creek is the haunt of a creature they call the 'massacuraman', which poses a dreadful danger to anyone foolhardy enough to enter the water.[7] I thought that they were referring to the *pirai*, fish that will attack any living thing with an open wound, being able to detect the scent of blood in the water from a great distance. They attack in great numbers, and possess the horrid reputation of being able to strip a man to the bones in a matter of a minute or two. However the massacuraman is a different being altogether. They say it has a round hairy head and paws with fearful claws that inflict appalling wounds. Not long ago, one of these monsters had seized hold of a woman who was washing her clothes at the water's edge, and dragged her beneath the surface in full view of her shocked companions. What manner of beast it must be, I cannot conjecture. Yinta has implored me not to swim, and I had no hesitation in acceding to her request!

June 5th. Morning. I am impatient to be moving on. We have packed everything into two bundles, and I have used some of our rope to fashion packs we can carry on our backs, leaving our hands free so that we can use our cutlasses if required. There is a good track that will take us south; we have all the provisions we require, so there is nothing to be gained by remaining here. We went to the captain and thanked him for his hospitality.

June 6th. In the deep forest, late afternoon. The prevailing impression is of a hot, lush green, in a variety of emerald shades that no artist could ever hope to capture on canvas. Shoots, vines, shrubs, bushes and palms – all are tangled in a dense, twisted, matted profusion. Out of all of this, the vast tree-trunks, hung with dangling creepers like thick ropes, rear up to the leafy canopy a hundred feet above, which greatly diminishes the light, so that one finds oneself in a steamy gloaming, cut through with sharp swathes of brilliant light where there is an opening in the foliage overhead. Here and there a tree has fallen, and the rotting trunk is covered with giant fungi.

I had imagined that the forest would be full of wild animals, as described so prettily in storybooks, but if it is so, then they take care to remain invisible. All manner of insects creak, hiss, chatter and buzz, and there are sounds which I assume to be bird-calls, though unlike any I have ever heard before – some shrill; some like the screech of metal on metal; one which utters a high piercing whistle with a questioning inflexion at the end, and of course the kiss-ka-dee, with which I am already familiar. The mosquitoes are a regular plague, and there is a very large kind of marabunta here, with a body the colour of polished amber.

The *smell* is hard to describe. It is entirely pervasive; there is no escaping it. I remember once being in a hot-house on a fine day, and the smell was similar – a clammy, humid scent in which growth and decay were curiously mingled – the soprano scent of vigorous green shoots, and behind it lurking the *basso profundo* essence of the warm, dark soil, redolent with rotten leaves and stagnant water. It is at its most intense after rain when the fierce sun generates a sultry, torrid incense from the living vegetation as it springs up like a phoenix from the putrefaction of dead growth.

The shade of the trees brings no respite from the heat, and one is soaked with sweat after taking only a few steps, so we have walked slowly and rested often. The track is a good one, but we are probably more tired than we think, so we stopped about an hour ago, and have made camp by the track. We had a supper of cassava bread and dried fish, and spoke about *wa'shikwa* – our house – the one we are going to build when we arrive at our destination, a village to the south of here, where Yinta is known. How incongruous it seems to be writing this account in the midst of such a wilderness!

June 15th. Unable to write these past nine days – it has taken me all my time to keep a tally of them. So many rivers and streams! So many winding paths! Such a profusion of trees and flowers, all outwith my previous experience!

We have come to a little village on the Potaro where we have been given leave to spend the night in the communal benab. I think I'm the first white man who has ever been here, to judge from the way in which the little children crowd around and stare. We've had the promise of a *kanoa* to take us up the river tomorrow. Yinta reminds me of the haven where we can finally unpack our bundles and build a home for ourselves. We should reach it in about ten days, all being well. It cannot come soon enough for me! My feet are sore and I am too tired to write much, but I am relieved to know that our journey will shortly be at an end.

June 17th. Today we entered a great gorge with precipitous sides which soar upwards, thickly clad with vegetation, and with crags and rocky outcrops which would have delighted the heart of Mackenzie[8] could he have but viewed it. The depth of the defile is hard to determine, but from my judgment of the perspectives around me, I would conjecture it to be some six or seven hundred feet. As for breadth, it is not much more than the width of the river which must have fashioned this place over endless aeons, the banks of which begin immediately to slope up to the bases of the cliffs to right and to left. There is a profusion of undergrowth everywhere, and our progress has been difficult. The current is so strong that paddling against it is of little avail, and indeed at times we have been fearful of being swept away. For much of the time we have been obliged to take to the shore and carry the *kanoa*, but this is slow work because of the tributaries that thunder down the slope. Although of no great breadth they contain such a volume of water that it is only with great labour that they can be traversed. There are huge fallen trees, black in colour, which have been carried here by the current, and these are either lodged in the bank, or swept along in the stream, almost completely submerged. I feel small and fragile in such a place. Even the *kanoa* men appear ill at ease. We are constantly plagued by a sort of small black fly of a type I have not met before, but which causes itchy swellings more troublesome than those of mosquitoes. The roaring of the stream, echoing and reverberating from the cliffs on either side, produces an eldritch effect.

Upstream the gorge curves round to the left, and we cannot see what lies ahead, but the men assure us that a great waterfall is only a day's journey away. Indeed it is possible to discern a faint sound, and at times a slight vibration in the ground. As I write, we have made camp, and the light is fading. There is no breeze here, so the heat is quite suffocating and made unendurable by the flies and the mosquitoes, which are everywhere in thick clouds. Our guide has lit a fire and thrown green leaves on it, and this has the effect of driving the wretched insects away, while smoking us like so many haddocks.

As darkness comes, I am gripped with a kind of ghastly, unreasoning horror. I have experienced it before, but never as strongly as this. When I read Swift's *Gulliver's Travels* I thought it very amusing, and keenly observed as a piece of satire, but as the last rays of the sun disappear from the lips of this chasm, I feel like Gulliver in Brobdingnag – dwarfed by the awful scale of the place. I have never felt so fragile and useless. Our little camp is by the water's edge, and I can hear the grindings, rumbles and crashes of boulders being swept past us in the torrent. The sweat pours from me as I write.

The light has gone, but the fire is still alight, and by its miserable flicker I am able to write. It is barely sufficient to illuminate the undergrowth for but a few yards around, and the lower parts of the great trees that surround us. Far above, I know, hang these awesome precipices, and that very knowledge thrills, oppresses and terrifies me. The sounds in the night are rendered all the more fearful for being concealed in utter darkness, echoing with the creaking and twittering of insects as well as the calls of other creatures whose identity I cannot even guess at. God knows, I could not have ventured alone into such a place for all the riches in the world.

June 18th. Evening. We are presently camped about a mile from the foot of the Kaituk fall[9] – so the *kanoa* men term it – to venture further would render writing impossible because of the dense spray. Since dawn I have gazed at this spectacle, which dramatically exceeds in grandeur anything I, or any human living, could have believed possible. I am flooded with a mightily humbling sense of being the first white man to witness what must surely be the one of the foremost wonders of the earth.

I have been considering how to set down my impressions of this elemental, natural Goliath – this Prometheus – this veritable Leviathan, beside which any other waterfall in the world must seem the feeblest trickle – but my Muse has deserted me. What can I say? I cannot believe what I have seen. It is simply *too big*. No, that is not the word. (Why does my Muse, the fickle bitch, jilt me at moments such as these?) Colossal? – vast? – no – I own myself utterly defeated. For when I ventured to the base of the fall, I found myself in an amphitheatre designed for veritable Titans. Behind me, I could discern the narrow gorge by which we had made our approach, and on both sides the most precipitous slopes imaginable; sheer-sided and clad in an abundance of vines and creepers, and everywhere great boulders wreathed in moss. To stand and look upwards is to risk falling down, overcome with vertigo. Ahead of me was the fall itself. I can only guess at its dimensions, but it must surely exceed seven hundred feet. An incomprehensible volume of water! It is dark brown where it hurls itself into space, and then huge foamy curtains emerge, turning into creamy white feathers, seeming to move and shift as the water descends, roiling and foaming in its descent, and even slowing – or so it seems. Indeed, if one stares at it for long enough, the eye is completely deceived into thinking that the flow is upwards rather than downwards. I have never witnessed such a scene of complete majesty, nor felt so humbly and completely insignificant in the face of nature. If there is a *spiritus loci* here, how awesome it is! – how vast its dominion!

Ah, Mackenzie! What fervent rhapsodies thou wouldst surely have composed, couldst thou have been here! As for me, poor Robert Burns, this was the humble result when I had finally found a dry spot in which to write:

On Seeing the Great Fall at Kaituk

What Titan's hand in ages past
Laboured to hew that beetling height,
And caused thy torrent, deep and vast,
To thunder thus in awesome might?

How many aeons fled their course
Whilst endless waters fell, unseen,
To carve this gorge with patient force
Amidst eternal forests green?

In lonely splendour keep thy state
Between these cliffs of mossy stone:
And thunder on, inviolate,
Leviathan, aloof, alone!

June 21st. Above the falls, morning. The kanoa men left two days ago, first indicating a way that would take us to the top of the gorge. It took us a full day to accomplish this, and at times I was more terrified than I have ever been before. If there was a path we were unable to find it, and the higher we climbed, the steeper the slope grew. We had to drag our bags behind us – they seemed heavier by the minute – they kept catching in branches – I was nearly blinded by the sweat running into my eyes. Yinta is more nimble than I, and mostly went ahead, calling back to me in encouragement as she found ways around stony outcrops and dense bushes. Once I made the mistake of looking down, and the vertiginous prospect gave me such an overwhelming sense of dizziness that I had to cling to a rock for several minutes until my heart stopped pounding. As we came nearer to the top we had to make our way upwards by climbing through the twisted branches and roots of trees and bushes that grew at the edge of the precipice. I was almost sick with relief when we finally reached the top.

Since then we have rested, and shall set out shortly for the last part of our journey. I am concerned about Yinta, whose belly is growing bigger by the day. I do not want her to come to harm through her exertions. So, despite her protestations, I have put all of our worldly goods into a single bundle, which I shall carry. We have come out of the forest now, and ahead of us lies a wide grassy plain which should make our progress easier.

June 28th. On the river Rewa. A week since I wrote, during which time we have made good progress. Three days ago we were able to obtain a *kanoa*, so we have been on the water once more.

A singular occurrence today as we were paddling upstream. The river is not very wide at this point, probably around ten yards, with the branches from the trees on either side arching to meet overhead. The dark water is very smooth and mirror-like, and the reflection of the trees on its even surface gives the disturbing impression of floating in a dark green tunnel where there is neither up nor down. At about noon we came to a place where a small creek, only a few feet wide, joined the stream along which we were proceeding. In itself this was nothing out of the ordinary, but as we drew level with the opening, I could see that the water was utterly black, and all the vegetation overhanging it had the appearance of being dead. Oddly enough, the pervasive sound of insects had suddenly ceased, creating the most uncanny feeling imaginable. Rotting white tree-trunks rose up from the water like the bleached bones of monstrous ancient creatures, and despite the heat of the day, I swear that the atmosphere had grown cold – I could see the gooseflesh on my arms, and I was suddenly afflicted with an unaccountable sense of morbid dread. I know that the others felt the same, for when I gestured to them to stop and investigate they became exceedingly agitated, declaring that the place was haunted by a *yawahü*, a word I recollect as signifying 'devil' in their language.

I had never lent the slightest credence to the deluded ramblings of the superstitious until that strange business with MacDuff's house, but I do know that I would have found it difficult to venture any distance into that strange, ominous waterway, and for exactly the same reasons. I have been told that every tree, every animal and every location has its own *koyaha*, or individual spirit. A year ago I would have laughed such a notion to scorn, but now I am no longer so sure of myself. It is hard at times to avoid an appalling realisation of the vast, immemorial antiquity of the endless forests by which one finds oneself surrounded. Who knows what fearful secrets they hold? At night, I have on several occasions heard a strange whistling sound, which Yinta insists is a spirit called the *mashishikiri*. I am told that there is even a plant named after it, which emits a similar sound as one passes close to it. I had thought that the woodland around Alloway Kirk was wild and mysterious, with all manner of ghouls and goblins reputed to lurk behind every bush, ready to pounce on the unwary traveller, but compared with this place Auld Scotia's ghosts and warlocks no longer hold any terrors, and the nocturnal experiences of van Leyden become insignificant.

June 29th. Onwards, ever onwards! We have been walking through rough terrain – it is twilight now – our hammocks are slung in a shady spot beside a little creek. How much longer must we travel, I wonder? How many weary miles have we travelled since we left Goed Intent? These weeks of walking have taken their toll of us both. My inclination is to seek out the nearest village and to remain there for a week or two until we are strong again, but Yinta, despite her condition, insists on pressing onwards. I have never known anyone, man or woman, possessed of such strength and determination!

This afternoon as we were walking I was very startled by the sound of three loud booms, like the discharge of artillery in the distance.[10] I thought it might be thunder, but the sky was perfectly clear. I asked Yinta what had caused it, but she does not know. What a strange country this is! I am sure that if I were to return home with an account of it I should be laughed at for telling fanciful stories.

Our stock of food is running low, so we have to conserve what we have until we reach the next village.

June 30th. We came across a village today, where we were made very welcome. Yinta tells me that the captain knows of the settlement towards which we are headed, and assures her that we can be there in a few days. We had a good meal – a hammock awaits us in our own hut – tomorrow we shall set out in a *kanoa* for a place called Shea, from which we shall have only a short distance to walk. How good it is to rest! – to hear the sound of friendly voices all around!

I am stiff from the journey, and hobble when I walk, but Yinta retains the grace that first drew me to her. Her movements are lithe, she smiles constantly and the signs of impending motherhood show clearly on her slender body. This afternoon she took my hand and placed it on her stomach so that I could feel the baby move inside her. '*Aichi*,' she said, which means that I am to have a son! I do not know how she can be certain, but I'm sure she is right, and oh! there was so much love in those dark eyes of hers as she spoke that one word!

July 1st. This has been a strange day! We have been on a narrow river, with very dense woodland all around. It the middle of the morning we heard a whistling sound, very plaintive, starting at a high pitch and falling away to nothing. I thought it was a bird of some kind, but the *kanoa* men looked very alarmed, saying '*di-di*' over and over again. They paddled more quickly and soon left the sound behind us.

At around midday we stopped to eat. I walked down the bank a little way, and found a little creek where I stooped to rinse my face, which was sore from the sun. Something made me look up, and to my astonishment I saw someone standing on the other side of the creek, watching me intently. I say 'someone' but this was not a person like myself. At first I thought it must be an ape of some kind, but it stood perfectly erect – at least five feet tall, naked, and obviously a male – in perfect proportion, differing only from a human by virtue of the fact that it was entirely covered with long, reddish hair. Its eyes were very dark, and it appeared both curious and nervous. I shouted out to attract the others, and it leapt back into the undergrowth and disappeared. When the others arrived I tried to explain what I had seen. Yinta was filled with consternation, and said that I could easily have been attacked and carried off into the trees, never to be seen again. The Di-di is a kind of man from long ago that lives in the forest, she said. Sometimes they come to villages and attack the inhabitants. I asked her what manner of creature it was, and where it came from – she says that they have always been here in the deepest parts of the woods, from the beginning of time itself.[11]

When we made camp tonight, the men were very nervous and I must admit that I too was fearful. We intend to take turns to take watch, and our cutlasses are in easy reach. What else remains to be discovered in this forest?

I think this is the second day of July, but I confess I am uncertain about the accuracy of the dates of my entries. I thought I had kept a proper count, but now I fear that I may have been careless. When I was on the plantation, it was hard to keep track of the days unless I took pains to maintain a most assiduous tally. Even then I discovered myself frequently in error unless I checked with my almanac, or when visitors came from Stabroek, where the passage of time was more efficiently regulated. Here in the forest the days simply merge into one another, and I do not have the leisure to write as often as I would wish, and I have been careless of keeping count of the days.[12] For long periods I have feared to open these pages at all in case the rain would cause the ink to run. The want of a table on which to work is another constraint. Any future author seeking to commit his impressions of this wild region to paper will have to come better prepared than I. As for my present situation, alas! what can I say?

Nobody slept well last night, but it passed without incident. We have been on a river – I do not know its name – and making our way upstream through a succession of little rapids, but what lies ahead of us I am unable to speculate. Yesterday we passed a most astonishing mountain that had the appearance of a stone pyramid of immense size, rising up many hundreds of feet from the dense mass of trees that covered its lower slopes. The *kanoa* men averted their eyes from it, saying that it was the abode of the devil, which made me wonder if this was the place that Pijpersberg had seen. However, I seem to recollect that Bos mentioned the Massaruny, which must be very many miles to the north of us. It is an eldritch sight, this colossal outcrop, rising as suddenly and abruptly as it does, and it has that same feel of vast, indifferent isolation that I noted as we passed Ailsa Craig, all these years ago.[13]

[Undated] I am sure that no white man can have visited these parts before, for when we stopped at settlements the people flocked out in a body to stare at me in wonderment and suspicion. Yinta was able to speak their language, and could assure them that I meant them no harm. They had most likely heard of the ways of the colonists, none of them agreeable, and generally assumed that I was the leader of

some party come to haul them off into a life of servitude. Once reassured, they were hospitable enough, and kept us pretty well provisioned with cassava bread and chickens, which they term *karinabe*, and of which there never seems to be any shortage. These we trussed, and take with us in the *kanoa*.

We have arrived at Shea, and have been given a hut to rest in for the night. The inhabitants here are of the Makushi tribe, so I understand nothing of their language, and even Yinta has had to make use of an intermediary to converse with the village captain. I am feeling slightly feverish, probably the effect of too much sun. I need to rest – so does Yinta. She says that we are nearly there – oh, for an end to this journey! It has begun to rain, and I do not really feel strong enough to continue, but we are only a day's walk from our destination, so I must force myself to go on.

[Undated] We are home at last! I do not think I could have dragged my weary body any further – we are soaked to the skin – I am exhausted and shivering – but we are here. We arrived this afternoon in a small village comprising seven huts surrounding a large benab. Everyone came running towards us, greeting Yinta with tears of joy. Such a welcome! Such relief!

Yinta and I are now partaking of the hospitality of a family of four, who have given us their mats on which to sleep. The father is a kind soul, with but a single tooth in his head, and he has brought me a plank of wood to serve as a table, on which I am writing this journal. He views my labours with amused incomprehension. Outside, the rain pours down incessantly. As I write, the mother suckles her youngest child and the other little one, who I guess to be five or thereabouts, sits staring at me in astonishment. Yinta fusses over me, bringing me food – a kind of porridge or gruel that I have to force myself to eat.

[Undated] My fever is very much worse, and despite the stifling heat of the hut I shiver constantly. I fear it will soon be over with me. There, I have written it down. How strange that the twisting, convoluted path of life should have brought me here. I had thought I would have been afraid, but there is nothing in me but a terrible weariness and resignation. After coming so far! I have to rest now.

[Undated] I cannot conjecture how many hours, or days, or indeed weeks have passed since my last entry. My health is shattered – my fever breaks, and I feel improved, but then it returns worse than before. It is light, and then it is dark, and always the monotonous

drizzle of the rain on the thatch. Most of the time I lie on my mat, drifting in and out of sleep. Yinta tends me with great solicitude, bless her. In lucid moments like these, I try to compose my thoughts, but it is hard. I no longer have any hope of supernatural assistance – I turned my back on God years ago, when Mary reached her own moment of extremity. These poor people, whose names I do not even know, are my true benefactors, together with Yinta, who would verily be a saint in heaven, if there were a heaven.

Today I saw a little girl squatting near the hut, very absorbed with the job of fashioning twigs and feathers into a little doll figure. I found myself moved by this and at first I was unable to understand why. Then I recollected the day I last saw Bess, and how she was occupying herself in a similar pastime. My Bess – a wee Scots lassie, at this very moment breathing the cold Ayrshire air and living in a very decent house with a bed of her own to sleep in! Here was another wee lassie: covered in mosquito bites; living in a leaking hut and knowing nothing but the rain, and this clearing in the forest. Two more different children it would be hard to imagine, and yet as I looked at this one, rapt in her little task, I recognised an air of preoccupation that I often used to notice in Bess, and I realised that they were just the same. Until I arrived, this child had never seen a white person before, and I hope for her sake that she never sees another. They only cause trouble.

I miss my Negro friends. When I think of Toby, or Gregory, or indeed any of the decent, good black people I have encountered and when I think of what white men have done to them, I am sickened. I think of Adah. Most of all I think of Ambrose. What will become of him? At the outset I was never comfortable with slavery, and now it appals me. What has been done to these people constitutes an act of vast criminality; an act so monstrous and terrible that it defies belief. How can a society that prides itself on its benevolence and its superior culture allow itself to be so inextricably bound up with – nay, *founded* upon! – such suffering, cruelty and indignity? As Equiano says, this infernal traffic spreads like a pestilence, and taints what it touches! – violates that first natural right of mankind – equality and independency – and gives one man a dominion over his fellows which God could never intend! What I have witnessed is so uniquely horrible and vile that generations of my countrymen in years to come will look back upon it in shame and self-loathing. Slavery cannot be undone. We have sown the seed, and the fearful harvest thereof shall be as bitter ashes in our guilty mouths.

I hope that my fellows never come here to this village. Maybe my imagination is fevered, but I can see them landing at the creek down there, and strutting around importantly. I can hear their loud, arrogant voices issuing orders and instructions as they hack down trees and ruin the tranquillity of this place forever. There is nothing here for white people. This tribe is gentle; they do not need rum, gunpowder and the pox.

I just want to be laid to rest in the forest, and to achieve peace at last. As for this journal, in which I have set down my thoughts and sentiments with unguarded freedom and candour, it is my hope now that it, like its poor author, shall be buried in oblivion. I would not have it bandied around by idle vanity or malevolence. I was, as Mr Cowper remarked, 'born to be forgot'.

God help me, I drifted into sleep, and I have just seen a kind of dreadful procession in my mind's eye – Allardyce with the look of death in his eyes – Mary after her struggle was over – Nancy – McLehose, writhing the last of his miserable life away – they have all gone down the road on which I am headed. If there is a world to come, will they be waiting for me? When was it I last saw my darling wee Bess? She will be quite the young lady now. I wonder if she ever thinks of me – her wretched father? Bless her. But what have I done for her that she should turn her thoughts to me? I know now that I shall never see her again on this earth. What an odd realisation, all of a sudden, when it should have been so obvious to me from the outset! What an inevitability, indeed, now that it has come to this! Up until the time that this infirmity seized me, I truly believed that I should return to Scotland one day. I never once gave a serious thought as to how, or when, or to the practicalities of the matter, and I certainly never thought that I was going to die in this country. There, I have written it. Foolish, foolish, foolish! Is this what LIFE means, after all? Waiting for a happy tomorrow, deluding ourselves all the while? All our yesterdays, quoth Macbeth – and we the fools with our brief candles! A tale told by an idiot. Must rest now – very weak.

[Undated] Yinta lays me down and bathes my temples. She was singing just now – such a sad, haunting air! The words were familiar – *D'anshihifa kiduaha, da bethetho*. I now realise that they are my words, and oh! how sincerely I meant them, and still mean them! What an irony that only on my deathbed have I come to understand what it is truly to love, and to be loved! It will be of great comfort to me when the darkness comes. Perhaps there is a God after all.

[Undated] I dreamt of that strange castle again. It was very vivid, and I could swear that this time I could smell the tingling air of a frosty Ayrshire day. I wonder if I shall be going there soon? I know that Gregory believed that after his death he would return to Africa, so perhaps the notion is not so very far-fetched after all.

[Undated] Just now I thought I was down at the creek when I heard someone approach – I looked up and it was Bess, dressed in her Sunday best, smiling sweetly, and holding her hands out towards me. I called her name, and ran to embrace her, but as I did so everything changed somehow, and I opened my eyes to see Yinta crouched by my bedside. In a voice sharp with anxiety, she told me that I had gone outside, and had fallen down. I am all covered in mud. I am confused – waking and sleeping merge into one. My imaginings are taking on the form of reality, while the real world grows more illusory. Is this what death is like? Do we enter into a dream from which we never awaken? Who knows? Shall I see Mary again? What of Nancy and James?

[Undated] I feel my time is at last expired. Yinta almost persuades me that I am better, but I fear that this affliction shall prove fatal to me. I stare into her kind eyes – I need that memory to carry with me into eternity! God help me! – a strange exclamation from one who has so abjured God. But if there is Another who is truly benevolent, then surely an honest man has nothing to fear from the terrible end of this last journey that I must shortly undertake. I have tried to be a good man. Whatever mitigated the woes, or increased the happiness of others, this was my criterion of goodness; and whatever injured society at large, or an individual in it, this was my measure of iniquity. If indeed I am to face my Maker in the next world, then I hope that I shall not be judged too harshly. I have tried to love my neighbour as myself, as we are bidden to do in the Good Book.[14] I hope that I may be forgiven my impulsiveness and foolishness – if I had failings, may they be the failings of a generous heart. Whatsoever things are lovely; whatsoever things are gentle; whatsoever things are charitable; whatsoever things are kind, think on these things.[15] I do not think I can write any more now.

[Undated]   Bess

NOTES

Editor's Note

1. Literally 'meeting place of the people': a circular, thatched building, where villagers would congregate. A replica of one was built by Wai Wai tribesmen, under the supervision of the architect George Henry, in the Kingston district of Georgetown in 1977 for the meeting of Foreign Ministers of the Non-aligned Countries.
2. A resinous, latex-like gum from the sap of the balata tree *(ecclinusa psilophylla)* found in sandy forests.

1796

1. The quotation appears at the foot of the title page of the journal.
2. Burns refers several times in the text to this poem, which was presumably written before the journal was commenced.
3. Robert Fergusson (1750-1774). Scottish poet, author of *Leith Races, The Farmer's Ingle*, etc.
4. Jean Armour, a Mauchline girl he had once offered to marry. See entry for 16th August 1786.
5. Presumably the parish minister in Mauchline.
6. This must be a quotation from an earlier work. William Fisher is mentioned several times in the journal as the living embodiment of hypocrisy, e.g., 17th July 1787.
7. The poet's daughter. The child would have been just over a year old at the time this entry was written. See entry for 22nd May 1787.
8. Richmond was a lawyer who helped Burns to obtain a bachelor's certificate, and who together with Hamilton, appears to have had his best interests at heart. See the entries for 16th August and 10th September 1786.
9. Such marriages by declaration *(sponsalia de presenti)* seem to have been recognised by some eighteenth-century church authorities. Whatever the legal position it is clear that Burns regarded it as binding.
10. Pleuritic? The humid atmosphere of the tropics can easily exacerbate any respiratory condition such as pleurisy.
11. See the *Greenock Register* (1786) No. 5, quoted in Wilkins, *Scottish Customs and Excise Records with particular reference to Strathclyde, from 1707 onwards*, p. 53 (1992).
12. The following verse has been crossed out:
    Here ilka ben and craggy glen
    Inspired my youthful rhymes:
    What [~~foreign~~] dusky Muse shall guide my pen
    In [~~sultry foreign)~~] far West Indian climes?
    A variant of these lines appears in the entry for 18th October 1786.
13. Samuel Richardson, *Pamela, or, Virtue Rewarded* (1740).

14. Joseph Knight had been brought to Scotland from Jamaica by John Wedderburn of Bandean, who saw to his education and treated him with 'particular kindness and favours'. Following his marriage to a servant girl, Knight indicated that he wished to leave Wedderburn's employment, as the law did not recognise slavery in Scotland. The Justices of the Peace in Perth upheld Wedderburn's contention that although Knight was no longer technically a slave, he was still obliged to provide 'perpetual servitude'. Knight appealed and the ruling was reversed. In 1774 Wedderburn's own appeal to the Court of Session was upheld and Knight was told he had to remain with his master. James Robertson has written an excellent semi-fictional account of the affair – see bibliography.

15. Present-day Haiti. The remainder of Hispaniola now forms the Dominican Republic, whose capital is Santo Domingo.

16. The name of this island derives from the Taino *cubanacan,* from *cu'*, 'a sacred place'; *bana*, 'a grand place', and *ca'n*, 'the centre'. Other theories, such as that the name 'Cuba' is of Hispanic-Arabic origin and signifies 'cupola', or is linked in some way with the Arabic *ka'bah*, the holy shrine at Mecca, are implausible. The Taino language also gives us 'hurricane', from *hura,* 'wind', and *ca'n,* 'the centre'.

17. The name Jamaica is derived from *xaymaca*, an Arawak word meaning 'island of springs'.

18. A hogshead is equivalent to 16 hundredweight (813 kilograms) and a puncheon is 110 gallons. So the estate produced about 160 tons of sugar and 65,000 litres of rum annually. This would have raised an income of around £4,500 – a huge sum in 1786.

19. It was not until 1880 that a protozoal parasite was found in the blood of a malaria sufferer. In 1898, William Ross discovered that this parasite was transmitted to humans through the bite of the female mosquito. Until then, the disease was thought to be caused by the bad air associated with stagnant water, hence the name.

20. The English *hammock* and the Spanish *hamaca* both derive from the Arawak *hamaka.*

21. Probably a quotation from the poem he mentions in the opening pages of the journal. The iambic pentameter is reminiscent of Gray, whose style he consciously imitates elsewhere. See entry for 5th June 1787.

22. The OED gives this as a Scottish dialect form of 'Negro' deriving from the Latin *niger*, recorded as early as 1568. It was quite possibly not considered to be a derogatory term at this stage, though the later variant 'nigger' is clearly offensive. This was first recorded in Britain in 1786. Within a few years the word was being widely employed to refer disparagingly to any member of a dark-skinned race.

23. The word derives from the Spanish *cimmarón*, meaning 'wild'. The first Maroon War was fought between 1720 and 1739.

24. Almost certainly the *Essay on the Slavery and Commerce of the Human Species* by Thomas Clarkson. It was written in Latin in 1785, winning a prize at Cambridge. The English translation appeared the following year, and was

extremely influential. Clarkson was one of the founder members of the Society for the Abolition of the Slave Trade, formed in 1787.

1787

1. The name given to the group made up of the strongest slaves on the plantation. They would undertake the heaviest work.
2. Typhus, characterised by petechial spots, and associated with crowded, insanitary conditions. Given the incubation period of around ten days, it seems likely that Mary contracted the disease during her visit to Port Antonio – ironically on her visit to the doctor.
3. Sadly these were, if anything, understated. Thomas Thistlewood died aged 65 on 30th November 1786. His diary runs to some 10,000 pages of manuscript in which his sexual exploitation of his slave women is described in exhaustive detail. An edition has been published by D. Hall (1989). See also *Mastery, Tyranny, and Desire* by Trevor Burnard (2004).
4. Jean Jacques Rousseau (1712-1778). In *Émile* (1762) he proposes the notion of the 'noble savage' living harmoniously with nature and only rendered degenerate by contact with 'civilisation'. This was a common theme of the eighteenth-century Enlightenment.
5. A term for a white man that quickly became derogatory. According to Chambers, the word derives from Calabar *efik mbakara*, meaning 'a European'. In modern Jamaican usage it can also mean rich, or belonging to high society.
6. Most probably Sir Alured Clarke, Lieutenant-Governor from 1784 to 1790.

1788

1. 'Seize the day, place as little trust as possible in tomorrow.'
2. Author of *Amazing Grace*. See bibliography.
3. Olney Hymns, Book I, no. 8.
4. It seemed as if from day to day,
   They were to eat and die;
   But still, though in a secret way,
   He sent a fresh supply.
   (Book I, no. 36)
5. Book I, no. 41.
6. From the information provided, this could be Hector MacNeill (1746 – 1818) who visited Jamaica at about this time. His pamphlet *On the Treatment of Negroes in Jamaica* appeared in 1788, offering a justification of slavery. On his return to Scotland he wrote the poem *Scotland's Skaith, or, The History of Will and Jean* (1795) and a semi-autobiographical novel *The Memoirs of Charles Macpherson Esq.* (1800).

1789

1. This castle dates from the 15th century, and was abandoned in the 17th century. It was further damaged by a storm in 1839, but stabilised a few years later.

2. The West African Ashanti spider-god Anansi embodies the qualities of hero and trickster. This oral tradition in Jamaica probably represents the most authentic and enduring aspect of African culture to have survived enforced removal to the Caribbean. Anancy stories also quite clearly formed the basis for the Brer Rabbit tales by Joel Chandler Harris (1840-1908). See also under Beckwith in the bibliography. The story of *The Old Woman and Her Pig*, published by Joseph Jacobs in 1895, is substantially identical to the tale told by Adah here, though it appears in a collection of 'English' fairy tales. It is difficult to say whether Adah's tale is an original Anancy story, or a local adaptation of an English version brought over by early colonists.

3. *The House That Jack Built* was first printed in 1755, and is said to refer to Cherrington Manor, near Shrewsbury, which had a malt house in the grounds.

4. See glossary.

5. The second and third volumes have no title pages.

6. Neonatal tetanus, probably caused by the use of a non-sterile implement to cut the umbilical cord.

7. William Pitt the Younger, Prime Minister from 1783 to 1801.

8. *Domestic Medicine*, by the Edinburgh-born physician William Buchan (1729–1805). It first appeared in 1769, and a fuller edition followed in 1785. It became extremely popular in Britain, as well as in America where for many years it remained the standard self-help medical text. It was even translated into Russian. Buchan is buried in Westminster Abbey.

9. 'Dragon's blood' was a resin obtained from an African palm of the genus *Daemonorops*, and was chiefly used to tint varnish, though its astringent qualities also made it a popular medicine.

1790

1. *The Interesting Narrative of the Life of Olaudah Equiano, or, Gustavus Vassa, the African, Written by Himself.* London, 1789.

2. Robert Adam (1728 –1792). Kirkcaldy-born architect famous for his fine buildings in the classical style. He worked with his brothers James, John and William.

3. *Trombicula alfreddugesi,* also known as chigger, jigger or red bug. A small insect whose larvae attach themselves to a human or animal host, injecting a digestive enzyme beneath the skin. This leaves a red welt around a white area that soon becomes hard and itchy.

4. Following Effingham's arrival, the House of Assembly voted to end this expenditure in future.

5. Genesis, 9:25.

6. Exodus, 20:17.

7. Such arguments were still put forward well into the nineteenth century.
   See under John C. Lord in the bibliography.

8. David Hume wrote in 1748, 'I am apt to suspect the Negroes and in general
   all other species of men (for there are four or five different kinds) to be
   naturally inferior to the whites. There never was a civilized nation of any
   other complection than white, nor even any individual eminent either in
   action or speculation. No ingenious manufactures amongst them, no arts,
   no sciences. On the other hand, the most rude and barbarous of the whites,
   such as the ancient GERMANS, the present TARTARS, have still some-
   thing eminent about them in their valour, form of government, or some
   other particular. Such uniform and constant differences could not happen
   in so many countries and ages, if nature had not made an original distinc-
   tion betwixt these breeds of men. Not to mention our colonies, there are
   Negroe *(sic)* slaves dispersed all over Europe, of which none ever discov-
   ered any symptoms of ingenuity, tho' low people, without education, will
   start up amongst us, and distinguish themselves in every profession. In
   JAMAICA indeed they talk of one Negroe as a man of parts and learning;
   but 'tis likely he is admired for very slender accomplishments like a parrot,
   who speaks a few words plainly.' See bibliography.

1791

1. Vincenzo Lunardi, the Italian balloonist, who flew from St Andrews Square
   in Glasgow to the Borders town of Hawick on November 23rd, 1785.

2. The original name for the Demerara was 'Malali', an Arawak word meaning
   'fast-flowing stream'. Under Dutch rule, the river was referred to as 'de
   Malali'. Later the two words were combined to form 'Demalali' and the 'l'
   sound modulated to 'r', giving 'Demerary' – a form still current in the
   1790s. See J. P. Bennett, *The Arawak Language in Guyanese Culture,*
   Georgetown, 1986.

3. *Chinchona succirubra*, known as Peruvian Bark in the 18th century, and
   prized for its febrifuge and tonic qualities.

4. The city was named after a president of the West India Company called
   Nicholaas Geelvinck, who held the title of Lord of Stabroek, a province of
   Antwerp in Belgium.

5. Alexander Lindsay, 6th Earl of Balcarres.

6. Victor Hugo's novel *Bug-Jargal* (1826) is set during the 1791 uprising in
   Haiti. It is one of the seminal works of colonial fiction, and the first
   European novel to have a black hero. It was originally conceived as a short
   story, first published in instalments in *Le Conservateur Littéraire* in 1820
   when the author was only 18, and later expanded.

7. *Verenigde West-Indische Compagnie* (West India Company). The Charter was
   drawn up in 1621. It gave the Company a monopoly on trade, as well as
   almost complete autonomy in the legal and administrative workings of the
   Dutch colonies.

8. J. C. de la Coste, an Attorney at Law, imported a printing machine in 1790 and attempted to establish a newspaper, but was unsuccessful. In 1796 the press was purchased by a Mrs Volkerts, who went on to publish the first newspaper in the colony, the *Royal Essequibo and Demerara Gazette*.

1792

1. A slave called Coffy led a revolt that began on the Marianenburg plantation in the Berbice in 1762. The insurrection was put down after considerable loss of life, though Coffy retains the status of a popular hero. There is a statue of him in Independence Square in Georgetown. See Jan Jacob Hartsinck, *Beschryving van Guiana, of de Wildekust, in Zuid-America*, Amsterdam (1770), reproduced in facsimile by S. Emmering, 2 volumes, Amsterdam (1974). Walter E. Roth produced an English translation of the relevant chapters under the title *The Story of the Slave Rebellion in Berbice – 1762*, which appeared in appendices to eight consecutive issues of *The Journal of the Guyana Museum and Zoo*, commencing in December 1958.

2. 'Salapenta' is the Creole term for any large lizard. Properly speaking, the salipenter is a tegu lizard *(tupinambis nigropunctatus)*of the Teiidae family, popularly known as racerunners, of which there are six species native to South America and Trinidad. In Guyana today it is sometimes referred to as the 'bush motorbike'.

3. Of the Dutch West India Company.

4. So called because of the small red or white pustules, resembling grains of millet, which form on the skin.

5. *Julius Caesar*, III, ii.

1793

1. Willem August Sirtema, Baron van Grovestins.

2. Strictly speaking the marabunta is a type of army ant, but the name is used in Creole to describe wasps. The common feature is that the bite of the ant and the sting of the wasp are both extremely painful.

3. Only anacondas that have been captured can be measured accurately, and the official 'longest specimen' was just over thirty-five feet in length. However there have been many reports of much larger ones. Matthew French Young saw one in Brazil that he estimated to be 'at least fifty to sixty feet'. The explorer Percy Fawcett claimed to have killed one that measured sixty-two feet, and to have heard reports of others that exceeded eighty feet.

4. Isaiah, 37:1.

1794

1. The OED gives the date of 1801 for the first written usage of this as an English word, but it was probably quite common in the Dutch colonies before that time.

2. Tonsilitis.

3. I know of a house in Hague, West Coast Demerara, which is reputed to be completely uninhabitable for precisely this reason. When our own house in Goed Intent was begun, the site manager, Mervin Lewis, insisted on carrying out a cleansing ceremony before he allowed a spade to enter the earth.

4. The OED gives a date of 1789 for the first usage of this phrase to mean 'gibberish'. Properly speaking, 'double' is an obsolete word meaning 'high'.

5. 'Ghosts! You can't catch me!'

6. The *rijksdaalder* of 50 *stuivers* was introduced as the colonial currency in 1701 in order to facilitate commerce. It was worth approximately four shillings and fivepence (22p) in sterling. Guilders were also in circulation.

1795

1. Mazaruni.

2. Van's Gravesande (see bibliography) wrote at some length about Pijpersberg's 'pyramid', and the abundance of unusual artefacts that he came across on the forest floor a short distance inland from Stabroek. He speculated that this might form evidence of colonisation by some ancient civilisation. Ataraipu, or Devil's Rock, was visited by Charles Barrington Brown in October 1869 (see bibliography). It is a striking (but natural) pyramid-shaped outcrop, and certainly answers the description. However, it is situated on the Kwitaro, many miles south of the Mazaruni, as Burns observes in a journal entry in 1796. No details of Tollenaer's sketch survive, and so there is no way of knowing what Pijpersberg and Tollenaer were describing.

3. Burns' phonetic version is understandably speculative and confused, so I have reproduced the conversation as it would be written today.

4. A large rodent, related to the guinea pig, native to the Guianas.

5. There are no tigers in Guyana. The word is used to refer to jaguars, or to the very dangerous wild cats that hunt in packs.

6. An insect similar to the bot-fly that lays its eggs under the skin of humans and animals alike. These hatch out as larva that thrive in the festering pus of the resulting abscess, but are very difficult to remove because of their stiff hairs that anchor them in place. A huge, itchy boil develops, with a hole on the top through which the larva breathes.

7. From the description given, this could only be a fully-grown example of *theraphosa blondi*, the world's largest spider, specimens of which have been reported with a leg-span of 28 centimetres. It is native to the coastal fringes of Guyana and Surinam.

8. Toussaint L'Ouverture was born a free black in 1743. Following the French Revolution, the principle of the 'Rights of Man' was extended in 1789 to all free blacks and mulattoes in the colony of Haiti, but furious plantation owners refused to implement the order. In 1791, the French authorities retracted the decision, which led to the successful slave uprising, led by

Toussaint. In 1793, the Jacobins, under Robespierre, announced the aboli-
tion of slavery, and Toussaint joined with the French to eject the British and
Spanish. At the period of this journal entry, he was effectively the governor
of Haiti. In 1802, under promise of safe passage, he was lured to a meeting
with the French authorities, arrested, and sent to France. Napoleon had him
imprisoned in wretched conditions, and he died of pneumonia in 1803.
During his own exile on St Helena many years later, Napoleon is reputed to
have commented, 'What does the death of one wretched Negro mean to me?'
Toussaint was the subject of a sonnet by Wordsworth, written towards the
end of 1802. In *The Black Jacobins* (1938), C. L. R. James provides an analysis
of the interplay between decolonisation, class struggle and the French
Revolution.

9. The poem in question is the second Epode:

> *Beatus ille, qui procul negotiis,*
> *Ut prista gens mortalium,*
> *Paterna rura bubus exercet suis,*
> *Solutus omni faenori.*

10. It was normal practice to set fire to the weeds surrounding the cane to make
the stems more accessible for cutting, and also to drive out rats and snakes.
This happens in Demerara today, where the cane is still cut by hand.

11. I transliterated the poem into 'correct' Arawak (Loco) with the help of J .P.
Bennett's grammar and dictionary, and was very fortunate to be able to check
my version over with Father Bennett himself when I visited him in the
summer of 1998 at his home in the Kabukabari Mission on the Pomeroon.
This is given below, together with a literal translation. Burns turns out to
have been remarkably accurate. His decision to divide words into individual
syllables is perfectly logical if the poem is to be read aloud, and as he says,
there was almost certainly no agreed written form of Arawak at the time.

Da Likiñ

Akhui! Da anshihi jiañ kore tokoro
Bohoya oloko maküralikhá:
Akhui! Da anshihi jiañ yeni semi
Hü'yentua maucha.

Bui hibi, da likiñ,
Kena d'anshihi hü.
Kena d'anshihifa hü, likiñ,
Barikoma Malali sakañ.

Barikoma Malali sekañ, likiñ,

Kena konokobe n'makawadowafañ:
D'anshihifa kiduaha,
Da bethetho, da likiñ

My Sweet One

O! My love is like a red flower
Fragrant in the hot season:
O! My love is like the tuneful song
You sing in the morning.

You are beautiful, my sweet one,
And I love you,
And I shall love you still, sweet one,
Though the Demerara runs dry.

Though the Demerara runs dry
    my sweet one,
And the forests disappear:
I shall always love you truly,
My friend, my sweet one.

1796

1. Antony Beaujon was Secretary of the Court of Policy. Despite his reservations, he did become Governor of the united colonies later in the year.

2. France invaded the Netherlands in 1795, renaming it the Batavian Republic under a puppet government made up of Dutch supporters of French Revolutionary principles. The Prince of Orange, exiled in London, urged Dutch colonists to support Britain, which was at war with France following the execution of Louis XVI on 21st January 1793. However many colonies continued to support the Batavian Republic.

3. Venezuela, so called because the first European settlers saw that the houses there were built on piles because of the danger of flooding, just as in Venice. At the time of this entry, the present day countries of Colombia, Ecuador and Venezuela together formed the Spanish Viceroyalty of Nuevo Granada, with its capital at Bogotá. The Republic of Venezuela was established in 1811.

4 . A reference to Thomas Gray's *Elegy Written in a Country Churchyard.*

5. Literally 'see-over-all' because of its commanding situation. In 1716, the administration was moved to Fort Island, in the Essequibo estuary. The abandoned buildings were largely demolished in 1748, and the bricks taken to construct a sugar mill on the Essequibo.

6. The first cascade on the Mazaruni is now called the Marshall Falls.

7. The massacuraman is mentioned several times by Matthew French Young in his book *Guyana, the Lost El Dorado* (1988). He gives an account of a spate of drownings in the Wismar-Christianburg area, some of the victims being found later with their hearts and livers torn out. Charles Barrington Brown mentions a 'water child' on the Upper Mazaruni that was reputed to have upset a canoe and carried off one of its occupants. Officially there is no such creature, and many of my Guyanese friends are inclined to view it in much the same way as Scots regard the Loch Ness monster. Others suggest that the circumstantial evidence points to the existence of a creature as yet unknown to zoologists.

8. Henry Mackenzie (1745-1831), the Scottish-born author of *The Man of Feeling* (1771), a seminal work in the sentimental movement. The hero is forced to consider the value of emotion and moral virtue in a world dominated by commercial and practical interests.

9. The Amerindian name by which the Kaieteur Fall was previously known. Kaieteur has a width of 400 feet, and a vertical drop of 761 feet. Until now, it has been assumed that the first European to see it was the surveyor Charles Barrington Brown, who descended the river Potaro and so came upon the fall from above on 24th April 1870. 'Not being prepared for anything so grand or startling,' he wrote, 'I could not at first believe my eyes, but felt that it was all a dream.' (See *Canoe and Camp Life in British Guiana*, London, 1876.) The Victoria Falls, discovered in 1855, have a height of 335 feet, and the Niagara Falls a mere 167 feet. The Angel Fall in Venezuela, named after the aviator who first sighted it in 1935, has a height

of 3,212 feet, but it is, properly speaking, a cascade. Kaieteur's claim to fame is that it is the largest single-drop fall in the world. It can be accessed overland, but only with difficulty, and the only practicable way of getting there is by chartered plane. No tourist development is permitted in the Kaieteur National Park, and so the present-day visitor sees the fall as it was in primeval times – an awesome experience.

10. This phenomenon occurs worldwide, and is of unknown origin. It is sometimes referred to as 'Barisal Guns' after the town in Bangladesh where it was noted in the 1870s.

11. The Di-di (pronounced 'dy-dy') is mentioned in 1876 by Charles Barrington Brown (see bibliography). Gary Samuels, a botanist working in the interior, claimed a sighting in 1987. It is supposed to be some kind of primitive anthropoid not yet recognised by zoologists, like Bigfoot or the Mono Grande.

12. At this point in the Journal, Burns abandons his habit of dating the entries.

13. From the description, this must be Ataraipu, sometimes called the Devil's Rock, on the west bank of the Kwitaro, some 160 miles south of Kaieteur. It rises 600 feet above the surrounding forest.

14. St Paul's Epistle to the Romans, 13:9, and Matthew, 19:19.

15. An echo of Paul's Epistle to the Philippians, 4:8.

BIBLIOGRAPHY

Armitage, David and Braddick, Michael J. *(editors)*, *The British Atlantic World, 1500-1800.* New York, 2002.

Augier, F. R. and Gordon, Shirley C., *Sources of West Indian History.* London, 1962.

Beckwith, Martha Warren, *Jamaica Anansi Stories.* New York, 1924.

Bennett, J. P., *The Arawak Language in Guyanese Culture.* Georgetown, 1986.

Bennett, J. P., *An Arawak-English Dictionary, with an English word-list.* Walter Roth Museum of Anthropology, Georgetown, 1994. Second edition: first edition published in 1989.

Bennett, J. P., *Twenty-eight Lessons in Loko (Arawak): A Teaching Guide.* Walter Roth Institute of Anthropology, Georgetown, 1995.

Braddick, Michael J., see Armitage, David (2002).

Brown, Charles Barrington and Lidstone, William, *Fifteen thousand miles on the Amazon and its tributaries.* London (Edward Stanford), 1878.

Brown, Charles Barrington, *Canoe and Camp Life in British Guiana.* London, 1876.

Buchan, W., *Domestic Medicine.* Second edition, London, 1785. The first edition was published in Edinburgh in 1769.

Burnard, Trevor, *Mastery, Tyranny, and Desire.* North Carolina, 2004.

Clarkson, Thomas, *Essay on the Slavery and Commerce of the Human Species, particularly the African.* 1786.

Cundall, Frank *(editor)*, *Lady Nugent's Journal: Jamaica one hundred and thirty years ago. Reprinted from a Journal kept by Maria, Lady Nugent, from 1801 to 1815, issued for private circulation in 1839.* London, 1934.

Curtin, Philip D., *The Rise and Fall of the plantation complex: Essays in Atlantic History.* Cambridge, 1990.

Devine, T. M., *Scotland's Empire 1600-1815.* London, 2003.

Essequibo and Demerara: Court of Policy and Combined Court Proceedings, 1797–1828.

These minutes exist only as a unique MS copy in the National Archive of Guyana, Main Street, Georgetown, reference AB1/1–641. The proceedings are set down in two columns per page, with Dutch to the left and English to the right. Each minute is signed by the secretary and the other members present. The first few pages of the minute book have degenerated into fragments, and the whole volume is yellowed and fragile throughout. It was an interesting experience to consult this document first-hand, though the book is in urgent attention of specialist treatment if it is to remain legible for much longer.

Equiano, Olaudah, *The Interesting Narrative of the Life of Olaudah Equiano, or Gustavus Vassa, the African. Written by Himself.* London, 1789.

Falconbridge, Alexander, *An Account of the Slave Trade on the Coast of Africa.* London, 1788.

Fawcett, P. H., *Exploration Fawcett.* Edited by Brian Fawcett. London, 1953.

Freeth, Zahra, *Run Softly Demerara.* London, 1960.

Gordon, S.C. see Augier F. R. (1962).

Goslinga, Cornelis Ch., *The Dutch in the Caribbean and in the Guianas, 1680-1791.* Assen, 1985.

Gravesande, (Laurens) Storm van's, *The Rise of British Guiana, compiled from his despatches to the Directors of the Zeeland Chamber of the West India Company 1738–1772.* Translated by C. A. Harris CB CMG and J. A. J. de Villiers. A reprint of the 1911 edition produced by the Haklyut Society, Liechtenstein, 1967.

Hall, D. *(editor)*, *In Miserable Slavery, Thomas Thistlewood in Jamaica, 1750-1786.* London, 1989.

Hart, Richard, *Slaves who abolished slavery: Volume 1 – Blacks in bondage.* University of the West Indies, Jamaica, 1980.

Hart, Richard, *Slaves who abolished slavery: Volume 2 – Blacks in rebellion.* University of the West Indies, Jamaica, 1985.

Hartsinck, Jan Jacob, *Beschryving van Guiana, of de Wildekust, in Zuid-America.* Amsterdam, 1770. Reprinted in facsimile by S. Emmering, Amsterdam, 1974. (Two volumes).

Henriques, Fernando, *Family and Colour in Jamaica.* London, 1953.

Hugo, Victor, *Bug-Jargal.* Paris, 1826.

Hume, David, 'Of National Characters' (1748) in *The Philosophical Works of David Hume.* ed. T. H. Green and T. H. Grose. London, Longmans, 1882.

James, C. L. R., *The Black Jacobins: Toussaint L'Ouverture and the San Domingo Revolution.* (1938). Vintage Books, New York, 1989.

Kovel, Joel, *White Racism: A Psychohistory.* New York, 1970. London, 1988.

Lewis, M. G., *Journal of a West Indian Proprietor 1815-1817*. London, 1843.

Long, Edward, *The History of Jamaica*. London, 1774. (Two volumes).

Lord, John C., *"The Higher Law" in Its Application to the Fugitive Slave Bill. A Sermon on the Duties Men Owe to God and to Governments*. Sermon given at the Central Presbyterian Church on Thanksgiving Day 1851, and subsequently published as a pamphlet. Issued as part of the *Making of America* project (MoA) in the Universities of Michigan and Cornell.

Mackenzie, Henry, *The Man of Feeling*, 1771

Menezes, Mary Noel, *British Policy towards the Amerindians in British Guyana, 1903-1873*. Oxford, 1977.

Netscher, Pieter Marinus, *History of the Colonies Essequibo, Demerara and Berbice: from the Dutch Establishment to the present day*. (1888). Translated by Walter E. Roth, 1929.

Newton, John, *Olney Hymns, in three books*. Book I. On select Texts of Scripture. Book II. On occasional subjects. Book III. On the Progress and Changes of the Spiritual Life. London, 1779. In Book I, Cowper supplied Hymn 3 (*O! for a closer walk with God!*) while Newton's Hymn 41 – now known simply as *Amazing Grace!* – is listed more fully as *Amazing Grace! (how sweet the sound)*. The tune to which it is now sung is called 'New Britain', written by William Walker of South Carolina in 1835, and based on earlier melodies. The words of the hymn have been added to, adapted and 'improved' over the years. The bicentenary of the hymnal was marked in 1979 with a facsimile edition published in Olney, Buckinghamshire.

Parry, J. H. and Sherlock, P. M., *A Short History of the West Indies*. London, 1956.

Pitman, F. W., 'Slavery on British West Indies Plantations in the Eighteenth Century' in the *Journal of Negro History*, Vol. 11, No. 4, October 1926, pages 584-668. In 2001 this Journal was renamed the *Journal of African American History*.

Ragatz, Lowell Joseph, *The Fall of the Planter Class in the British Caribbean, 1763-1833*. The American Historical Association, New York, 1928.

Ralegh, Sir Walter, *The Discoverie of the Large, Rich and Beutiful Empyre of Guiana, with a Relation of the great and Golden Citie of Manoa which the Spanyards call El Dorado . . . performed in the yeare 1595*. Imprinted at London by Robert Robinson, 1596. Transcribed, annotated and introduced by Neil L Whitehead (Volume 77 in The American Exploration and Travel Series, Manchester University Press, 1997).

Robertson, James, *Joseph Knight*, London, 2003.

Rodway, James, *History of British Guiana from the year 1782 to the present time*. Georgetown, 1893.

Roth, Walter E., 'The Story of the Slave Rebellion in Berbice – 1762.' (Appendices in eight consecutive issues of the *Journal of the Guyana Museum and Zoo*, December 1958 onwards. A translation of Hartsinck's *Beschryving . . .* Vol I, 361–520).

Roth, Walter E., see also Netscher, Pieter Marinus (1888).

Schaw, Janet *(edited by Andrews, E. W. and Andrews, C. McL.), Journal of a Lady of Quality, being the Narrative of a Journey from Scotland to the West Indies, North Carolina and Portugal, in the Years 1774-1776.* Yale, 1922.

Schomburgk, Robert H., *A description of British Guiana, Geographical and Statistical.* London, 1840. Reprinted London, 1970.

Smout, T. C., *A History of the Scottish People 1560-1830.* Glasgow, 1969.

Thistlewood, Thomas, see Hall D. (1989) and Burnard T. (2004).

Thomas, Hugh, *The Slave Trade: The History of the Atlantic Slave Trade: 1440-1870.* London, 1997.

Walvin, James, *Black Ivory, A History of British Slavery.* London, 1992.

Ward, Edward, *A Trip to Jamaica, with a True Character of the People and Island.* London, 1700. (Reproduced by the Facsimile Text Society, Columbia University Press, New York, 1933).

Whitehead, Neil L., see Ralegh W. (1595).

Whitely, Henry, *Three Months in Jamaica in 1832.* London, 1833.

Wilkins, Frances, *Scottish Customs and Excise Records with particular reference to Strathclyde, from 1707 onwards.* Wyre Forest Press, Kidderminster, 1992.

Williams, Denis, *Icon and Image: A study of sacred and secular forms of African Classical Art.* New York University Press, 1974.

Williams, Denis, *Prehistoric Guiana.* Kingston, Jamaica, 2004.

Young, Matthew French, *Guyana: The Lost El Dorado.* Peepal Tree Press Ltd., Leeds, 1998. With a Foreword by Joseph G. Singh, then Chief of Staff of the Guyana Defence Force.

GLOSSARY

A

Ae, *adj.* one.

Ahent, *prep.* behind.

Airns, *n.pl.* shackles.

Aye, *adv.* always; still.

B

Backra, *n* a white man *(contemptuous)*; also **buckra.**

Bagasse, *n.* cane from which the juice has been extracted, often burned as fuel.

Bairn, *n.* a child.

Bammy, *n.* deep-fried cassava bread in the shape of a pancake.

Bandileers, *n.* bandoliers; colloquially, the testicles.

Barbecue, *n.* originally, any raised storage or drying platform. From the Arawak *barabakua.*

Bardie, *n.* a minor poet.

Ben[1]**,** *n.* a mountain.

Ben[2]**,** *adv.* in; inside; *prep.* within; *n.* an inner room.

Benab, *n.* A shelter thatched with palm fronds, usually circular and with open sides.

Bield, *n.* a shelter; a refuge.

Birl, *v.* to spin.

Bouse, *n.* strong drink. *v.* to drink alcohol.

Bow-leggit, *adj.* bow-legged.

Brawly, *adj.* excellent; splendid.

Breeks, *n. pl.* trousers; breeches.

Brunstane, *n.* brimstone.

Buckie, *n.* a boy.

But *n.* the outer room of a house.

But and ben, *n.* a two-roomed cottage.

C

Calaloo, *n.* a soup or stew made with vegetables, sometimes with pork, salt fish or dumplings added.

Camoodie, *n.* an anaconda.

Canna, *v.* cannot.

Canty, *adj.* cosy; neat; pleasant.

Cayman, or **caiman,** *n.* a South American alligator.

Chaumer, *n.* room; chamber.

Chiel(d), *n.* a child; a man; a fellow.

Cloot, *n.* a cloven hoof; a cloth rag.

Clootie, *n.* the devil.

Cotter, *n.* one who lives in a cottage.

Cyan, *v.* to be able. Also *neg.* **cyan't.**

D

Deil, *n.* the devil; Satan.

Dominie, *n.* a schoolmaster.

Doup, *n.* the posterior.

Dour, *adj.* sulky; sullen.

Drave, *v. pp.* drove.

Dreich, *adj.* miserable.

Duddies, *n. pl.* ragged clothes.

Duppy, *n.* a ghost; a zombie.

Dutty, *adj.* dirty.

E

E'e, *n.* eye. *pl.* **e'en.**

Eldritch, *adj.* eerie; ghostly.

Emerods, *n. pl.* haemorrhoids; see Samuel I, 5:6 *et seq.*

F

Fairing, *n.* one's just deserts.
Fand, *v. pp.* found.
Fash, *v.* bother.
File, *v.* to soil.
Fooshtie, *adj.* musty; mouldy.
Forbye, *prep.* also.
Fower, *adj.* four.
Fushionless, *adj.* effete; useless.

G

Gaff, *v.* to chatter; to while away the time in conversation.
Gar, *v.* to make; to cause. 'It wad gar ye grue' = it would make you sick.
Gie, *v.* to give.
Girn, *v.* to complain; n. a petulant complaint.
Glaur, *n.* mud.
Glower, *v.* to stare; to frown; to fix with a gaze intended to intimidate.
Gowk, *n.* a foolish person.
Grue, *n.* nausea; fear; revulsion; *v.* to shiver in horror or disgust.
Guid-willie, *adj.* literally 'good-willed'; friendly; cordial.

H

Hae, *v.* have.
Hizzie, *n.* a hussy (*contemptuous*).
Houghmagandie, *n.* sexual activity; fornication.
Howff, *n.* a drinking-den; a meeting place, often a tavern.

Hungan, *n.* in Haiti, a voodoo priest.

I

Ilka, *adj.* every, each.

J

Jalouse, *v.* to guess.
Jo, *n.* darling; dear one.
Jouk, *v.* to swerve; to evade a blow.
Jumbie, *n.* a ghost; a zombie.

K

Ken, *v.* to know.
Koker, *n.* a sluice gate. From the Dutch meaning 'container'.

L

Licht, *n.* light.
Lowp, *v.* to leap. Also **loup**.

M

Maist, *adj.* most
Mak, *v.* to make.
Maun, *v.* must.
Mauna, *v.* must not.
Micht[1], *n.* might; power.
Micht[2], *v.* might.
Mischanter, *n.* ill fortune.
Mou, *n.* the mouth.
Muckle, *adj.* large.

N

Na, *adv.* not. Also as negative suffix, e.g, didna = did not.
Nane, *adj.* none.

O

Ower, *prep. and adv.* over; too.

P

Paal, *n.* a structure of driven wooden piles and heavy planks designed to shore up the soft bank of a waterway; also **paal-off**.

Pego, *n.* the penis.

Pen, *n.* an enclosure or a farm where vegetables are grown, or animals raised.

Pickney, *n.* a child.

Pintle, *n.* the penis; a wooden peg.

Pleuk, *n.* a pimple; acne.

Primsie, *adj.* conceited; affected; 'stuck up'.

Q

Quean, *n.* a woman, usually young. Also **quine**.

R

Randy, *n.* a reckless person; a loose woman; lively merry-making. *adj.* wild; abusive.

Rodger, *v.* to beat vigorously; to copulate.

S

Salapenta, *n.* a large lizard; *tupinambis nigropunctatus*.

Saut, *n.* salt; adj. salty.

Shair, *adj.* sure.

Sic, *adj.* such; *adv.* so.

Sicht, *n.* a sight.

Skelp, *v.* to slap; to go quickly.

Slaistery, *adj.* wet; messy; untidy.

Snell, *adj.* cold; sharp; piercing.

Sonsie, *n.* plump; pleasant. When applied to a woman it suggests a cheerful, buxom attractiveness.

Spleuchan, *n.* literally a tobacco-pouch; colloquially, the vagina, or the scrotum.

Splore, *n.* a heavy drinking-bout.

Stelling, *n.* a landing stage.

Stoup, *n.* a jug; a drinking vessel.

Straik, *n.* a blow.

Sumphish, *adj.* stupid.

Swall, *v.* to swell.

Syke, *n.* a small stream.

T

Tassie, *n.* a drinking vessel.

Tauld, *v. pp.* told.

Thairm, *n.* the gut; the stomach.

Thocht[1], *v. pp.* thought.

Thocht[2], *n.* a thought.

Thole, *v.* tolerate.

Throng, *adj.* busy; very preoccupied. Also **thrang**.

Tippenny, *n.* a kind of beer sold for twopence a pint, hence the name.

Tirlie-whirlie, *n.* literally, an ornament, but used colloquially to denote the female genitalia.

U

Unco, *adj.* very; strange; peculiar.

Usquebaugh, *n.* whisky.

V

Voustie, *adj.* boastful; bragging.

W

Wame, *n.* the stomach.

Wanga, *n.* in voodoo, an object designed to cause harm to an intended victim.

Waucht, *n.* a very large drink.

Weel, *adj.* well.

Whaur, *adv.* where.

Y

Yestreen, *n.* yesterday evening.

OTHER HISTORICAL TITLES FROM PEEPAL TREE

Kevyn Alan Arthur, *The View from Belmont*   £7.99
Set on a Trinidadian estate in 1823, the novel explores human relation-
ships under slavery and raises questions about the contemporary
Caribbean, the nature of history and its interpretation.

Kevin Baldeosingh, *The Ten Incarnations of Adam Avatar*   £10.99
Five hundred years of Caribbean history are told through the lives of
Adam Avatar, who believes he has been reincarnated as an Amerindian,
a conquistador, a Portuguese slaver, a Yoruba slave, a female pirate, and
a female stickfighter in nineteenth century Trinidad.

David Dabydeen, *The Counting House*   £8.99
Set in 19th century Guyana, the novel follows the lives of Indian
indentured labourers as they encounter the truths about their aban-
doned condition. 'Beautifully written ... Dabydeen's grace is to give his
chararcters imaginations and inner living voices...' Michele Roberts.

Beryl Gilroy, *Inkle and Yarico*   £6.99
Inkle and Yarico retells, through a Black woman's perspective, the 17th
century 'true' story of a shipwrecked Englishman who is rescued by an
Amerindian woman and repays her kindness by selling her into slavery.

June Henfrey, *Coming Home and Other Stories*   £6.99
Set mainly in Barbados, these are strong and moving portrayals of
women from the slave period to the present, attempting to define
themselves in situations where power is determined by race and gender.

Carl Jackson, *Nor the Battle to the Strong*   £8.99
In this powerful work of grief and hope, told through five generations
of an African Barbadian family from slavery up to the workers' rebel-
lions of the 1930s, Jackson sings a redemption song out of the darkness
of suffering into freedom and forgiveness.

All Peepal Tree titles are available from our website: www.peepaltreepress.com

Explore our list of over 200 titles, read sample poems and reviews, discover new
authors, established names and access a wealth of information about books,
authors and Caribbean writing. Secure credit card ordering, fast delivery
throughout the world at cost or less.

You can contact us at:
Peepal Tree Press, 17 King's Avenue, Leeds LS6 1QS, United Kingdom
Tel: +44 (0) 113 2451703 E-mail: hannah@peepaltreepress.com